William Nicholson
RECKLESS

Quercus

651503

First published in Great Britain in 2014 by Quercus Editions Ltd
This paperback edition published in 2015 by

Quercus Editions Ltd
55 Baker Street
7th Floor, South Block
London W1U 8EW

A CIP catalogue record for this book is available
from the British Library

PB ISBN 978 1 78206 645 3
EBOOK ISBN 978 1 78206 644 6

10 9 8 7 6 5 4 3 2 1

Printed and bound in Great Britain by Clays Ltd, St Ives plc
Typeset by Ellipsis Digital Limited, Glasgow

Why I chose the name is not clear, but I know what thoughts were in my mind. There is a poem of John Donne, written just before his death, which I know and love. From it a quotation:

'As East and West
In all flat maps – and I am one – are one,
So death doth touch the resurrection.'

That still does not make a Trinity, but in another better known devotional poem Donne opens, 'Batter my heart, three-person'd God . . .'

> J. Robert Oppenheimer, on why he named
> the first atom bomb test 'Trinity'

Batter my heart, three-person'd God; for you
As yet but knock . . .
Yet dearly I love you, and would be loved fain,
But am betrothed unto your enemy;
Divorce me, untie me, or break that knot again,
Take me to you, imprison me, for I,
Except you enthral me, never shall be free,
Nor ever chaste, except you ravish me.

> John Donne, Holy Sonnet XIV

PRELUDE

Tea at Cliveden: September 1943

Rupert Blundell did not want to go to tea with the princess. He was unsure how to address her, and he was shy with girls at the best of times. Lord Mountbatten, his commanding officer, brushed aside his murmurs of dissent.

'Nancy wants some young people,' he said. 'You're a young person, and you're available.'

Rupert was twenty-six, which felt to himself both young and old. Princess Elizabeth was of course much younger, but being heir to the throne she was unlikely to be short of savoir-faire.

'And anyway,' said Mountbatten, 'you'll like Cliveden. They still have a pastry cook there, and it has one of the best views in England.'

So Rupert put on his rarely worn No.2 dress uniform, which fitted poorly round the crotch, and reported to COHQ in Richmond Terrace. A car was to pick him up from here and drive him to Cliveden, Lady Astor's country house.

'Very smart, Rupert,' said Joyce Wedderburn, passing through on her way back to her office.

'I'm under orders,' said Rupert glumly.

'Aren't the trousers a bit small for you?'

'In parts.'

'Well, I think you look very dashing.'

She gave him one of her half-smiles that he could never interpret, that suggested she meant something other than what she seemed to be saying. But Rupert liked Joyce. He could talk to her more freely than to the other girls. There was no nonsense about her, and she had a fiancé in the Navy, in minesweepers.

The car arrived: a Humber Imperial Landaulette, driven by one of Lady Astor's chauffeurs. Its rear hood was down, and sitting in the wide back seat was an American officer of about Rupert's own age. He introduced himself as Captain McGeorge Bundy, an aide attached to Admiral Alan R. Kirk, commander of the Allied amphibious forces.

'Call me Mac,' he said.

He revealed to Rupert that they were to represent the wartime allies at this tea party. There was to be a Russian too. All this in a crisp monotone, as if to impart the information in the most efficient way possible.

The Russian was news to Rupert.

'I've no idea what we're supposed to do,' he said. 'Have you?'

'I think the idea is the princess wants to meet people nearer to her own age,' said Bundy.

'What for?'

'Maybe it's a blind date.' Bundy smiled, but with his mouth only. 'How'd you like to marry your future queen?'

'God preserve me,' said Rupert.

Mac Bundy was trim and sleek, with sand-coloured hair brushed back smoothly over his high forehead. He wore wire-rimmed glasses. His navy-blue uniform had every appearance of being excellently cut. Looking at him, Rupert felt as he did with so many Americans that they were the physically perfected version of the model, while he himself was a poor first draft.

He shifted on the car seat to ease the itching in his trousers. The landaulette drove through Hyde Park, past the Serpentine. From where he was sitting he could see himself reflected in the driver's mirror: his long face, his thick-rimmed spectacles, his protruding ears. He looked away, out of long habit.

'So who got you into this?' said Bundy.

'Mountbatten. He's a friend of Lady Astor's.'

'Kirk fingered me,' said Bundy, adding in a lower tone, with a glance at the driver, 'His actual order was, "Go and humour the old bat."'

They exchanged details of their postings. Bundy confessed he owed his staff job to family connections.

'I wanted a combat posting. My mother had other ideas.'

His father, Harvey Bundy, was currently a senior adviser in the US War Department under Henry Stimson.

'So this princess,' he said. 'I hear she's all there.'

'All there?' said Rupert.

Bundy curved one hand before his chest.

'Oh, right,' said Rupert. 'I wouldn't know.'

He had never thought of the seventeen-year-old Princess Elizabeth as a sexual being.

'Don't worry,' said Bundy. 'I'm not going to wolf-whistle.'

Rupert looked at the passing shopfronts and was silent. War-time was supposed to change things, break down the barriers. But even when the barriers were down, you had to do it yourself. No one was going to do it for you. There was no one you could talk to about these things. No one in all the world. About feeling ashamed. About wanting it so much.

The car emerged onto the Bayswater Road.

'I asked round for tips on meeting royalty,' said Bundy. 'Apparently you call her ma'am, and you don't sit until she sits.'

'Ma'am? The poor girl's only seventeen.'

'So what are you going to call her? Liz?'

'In the family she's called Lilibet.'

'How'd you know that?'

'Mountbatten told me.'

'Okay. Lilibet it is. Have another slice of pie, Lilibet. Want to take a walk in the shrubbery, Lilibet?'

Rupert glanced nervously at the back of the chauffeur's head, but he showed no signs that he was listening.

'Is that what you do with girls?' said Rupert. 'Take them into the shrubbery?'

'I'll be honest with you,' said Bundy. 'I'm no expert.' He leaned closer and spoke low. 'When I was twelve years old we went to Paris, and my mother took me to the Folies-Bergère. The way she tells it, I got bored by the naked girls and went outside to read a book.'

'And did you?'

'That's her story.'

The car was now turning into Kensington Palace Gardens. There on the pavement outside the Soviet embassy was a young Russian officer, standing stiffly, almost at attention.

'Our noble ally,' said Bundy.

The Russian had a square, serious face and heavy eyebrows. He gazed inscrutably on the open-backed car as it pulled up beside him.

'You are the party for Lady Astor?'

He sounded exactly like an American.

'That's us,' said Bundy. 'Jump in.'

He squeezed onto the seat beside them, and the car set off down Notting Hill Gate to Holland Park. His name was Oleg Troyanovsky. His father had been the Soviet Ambassador in Washington before the war, and he had been sent to school at Sidwell Friends. Within minutes he and Bundy had discovered mutual acquaintances.

'Of course I know the Hayes boys,' said the Russian. 'I was on the tennis team with Oliver Hayes.'

'So what are you doing in London?'

'Joint committee on psych warfare.' The wrinkles between

his eyebrows deepened as he spoke. 'My father arranged it, to keep me away from the eastern front.'

'Check,' said Bundy. 'Privilege knows no boundaries.'

'And here we are, going to tea with a princess.'

They grinned at each other, bound together by a shared awareness of the absurdity of their situation. The car picked up speed coming out of Hammersmith and onto the Great West Road. The wind blew away their words, and conversation languished. They looked out at the endless line of suburban villas rolling by, and thought their own thoughts.

The war had gone on too long. It was no longer a crisis, with the excitement that crisis brings with it, and the promise of change. It had become an intermission. The phrase most often heard was 'for the duration'. Shops were closed 'for the duration'. Trains ran a restricted service 'for the duration'. Life had paused, for the duration.

Meanwhile, thought Rupert, my youth is slipping away.

Last month Mountbatten had accepted a new appointment, as Commander-in-Chief, South East Asia.

'You'll come with me, won't you, Rupert? I must have my old team round me.'

Rupert was more than willing to go. A brighter sun, a bluer sky. Maybe even a new dawn.

The landaulette turned off the main road at last and made its way up a wooded hill, through the pretty red-brick village of Taplow, and so to the great gates of Cliveden. A long drive wound through a wilderness of untended woodland, until quite suddenly there appeared before them a fountain, in which winged and naked figures sported round a giant shell. No water flowed, and the angels, or goddesses, wore an embarrassed air, as if sensing that their nakedness was no longer appropriate. The car made a sharp left turn. Ahead lay a broad beech-lined avenue, at the end of which stood a cream-coloured palace.

'Ah!' sighed Troyanovsky. 'What it is to be rich!'

'Not rich,' said Bundy. 'Very rich. They don't come richer than the Astors.'

The house grew as they approached it, revealing on either side of the central block two curving wings, reaching out as if to embrace the awed visitor. To the right there rose an ornate water tower, faced with a clock that had perhaps once been gold, but was now a tarnished brown. The grass of the flanking lawns grew long round ancient mulberry trees.

The chauffeur drew the car to a stop before the porte cochère, and a butler emerged from the house to greet them.

'Her ladyship and her Royal Highness will join you shortly, gentlemen.'

They followed the butler into an immense oak-panelled hall, hung with faded tapestries. At one end, before a carved stone fireplace, tea had been laid out on two small tables. To the left of the fireplace hung a full-size portrait of a young woman in a gauzy pale-blue dress, her hands clasped behind her back, her head turned coquettishly to the viewer.

'That is Nancy Astor,' said Bundy with crisp authority.

'But she's beautiful!' exclaimed Troyanovsky. He stood back to appreciate her, evidently as a woman rather than as a work of art.

'She was younger then, of course.'

Rupert was puzzled by the painting. The pose was unusual: a slight forward tilt from the waist, as if she was on the point of running away.

Bundy examined the waiting tea. There was fruitcake topped with marzipan. A silver dish with a lid stood warming on a spirit lamp. He lifted the lid to discover a nest of small scones.

'What do we have to do to deserve this?'

'We could link arms and perform a dance,' said Troyanovsky gravely. It took the others a moment to realise he was making fun. 'Or perhaps we could sing together, to represent the harmony of the Alliance.'

They grinned at that.

'And youth,' said Rupert. 'We're here to represent youth.'

'I'm not young,' said Bundy. 'Who wants to be young? I want to be a grown man, in charge of my own destiny.'

'Only an American could say that,' said Troyanovsky. 'We who come from older civilisations know that we will never be in charge of our own destinies.'

He looked to Rupert as he spoke, his heavy brow wrinkling. Rupert nodded to be friendly, unsure whether or not he agreed.

'But you know what?' said Bundy. 'I'm all for this idea of us singing together.'

He started to croon the current hit by the Andrews Sisters, making small hand movements before him in the air.

> 'There were three little sisters
> Three little sisters
> And each one only in her teens—'

A door opened, and he fell silent. In swept a small tornado of a woman, followed a few paces behind by a young girl.

'Oh my God! They're here already! Make yourselves at home, boys! Which one of you is Bundy?'

Mac Bundy presented himself.

'I knew your father, I knew your mother, I warned them not to marry, and if they had to marry, not to produce any children. Bound to be morons. Are you a moron?'

'No, Lady Astor,' said Bundy, smoothly unperturbed. 'I don't believe I am.'

'Humph. We'll see about that.'

She was in her mid-sixties, her face now bony, but her bright blue eyes as brilliant as in the portrait. She held her head high,

7

and moved in hops and starts, as if unable to contain the energy within her. Her voice was thin and crackly, half American, half English.

'This is just an informal get-together. No need to stand on ceremony.'

The three young officers were introduced to the young girl, who turned out to be Princess Elizabeth. She was even smaller than Lady Astor, and had wavy dark-brown hair, and very white skin. Her modest knee-length white dress, patterned with pink flowers, could not disguise the fact that she was, as Bundy had put it, 'all there'.

'Come along, Lilibet,' said Lady Astor. 'You sit here. You know no one can sit down until you've sat down. God, what a country! How I've stood it all these years I'll never know.'

They sat down. Their hostess poured out tea, talking as she did so.

'I've told Lilibet that family of hers keeps her far too shut away, she never meets anyone at all, so I promised her some young men, and here you are. You must help yourselves to the scones. It was Lilibet's idea to invite our allies, and a very good idea if I may say so. You three' – teapot in mid-air, piercing blue eyes fixed on the young men – 'you are the future of the world. You must make a better job of it than we have.'

'With Her Royal Highness's help,' said Bundy, leaning his upper body forward as if attempting a bow while sitting down.

'Oh, the royals can't do a thing,' said Lady Astor. 'No one pays the slightest attention to a word they say. Of course, everyone loves them, but only in the way you love a family pet.' She reached out one hand to pat the shy young princess. 'Do you mind me going on like this, darling? Are you shocked?'

'Not at all,' said the princess in a small clear voice. 'But I'd like to hear what the gentlemen have to say.'

So she wasn't such a little girl after all.

'That's telling me,' said Lady Astor. 'What have you got to say, boys?'

There followed a brief silence.

'Well, ma'am,' said Bundy. 'I think we all agree that this war will be over sometime next year.'

'Oh, I do hope so,' said the princess. 'That's what the officers at Windsor tell me too.'

Rupert was looking at the princess's hands. Her hands were so delicate, the nails varnished a very pale pink. She was interlacing her fingers in her lap, nervously squeezing them.

'I'm so bored by the war,' said Lady Astor. 'Can't we talk about something else?'

'I'm not sure I would say I was bored exactly,' said the princess.

Her enunciation was so clear that everything she said sounded carefully considered. Her earnest gaze fell on Rupert, as if inviting him to complete her thought.

'It's a hard feeling to describe,' said Rupert. 'One feels bored and frightened at the same time. And then beneath it all there's this feeling that one's real life is waiting to begin.'

The princess looked at him in surprise.

'Yes,' she said.

Then she smiled. Rupert realised for the first time that she was pretty.

'It's all right for you young people,' said Lady Astor with a grunt. 'Some of us are waiting for our life to end.'

'Not for many years yet, I hope,' said Bundy.

'Look at that!' She pointed at the portrait hanging by the fireplace. 'I have that staring at me every day, reminding me how old I am.'

'But it's a wonderful portrait,' said Troyanovsky. 'I have been admiring it.'

'Don't you think I'm standing in an odd way? It's because

9

Sargent had this idea of painting me with my little boy on my back.' She stood up and assumed the same pose as in the painting, hands clasped behind her back. 'But Bill was only one year old at the time, and he just wouldn't keep still, so Sargent painted him out.'

'It is a very fine portrait,' said the princess, gazing at it.

'I can't look at it any more,' said Lady Astor. 'Don't grow old, my dear. It's too tiresome.'

'I would like to be a little older,' said the princess.

As she spoke she glanced at Rupert. This gave him an odd feeling. It was as if some secret understanding had sprung up between the two of them.

The princess turned to Troyanovsky.

'Tell me about Russia,' she said. 'I know so little about your country.'

'Well, ma'am,' said Troyanovsky, 'if I'm to tell you about my country I must speak about the war. We have been fighting a life and death battle.'

'Yes, I know,' said the princess. 'We all so admire Mr Stalin.'

'Humph!' said Lady Astor. 'I met Joe Stalin.'

'Did you?' said Troyanovsky, much surprised. 'When was that?'

'1931. I went to Russia with George Bernard Shaw. We were both introduced to Uncle Joe. Shaw was all over him, of course. When it came to my turn, I said, "Mr Stalin, why have you slaughtered so many of your own people?"'

The Russian's teacup froze halfway to his lips.

'What did he reply?'

'Some nonsense about defending the revolution. What could he say? The man's a mass murderer.'

Troyanovsky was silent. The groove deepened between his eyebrows.

'The Russians are fighting like lions,' said Bundy. 'We owe them a great debt.'

'The revolution is still young,' Troyanovsky said.

'I hope,' said the princess, speaking earnestly, 'that after the war we can all go on being friends.'

'I believe our nations can and must be friends, ma'am,' said Bundy. 'I think we've all had our fill of hatred. We may not always see things the same way, but I believe we can agree to disagree.'

'I expect you'll think I'm very naive,' said the princess, 'but I do so much want this to be the last war we ever have to fight.'

'There will always be war,' declared Troyanovsky.

'But why?'

'Human nature, ma'am.'

'I disagree,' said Bundy. 'I believe we have the power to control our impulses.' Quite suddenly he became vehement. 'There's evil in all of us, no doubt about that, but we must grow up, and accept it, and manage it. We have to live with our imperfections. You people' – this was to the Russian – 'you're perfectionists. You believe you're creating the perfect society. I think that's dangerous. It permits your leaders to take extreme measures.'

'War is an extreme measure, I think.' The Russian nodded his big head, frowning. 'In the West, you are pragmatists. We are idealists. But you know, in spite of this, we want much the same as you. To eat. To sleep safe in our beds. To go dancing. To talk late into the night about the wrongs of the world.'

'So after the war,' said the princess, 'when we who are young now are old enough to influence the affairs of the world, let's agree that we'll have no more wars.'

'Hear, hear!' said the young officers, raising their teacups.

Rupert was touched by the young princess's gentle diplomacy. He sensed that it was more than good manners, that she was genuinely distressed by conflict. What a curious mixture she was, he thought. Scrupulous in the performance of her duty; her face so serious, but still lit by the lingering innocence of childhood.

Lady Astor now rose. This was the cue for the gentlemen to rise.

'I must show our guests the view from the terrace,' she said.

The princess rose, smoothing her dress down as she did so. Lady Astor led the way across the adjoining library and out through French windows.

Rupert found the princess was by his side.

'So you feel your real life is waiting to begin,' she said to him, speaking softly.

'I do, ma'am,' he said.

'And what will it be, this real life?'

'I wish I could tell you it'll be a life of honourable service to my country,' said Rupert. 'But I'm afraid all I mean is love.'

'Ah, love.'

They came out onto the terrace.

'There it is,' said Lady Astor with a sweep of one arm. 'England. The land we're fighting for.'

The view was indeed spectacular. Below the terrace stretched a long formal lawn, laid out in two parterres. To the east rose a wooded hill. The river flowed round the foot of this hill, concealed by trees, here and there glinting into view. Beyond the river the land stretched for miles to the south, to Maidenhead and beyond. Above it all rose a peaceful late-afternoon sky.

'Did you know,' said Lady Astor, 'that the first ever performance of "Rule Britannia" took place right here? Two hundred years ago, at a big party down there, given by the Prince of Wales.'

She pointed at the long lawn below them.

'So beautiful, so untouched by war,' said Troyanovsky. 'Hitler could have marched his armies up this valley. Instead he turned them on my homeland.'

They strolled slowly down the length of the terrace. Once again Rupert found himself by the princess's side.

'So you're not married, Captain Blundell?'

'No, ma'am.'

'That is a happiness still to come.'

A conventional enough remark, but there was a wistfulness to her tone.

'I hope so, ma'am.'

She then turned to make conversation with Bundy, and Rupert was left with his thoughts.

'There's someone for everyone, Rupert,' his mother used to tell him. But all you had to do was look around you to know this was not true. Add together the solitary young, the unmarried, the divorced, the widowed and the solitary old, and it was hard not to conclude that loneliness was the natural condition of humanity.

It was now time for the princess to return to Windsor Castle. Her detective appeared as if by magic.

'I'm ready, Mr Giles,' she said.

She shook hands with each of the young officers.

'Remember,' she said. 'No more wars.'

Lady Astor accompanied the princess to her car. Left alone, the young men relaxed. They stood looking out over the great view, reluctant to leave.

'So where do you go next, Rupert?' said Bundy.

'India. Mountbatten's taking command out there.'

'Me, I'm in London until the second front.'

'Pray it may come soon,' said the Russian.

'My dad says one more year,' said Bundy, 'and it'll all be over.'

Troyanovsky took out a pack of cigarettes and offered them to the others. They both declined. He lit up, and inhaled deeply.

'Your princess,' he said to Rupert, 'she is charming.'

'I agree,' said Rupert. 'I thought she was lovely.'

'No life for a girl, though,' said Bundy. 'She should be out every night dancing, not fretting over the future of the world.'

'Leave that to Lady Astor,' said Rupert.

They laughed at that. Then the Russian shook his head.

'What she said to Stalin, that I find it hard to believe.'

'But she's right,' said Bundy.

Troyanovsky puffed on his cigarette, frowning.

'The day will come,' he said slowly, 'when you will ask yourself not what is right, but what is possible.'

'Who's the pragmatist now?' said Bundy.

'I think I can claim that honour,' said Rupert, peacemaking. 'We British have a long history of calling a spade a spade, and then getting some other fellow to do the digging.'

Bundy smiled his smile at that.

'But your princess,' said Troyanovsky, 'what she said to us, that was good. No more wars.'

'We're all with you there,' said Bundy.

'So we must make it be so,' said the Russian. 'We three.'

He put out one large hand. Rupert understood his meaning, and clasped it. After a moment Bundy put his hand on top of theirs.

A solitary plane appeared in the far distance and buzzed slowly across the sky. The sun dropped below the clouds and threw shafts of golden light over the landscape. Rupert felt a sudden rush of fellow feeling for the other two. Partly it was this odd triple hand-clasp that they seemed unable to break, and partly the conviction that such a moment would never come again. There really was a symbolic power to their presence, joined together on the long terrace, looking out over England.

'No more wars,' said Rupert. 'Wouldn't that just be something?'

PART ONE

Warning

1945 − 1950

1

It was the colours they all talked about, the ones who witnessed the Trinity test. A brilliant yellow-white light, a searing light many times brighter than the midday sun. Then a ball of fire, an orange-red glow. Then a cloud of coloured smoke pouring upwards, red and yellow, like clouds at sunset, turning golden, purple, violet, grey, blue. Observers ten miles away saw a blue colour surrounding the smoke cloud, then a bright yellow ring near the ground, spreading out towards them. This was the shock wave. When it arrived there was a rumbling sound, as of thunder.

Brilliant white, fire-red, orange, gold, purple, violet, grey, blue. Sunset skies and thunder at dawn in Alamagordo, New Mexico.

President Harry S. Truman was not in the country. He had sailed for Europe a week earlier on the USS *Augusta*. It was an uneventful crossing, with an orchestra to play during dinner, and a different movie shown each evening. *A Song to Remember*, *To Have and Have Not*, *The Princess and the Pirate*, *Something for the Boys*. The president was on his way to the final meeting of the wartime Allies at Potsdam, just outside Berlin. He was dreading it.

Truman had never wanted to be Roosevelt's vice president. 'Tell him to go to hell,' he replied to the offer. 'I'm for Jimmy Byrnes.' But Roosevelt wanted the plain-speaking man from Missouri, and he got his way. During Truman's brief three months in the vice presidency, Roosevelt neither informed him nor consulted him. When Roosevelt died and he found himself president, Truman told reporters, 'Boys, I don't know if you fellas ever had a load of hay fall on you . . .'

After a further brief three months as the leader of the free world, with the war in the Far East still raging, Truman now faced the task of standing up to Stalin. The Potsdam Conference would decide the shape and future of the postwar world.

The *Augusta* sailed up the Scheldt estuary cheered by Belgian and Dutch crowds, and docked at Antwerp on Sunday, July 15 1945. A C-54 plane called the *Sacred Cow* flew the president and his party to Berlin that same day. The Potsdam Conference was due to begin on Tuesday, July 17. Harry Truman felt seriously out of his depth.

The presidential entourage took up residence at No. 2 Kaiserstrasse, in the movie colony of Babelsberg. The grand but ugly yellow-painted villa had been built in the 1890s by a wealthy publisher, and most recently was occupied by the head of the Nazi film industry. It stood in tree-studded grounds on the banks of Lake Gribnitz. Truman said the building put him in mind of the Kansas City Union Station.

That evening, Secretary of War Henry L. Stimson received a coded telegram from General Groves, who led the Manhattan Project, the top secret mission to build the atomic bomb.

Operated on this morning, diagnosis not yet complete but results seem satisfactory and already exceed expectations.

Stimson at once took the message to Truman. Truman was pleased but cautious. He would wait for the full report.

Stimson ate privately that evening with his assistant, Harvey Bundy. Stimson was now in his late seventies, and in poor health. He had his suspicions that he was being cut out of the key decisions on the war. Bundy, brought in by him as his Special Assistant on Atomic Matters, was an old friend, and like himself a Yale man, a Skull and Bones member, and a lawyer.

'You think we're going to have to do this, Harvey?'

'Have to, no,' said Bundy. 'Going to, yes.'

'You think the Japs'll surrender anyway?'

'You've read the Purple intercepts,' said Bundy. 'We all know they're desperate for a way out.'

'It may take an invasion.'

'Please God, no,' said Harvey Bundy. 'My boy Mac's joined the Ninety-Seventh; he's determined to get in some real fighting. His division's slated for the push into mainland Japan. Kay's half crazy with worry.'

'If this gadget's half what they say it is,' said Stimson, 'there's no way your boy's going to see action. You tell Kay to relax.'

The next day Truman had his first informal meeting with Stalin, at what was now called the Little White House. They discussed how to handle the continuing war with Japan. Intercepted cables revealed that the Japanese were pleading with the Soviets to broker a peace deal short of unconditional surrender, that would leave the emperor in place. The Allies wanted the Soviets to enter the war against Japan, late though it was. Stalin readily agreed. The declaration would be made by August 15, he said.

Fini Japs when that comes about, wrote Truman in his diary.

That evening a courier arrived carrying General Groves' full report on the Trinity test. Truman read it at once, and gave it to his secretary of state, Jimmy Byrnes, and to Henry Stimson. Stimson showed it to Harvey Bundy. It was electrifying.

'For the first time in history,' Groves wrote, 'there was a nuclear explosion. And what an explosion!' He estimated its power at the equivalent of twenty thousand tons of TNT. He described the blast effects with memorable details. A steel tower evaporated. A window was broken over a hundred miles away. The light of the explosion was visible from El Paso, almost two hundred miles away. A blind woman saw the light. Groves called it 'the birth of a new age, a great new force to be used for good or evil. No man-made phenomenon of such tremendous power has ever occurred before.'

Later, alone with Harvey Bundy, Stimson pondered the mighty issue before them.

'Are we unleashing a monster here, Harvey?'

'You want my opinion,' said Bundy, 'I'd say we can't come this far and spend this much money and not use it. And that's not even an opinion. Once it can be used, it's going to be used.'

'But why?'

'You ever get given a new toy for Christmas? You ever got told you can have the shiny new toy, but you can't play with it?'

2

In the Botanical Gardens at Peradeniya, near Kandy, the old capital of Ceylon, the midday monsoon had just begun. Captain Rupert Blundell, caught by the sudden downpour on his way from Forward Projects Planning to the main gate, where a staff car was waiting for him, took shelter in the arch between the twin trunks of a giant Java fig tree. Crouching in the embrace of its rough bark, he watched the torrents of water hammer the brown earth and form miniature cascades between the tree's spreading roots. Overhead the branches reached outwards and curved down, forming a natural pavilion. All round him the humid air hissed and the stiff leaves crackled, the ground popped and bubbled and the run-off gurgled, as the monsoon rain streamed through bamboo groves and palm avenues, past the huts and tents of Divisional HQ, to the looping embrace of the Mahaweli river.

Beyond the veil of rain he saw two men go by, moving in slow circles, as if dancing. Both were drenched to the skin, beyond caring about shelter, laughing, shouting to each other. He watched their rotations as they came nearer, and saw that between them they had a monkey on a string. The monkey bounded up and down and from side to side, but with each bound they tugged on its string, forcing it back to its position between them.

'Oh, no, you don't!' they cried. And, 'A right crackerjack we've got here!'

It was like watching two parents taking their toddler for a walk in the rain, only without the love.

As the monkey passed by it made a sudden spring for the fig tree and got its fingers round one of the low bendy branches. For a moment Rupert saw its face. Its big black-rimmed eyes were staring in terror, and it was uttering shrill screeching noises. Then the string jerked and it fell back, shivering the branches, causing a spray of water to fill the air.

Rupert left his refuge and pushed out through the canopy into the rain.

'You!' he shouted. 'Stop that! Release that animal!'

He saw now that the two men were army cooks. They came to attention, rain streaming down their faces.

'Yes, sir!'

'Just a bit of fun, sir!'

They pulled in the string and untied the monkey. The trembling animal, now released, gave its drenched fur a single vigorous shake, and bounded away into a nearby tree.

'Names!'

'Chappell, sir.'

'Price, sir.'

'Do that again and I'll have you up on a charge.'

'Yes, sir.'

'Bugger off, then.'

'Yes, sir!'

They saluted and ran away towards the mess hall. Rupert remained standing motionless in the rain. He was shaking with rage. He had acted on an impulse that he didn't fully understand. Now he was too wet to proceed to HQ as ordered.

No longer hurrying, he passed down the double coconut avenue towards the main gate. The rain was warm. He felt his anger pass. He walked slowly between the palms, lost in the hum of rain, and the world blurred and softened round him. He found his staff car and instructed the driver to take him to his billet in town, so that he could change into dry clothes.

Only when seated in the back of the car did he feel uncomfortable in his soaked clothing. He wanted to stop the car and get out and walk. But Kandy was a good five miles from Peradeniya, and he must make at least a token appearance at the meeting. Mountbatten had called a final briefing before his departure to join Churchill in Potsdam.

The car hissed its way through deep puddles past Bowala and Primrose, down into the cup of green hills. Ahead and below lay the lake round which the old capital's buildings clustered.

Oh Christ, thought Rupert. I suppose I identified with the monkey.

Alone on the back seat, he grimaced at the realisation. With his lugubrious features and thick-rimmed spectacles, he was not unlike a monkey. Moreover, he had known as a boy what it was to be tormented by bigger boys. The monkey's desperate staring face, its sharp bark of fear, had struck a familiar chord. The bullied child still lived on inside him, flinching, appeasing, dreaming dreams of revenge.

Beware the fantasies of weak men.

He could see his own absurdity all too well: the comedy of his little display of anger, his sodden clothing. Instinctively he distanced himself from his feelings, placing them in the ironic context of one whose job it is to analyse but not to judge. Why should a monkey on a string be so much more offensive than a dog on a lead? Because the monkey is a wild animal, not a pet. Rupert hated to see wild animals in cages or tethered to trees.

So do I flatter myself that I too am some kind of wild animal?

This only served to extend the joke. He knew well enough

how others saw him. The oddball, famous for his absent-mindedness, teased for his lack of physical grace. Clever, of course, but a little to be pitied. The story would get about, how he had rescued a monkey from its persecutors, and they would say, 'Did you hear about Rupert's heroic deed? He took on the might of the Army Catering Corps!' The joke being that he was the last among them anyone would describe as a warrior; or indeed as a wild animal.

Just a bit of fun, sir.

Chappell and Price: laughing, thoughtless bullies. Exemplars of the power wielded the world over by the stupid and the strong.

'You don't win a war by seeing the other fellow's point of view, Rupert.'

Who was it who said that? Not Dickie Mountbatten, who was forever quoting Maeterlinck's *The Life of the Bee* and urging his team to work in harmony. It was either Leese or Browning, army men who believed in overwhelming force; or maybe the American, Stillwell, who called the British 'pig fuckers'. Plain speaking and brute force, the doctrine of real men.

'But if you don't see the other fellow's point of view,' Rupert countered, 'you can't predict what he's likely to do.'

Rupert was accustomed to being overruled. His attempts to broaden his superiors' understanding of their own war aims, let alone the objectives of the enemy, made very little impression on their single-minded pursuit of their own interests. As a lowly captain with no men at his command and the jerry-rigged title of Adviser to CINCSEAC, Forward Planning, his only influence lay in the accident that Dickie Mountbatten had taken a liking to him.

'You're the chap who tells me the things I don't want to hear,' he said to Rupert. 'And that's just what I want to hear.'

So Rupert came and went among the officers of the High Command, seeing without being seen, knowing without being known. The price he paid was loneliness, but this was nothing new. As a child he had once asked for a bed with curtains round it. He thought that if he drew the curtains he could protect himself from the eyes of the unkind world.

Why else do I like walking in the rain?

The meeting took place in the main conference room of the King's Pavilion, a pillared monstrosity built in the early nineteenth century to house the Governor of Ceylon. The conference room was designed for imperial receptions, with tall windows that looked down the hillside to the lake. The staff sat on either side of a long baize-covered table, with Mountbatten at the head. Boy Browning, Army Chief of Staff, reported on the current status of Operation Zipper, the planned amphibious invasion of the Malay peninsula.

'As you know, sir, the light-fleet carriers have been transferred to the Pacific fleet, at Fraser's insistence.'

'Damn Fraser!' exclaimed Mountbatten. 'He doesn't need them.'

'We've also lost over thirty thousand men with the reduction in service time that came in on June the eighth.'

'Can you believe it?' said Mountbatten. 'It's bare-faced electioneering! Grigg thinks the returning troops will all vote Tory. He's got a nasty surprise coming.'

The discussion became technical, revolving round troop numbers and favourable dates for an assault on Singapore.

'We've already delayed Zipper twice. Mid-August is our last chance.'

As the meeting wound up, Mountbatten rose to his feet. He smiled at his staff, projecting his usual air of invincible self-confidence.

'I leave for Germany this afternoon. My message to Churchill is simple. If we fail to reconquer at least one colony before the end of the war, our prestige in the Far East will be lost for ever.'

Rupert followed Mountbatten at his request out onto the terrace. The rain had stopped. Kandy shimmered in bright sunlight.

'Mark my card, Rupert.'

'Nobody at Potsdam will care a rap about Operation Zipper, sir.' Rupert knew that Mountbatten was inclined to listen most attentively when shocked. 'They'll talk a lot about the defeat of Japan, but everyone knows that's just a matter of time. Anyway, that's an American show. The real hot potato is containing Stalin. The Americans want to get the Russians into the war on Japan, but at the same time they don't want them to take any more of Europe than they've already got. That's where the dealing will get tough.'

'They don't care about the Fourteenth Army in Burma?'

'No, sir. They don't even know where Burma is.'

'How do you know this?'

'I don't. All I do is put myself in Truman's place and ask myself how the world looks to him. Hitler's gone. Japan's on its knees. Stalin's all he cares about. He'll be looking ahead, to the next war.'

'The next war! God help us!'

'Your best bet is to hitch Burma and Malaya and Singapore to the wagon. Tell the Americans that if they don't watch out, the whole of South East Asia will turn into Soviet satellite states. Then India will follow. They'll pay attention to that.'

Mountbatten nodded as he listened. None of this was new to him, but Rupert had a knack of putting matters in a way that he could recall later.

They left the terrace and re-entered the conference room.

'Did you see the March of Time film, *Back Door to Tokyo*? Never even mentioned me. You'd think Joe Stillwell and the Americans were the only ones fighting out here. Extraordinary!

And I'm Stillwell's superior officer! Or was, until I got rid of him.'

As they passed through the hallway to the main doors, Joyce Wedderburn was waiting for Mountbatten with a copy of his schedule.

'What do you think will happen in the election?' Mountbatten said.

'Labour's going to win,' said Rupert.

'Peter Murphy says so too. Poor Winston. He has no idea.'

Rupert shared a car back to Divisional HQ with Joyce.

'Is he still going on about how he wasn't in that news film?' Joyce said.

'Yes,' said Rupert.

'He's terrifically miffed about it, poor dear.'

Joyce affected a motherly style with Mountbatten, despite being, at twenty-six, almost half his age. Rupert and Joyce shared the same protective instinct towards Mountbatten, partly prompted by witnessing his treatment at the hands of Edwina, his wealthy and strong-minded wife.

'Why's he going to Potsdam?' said Rupert. 'He'll be a small fish there, and he won't like it.'

'The PM wants him.'

The car delivered them back to the Botanical Gardens. They walked together from the gates to the Grand Circle, where the main Divisional HQ buildings stood.

'Is Edwina still seeing that chap of hers?' asked Rupert.

'When she gets time,' said Joyce. 'Which isn't often.'

'Dickie is extraordinary.'

'What no one understands about him,' said Joyce, 'is that he's shy with women. He really doesn't think he's much of a success in that department.'

'Oh, well,' said Rupert. 'None of us think we are. Not really.'

'But it's so silly,' said Joyce. 'It's not hard. All you have to do is pay us a little bit of attention. We don't expect it to be like in the pictures.'

Rupert wondered if this was meant for him. Joyce's fiancé had gone down with his ship in '43. She wasn't exactly a looker, but then, nor was he. She was trim and brisk and entirely without personal vanity. She would make an excellent life companion.

But I don't want a life companion. I want a lover. I want an end to loneliness.

A childish dream, of course. It was like wanting not to grow old, or not to die. Rupert was now settled in the self-protective belief that all people are by their nature alone. To know me truly, he liked to say, wearing his philosopher's hat, you would have to be me. Each of us is an undiscovered universe, lost in the darkness and silence of space.

'What about you, Joyce?'

'Oh, I expect someone'll turn up some day,' said Joyce. 'Someone who keeps his underwear clean and doesn't smoke in bed.'

'High standards,' said Rupert.

He came to a stop before a talipot palm tree.

'You know what that is?' he said.

'A palm tree,' said Joyce.

'It's called a talipot. You know why it's special?'

Joyce examined the big raggedy palm with its immense broad leaves.

'Tell me,' she said.

'They only flower once in their lives. They can live for up to forty years without flowering. But when they do flower, it's spectacular. The talipot produces the largest cluster of blooms of any plant in the world.'

'Really?' She looked from Rupert to the palm tree and back. 'I bet you're just making it up.'

'No. It's true.'

'Well, I'm not waiting forty years, I can tell you.'

As she said this she shot Rupert a comical look that entirely disarmed him. She gets it, he thought. Not that his meaning had been obscure. But Rupert was so unaccustomed to being the object of attention that he was caught unawares, as if she had come upon him half undressed.

He realised he was blushing.

'Oh, Rupert,' she said. 'You are sweet.'

They walked on towards the main hut.

'It'll be quiet while Dickie's away,' Rupert said.

'I shan't complain.'

'How about a Chinese one of these evenings?'

He heard himself utter these words in some amazement. They came out unpremeditated, almost not of his own volition.

'I'd love that, Rupert,' said Joyce.

'Saturday?'

'It just so happens I'm free Saturday evening.'

Another of those comical looks, and she headed off into the hut. Rupert continued towards his own quarters, now in a state of considerable confusion. He felt as if he had stumbled upon some renegade part of himself that was not subject to his authority. He had, it seemed, made a date with Joyce Wedderburn. This generated certain expectations; hopes, even. And hopes could be dashed. Better to expect nothing. Just a friendly meal in a Chinese restaurant in old Kandy. Two bored army colleagues passing the time. What could be more natural than that?

A single man and a single woman eating alone together. What could be more thrilling, more terrifying, more potentially life-changing than that?

3

Admiral Mountbatten duly arrived in Babelsberg, and was assigned a room at 23 Ringstrasse, where Churchill was lodged. At the first opportunity he met General George Marshall and the US chiefs of staff, to begin preparing a joint report on the final stages of the war in the Far East. Marshall told Mountbatten that Stalin had committed the Soviet Union to war against Japan, but that no announcement would be made until later in August.

'It would be good if we could finish the job ourselves first, don't you think?' he said to Mountbatten.

'Oh, we can finish it all right,' said Mountbatten. 'All we need is the political will. I've got Slim and his army doing wonders in Burma, and no back-up of any kind whatsoever.'

The next courier to arrive from New Mexico informed the president that there would be a 'gadget' ready for use on or after August 2. This was only a matter of days away. Henry Stimson was authorised to brief Mountbatten about the atom bomb, swearing him to secrecy.

Mountbatten was thunderstruck.

'One bomb can destroy an entire city!'

'It's the wrath of God. It's like nothing you've ever dreamed of before.'

'My God!'

Mountbatten felt flattered to be one of the few let in on the secret, but he couldn't help seeing it in terms of his own role in South East Asia Command.

'So what happens to Operation Zipper?'

'What's Operation Zipper?'

'The invasion of the Malayan peninsula. The recapture of Singapore.'

'Oh, we won't be needing any of that.'

Mountbatten then had a private meeting with Churchill.

'Are they really going to drop this new bomb?' he asked him.

'I bloody well hope so,' said Churchill. 'It's the only thing that'll stop Stalin.'

'And the Japs.'

Churchill made a dismissive gesture with one hand.

'The Japanese war will be over within the week.'

'Right,' said Mountbatten, trying to look more pleased than he felt. 'So what happens to my outfit in Kandy?'

'Everyone goes home.' Then seeing the look on Mountbatten's face, Churchill added, 'Don't worry, Dickie. We'll find something for you to do.'

'Thank you, Prime Minister.'

'What do you reckon to the election? Could be a close-run thing, they tell me.'

'You've led us through the war, Winston. You've won the nation's everlasting gratitude.'

'Let's hope they bloody well show it.'

Mountbatten sent a telegram to Boy Browning in Kandy, instructing him to prepare for an imminent Japanese surrender. He was unable to give his reasons.

The cable was met with bewilderment in Kandy.

'What on earth does he mean?' exclaimed Boy Browning. 'Is

he cancelling Zipper? Rupert, you're in on all the secret plans. What the hell's going on?'

'I don't know,' said Rupert, equally puzzled. 'Maybe it means the Soviets are coming in against Japan.'

'All the more bloody important that we get boots on the ground in Malaya first. Does he want the whole of South East Asia to go red?'

Pending further orders, there was nothing to be done but put all plans on hold. This, combined with the absence of the commander-in-Chief and the persistence of the monsoon rains, cast a spell over Divisional Headquarters. The enormous staff that Mountbatten had gathered together, over seven thousand, counting all ranks, settled down to grumble and drink and wait.

Rupert, whose job was forward planning, now understood that the war would soon be over. He was in need of some forward planning of his own. In the gaps between the downpours he walked the avenues of the Botanical Gardens, breathing in the rich scent of the soaked earth, and finding strength in the luxurious growth of the plants.

In the three days since he had made his dinner date with Joyce, neither of them had referred to it again; but Rupert had thought of little else. He was both ashamed and excited by how much of his time was now given over to thoughts of Joyce. Absurdly, she even looked different now. She had become more attractive. He had discovered what finely formed hands she had, and how her face in profile, with her high cheekbones and slightly curved nose, was characterful, even beautiful. Most of all there was that mischievous look in her eyes, which seemed to collude with him – but about what? All he could say for certain was that they were behaving as if they shared knowledge of each other that no one else possessed. What knowledge? He knew next to nothing about her.

But of course the secret was not hard to find. By accepting

the dinner date for Saturday evening they had both taken the great risk of admitting an interest in the other, and this had changed everything. A new door had opened. Beyond it stretched a new road to what could be a new life. However many times he told himself they had not even begun any kind of relationship, he couldn't stop himself from gazing through that door, and down that road, to the very end.

At the end was married life. Joyce, his wife, sharing a home with him. Joyce the mother of his children. This prospect filled him with joy and wonder. This was not because he was in love with Joyce: he hadn't yet had the chance to know enough of her for that. It was because he had always pictured his life as a solitary one. This new vision of companionship was almost unbearably sweet.

And why not? There was many a marriage built on friendship.

He sighed a little to himself, as the warm wind rustled the leaves of the palm trees. Not exactly the thoughts of a lover. And yet there was passion enough in him, waiting for its cue to come on stage. Waiting, as it were, for permission.

He had never in all his twenty-eight years made a romantic approach to a girl. No girl he had ever known had given him reason to think such an approach would be welcome. He had a deep horror of what he called 'making an ass of myself', which meant exposing himself to rejection. Like the mirrors over which his gaze slid unseeingly, he did all in his power to protect himself from meeting his own unloved image in the eyes of others.

This left him in a dilemma. To fall in love, he had to know that he was loved. But he couldn't know if he was loved without declaring his own hopes. And he dared not voice such hopes without the certain knowledge that they would be reciprocated.

How to break out of this vicious circle? For some time now he had been developing a more elevated concept of friendship.

It was customary to place friendship in a different class to love. Those who look to be loved are bitterly disappointed by the offer of friendship. But it struck Rupert that this was not the way life was actually lived. Most marriages settled down, surely, into what was really a friendship. Why then should friendship not evolve into marriage? If only the expected first stage could be skipped, the romance and the passion, he felt well able to offer the steady companionship that followed. It seemed to Rupert that while he might cut a comical figure as a lover, he would make a thoroughly respectable husband.

All girls wanted husbands, didn't they? Joyce Wedderburn must want a husband. If he presented the plan in the right way, might she not find it worth her consideration?

Beneath this line of thinking, modest and sensible as it was, lay a secret dream that he barely dared to admit even to himself. In this dream Joyce revealed she had been nursing a lonely passion for him for years, that she adored him, that her lips ached to kiss him, that she had never dared to hope for the bliss of holding him in her arms. Were this wild dream ever to come true – his whole lanky frame shuddered with the thought of it – his heart would explode – the fiery lake of love within him would erupt – the world would melt before the force of his passion – he would, in short, fall in love.

In the meantime, there was friendship. A tepid first stage, but manageable. The great thing was to plant the idea in Joyce's mind, and let time do its work. He dreaded the end of the war, the return to solitary rooms in Cambridge. Why should Joyce not have a similar fear? Together, friends, companions, and one day lovers, they could face the future.

At this point in his musings, Peter Wilson passed him, heading in the opposite direction.

'Do you play golf, Rupert?'

'A little,' said Rupert.

'There's a funny old course up in the hills of Nuwara Elya, I was up there yesterday morning. The ninth hole runs right across the front of the clubhouse veranda. Par three, about a hundred and sixty yards. I played it with a five iron, all the planters and their wives watching, knocking back the John Collinses. I took one great whack at the ball, and up it went, and onto the green, and plopped into the hole. My God! What a cheer I got! Never done it before, never do it again.'

'Well done, Peter,' said Rupert.

'So what do you make of Dickie's latest? More hurry up and do nothing, eh?'

The Chinese restaurant was half empty in the early evening, as Rupert and Joyce sat down at one of the stained oilcloth-covered tables. They'd come early knowing that it filled up quickly. Both were still in uniform. They agreed to share a large plate of the Special, which consisted of fried rice, boiled eggs, and whatever was currently being cooked in the kitchen.

'The remarkable thing about the Special,' said Rupert, 'is that it's not special at all. If anything it's universal. All-inclusive.'

'Oh, I always have the Special,' said Joyce. 'I never know what I want to eat until I see it.'

They drank green tea to start with, and then shared a bottle of the local beer. The lighting was poor in the room, and Joyce sat partly with her back to such light as there was.

'Good idea, Rupert. This way we halve the cost.'

'And it's more friendly. After all, we have known each other for ages.'

'Years,' said Joyce. 'God, this war has gone on for ever. It makes me feel so old.'

The large greasy platter arrived with suspicious speed, mounded high with nameless lumps. They both gazed at it in awe.

'I think this is what's called fodder,' said Rupert.

'Anything's better than the mess,' said Joyce.

They sipped at their beers and picked at their fried food as the restaurant filled up.

'Looks like it's going to be over soon now,' said Rupert.

'By Christmas, everyone says,' said Joyce.

'What will you do after the war?'

'Help! I don't know. Get a job, I suppose. How different everything will be.'

'You don't sound all that excited about it.'

'I don't mind admitting it,' said Joyce. 'I'll miss some things. I'll miss Dickie rushing in and out all the time.'

'Me too,' said Rupert. 'Dickie does have a way of making you feel like you're at the centre of the known universe.'

'So what about you, Rupert? What will you do?'

'Pick up where I left off before the war, I suppose. I was at Cambridge, doing a doctorate in philosophy.'

'That sounds so brainy. What was it about?'

'Free will. Determinism. Is everything we do really caused by things that have happened before?'

'Is that what you think?'

'It's certainly not what I feel. I feel as if I make my own decisions. But when you start to look into it you find that what you want is influenced by your upbringing, your culture, your social circle. Even by the size of your nose.'

'The size of your nose!'

'Well, I've got a funny pointy nose. It's not a beautiful nose. That's going to influence my decisions when it comes, say, to finding a wife. No one's going to pick me out in a beauty parade. So I have to manage some other way.'

'Oh, Rupert. Don't be so silly.' He couldn't make out her face very well, but her voice sounded as though she was smiling. 'It's a noble nose.'

'My point is, if I looked like Clark Gable I would make a different set of decisions.'

'So there isn't a girlfriend waiting faithfully at home?'

'Alas, no.'

'Me neither. Boyfriend, I mean.'

'Oh, you won't have any trouble, Joyce,' said Rupert. 'Plenty of chaps would be glad to nab you.'

'Well, I'd like to know where they are,' said Joyce.

'They're probably just too shy to say so.'

'Oh, bother shyness. Don't you think it's just the biggest swiz there is? If only everyone would just say what they wanted, life would be so much simpler.'

'Do you really think so?'

'Yes. I do.'

'What do you think about friendship, Joyce?'

'I'm all for it. Isn't everybody?'

'Do you think friendship can ever turn into something more?'

'What, like love, you mean? Yes, of course. Happens all the time. You know Doreen in Movement Control? She was best pals with the sergeant there, and now they're engaged to be married. Most couples start out as friends, I should say.'

Rupert listened as she chatted on, trying to gauge whether she had any inkling that the conversation might have a personal bearing.

'So what is it, you think, that makes some friendships take that next step?'

'Well, it's nothing to do with noses, I can tell you that.'

She laughed and met his eyes, and then the laugh froze. He saw in that instant that she had suddenly understood what he wanted to say, and that she didn't want him to say it, and was acutely, blushingly embarrassed. In the instant that followed, he in his turn was suffused with dread and humiliation at the thought that his foolhardy hopes were now exposed to the awkward stumblings of her pity.

A silence fell. Rupert found himself entirely unable to speak. To cover his shame he took a mouthful of fried rice, and found himself unable to swallow.

'Some friendships,' said Joyce, looking down now, speaking hurriedly, 'are much better staying as friendships, aren't they? And really, truly, I do sometimes think that good friends are more important than boyfriends or husbands. I mean, with a boyfriend you have to fuss over them and look after them and so on, but with a friend you can be equals. You can say what you really think. And you're not tied down, are you? You're free. It's like what you were saying about free will. Friends are all about free choice, aren't they? And that makes them special.'

As she uttered the word 'special' she looked at the platter between them.

'Oh, Lord. We haven't eaten very much, have we?'

'It's the monsoon,' said Rupert. 'The humidity takes away the appetite.'

'I got caught the other day!' Joyce gladly followed his lead into neutral territory. 'I cantered for shelter, but I still got a soaking.'

'Me too,' said Rupert. 'That's why I was late for Dickie's last briefing.'

He remembered the cooks, and the monkey on a string with its frightened staring face. He could feel the misery gathering like a distant storm, swelling across the sky, casting its approaching shadow. Only his pride, and the sustaining power of good manners, kept him smiling, exchanging commonplaces, at the grease-stained table.

Neither of them had the will to continue for long. Rupert paid the bill for both of them, brushing aside Joyce's protests.

'My pleasure,' he said. 'Good to have company once in a while.'

He walked her back to her billet. When it was time to part she darted forward and pecked him on the cheek.

'You're so sweet, Rupert,' she said. 'You'll make some lucky girl a wonderful husband.'

Then she ran into the house.

Rupert walked down to the lake, and stood for a long time gazing unseeingly at its dark surface. He told himself he had not been in love with Joyce, and therefore he had lost nothing. His life was just as it had been before. But why then did he want to cry? Why did he feel this dread when he looked ahead to the rest of his life?

He didn't cry, that night by the lake in Kandy. Instead his rational mind took charge once more. What is it you fear? he asked himself. The answer came back: loneliness. You will be lonely, he told himself. That's just how it is. So the choice you get is what you do with your loneliness. You can call it your sickness, and let it imprison you. Or you can call it your strength, and let it set you free.

Bats passed flickering over the water. On the island in the middle of the lake the fireflies were out in clouds. From an open window nearby came the strains of a big band, probably Radio Jakarta, the Japanese-run propaganda station. Rupert shook out a cigarette and lit it, drawing the harsh smoke deep into his lungs, feeling the nicotine calm his trembling body.

Oh, Joyce.

Now that she was for ever out of his reach it turned out he had been in love with her after all.

4

It was a warm late afternoon in early August, but for all it was high summer you didn't get to see so much of the sun here in County Donegal. Clouds you had and more than you wanted, and rain of course. But sunshine that pricked right through your cotton pinafore dress and made your skin itch, that was special. Mary Brennan was making her way home from Clancy's farm, carrying the can of milk for which her mother had sent her. She did not hurry on the road.

Mary was just twelve years old and shy and quick-thinking and a little wild inside. She had an elder brother called Eamonn and an elder sister called Bridie and a mother called Mam, but no Da because he had been lost at sea just before she was born. So Mary was the baby, and everyone told Eileen Brennan she spoiled that child and Mam said the good Lord took my man but he gave me my baby, so I'll be duly grateful thank you very much.

You could see the sea from their cottage windows, and from the road, and from just about everywhere round Kilnacarry. Mary could see the sea now, walking back down the road from Clancy's, the milk can bumping cold against the side of her hot leg. It was the sea where Da was lost, which made it frightening. What was it like to be lost at sea? She thought it must be like being in a mist, where you can't tell anymore which way you're going, except instead of ground beneath your feet there's water.

A low dry-stone wall ran alongside the road, and the stones of it were warm in the sun. On the other side of the wall, half-way up the slope of the hill, grew a single wych elm. It was very old and had some branches broken by the winter gales. Bridie said a man had hanged himself there and suicides went to hell, and the devil sat up in the old elm's branches and whispered to you so you'd hang yourself too and become one of his minions for all eternity. Certainly there was something unnatural about the way it stood on the hillside like that all on its own, leaning sideways, or it was the hill that leant sideways. Maybe the devil was there now.

On an impulse Mary climbed the stone wall and set off up the slope. Her skin was tickling in the sun and she felt bold as a banshee. At the foot of the tree she put the milk can down, snug in a crook of roots, and she looked up into the black branches and yellow-green leaves. Her heart thumped in her chest even though she didn't believe the devil was crouched above her. But you could never be sure.

'Hey, old devil man!' she called aloud. 'Come and get me!'

She felt a thrill of excitement as she spoke these words, which were sinful, no question about it. Except she was only teasing the devil, she had no intention of letting him have her soul. If he jumped down out of the tree she would cry out, 'Jesus, Mary and Joseph protect me!' and the devil would be defeated.

She wondered what it would be like to be the devil's minion. He would make you commit sins. That was what the devil wanted from you. Then your soul was damned, unless you made a true act of contrition together with a firm intention of amendment.

'Hey, old devil man!' she called. 'Make me do a sin!'

She was moving round the tree trunk, staring up into the branches, and the sun suddenly dazzled her eyes. In the heart of the dazzle she thought she saw something move in the tree, but then it was gone.

'Bet you can't make me do a sin!' she called. And to show how she wasn't afraid of the devil she started to dance a little skipping dance. Then as she danced she flicked her frock up so she could feel the sun on her bare legs, and it was such a good game she did it some more, lifting her skirt up all the way so the devil could see her knickers. This wasn't a sin because it was rude, and being rude to the devil was brave and good. Father Flannery had once told her when she was a little girl and afraid of the dark, 'If you meet the devil you just give him a raspberry,' and he'd made the raspberry sound with his lips. 'Get thee behind me, Satan,' he said.

'Get thee behind me, Satan!' called out Mary Brennan, and turning round she hitched up her skirt and showed the devil her bum.

Then there came a noise out of the tree and something was moving and suddenly Mary was mortally afraid. She turned and ran off down the hill and over the wall and down the road to the village. There was her mam outside the cottage bringing in the washing from the hedge, and Mary ran all the way to press herself against her warm and comfortable body.

'Why, what's got into you, girl?' said her mam.

'I saw the devil in the witch tree,' said Mary, gasping for breath.

'The devil? And what did he say to you?'

'Nothing. I ran away.'

Her mother stroked her hair.

'What a dreamy young missy it is,' she said. 'And did the devil drink the milk?'

'Oh,' said Mary, her face muffled in her mother's apron. 'I forgot the milk. It's standing by the witch tree.'

'And how are we to have our tea?'

But Mary would not go back, nor would Bridie, so Eamonn had to be fetched from the yard where he was cutting sticks for the winter woodpile. Eamonn wasn't afraid of devils.

The cottage was whitewashed on the outside and had three rooms: one for Bridie and Mary, one for Mam, and Eamonn slept in the kitchen. Two barrels, at the front and back, collected rainwater for washing. Drinking water came from the well. The yard was planted with King Edwards, and the laying hens scratched about between the bushes by the road. This was how home had been for as long as Mary could remember, and she loved the cottage and Kilnacarry and the bay between the two headlands that reached out into the sea, and the sea itself. But there was another feeling too, that came with the warm summer days and the long light evenings. She felt restless and itchy, the way she felt when she danced under the tree.

While they were eating their tea Mary got into a quarrel with Bridie because Bridie said she had made a bags of getting the milk and was a baby to be seeing devils in trees. Mary didn't take offence about forgetting the milk, but she was not a baby any more and said it was false of Bridie to say so and a lie. 'So why are you still in pinafores?' Bridie said, when she knew very well that Mary was waiting to grow into Bridie's old frocks and Mam had said there wasn't the money nor the call to go buying new for her. In this way Mary became upset because Bridie was showing up that they were poor, and that wasn't Mam's fault, it was on account of Da being lost at sea. And now Eamonn had to work all the hours of daylight and still life was hard and it was too bad of Bridie to make them feel this way. Mary felt hot tears of self-pity, or rather family pity, stinging her eyes and a powerful desire to pinch Bridie or cut her. She knew she had gone red and that always made her face blotchy and she hated it, but the more she minded the longer she stayed blotchy.

After tea she went out and didn't tell anyone where she was going. That way if she died they wouldn't find her right away and would be sick with worry, and then they'd find her and she'd be dead and they'd be sorry, Bridie most of all. She went out of the village past the church and on round the bay, past the beached fishing boats where the men were mending their nets. Michael Gallaher hallooed her as she ran by, and she waved back but didn't stop. Once Michael Gallaher got going on one of his fishing stories you could never get away.

Round the little headland she trotted, her dark hair flying free in the light of the descending sun. It was August already, which wasn't midsummer at all but almost autumn, and the days had been shortening for six weeks now. Down the far side of the hill, on the sheep track now, passing between the great boulders that lay on the brown grassland, and there ahead was her own special private place, where she came when she was hurt or angry or just wanted to be alone. It was a small sandy cove, protected by two lines of rocks, and between them the waves came rushing in, making white foam on the beach. It was called Buckle Bay, no one knew why. Sometimes when it was high tide the sand was all covered with frothy white water, but mostly there was some beach to walk on. She loved the feeling of the firm wet sand beneath her bare feet. She loved to stand just where the waves reached, and feel the cool water rush over her feet and ankles, and then the water sucking the sand from under her heels and toes as the wave ebbed.

If you stood and looked out to sea at a time like this, you saw the sun going down. That was grand, and also a little bit melancholy, because the brightness of the day was fading, and you knew in a while it would be dark. But before the darkness there came the colours, the reds and golds and purples of sunset.

Mary stood on the sand and watched the sun descend and the

agitation that had filled her all day slowly passed. The horizon was straight and strong and clear, and the sea big and calm, and the sky above bigger still, and the long warm day was ending.

Mary thought of how she had flicked up her skirt to show the devil her knickers and she knew it had been wrong. There was a spirit of wickedness in her, no denying it. Also, although she was always saying in her prayers thank you for her home and her family, secretly it made her sad that they had no da and were so poor. You had to be brave and put a smile on your face the way Mam did, but surely it wasn't fair. What had they done to deserve it?

That meant she was having blasphemous thoughts about the goodness of God, and that was a mortal sin. So maybe she'd end up as one of the devil's minions after all.

The sun was near the horizon now. It had grown bigger and more gentle as it had descended. There were lines of cloud above it, come out of nowhere, pink streaks beneath the softening blue. It was good to stand here on the warm sand and listen to the hiss of the waves and feel the kindness of the sun.

Such a calm evening. The sea so still you'd say it wasn't moving at all, but for the ripple of water over her bare feet. Then even that became still, and all the world was hushed before the coming of night. The stillness moved her deeply. All is well, said the stillness. All is for a reason.

Then across the water, out of the red glow of the setting sun, came the figure of a man walking towards her. He was far away but she could see him clearly. He wore a loose white robe, and he had his arms reached out before him, as if he wanted to touch her. She thought she could see his face, though he was too far off and surely that wasn't possible. It seemed to her that his face was filled with love, and that he was speaking her name.

'Mary. My beloved, my Mary.'

No movement anywhere in the whole wide world, only the

slipping down of the sun and this beautiful man coming towards her. She felt her heart melt with joy. She reached out her hands towards him.

'Here I am, Lord,' she said.

Then she saw that even as he was beautiful, even as his face was filled with love, he was weeping tears of sorrow. She knew he was Jesus, her Lord and Saviour, and that he was weeping for the sins of the world. She knew that he was coming for her, and that when he reached her, when he took her in his strong arms, she would experience a pure and intense bliss, and her life would be over.

'Take me, Lord,' she said.

Closer he came, over the still water, and closer still, but not yet close enough to touch her.

'Be my voice, Mary,' he said. 'Warn my children. A great wind is coming.'

Then the sky went dark and the wind swept in off the sea, but it never touched Mary. She stood on the beach, her pinafore dress quiet about her, as the wind swept over the land and stripped it clean, scoured it of all the works of sinful mankind. Mary understood that she was made to see this so that she could be the voice of the Lord, and give the warning. Then the wind passed and all was as before.

'Time is running out,' said Jesus. 'Tell my children they must love each other or perish. Tell them, Mary. Be my voice.'

'Why me, Lord?'

'Because your heart is open wide, my child. Because you have faith.'

Jesus was near now, she could see his kind face so clearly, and the shine of the tears on his cheeks. She wanted to run into his arms, but her legs would not move.

'Come here again, Mary. You will see me twice more, as you see me now. After that you will see me no more in this world.'

His voice was close, a gentle whisper in her ear, but he was still many paces away from her. She reached out to him in yearning, and as she did so he faded before her, and the golden light of the setting sun wrapped him round, and he was gone.

The stillness ended, and the sea was moving once more. She felt the breeze on her cheek, and flurrying her hair. The tide had gone out, she was standing far from the waves' edge. She must have been here for a long time. Soon it would be dark.

Slowly, dreamily, Mary Brennan made her way home. She knew what she must do now. She must tell everyone what Jesus had said to her. She knew she would not be believed, not at first, but she had no worries on that score. She had become an instrument of God. She had only to obey. God would do the rest.

They noticed the change in her as soon as she came into the cottage. Bridie was just lighting the oil lamp on the wall. Eamonn was on the wooden seat smoking a cigarette. Mam was at the table, making an apron in a crossover design, every stitch sewn by hand. She sold her aprons for half a crown each, which provided for a few little extras.

'What's become of you, missy?' said Mam. 'We thought the fairies had got you.'

'No, Mam,' said Mary. 'I was down by Buckle Bay and I saw Jesus.'

'You did no such thing!' exclaimed Bridie sharply. 'That's taking the name of the Lord in vain.'

'A great wind is coming,' said Mary.

It was the way she didn't snap back at Bridie that made them sit up and listen.

'What great wind?' said Eamonn.

'Come here, my chick,' said Mam.

Mary went to her, and her mother looked her in the face.

'Is this one of your tricks?'

'No, Mam,' said Mary.

'Then you'd best tell your story to the priest.'

Father Dermot Flannery was not absolutely in bed when the knock came on his door. He was sitting in a deep-cushioned chair, a tumbler of Jameson's balanced on the arm, reading the sports pages of the newspaper by the light of a tilley lamp. But his body, following many years of regular habit, was halfway through the routine that suspended his waking self, stage by stage, until it took only the final act of lying down in bed to release his spirit to sleep. For this reason the knock on the door made him irritable.

Father Flannery was a martyr to his irritability. He hated it and was ashamed of it, but seemed unable to control it. In his own mind he was a humble and charitable shepherd to his flock. Why then this peevish snapping?

'What in God's name time do you call this?' he barked at the door.

'It's us, Father,' came a muffled voice from outside.

'Oh, us, is it? Us should be in their own homes, in my opinion. Well, then, well, then, let's be seeing you.'

In shuffled Eileen Brennan and her three children, the entire Brennan clan, great gawky youths that filled up his parlour with their loose limbs and their odour of poverty.

'Sorry, Father, but it's our Mary,' said the mother, blinking in the bright hissing light of the tilley lamp.

'Is it now?' said the priest, scowling.

He had turned fifty years of age in the last twelve months, and also his mother had died, and so it was he had discovered to his great surprise that he had become a priest not so much to serve the Lord as to please his mother. Her pride in his status had never faded. But now that she was gone there seemed not so much point to it all somehow. He was not a learned man, but he

48

was honest. He did not deceive himself that he made any real difference to the souls in his care. Their lives were hard, his heart bled for them, but you couldn't go on bleeding out your heart for ever, and the suffering went on in the same way. After twenty-five years as a parish priest there was nothing new to discover. Misery had ceased to be interesting.

'So what's ailing your Mary?' he said. 'She's looking well enough.'

And better than well. The youngest of the Brennans was a sturdy lass with a round pink face and a look in her eyes that made him put his head on one side. It was a bold look, but not at him.

'Tell Father, Mary,' said her mother.

'Mary's seen Jesus,' blurted out Bridie Brennan.

'Is that a fact?' said the priest.

'Yes, Father,' said Mary. 'It was over by Buckle Bay. He came walking to me over the water.'

So the priest got her to tell the whole story, which of course was all just so much nonsense, but there was no need to injure the child's young faith. Also there was a way she had of speaking about her experience that touched him, weary though he was and wishing for his bed. Her eyes shone as she spoke, filled with the wonder of it, and there wasn't so much wonder in the world.

'The whole sea was still, Father, and he was so beautiful, and I did feel his great love.'

'And he gave you a warning, you say?'

'There'll be a great wind, Father. We must love each other or perish.'

'Well, I'll not be disagreeing with that.'

'Should we be telling the Holy Father, Father?' said Mrs Brennan.

'One step at a time,' said the priest. 'First you must go home, and say your prayers, and get a good night's sleep. Then we'll see what the world looks like tomorrow.'

'I shall see him again,' said Mary. 'And once more after that.'

So the Brennan clan departed, and Dermot Flannery went thoughtfully to bed. The girl had said nothing of any significance, of course, but she had impressed him even so. Kilnacarry was a village at the end of the road, and no one came down the road who didn't already live there, and the folk of Kilnacarry were too poor to go up the road to anywhere else. The outcome was that every day God sent looked much like every other day, except that some days it rained and some days it didn't. And now here was a child who said she'd had a vision of Our Lord himself. A little stir and bustle and a few sixpences from the curious would make a welcome change for the good people of the parish.

5

Colonel Paul Tibbets handpicked his crew from guys he had flown with in bombing missions over Europe. He asked for Dutch Van Kirk as his navigator and Tom Ferebee as his bombardier. These three knew each other well. Then there was Wyatt Duzenbury for flight engineer, and Deak Parsons looking after the weapon. Tibbets had spent time at Los Alamos, he had been at meetings where Robert Oppenheimer chainsmoked, and General Groves, who hated people who smoked, worked alongside him, and he knew about the atom bomb. He knew it was a big deal, and would shorten the war, but mostly it was a bunch of technical challenges. The bomb was so heavy that the plane that carried it would have to be stripped down to its shell. Then there was the matter of getting away after the drop. The usual bombing pattern was you dropped your load and went on flying straight ahead over the target, but you couldn't do that with this new gadget, because it was going to be a big bang. Oppenheimer told Tibbets he had to turn tangent to the expanding shockwave, 159 degrees in either direction, and get the hell out of there. They timed the drop with dummy bombs and reckoned he had forty to forty-two seconds to make that turn, which was not an easy matter in a B-29 Superfortress at twenty-five thousand feet. Tibbets practised turning, steeper each time, until the big plane's tail was shaking, but he got so he could make the turn and get eleven miles away in forty seconds. Eleven miles from the detonation and the plane could ride the shockwave.

'I sure am happy to hear that,' said Dutch Van Kirk.

'You just get us there on time,' said Tibbets. 'I'll get you home.'

The crew shipped out to North Field airbase on Tinian in the west Pacific to await orders. The words 'atom bomb' were never spoken. They had been told the weapon they were going to drop would destroy an entire city. So the Japs would finally get paid back for Pearl Harbor, and the Bataan death march, and all the cruelties they'd inflicted on American POWs. Everyone knew the Japs were monkeys. Just about everyone back home wanted to see the whole bunch exterminated, men, women and children. Tibbets told his crew what General Uzal Ent told him at Colorado Springs.

'Paul, be careful how you treat this responsibility, because if you're successful you'll probably be called a hero.'

'And if we fail?' said Tom Ferebee.

'Our worries are over,' said Tibbets.

He named the B-29 after his mother, Enola Gay Haggard, who herself had been named for the heroine of a novel called *Enola, Or Her Fatal Mistake*. His mother had backed him up in his dream to be a flyer even when his father said he was going to be a doctor. He did some time at med. school in Cincinnati but he quit to join the Army Air Corps. His father was angry and said, 'If you want to kill yourself, go ahead, I don't give a damn.' But his mother said, 'Paul, if you want to go fly airplanes, you're going to be all right.' So he called the plane the *Enola Gay*; had it painted on the side.

The order came through on August 3, requiring the delivery of 'the first special bomb as soon as weather will permit visual bombing'. It was authorised by Henry Stimson, Secretary of War. No order was ever signed by President Truman.

The weather station on Guam predicted that the skies over Honshu would be clear on the sixth day of August. On August 5 Tibbets was cleared to go. Target time was 09.15 next morning, Tinian time, 08.15 Japanese time. Tibbets told Dutch to figure out what time they had to take off to be over the target at 09.15 and Dutch calculated 02.45. The crew were then ordered to get some sleep. Tibbets, Van Kirk and Ferebee had no inclination to sleep. They stayed up playing poker.

Deak Parsons, the weaponeer, oversaw the loading of the bomb into the aeroplane. This was an anxious time. 'Little Boy' was three metres long, weighed almost ten thousand pounds, and was extremely vulnerable to accidental detonation. Crash impact, or an electrical short, or fire, or lightning could all set it off, and if it blew it would take out Tinian Island and all five hundred Superfortresses based there. So Deak did not load the four silk powder bags, each containing two pounds of slotted-tube cordite, into the gun breech, and he instructed Morris Jeppson to remove the three safety plugs that connected the bomb's internal battery to its firing mechanism.

That night the airstrip was floodlit as if for a Hollywood premiere or, as Dick Nelson said, 'like a supermarket opening.' The crew were filmed and photographed as they climbed on board, but none of them had too much to say. They each had their job to do and their minds were on the mission.

The *Enola Gay* took off right on time and made its rendezvous in mid-air with the instruments plane that would measure the blast and the picture plane that would take the pictures. Flying time to target was six hours, if Dutch had got it right. When the three planes were in formation, Tibbets left the pilot's seat and crawled down the tunnel to speak to the crew. Eight of the twelve men on board had been kept in ignorance of the nature of the bomb, at least in theory. But they weren't stupid. No one had ever before seen a bomb like the one they were carrying.

'We're going on a bombing mission,' Tibbets told them. 'But it's a little bit special.'

Bob Caron, the tail gunner, said, 'Colonel, we wouldn't be playing with atoms today, would we?'

'Bob,' said Tibbets, 'you've got it just exactly right.'

Then Deak Parsons loaded the bags of cordite into the bomb's gun breech, and Morris Jeppson climbed down into the bomb bay and pulled out the green testing plugs and put in the red firing plugs. After that the bomb was armed. There was a timer device that stopped it going off for fifteen seconds after release, then a barometric switch took over, a thin membrane that got pushed in as air pressure increased during descent, and closed the final circuit at two thousand metres. Then the three gun primers ignited and blew the cordite, which shot the uranium projectile down the gun barrel inside the bomb at three hundred metres a second to smash into the solid uranium target, and set off a chain reaction. Once the bomb was armed, who knew what might go wrong? Some random radar signal could do it, or plain old water leakage.

Tibbets had orders not to use the radio but he reckoned he owed it to his crew to talk them down to the drop. So the *Enola Gay* flew on, and the sun rose, and it was a clear day down there. Japanese early warning radar picked up the incoming planes and sounded the alert, but when they confirmed that it was only three aircraft they assumed it was a reconnaissance mission and lifted the alert. The Japanese Air Force was so short of fuel they no longer made any attempt to intercept small formations.

Then the rivers and the bridges and the big shrine of Hiroshima came into view and Tibbets began the countdown. They were over the target at 08.15:15 local time and that's when the bomb dropped. As soon as it was away the whole plane gave a great jump and Tibbets took it into its tight turn, losing height fast. Then the bomb went off with a bright flash and the shock wave chased the plane and Bob Caron in the tail said, 'Here it comes!' and when it hit them the plane snapped all over, even though by then they were ten and a half miles away. They looked back to see what had happened to the target but all they could see was black smoke and dust and this tall, tall cloud, and right at the top, the colours. Salmon and pink and yellow flame. Then they headed away over the Sea of Japan.

'Dutch,' said Tibbets, 'what time were we over the target?'

'Target time plus fifteen seconds,' said Dutch.

Tom Ferebee snorted.

'What lousy navigating. Fifteen seconds off!'

No one spoke about what was happening on the ground. Don Albury, co-pilot on the picture plane flying with the *Enola Gay*, looked down at that great cloud, and the rainbow colours streaming out of it at the top, and said a little prayer.

'Lord, please take care of them all down there.'

General Groves phoned Dr Oppenheimer at 2 p.m., Santa Fe time, that same day.

'I'm very proud of you and all your people,' Groves said.

'It went all right?' said Oppenheimer.

'Apparently,' said Groves, 'it went with a tremendous bang.'

The president learned the news while he was at lunch on the USS *Augusta*, en route to Newport, Virginia. Excited, he turned to shake Captain Graham's hand.

'This is the greatest thing in history!' he said.

He then made an announcement to all the crew gathered in

the mess hall that a successful attack had taken place on Japan with an extraordinary new weapon that was twenty thousand times more powerful than a ton of TNT. The crew cheered and clapped. The president and his party then attended a programme of boxing bouts on the ship's well deck. The display came to an abrupt close when the ring collapsed, injuring a crew member, who was struck on the head by a post. The president and Secretary Byrnes visited the injured man in the sickbay to be sure he wasn't seriously hurt.

In his statement released to the press, Truman said, 'The Japanese began the war from the air at Pearl Harbor. They have been repaid many fold.' He revealed the scale of the Manhattan Project: up to 125,000 individuals working for two and a half years. 'We have spent two billion dollars on the greatest scientific gamble in history, and won. It is an awful responsibility which has come to us. We thank God that it has come to us, instead of to our enemies; and we pray that He may guide us to use it in His ways and for His purposes.'

6

On the second evening of Mary Brennan's visions the priest was out on the sand of Buckle Bay as the sun was setting, along with Ned and Betty Clancy, who'd heard the tale from Eileen Brennan, and Michael Gallaher, who had followed out of mere idle curiosity. As the sun went down in the west Mary Brennan walked out alone towards the water's edge and stood there, very still. They couldn't see what she saw, but they could see the way her arms went out, and the look in her eyes that shone like the setting sun. They heard her speak, she said, 'Yes, Lord,' and, 'I'll tell them, Lord.' The priest watched closely and he was moved. This is true faith, he told himself. Whether the vision was real or not, he could not doubt the child's ardent and innocent surrender to her God.

Then Eileen Brennan was nudging him and saying, 'The sea! The sea!' The priest turned his gaze from the girl to the sea, and saw to his amazement that it was no longer moving. Just as the girl had said, a stillness had fallen over the world. He looked at the others and saw that they saw it too.

Mary Brennan let out a cry, and fell to the sand.

'Mary!'

Her mother ran to her, and drew her up to her feet again.

'What is it?' she said. 'What did you see?'

'The chastisement,' said Mary. 'Oh, Mam, it was terrible! The great wind will take everything!'

'Our Lord is warning us,' said Eileen Brennan, turning to the priest. 'You must tell the Holy Father what my child has seen.' And to Mary, 'When will it come, this great wind?'

Mary shook her head. She didn't know.

'Sure, you should ask him,' said Eamonn, who saw matters in a practical light.

'The sea was still,' said Eileen Brennan. 'Just like you said. The father saw it too.'

'I did so,' said the priest.

'He'll come again,' said Mary. 'One more time. Oh, Mam, I do love him so.'

'I'm sure we all do,' said her mother.

'Wouldn't it be the war?' said Bridie. 'There's terrible things been doing in the war.'

'There's always war,' said Father Flannery. 'I'm thinking it's the godlessness. The young people today have no respect.'

'Our Mary has respect,' said Eileen Brennan.

'Your Mary is a child of God,' said the priest. 'When she lifted up her sweet face to the west I saw the light of heaven in her eyes.'

'You must send word to the bishop, Father.'

'I shall send word to Monsignor McCloskey,' said the priest. 'In Donegal.'

Monsignor McCloskey drove up to Kilnacarry the very next afternoon and met Mary Brennan in the priest's house. Monsignor McCloskey was much of an age with Father Flannery, but he was a varsity man with a narrow face and sharp little eyes. Father Flannery begged him to go easy on the girl, aware as he was that these varsity men had little time for peasant superstitions.

'If this is a true revelation, Dermot,' said Monsignor McClo-skey, 'it will be proof against my reasonable doubts. If it is nonsense, then the sooner we put a stop to it the better.'

The monsignor requested that he interview Mary Brennan alone; which is to say, without the rest of the clan. Father Flan-nery remained in the room, and took notes. Mary bore herself with great composure, and seemed unafraid of the monsignor, for all his close-fitting cassock and his wire-rimmed spectacles.

'Now then, Mary,' said the monsignor. 'I'm sure I don't need to tell you that sometimes we think we see things when we don't. Just the same way we have dreams that feel so real, but when we wake we know it was all in our imaginations.'

'Yes, Monsignor,' said Mary.

'Having a dream of Our Lord is a holy thing, and a blessing, and shows what a good girl you are.'

'It was no dream, Monsignor.'

'Dreams don't only come when we're in bed at night, Mary. They can come in broad daylight, when we're wide awake and have our eyes open.'

'Then am I dreaming now, Monsignor?'

'No, Mary. Not now.'

'How am I to know when it's a dream and when it's real, Monsignor?'

'Ordinary life is real, Mary,' said the monsignor. 'When some-thing extraordinary happens to us, we have to ask ourselves if maybe we're dreaming.'

'Maybe Jesus came to me in a dream, Monsignor.'

'That is what I'm trying to establish, Mary.'

'But Monsignor,' said Mary, her innocence striking like a sword, 'if Jesus wanted to come to me, it would never be ordi-nary. So it would have to be a dream.'

'Well, yes, Mary . . .'

'I don't see that it matters what you call it,' the girl went on.

'What matters is that he was so beautiful, and so loving, and I am to be his voice and give his warning, before it's too late.'

The monsignor fell silent, perplexed.

'He was crying, Monsignor. The sins of the world made him cry for us. He told me we must love each other or perish. He told me a great wind would come. He showed me the great wind. The sun went out and the wind swept over the land and all the trees and the houses and the people in them were destroyed. He told me I must tell everyone, Monsignor, before it's too late.'

'When will it be too late, Mary?'

'I don't know, Monsignor. I think he may tell me that this evening.'

'This evening?'

'He'll come to me for the last time. He promised.'

'May I be there, Mary? Would you mind?'

'No, Monsignor.' She sounded genuinely puzzled. 'Why would I mind? I would wish that all of you could see him as I see him.'

'Why do you think he has chosen you, Mary?'

'I asked him that, Monsignor. He said, because my heart is open, and I have faith.'

The monsignor sighed, and looked round to meet Father Flannery's eyes.

'I shall join you this evening,' he said.

On the final evening of Mary Brennan's visions the little beach was crowded. Word had spread far beyond the village. There were people from Rosbeg and Portnoo and Ardara and Kilkenny, such a scrum that Eamonn Brennan and the priest had to make a space for Mary to walk clear to the water's edge. Monsignor McCloskey was there, and a man from the newspaper come up from Donegal with a flash camera.

'You'll not be making flashes at her when she's talking to Our Lord,' said Father Flannery, and the cameraman said no, he would take his pictures afterwards.

Mary Brennan was not disturbed one bit by the crowd. The priest asked her if she would like them sent away, and she said, 'No, Father. The more who come the better. I have so many people to tell.'

It was this that impressed the priest as much as anything, the humble practical way in which the girl saw the whole business as a task entrusted to her, much as you might give her a letter to take to the post. There was no vanity in her. So supposing Jesus had a message to give to the world, who would he choose? Surely just such an innocent child as this.

As they waited for sunset there was much talk in the crowd about the now famous stillness. They all knew that at the moment Jesus came walking on the water, the sea would become still. Only Mary Brennan would see and hear Jesus, but all of them would witness the stillness.

And so it proved. Mary went forward, apart from the crowd, and reached out her arms. The sun, partly in clouds, sent out its golden setting light over the water. And the sea became still. Not everyone saw it, but many did. Father Flannery saw it. The monsignor thought he did not see it, there were waves still washing in to the beach, and out to sea there was the gentle heave of the swell. But then for a moment there did seem to come a pause, and a silence. But perhaps he only imagined it.

Mary spoke to Jesus, they saw her lips move, but no one heard her words. Then after a little time, in the afterlight of the sunset, she turned and faced them all, gathered in the little rock-girt bay.

'Dear friends,' she said. 'I'm not speaking to you in my own words, but in the words of our Lord Jesus Christ. I'm only the voice.'

This voice was soft and small, and partly obscured by the hiss and rush of the waves. Those who were nearest to her remembered what she said and repeated it afterwards, and out of these repetitions came the prophecy, which took several forms. However, everyone who had been present that evening agreed that Jesus, speaking through the child, was saddened by the sinfulness of mankind.

'Why do you hurt each other so, when I made you to love each other?'

Mary spoke of Noah and the flood, when God looked upon the earth and saw that it was corrupt and filled with violence and said, I will destroy man who I've created. Now such a time had come again. This time all living things would be destroyed by a great wind. Everyone remembered Mary speaking of the great wind.

'When this great wind sweeps over the land,' she said, 'it will be made clean. Jesus told me these things weeping.'

They remembered that most of all, how Jesus wept for the child, there in Buckle Bay.

'Tell my children,' said Mary, speaking in the words given her by Jesus, 'you must love each other or perish. Time is running out. I asked my Lord, When will this happen? He told me, Yours is the generation that will perish. I asked my Lord, What can we do? He told me, Love each other, and love my Father in heaven. I asked my Lord, will there be a warning given to us before the great wind comes? He told me, When the time is near I will speak with you again.'

So there it was: the warning, the prophecy, the promise. All this was felt to be a great honour and a responsibility by the people of Kilnacarry.

'Now I've done as I was told,' said the child in her soft voice. 'I've spoken all the things he said. There's nothing more.'

As she fell silent the flash camera exploded with a pop, and her ecstatic face was lit up for a second, and they all saw. The girl's simple clear speech had a profound effect on all who heard it.

'Jesus, Mary, Joseph and all the Holy Martyrs!' murmured old Molly Lynch. 'Haven't I been saying it for years? The world has gone to the bad.'

In low voices they repeated to each other the words of Mary's warning, crossing themselves as they did so. The two priests conferred in undertones as the crowd dispersed into the night.

'There's nothing against the doctrines of the Church in what she says,' said the monsignor. 'A call to repentance is always timely. But this talk of a great wind disturbs me.'

'That's the part they'll all be spreading,' said Father Flannery.

'We have to guard against needless panic.'

'That, and the stillness.'

Monsignor McCloskey said nothing to that, but Father Flannery could tell that he had been affected by the evening's events.

'I believe her to be honest,' said Father Flannery.

'Oh, she's honest, all right,' said the monsignor. 'But even an honest person can be deluded.'

'Did she sound deluded to you?'

'Time will tell. The Church in her wisdom does not rush to judgement on such matters. It was thirteen years before the visions of Fatima were declared worthy of belief.'

The next day, August 9 1945, the local newspaper carried an account of a terrible new weapon that had been dropped on Hiroshima to end the war against Japan. Father Flannery read about the 'cosmic bomb' which harnessed 'the force from which the sun draws its power'. He read how a single bomb had destroyed an entire city, 'wiping it off the face of the earth'. He read how there were many more such cosmic bombs waiting to be unleashed.

'The great wind,' he murmured to himself.

On that day the lethargy dropped off him, and he made a resolution. He would break himself of the little selfishnesses of the priestly life. He would devote the rest of his days to propagating this message God had seen fit to put into the mouth of a child of his parish. He would build a shrine at Buckle Bay, and make it a place of pilgrimage so that the word might be spread far and wide. And he would protect Mary Brennan, so that her purity of heart might remain untouched, and God continue to find in her a vessel for His word. There was after all, by her own account, one final warning to come before the prophesied destruction.

Ours is the generation that will perish.

7

His name was Rupert, which she found funny because it was like Rupert Bear. But even at the age of seven Pamela understood that he was not a funny man but a sad man. She liked this about him. She too was sad, as was only proper for a child whose father had recently died. She also liked Rupert for not being in love with her mother, the way everyone else was.

'Mummy, why doesn't Rupert like you?'

'Who says he doesn't like me?' said Kitty Avenell, sitting before her dressing table in her bedroom, brushing her hair.

'Well, he doesn't look at you that way.'

Kitty laid down her hairbrush and met Pamela's eyes in the mirror.

'What way?'

Pamela obliged with a simpering ogle. They both burst into laughter. Pamela loved to see her mother laugh. She was so pretty anyone would fall in love with her.

'Well, thank goodness he doesn't,' Kitty said. 'That just goes to show how sensible he is.'

'I think he's sad.'

'Why should he be sad?'

'Because he doesn't have a wife, of course.'

'Maybe he doesn't want a wife.'

'Of course he wants a wife! He's old!'

The year, which was 1950, had excited Pamela very much when it first began. It seemed so different from 1949, so new and full of possibility. Forming that big round O in her exercise book at school had felt grand and noble. But then everything had gone on just the same.

Not just the same. Daddy had his accident. Funny how she kept forgetting about that.

Rupert was only visiting them for the day. Really he had come down to Sussex to talk to Larry Cornford, who just about lived with them these days. Larry was supposed to be married to Rupert's sister, but now they were getting a divorce, which meant Larry wouldn't be married any more.

Pamela found Rupert in the room called the study, that was full of her father's books. It still had her father's smoky smell even though no one used it now. Rupert was gazing at the bookshelves.

'Hello,' said Pamela.

She wasn't shy with grown-ups. It was one of the things everyone remarked about her.

'Hello,' said Rupert.

'Are you looking for a book?'

'Not really. But there are some very interesting books here.'

'I'm not really interested in books,' said Pamela.

'I am,' said Rupert.

This surprised Pamela. Her response had been of the kind that usually elicited a smile, a knowing glance, as if to say: She's very sure of herself for her age. But Rupert simply took it at face value.

'Why?' she said.

'Books help me make sense of my life,' he said. Then he added, 'Well, some books, anyway.'

This rather impressed Pamela. She felt he had raised the stakes of their conversation, and it was up to her to follow suit.

'My daddy died,' she said.

'Yes, I know,' said Rupert. 'I'm sorry.'

'You could marry my mummy if you want.'

She had learned that this sort of suggestion caused a subdued consternation among the grown-ups, which added to her prestige. But once again, Rupert took her seriously.

'Your mother's a wonderful person,' he said, 'but I'm quite sure she doesn't want to marry me.'

'But she's sad,' persisted Pamela. 'And you're sad.'

Rupert gazed at her through his spectacles in a way that made her feel he was thinking not about her but about what she'd said.

'Sometimes I'm sad,' he said, 'and sometimes I'm happy. Isn't that how it is for you?'

'Yes,' said Pamela. 'But I'd rather be happy.'

His words stayed with her. Simple though they were, they seemed to her to be important, perhaps because of the serious way he looked at her when he said them. She wondered if they were true. Then it struck her that although she was often cross she was rarely sad. In fact, sometimes she wasn't nearly as sad as she should be. Her father dying was very bad, and everyone looked at her sorrowfully, but the truth was that for most of her young life he had been away. He was always going away. This dying felt like just another going away.

Already she was forgetting him. That showed that deep down she was a bad person, which she had long suspected. She made herself cry because of forgetting him, but then realised she was crying for herself, not for him, and stopped and wiped her eyes.

There was a little house at the end of the yard that had been an outside lavatory, which she had taken over as her secret place. She would often sit there on the warped wooden seat and listen to the rain on the tin roof and watch the spiders in their webs in the single-paned window. She wasn't sure why she liked going there, it was boring and she never stayed long, but it was while perched in that musty-smelling gloom that she wondered about her own badness. The main form her badness took was only really caring about herself. Good people cared about other people. She pretended to, but she didn't. It was just one of those things about her, like her brown eyes and her skinny legs, and being pretty like her mother. It never struck her that there was anything she could do about it.

Her five-year-old sister Elizabeth kicked at the closed door of the outhouse.

'Pammy? You there?'

'Go away, Monkey.'

'Mummy says Rupert's going and you're to say goodbye.'

'I said go away.'

She waited until her sister had gone back into the house and then emerged. That was an example of her badness. She wouldn't come out when told to by her sister, even though she wanted to come out. Now why was that?

Rupert shook her hand to say goodbye, which she liked better than the grown-ups who expected to be kissed. Then Larry drove him to the station. Hugo turned up in his big white van and started unloading boxes of wine into the garage. He and her father had been partners in the wine business. Now, after the accident, Larry was going to be his partner instead.

Pamela liked Hugo, and knew he liked her.

'How's my little sweetheart today?' he said.

They had an agreement that when she was old enough he would marry her, but of course it was only a game. It was her mother he really loved. Once he had kissed her, and she had seen.

'Darling Hugo,' said her mother, 'he's only a boy.'

But he wasn't a boy, he was a grown-up.

'Do you want to play with the families?' said Elizabeth.

'Not with you, Monkey,' she replied.

Elizabeth burst into tears.

'Why do you have to be so mean?' said Kitty.

Why did she? It was a mystery. But now she had a way of silencing all criticism.

'I miss Daddy,' she said.

'Oh, darling.'

Tears sprang into her mother's eyes, but didn't fall.

'So do I,' said Elizabeth, which was a lie.

'He's watching over you both,' said Kitty. 'He's in heaven, watching over all of us.'

But he wasn't. He was where he always went, which was away.

Then quite suddenly Pamela had a memory of him that was so clear and strong it made her gasp. They were on the side of Mount Caburn playing Aeroplanes. Her father was below her down the slanting hillside, standing with his arms reached out on either side, squinting into the sun. She was further up, waiting to run. The grass was long on either side of the track, and the air was warm. Monkey was there, and their mother, but all she saw in this memory was the tall lean figure of her beautiful father, waiting to catch her.

'Off you go!' he cried.

She set off running down the close-grazed track. She ran and ran, until she was running so fast she couldn't stop. It was like falling, tumbling down that track, windmilling her arms and laughing as she went. All the way, her skirts flying, her chest tight, all the way watched by his beautiful face and bang into his strong arms. He caught her and swept her up and swung her round and all the world was dancing.

'Don't go, Daddy! Don't go!'

Now, remembering, she cried real tears, and she was crying for him and it hurt, and she didn't like it at all. She ran to her

69

mother and cried in her arms, which made Kitty cry too. Then Monkey joined them and of course she cried to be like them, but it was false crying. Then Hugo came in and found them and said, 'My goodness, it's a weeping family.'

Hugo was nice like that. He said ordinary things in an ordinary way.

A few days later she and Hugo were alone in the yard and she said to him, for no reason at all, 'I suppose you'll marry Mummy now.'

'Oh, no,' he said, blushing red. 'I'm not the one who'll be marrying Kitty.'

That was when she knew it would be Larry. She was glad about that because she liked Larry, and because it meant Hugo could marry her. But selfish though she was, she knew enough to understand that this must be hard for Hugo.

'Does that make you very sad, Hugo?'

'Oh, Lord, no,' he said. But she could see it did. 'And anyway, I'm going to marry you.'

'Not until I'm sixteen. That's nine more years.'

'I shall wait,' said Hugo gallantly.

The next year Kitty married Larry and became Mrs Cornford. Then one year after that Hugo married someone quite unspeakable called Harriet. Rupert didn't marry anybody.

PART TWO

Deterrence

January 1961 – June 1962

8

The yard outside was deep in snow. A light patter of flakes was still falling. It had been snowing since the night before the inauguration.

McGeorge Bundy stepped out of the house onto the porch to retrieve the newspaper. His breath made clouds in the sharp cold. Back inside, he stamped the snow off his shoes and shook the snow off the paper.

Mary was in the kitchen, fixing breakfast for the boys. Bundy took his usual place, unfolding the *New York Times* as he sat down. Mary placed a mug of coffee before him and he sipped at it in silence, his eyes scanning the columns.

'Oh boy!' he exclaimed softly.

He read on.

'Someone screwed up big time,' he said.

'Finish up, Stephen,' said Mary to her eldest, who was dawdling over his French toast.

'I'll have it if he doesn't want it,' said Andrew.

'No, you won't,' said Stephen, reaching an arm round his plate. 'You've got your own.'

Four boys between the ages of five and ten. Their racket filled the big house from morning to night, but to look at Mac you'd think he didn't even notice.

'What is it?' said Mary.

He showed her the headline in the paper.

KENNEDY DEFENSE STUDY FINDS
NO EVIDENCE OF A 'MISSILE GAP'

'Jack just about built his campaign on the missile gap.'

'What's a missile gap?' said Stephen, interested.

His father demonstrated, holding one hand a few inches above the table.

'We have this many missiles.' He raised his other hand to twice the height. 'The Russians have this many. The difference between them is the missile gap.'

The boys all stared at him wide-eyed.

'So the Russians have got more than us.'

'They would have if it were true.'

'Is it true, Dad?'

'No, Stephen. It's not true.'

He gulped down the rest of his coffee and jumped up.

'Quick march, boys! The car'll be here soon.'

The chauffeured Mercury sedan picked him up at 7.45 each morning. On school days the three eldest boys scrambled into the car with him and he dropped them off at St Albans on the way. Usually he was at his desk in the Old Executive Building next to the White House by 8.15, which gave him time to go through the early-morning cable traffic before the staff meeting at nine.

This morning would be different.

Sitting in the car, hissing over the snowy side roads of Spring Valley into the wide cleared streets of downtown DC, he ran through the possible sources of the leak. He concluded that it had to be Bob McNamara.

On reaching his office he telephoned Bob and got the full story. Then he crossed to the White House and took the elevator directly to the president's private quarters. He found the president sitting up in bed reading the *New York Times*.

'What the fuck's going on, Mac?'

'I'm afraid it's Bob's screw-up, Mr President.'

Bob McNamara was Secretary of Defence in the new administration. As national Security Adviser, Bundy was technically McNamara's junior, but the Bundys and the Kennedys had known each other a long time.

'Bob had a bunch of reporters round yesterday,' he told the president. 'He told them the briefing was NFA, Not For Attribution. He didn't realise that meant they could still run the story so long as they didn't name the source. He thought it was the same as Off the Record.'

'For fuck's sake!' groaned Kennedy.

He held up the newspaper.

'He's telling the world we can absorb every missile the Russians can throw at us and still have enough firepower to wipe out 80 per cent of the Soviet Union.'

'That's right.'

'Is it true?'

'Sure it's true,' said Bundy. 'I know it and you know it.'

This was why Kennedy listened to Mac Bundy more than any of the others. He got to the point fast. Kennedy had told him he would have made him his Secretary of State if he hadn't looked so young. 'Two baby faces like yours and mine are just too much.'

'It doesn't matter what I know,' said Kennedy. 'What matters is what the American people know, and what the Russians know. I should sack Bob for this.'

'Bob's good. We need him.'

'So what do I do? I campaigned on a missile gap.'

'Well, Mr President,' said Mac Bundy, thinking fast, 'this defence study is based on the findings of surveillance flights over the

Soviet Union. The U2s can't fly over every inch. It stands to reason we can't know for sure how many missiles there are down there. And as long as we're not a hundred per cent sure, we do what we have to do to defend the American people.'

'I buy that,' said Kennedy. 'That's good.'

'Our best today. Better tomorrow.'

This was the motto of the Dexter Lower School, which both Bundy and Kennedy had attended as small boys. Kennedy grinned.

'Ask not what your school can do for you, ask what you can do for your school.'

This was the motto of Kennedy's prep school, Choate. Bundy himself had been at Groton, which was rather more distinguished, and had as its motto 'To serve is to rule.'

'You said it, Mr President.'

'I pledged in my campaign to close the missile gap with a major build-up of defence spending. So that's what I'm going to do.'

After Bundy had left him, Kennedy got out of bed and got dressed. His back problems made it hard for him to get his socks on, but he didn't call for help. His morning struggle with his socks, which led through pain to victory, set him up for the day.

9

From a distance, the base looked like a prison. On all sides stretched the fields of Norfolk, still winter grey. The road ran straight and narrow, the three military cars carrying the inspection group bunched close together. RAF Feltwell, their destination, was ringed by a high wire fence from which rose thin steel gantries bearing floodlights, and stubby observation towers. Beyond the fence loomed grey hangars, with flat-roofed brick buildings alongside.

'It was an airfield in the war,' said Mountbatten, sitting beside Rupert Blundell in the back of the lead car. 'Totally rebuilt, of course. Must be a strange life for the men here. If they ever carry out the job they're trained to do, it'll all be over.'

'I don't see any missiles.'

'They'll be sleeping. They'll wake them up for us.'

Rupert believed he knew all there was to know about the missiles, but he had never actually seen one. They were called Thor, after the Norse god of thunder. There were sixty of them, deployed in RAF bases spread over Norfolk, Lincolnshire and Yorkshire, all targeted on the Soviet Union. Three-quarters of the Thor force was held at T-15, which meant they could be launched within fifteen minutes of the order to scramble. Each missile carried a 1.45 megaton warhead, and would detonate over its target in Russia eighteen minutes after launch. The Thor force carried more explosive power in a single strike than had been delivered in all wars in all history.

The RAF called them the Penguin squadrons: 'All flap and no fly.' The chiefs of staff viewed them as a liability. Earl Mountbatten, now elevated to the post of Chief of Defence Staff, took an even dimmer view.

'You might as well put a bloody great sign over the east of England saying, "Hit me."'

The convoy drew up to the gates of the compound. An RAF police sergeant was waiting by the guardroom at the salute. All security procedures were followed to the letter. The gates then opened and they drove in, past fire tenders and fuel tanks, past a fenced storage enclosure guarded by USAAF personnel, to the main RIM building, beside which stood the Mission Control Centre. Outside on the tarmac stood the officer in command, flanked by two squadron leaders and two launch control officers.

Mountbatten and his party emerged from their cars and took the salute. The wing commander introduced his staff, and led the visitors into the building.

Tea was served. Mountbatten's style was informal.

'So what have you laid on for us today?'

'We're going to run a wet countdown on one squadron, which is three missiles. In theory this is a no-notice exercise, but of course the men know you're here. I think you'll find they're pretty sharp.'

'Wet?'

'Fully fuelled. We aim to get the birds into firing order in eight minutes.'

There followed a tour of the base, in which the visitors were shown one of the launch pads, with its missile still horizontal beneath its protective cover. The Chief of Defence Staff then had an opportunity to talk to some of the men training in the missile flight school on the base, and to meet the members of the USAAF 99th Support Squadron, who had charge of the nuclear warheads. Captain Jerry Kreiss showed Mountbatten a key hanging on a chain round his neck.

'The missile isn't armed until I turn this key,' he said.

'And where do you get your orders?' said Mountbatten.

'Omaha, Nebraska,' came the reply. 'Offutt Air Force Base.'

This was the famous war/peace key, the physical embodiment of the policy of dual control. The British independent nuclear deterrent could only go bang if the Americans said so.

The group watched the wet countdown exercise from the control centre. Mountbatten himself gave the order, which in war conditions would have come down a dedicated phone line in coded form. The code was in two parts, one part held by the prime minister and one part held by the Chief of Defence Staff. Only when both codes were combined could an order to fire the nuclear missile be given. A similar code-based order had also to be received by the American authentication officer.

'Not exactly snappy, is it?' said Mountbatten.

'You'll see,' said the wing commander. 'We're got it down to a pretty slick operation.'

The go order was given. The teams on the bases exploded into action. Men in white protection suits, looking like spacemen, swarmed over the launch pads. A klaxon began to sound as the first shelter rolled back on its tracks to reveal the immense white rocket beneath. The launch mount arms locked onto the rocket, and hydraulic pumps began to raise it from horizontal to vertical.

'See that, sir?' said the flight control officer with a chuckle. 'There'll be fun in the married quarters tonight.'

The klaxons sounded on the other two pads, and two more rockets began to rise.

'When are they assigned targets?' asked Rupert.

'Three times a day,' said the wing commander. 'On every shift change the target data is checked. Each missile is given a fifteen-digit number to feed into the guidance system.'

'So the crew has no idea where their missile will land?'

'No idea at all. Frankly, they're happy to keep it that way.'

'I can tell you, if you're interested,' said Rupert. 'The current Thor force allocation is six air defence facilities, three missile bases, three long-range airbases, and forty-eight cities.'

The three missiles were all now erect. Electric motors automatically unscrewed the holding bolts, allowing the lifting arm to drop away.

'Big buggers, aren't they?'

'Eight-foot diameter,' said the launch control officer. 'Sixty-five foot tall. They say when they take off the ground will shake for three miles all round.'

'That'll make a mess of the launch pad, won't it?' said Mountbatten.

'Oh, these are single-use weapons,' said the wing commander. 'If we ever fire them, I'll send the men home to their families right afterwards. Their job will be over.'

A series of strange noises now came from the launch pads, groans and screams and creaks. Clouds of white vapour shrouded the rockets.

'They're pushing in the liquid oxygen now. It's super-cold, which makes the pipes set up that caterwauling. The cloud you can see is the boil-off.'

The fuelling phase lasted for several minutes. Then Captain Kreiss stepped forward with his war/peace key and ceremoniously armed the warheads.

'There are no warheads today, you'll be relieved to hear,' said the wing commander. 'Just dummies.' He checked the clock. 'Eight minutes. Fast work.'

'What if the American officer and his key can't be located?' said Mountbatten.

The missile technician at the console tapped the war/peace switch.

'I can fix this with a screwdriver,' he said.

Kreiss laughed.

'You better not, buddy.'

Signals sounded.

'Ready to go,' said the wing commander. 'I get the coded go order, and that's it. The bird goes up vertically over eighty thousand feet, rolls over and hits a speed of ten thousand miles an hour, climbs to three hundred and ninety-nine miles, travels seventeen hundred miles, and lands within two miles of its target.'

Mountbatten led his visiting team in a round of applause.

'Please take this the right way, Wing Commander,' he said, 'but I sincerely hope your men never get the opportunity to see the fruits of all their fine work.'

'We're all with you there, sir.'

As they drove away from the complex Mountbatten said to Rupert, 'You see now why I need you.'

'What are we doing with these monsters?' said Rupert. 'They must be number one on any Soviet target list. If we don't fire them first they're scrap metal.'

'That's why we have to rethink our entire strategy. Everyone knows it. But I'm one of the only two men in the country who's going to have to push the button. Believe me, that concentrates the mind.'

Rupert's position in Mountbatten's entourage was not clearly defined. His official title was Strategic Adviser to the Chief of Defence Staff, but as in all the former roles he had filled for Mountbatten, from Combined Operations to the ending of empire in India, his value lay in their personal relationship. They were not friends in the usual meaning of the word. They did not socialise. But Mountbatten spoke his mind more freely to Rupert than to anyone else, and he expected Rupert's best truth in return.

When he took on this latest position, Rupert had plunged into the fledgling field of nuclear strategy. To his amazement he found that there was no existing academic discipline supporting the decisions made by the military leaders. The staff colleges taught how to fight and win wars; but this was a new age. For this there was no rule book.

He read Schelling's *Strategy of Conflict*, and papers by Sherwin and Rapoport. He read Bernard Brodie's *Strategy in the Missile Age*, and familiarised himself with Clausewitz's classic *On War*. He studied papers issued by the RAND Corporation, by Daniel Ellsberg, Herman Kahn and Albert J. Wohlstetter. He was currently reading Henry Kissinger's *Nuclear Weapons and Foreign Policy*, a work commissioned by the US Council on Foreign Relations, which as far as he could tell argued for the benefits of waging a limited nuclear war. What had started out sounding like suicidal insanity was turning into something else. But what?

The more he read, and the more he thought about what he had read, the more convinced he became that the debate was no longer connected to any recognisable reality.

Everyone made jokes about nuclear weapons. The joking was a mix of dread and apology. Everyone understood that the deployment of such devastating destructive power was a kind of madness. And yet there they were, nuclear bombs in their thousands, the mainstay of an entire strategy of national defence.

In the little office allocated to him in the Department of Defence in Whitehall, Rupert wrote out the most blatant absurdities on cards, and pinned them up on the walls round his desk. He called them his 'jokes'.

1. The Deterrence Joke
   We'll never use our nuclear weapons, but don't tell the enemy.

So long as he believes we'll use them, he'll be afraid. The more he fears us, the more likely he is to attack us.

2. The Security Joke

Our nuclear weapons must be secure against attack, so the enemy is always afraid of our power to retaliate. The more he fears us, the more likely he is to attack us.

3. The Reasonable Leader Joke

A reasonable man would never risk nuclear war, so a reasonable leader would not be feared by the enemy. Our leader must therefore be a madman, so the enemy will be afraid. The more he fears us, the more likely he is to attack us.

Rupert also had an actual joke on his wall.

What should you do in the event of a nuclear war?
Cover yourself with a sheet and crawl slowly to the nearest cemetery.
Why slowly?
To avoid panic.

Behind the paradoxes and the jokes, or above and beyond them, loomed the grim and almost unimaginable reality called SIOP. The Single Integrated Operational Plan, devised and controlled by the Americans, stood ready to deliver 3,267 nuclear warheads on as many targets in a single strike.

Rupert's first report to Mountbatten was his most radical. He argued that no democratic government would ever choose to destroy civilian populations on such a massive scale. Since the weapons were unusable, they might as well be given up.

'What you have to understand, Rupert,' said Mountbatten, 'is that these weapons aren't for fighting wars at all. They're political weapons. They're for perceived power. Perceived prestige.'

'But if the Russians know we'll never use them, what power can they wield?'

'The Russians must never know we won't use them.'

'So all that matters is that Khrushchev thinks we have overwhelming power, and that we have the will to use it.'

'Precisely.'

'Well, then,' said Rupert, 'I'd like to repropose a scheme I've just dug up in the records. It was put forward seven years ago by one Lieutenant-Colonel S. E. Spey. His plan was that we pretend to build an imaginary weapon that could destroy all forms of attack, some sort of death ray, he suggested. He proposed a massive research programme, with occasional leaks to the Soviets about the success of this remarkable weapon. Of course it wouldn't exist. But as Spey pointed out, it didn't need to exist. It had only to be believed.'

Mountbatten was duly amused.

'I take it poor Colonel Spey failed to convince anyone.'

'So it seems. But is he wrong?'

'I think our friend Khrushchev would need harder evidence than leaks and rumours. Remember the prestige of nuclear weapons rests on the ultimate experimental demonstrations. Hiroshima and Nagasaki.'

'You know it's all a kind of madness, don't you, sir?'

'Yes.' Mountbatten sighed. 'But it's our madness. We have to do the best with it that we can.'

The image of Colonel Spey's imaginary death ray haunted Rupert in his ponderings. He was sure that there was a clue here, a way out of the trap in which they had all been caught. Somehow, he sensed, they were asking the wrong questions, or using the wrong tools. Defence strategy in an age of nuclear weapons could no longer be understood as the winning of battles. In an age of deterrence, the only victory was not to have a war.

10

Oleg Troyanovsky stood on the long first-floor balcony of the main villa and watched a car pull up in the drive outside. Now into his forties, his body had thickened, and the creases between his thick eyebrows had deepened into permanent furrows. Frowning, he looked down as the visitor emerged stooping from the car. It was Rodion Yakovlevich Malinowsky, Minister of Defence and Marshal of the Red Army. Troyanovsky knew perfectly well why he had come.

From the balcony he could see the tree-filled grounds of the estate, and the narrow boardwalk known as the Tsar's Path that ran for half a mile or so along the gravel beach. He could see the line of blue-and-white canvas-covered cabins used in summer as dressing rooms for swimmers. And some way off, making his way slowly along the boardwalk, he could see the short stout figure of his boss, Nikita Sergeyevich Khrushchev, General Secretary of the Communist Party and Chairman of the Presidium of the Soviet Union.

Khrushchev was making vigorous movements of his arms as he walked, which meant he was arguing aloud with himself. Troyanovsky could guess at what was agitating him. He himself had passed on the report from Khrushchev's son-in-law Aleksei Adzhubei, who had recently returned from a trip to the United

States. To general astonishment this Adzhubei, who was considered a fool, had succeeded in getting a meeting with President Kennedy. Kennedy had banged his fist on the table, and said, 'We should learn from you Russians! When you had difficulties in Hungary, you liquidated the conflict in three days!'

The source of Kennedy's agitation was Cuba.

Cuba was much on Khrushchev's mind in this April of 1962. He had retired to his dacha at Pitsunda to consider how best to resolve the problem.

'A chicken has to sit quietly for a certain time,' he liked to say, 'if she expects to lay an egg.'

Such pithy remarks were part of his tiresome man-of-the-people act. And yet Troyanovsky, so much more sophisticated, so much better educated, had a real respect for his boss. He had come to appreciate, first as his interpreter, now as his foreign policy adviser, the subtle way in which this semi-literate son of a miner deployed his crudity.

'Where I come from, in Kalinovka,' Khrushchev told him, 'it's the dream of every villager to own a pair of boots. So how do you think I made it to the top? What do you think saved my skin under Stalin?'

'Your political instincts, Nikita Sergeyevich.'

'Political my arse! Instinct plain and simple. I'm no intellectual. I don't go in for argument and analysis, papers for and papers against. I just follow my nose.'

'Lenin himself urged us,' said Troyanovsky, 'to engage in battle first, and see what happens.'

'Did he? Did he? What a great man he was.'

Troyanovsky descended from the first floor to find the marshal pacing irritably up and down the veranda.

'So where is he?'

'Walking by the beach, Rodion Yakovlevich.'

'I've brought him what he asked for.' He waved a plump paper file. 'He's not going to like it.'

'The report on the missile programme?'

Malinowsky grunted.

'How long's he going to be walking?'

'Would you like me to let him know you're here, Marshal?'

Malinowsky stared round at the surrounding trees and sea with a look of disgust.

'No food, no drink, no women. Might as well talk business.'

Troyanovsky set off down the path to the beach. As he came nearer to the arm-waving figure on the boardwalk he could hear the chairman's words sharp on the spring air. Khrushchev was haranguing the young American president.

'Cuba is now a socialist country, Mr President. The only one so far in the Americas. That is a fact, Mr President. Tiny though it is, it upholds with pride the prestige of international socialism. Furthermore, Mr President, you must consider my position. It was I alone who made the decision to support the Cuban revolution. My colleagues were both timid and penny-pinching. I alone saw that as the father of socialism, the Soviet Union could not stand aside and watch our new child falter as it took its first steps. You must therefore appreciate, Mr President, that if you attack Cuba, you attack the Soviet Union. You attack me.'

He came to a stop and took in Troyanovsky, now standing before him blocking his way.

'Well?'

'Rodion Yakovlevich has arrived, Comrade Chairman.'

'He can come and talk to me here. I'm walking.'

He continued down the boardwalk, his short stout figure now joined by the taller figure of his aide.

'I've never forgotten something Stalin said to us,' he told Troyanovsky. 'He said, "After I'm gone, the imperialists will strangle you like kittens." Like kittens!'

Troyanovsky said nothing. He understood very well that Khrushchev, the inheritor of Stalin's absolute power, accustomed to unquestioning obedience, had formed the habit of conducting his debates with himself.

'Stalin was mad, of course. We found that out too late. Quite mad.' Suddenly he began to beat the air with his fists, and his face went red. 'That Mudakshvili! That prick! Does anyone have any idea what shit he dumped on our country? Do you realise that it's only by the skin of my teeth that I'm here in Pitsunda and not in a grave in Vagan'kovskoe? The prisoners wept as they dug their own graves. The guards had to be drunk before they shot them.'

Just as suddenly he was calm again.

'Nonetheless, we must work. We must do everything in our power for the happiness of the people.'

When they returned, Malinowsky was standing by the gate in the wall. Behind him rose the high Caucasus mountains. He held the plump paper file in one hand.

'Another report, Rodion Yakovlevich?' said Khrushchev.

'Don't pull that sour face with me, Nikita Sergeyevich. You asked for it yourself. Much good may it do you.'

Malinowsky was an old friend, and dared to speak to Khrushchev in this way. They had survived the purges together, and they had come through the Battle of Stalingrad alive. They had been instructed to spy on each other by Stalin, and had done so, and still they were friends. You had to have been alive in those days to understand how it was.

'Well, then, I'd better take a look,' said Khrushchev.

He led them back into the house, across the veranda and through French doors to his mahogany-panelled study. Here he sat himself down at his big desk, pushed a cluster of phones to one side, and patted the mahogany desktop. Malinowsky unpacked the pages of the report and laid them out as if they had already been scanned. He was familiar with Khrushchev's habits. The chairman rarely read long reports. He liked it to be understood that he was too busy to read.

'To put it plainly, Nikita Sergeyevich,' he said, 'as far as our long-range missile programme goes, you'd have better luck fucking a goat with a telephone pole.'

Khrushchev frowned.

'I accepted the R-7 had to be abandoned,' he said. 'What about the R-16?'

'The R-16 functions perfectly, so long as it's set up and fully fuelled eight hours before launch. So if you could request the Americans to give us eight hours' notice of any attack, and not to target the R-16 sites, I'm told the missiles could be effective.'

Khrushchev threw up his arms.

'Take this shit paper away! Just tell me one thing. How long before we have long-range missiles that actually work?'

'Ten years,' said Malinowsky.

'Ten years! For ten more years the imperialists can shit nuclear bombs at us any time they like, and we can do nothing?'

'That's how it is.'

'I don't like how it is!'

Now Khrushchev was shouting again. Malinowsky shrugged.

'They don't know,' he said. 'Which is almost as good.'

'Of course they know! They're not idiots!'

He got up and stamped out onto the veranda. Malinowsky followed. Troyanovsky came discreetly at the rear.

'When will it ever end?' cried Khrushchev at the sky. 'They armed the enemies of Bolshevism in the Civil War! They waited sixteen years to recognise the Soviet Union! They kept out of the Great Patriotic War as long as they could, so we'd be bled dry! They dropped atom bombs on Japan when Japan was already defeated, just to intimidate us! They build up their armed forces so we're forced to respond, even though it means starving our own people. Has their hatred no end?'

Without thinking, he set off back down the waterside board-walk.

'I should also report,' said Malinowsky, 'that the Jupiter missiles deployed by the Americans in Turkey have now become operational.'

Khrushchev stopped and pointed dramatically out to sea.

'I can see them, Rodion Yakovlevich! I can see them!'

Of course he couldn't see them. The coast of Turkey was a hundred miles away.

'That sticks in my throat,' growled Malinowsky. 'Right in our backyard! How would they like it if we put nuclear missiles in their backyard?'

Khrushchev turned to him. His bright piercing eyes had all at once become focused. He had had a single brilliant idea.

'You're right,' he said. 'What if we were to put nuclear missiles in their backyard? That would throw a hedgehog in Uncle Sam's pants!'

Suddenly he was all smiles. He was bubbling with excitement.

'Our medium-range missiles work well enough, don't they? What's the range of the R-12?'

'A thousand nautical miles.'

'And the R-14?'

'Two thousand.'

Malinowsky knew what Khrushchev was thinking, but he took care not to speak the words first. His friend liked it to be known that he was the one who had the ideas.

For a long time, Khrushchev didn't speak. He was filled with amazement at the brilliance of the idea that had just come to him.

Ever since Truman had demonstrated to the world the awesome destructive power of the atom bomb, the Soviet Union had been struggling to catch up. So long as America had nuclear superiority, the Soviet Union was doomed to be a second-rate power. And this, the country that had almost single-handedly defeated Nazi Germany at such a colossal cost in blood! Stalin had vowed to match the Americans' new super-weapons, and then to surpass them. But however much of the nation's precious resources they poured into the programme, the Americans were always ahead.

Ten years! Ten more years of weakness! The great experiment launched by Lenin, the hope of the world, would be smothered in its cradle. Stalin was right. They would be strangled like kittens.

'There is a way,' he said to Malinowsky. 'There is a way to defend socialism, and match the might of America, and reduce our defence budget, all in a single stroke!'

'What is that way, Nikita Sergeyevich?' said the obliging marshal.

'We put nuclear missiles on Cuba!'

So simple. So perfect. The medium-range R-12s and R-14s were no threat to America here on home soil. But plant them in Cuba and they could reach half the cities in the United States.

'Do you think,' said Malinowsky, 'that the Americans would allow us to do that?'

'Why should they know? We'll do it in secret. Then by the time they find out, it'll be too late.'

The more Khrushchev thought about it, the better he liked it.

'Kennedy did nothing when the Berlin Wall went up. He'll do nothing again. What can he do? Risk a war that would blow up half his own people?'

He turned to Troyanovsky.

'Well, Oleg Alexandrovich? What have you got to say? You know the way the Americans think.'

Troyanovsky thought the plan insane. But he also knew that direct opposition only served to make Khrushchev more determined to have his own way.

'It's a bold idea, Comrade Chairman,' he said. 'But there are definite risks.'

'Of course there are risks! Fortune favours the bold! Even Stalin never thought of such a move! Get your people onto it at once, Rodion Yakovlevich. There's no time to lose. Work out everything we're going to need. The missiles, the warheads, the support teams, the transport, the ships.'

He gestured over the sea towards Turkey.

'This'll give them a taste of their own medicine!'

Khrushchev flew back from Sochi to Moscow that same day. He called a meeting of the Defence Council in the Oval Room, the large amphitheatre next to his first-floor Kremlin office. The meeting brought together the twelve-man Presidium and the heads of the Ministry of Defence. Here he outlined his new and top-secret plan.

'The Soviet Union is dedicated to world peace,' he said. 'We would have no intention of ever using these weapons. I am not a lunatic. The nuclear missiles would act as a threat and a deterrent. In this sense, they are truly weapons of peace.'

The deputy premier, Anastas Ivanovich Mikoyan, the great survivor from the early days of Lenin, urged caution.

'You think this can be done without the Americans knowing?'

'*Maskirovka*, Anastas Ivanovich. The art of deception and disguise.'

Khrushchev's overwhelming self-confidence forced the plan through. Approval, as was customary, was unanimous.

'I'll wait until the American mid-term elections are over,' said Khrushchev, 'then I'll go to the United Nations and announce the deployment in the General Assembly. Then I'll fly to Havana and pose for photographs with Fidel in front of an R-14 in firing position.'

He slapped the table and hooted with laughter.

'Comrades,' he concluded, 'I trust you see the enormous advantages that flow from this one simple idea. Not only do we secure the revolution in Cuba in perpetuity, but by placing existing medium-range missiles there we achieve, at a single stroke, full nuclear parity with the United States. All this at virtually no cost! The money we save from our defence budget can now flow into our economic and agricultural programmes. We will beat our swords into ploughshares. There will be no need for so many tank regiments, so many destroyers, so many fighter aircraft. You see how progressive my plan is? You see how truly it's in the interests of world peace? With this one move, we will make socialism safe for a generation!'

11

In the enclosed all-male world of a boy's boarding prep school in rural Sussex she might as well have been an alien descended from outer space. A beautiful alien, an emissary from a more advanced civilisation perhaps, sent to enslave mankind. At this moment she was sitting hunched over a stool in the school's art room, at work on a still life. Her subject, an empty wine bottle behind two apples, stood on the windowsill. Dappled light filtering through the branches of the lime trees outside made patterns on the apples' shiny surfaces. She worked with frowning concentration, smoking a cigarette, letting the ash fall unnoticed to the floor.

The art teacher, once craggily handsome, now a ghost of his former glory, slouched in a canvas chair and watched her with a dulled and hopeless longing. She was well worth the watching: eighteen years old, slim, distractingly beautiful. Black slacks, a tight black jumper, almost black hair. Not much good at art, of course.

Maurice Jenks, known in the school as the Magnificent Wreck, was not much good at art himself, but he was good enough to hold down a job overseeing the sons of the privileged in what was essentially a leisure activity. The goddess on the stool was called Pamela Avenell. She had come to him for private lessons because she had two younger brothers in the school, and lived nearby, and like so many pretty girls with no qualifications, supposed she might have a future in something to do with art. For example, thought Maurice Jenks in a burst of aching lust, she could peel off that tight black jersey and show me her artistically interesting naked body. Ah, if only. Twenty years ago he would have given it a shot. As matters stood, restraint was the order of the day. At least she gave him a break from the company of small boys, who merely bored him, given that he was not queer. Though considering his record of decline, no doubt that was to come.

He could hear them now, flocks of them, their thin voices calling in the sharp spring air from the playing fields beyond the lime trees. The Magnificent Wreck hoisted himself to his feet to attend to his charge. Time to check her work and tell encouraging lies.

'Better,' he said. 'Much better. Take a closer look at the apples.'

'I hate apples,' said Pamela.

'They're just forms. Look for the light and dark.'

He looked at the light and dark of her curving neck, her tumble of hair. It would be so easy to lean down and kiss that soft skin. He watched her pencil scratching away over the sketchpad, steadily making her first passable rendering a great deal worse. What was it about art that made everyone think they could do it? Indulgent parents, presumably. Confronted with offspring who failed at long division and Latin grammar, they fell back on the consoling nostrum that they were artistic. In the upper middle classes the stupid boys went into the City, and the stupid girls did art.

The Magnificent Wreck wondered if Pamela would tell on him if he took a swig from the bottle in the paint cupboard that was mendaciously labelled White Spirit.

'Oh, bother!' exclaimed Pamela, laying down a pencil, stubbing out her cigarette. 'It's all gone wrong.' She turned her limpid gaze onto the art teacher. 'I'm such a washout, aren't I?'

'Not at all,' he lied gallantly. 'You're just impatient.'

'I can't help it,' said Pamela. 'I can only really do the things I want to do.'

She gave him a mischievous grin that sent shudders through his ravaged frame. Sweet Jesus, he thought, if only these girls knew the power they possess. Now and for a few short years to come the world is theirs to command.

'Mr Jenks?'

He jumped. He realised he'd gone into some kind of trance, staring at her.

'Yes. Of course.'

'I think I should be getting home.'

He looked at the clock. In fifteen minutes' time he was supposed to be on duty supervising the lower changing room. Even art teachers bear their share of the domestic chores.

'I don't suppose you could give me a lift?'

There was insufficient time to run Pamela to Edenfield and be back by 3.30. Why couldn't she walk?

'All right,' he said.

They walked out together to the open space beside the main building where his Morris Traveller was parked. It was a battered half-timbered vehicle with room for a bedroll in the back. There had been times when he had had nowhere else to sleep.

Pamela got into the passenger side and he got into the driver's side.

'We could take the old coach road,' she said.

The old coach road was slower and more twisting than the main road, and therefore would make him even later than he would already be.

'All right,' he said.

He drove out past the playing fields, where troops of small and muddy boys were being rounded up by large and muddy teachers, and turned onto the rutted tree-lined track.

'I'm not really much good at art, am I?' said Pamela. 'Actually I'm not sure I'm really much good at anything.'

'Don't be silly,' said Maurice Jenks.

'The awful thing is I feel as if I should be. I have this feeling I'm going to do something brilliant and wonderful, only I don't know what.'

Ah, youth, thought the art teacher. He too had once dreamed heady dreams. Believe them while you can, my dear.

'I don't want just to be ordinary,' she said.

'I'm sure you won't be, Pamela.'

'Yes,' she said, 'but what am I to be not ordinary at?'

'You could do anything.'

Patently untrue, and quite rightly she stamped all over it.

'No, I couldn't. I couldn't be prime minister, or win a Nobel Prize, or be the first person on the moon. All I can do is get married and have children, which I do want to do, of course I do, but not yet. I want there to be a time before when I do . . . when I can be . . . oh, I don't know. Just something more.'

'Well, if you really want it,' said Maurice Jenks, 'then I'm sure it will happen.'

'I do really want it,' said Pamela. 'Only I don't know what *it* is.'

She wriggled in the car seat. The Magnificent Wreck kept his eyes on the bumpy road ahead.

'I'll tell you what I sometimes think,' she added after a pause. 'I sometimes think maybe it's wrong to think what we *do* is all that matters.'

She looked up, at the farm buildings ahead.

'Oh, God! We're nearly home. Would you mind stopping, just for a minute?'

Maurice Jenks stopped the car. She turned her lovely eyes on him.

'Would you mind if I asked you a personal question, Mr Jenks?'

'I hope not,' he said.

'I know I don't really know you. But you're not like the others. You've lived your own life, haven't you?'

'I've tried.'

'There's really no one else I can ask. You see, I have this really stupid feeling about what's going to happen to me, and I have to tell somebody. Then you can say how silly I'm being, and tell me to forget all about it.'

'I'm really not very wise, Pamela. I shouldn't pay too much attention to anything I say.'

'I think you are wise, Mr Jenks. You've got a wise face. I often look at your face, you know?'

Oh God, save me. What am I to do with this enchantress who weaves her spells all unaware? Dare I tell her how long I've gazed at her sweet face?

'Well, here goes.' She took a breath, like someone about to jump into water. 'I think I'm going to have a great love affair. I mean, really great. The kind of thing people write about in books. Only of course I don't know who it'll be with, because I never meet anybody, stuck at home all the time. But he's out there, somewhere. And when we meet it's going to be the start of my real life. And, oh,' seeing he was preparing to respond, 'you don't need to tell me it won't last, I know that. That doesn't matter. All I want is for there to be a time in my life that takes me over, that sweeps me up and carries me away. A time of such power, such overwhelming *power*, that I'll never forget it for the rest of my life. Then after it's over I can do all the ordinary things, and have babies and fuss about clean sheets. But I'll know – do you see, I'll always know – that for a time I really was alive!'

Her eyes shone with the passion of her dream, and at the same time she laughed, laughing at her own absurdity.

'You must think I'm such a child! But really I'm not a child, you know? I'm eighteen.'

'I don't think you're a child, Pamela. And I don't see anything so unlikely about you having a great love affair. I think there'll be many men who'll prove all too eager to kneel at your feet.'

'Oh, no! I don't want them kneeling at my feet.'

But she looked at him curiously all the same. He had given away a little more than he intended.

'So you do think someone might fall in love with me?'

'Yes,' he said.

She went on gazing into his eyes, and all at once he saw it: this girlish innocence was a pose. She was entirely aware of the effect she had on him.

'You're a very pretty girl,' he said. 'You could have any man you wanted. There. Does that answer your question?'

'Any man I wanted?' she said.

'Now, let's get going. I'm already late.'

She laid one hand on his shoulder.

'Any man?'

'No. Don't do this.'

'What am I not to do, Mr Jenks?'

Oh, God! She's practising on me.

She wriggled again, as she had done before.

'That itch!' she said. 'I've got an itch in the middle of my back, and I can't reach it. Will you scratch it for me?'

He closed his eyes.

'Please,' he said.

'It won't take you a moment.'

He reached out his hand, round her slender wriggling body. She moved closer, so that he could feel the tickle of her hair on his cheek, and smell her sweet smell. His fingers felt over

99

her back, over the ridge of her spine, over the buckle of her bras-siere.

'There,' she said. 'Just there.'

He scratched her back, helplessly obedient. Then he with-drew his hand and started up the car once more and drove on down the road. She didn't stop him this time, and didn't speak.

When the car pulled into the yard of River Farm, Maurice Jenks was already so late for his changing-room duty that some other teacher would have had to cover for him. Pamela's mother came out to see who had arrived.

'Oh, it's you, Pammy. You shouldn't make Mr Jenks drive you. You can easily walk.'

'He offered, Mum. It was very kind of him.'

She ran on into the house. Pamela's mother went to thank the art teacher, who had not got out of his car.

'Don't let her impose on you, Mr Jenks. She can be such a little madam.'

The Magnificent Wreck gazed up at her with faintly blood-shot eyes.

'She's a sweet girl,' he said. 'It's no trouble.'

Pamela was in the kitchen making herself a golden syrup sand-wich.

'Did you see William or Edward at school?' said her mother.

'Heavens, no,' said Pamela. 'They don't come anywhere near the art room.'

'Are these art lessons doing you any good at all?'

'Not really,' said Pamela. 'He's a darling, but he's not teach-ing me much. I keep saying, Mum, I should go to art school in London. I can stay with Susie.'

'I'm not having you stay with Susie.'

This was a long-running argument. Kitty Cornford thought her daughter was too pretty and too immature to be let loose in

London with a girl of her own age. Certainly not with giddy little Susie.

'Well, I don't know what I'm going to do then, other than go mad with boredom.'

Later that afternoon Simon Shuttleworth phoned and said why didn't they meet up for a drink. Simon was one of those people who had always been there in her life, since she had started going to dances. For a time she had told her friends he was her boyfriend, at that stage when it seemed necessary to have a boyfriend. His great merit more recently was that he had a car.

'I'll be back for supper, Mum.'

'Don't be late, darling. You know Larry hates to wait.'

Simon showed up in his little red MG. He wore a tweed jacket and cavalry twill trousers the same colour as his hair. He was what was called a 'suitable boy', which made Pamela treat him badly, without quite knowing why. He was twenty-two years old, training to be a solicitor in the old established Lewes firm of Adams & Remers.

'Where do you want to go?' he asked her as he opened the car door for her.

'Anywhere,' she said.

'How about the Cricketers?'

'God, no. Let's go to the Riverside.'

The Riverside was the most expensive hotel in the area, a former abbey turned into a luxury retreat. The drinks in the bar were stupid prices.

'Great. The Riverside it is.'

The short drive in the MG was cold, noisy and uncomfortable. The hotel was agreeably pampering. They sat in a long room got up like the drawing room of a stately home, in deep chintz-covered armchairs, looking out over the river at twilight. Pamela had a gin and tonic and lit up a cigarette. The waiter brought a small dish of peanuts, which Simon ate one by one in a steady stream, unaware that he was doing so. He talked about mutual friends in the area, about office life, about a house he and some others were planning to rent in France in August.

'I'll tell you what,' he said, as if the idea had just come to him. 'Why don't you come too? Heaps of room.'

'I don't know,' said Pamela. 'I'm not sure of my plans for the summer.'

'There's a pool there, and a tennis court. You could drive down with me.'

'I'll think about it.'

'Oh, do say yes. It would be so great if you came. Roger and Jill are coming. And the Maynards.'

'We'll see,' she replied.

'So are you going to the Kinrosses on Saturday?'

'Maybe.'

'I must say, you seem very vague about your life, Pammy.'

'I am vague,' she said. 'My life has yet to come into focus.'

The gin and tonic was doing its work. She was surrounded by a haze of smoke. She felt unfocused.

'Lucky you,' he said. 'I have to focus like mad. But not for ever. I plan to make partner by thirty-five. Then it's hello golf and long lunches.'

'God, Simon, you sound middle-aged already.'

'Once you start an actual job things have a way of getting serious. It'll be the same for you.'

'I may not do a job.'

'But you'll get married. You'll have children.'

'I may not.'

'Of course you will.' He smiled at her, and ate peanuts. 'You'll be a gorgeous wife and a gorgeous mother.'

'Will I?'

She couldn't see herself as a wife and mother at all. But if not that, what?

'I may become an artist,' she said. 'Or a film star. Or a spy.'

'You'd make a beautiful spy,' he said. 'I'd tell you all my secrets.'

'You don't have any secrets,' she said.

'That's what you don't know.'

'Go on, then. Tell me a secret.'

He shook his head, and ate the last of the peanuts. For some reason this annoyed her more than it should.

'There. You don't have any secrets.'

'Not from you.'

Everything he said was slightly loaded. It was all very tiring.

'I can never be sure with you, Pammy,' he said. 'Either you're much deeper than you appear, or much shallower.'

'Oh, much shallower,' she said. 'I'm terribly shallow. I'm vague and shallow. I'm sort of a puddle, really.'

Even this appeared to enchant him.

'You're a mystery,' he said. 'I don't know any other girl like you.'

She took out a fresh cigarette, and he leaned forward to light it.

'That's me,' she said, exhaling a thin stream of smoke. 'The mystery girl.'

'A beautiful mystery.'

Someone must have told him that a girl can never have too many compliments. But you can't dish out praise like payments on an instalment plan. Not everyone wants to be bought.

'Better take me home, Simon.'

In the car he said, as she had known he would, 'When can I see you again?'

'I'm not sure,' she said. 'My plans are still up in the air.'

She had no plans at all. What she had up in the air was a lot of nothing. That was the problem. A lot of nothing, and this burning feeling that there had to be *more*.

She could see from Simon's face as they parted that she had

disappointed him. But that was how it would always be with Simon: he would always want more than she was prepared to give.

'I'll call you,' he said.

'You do that.'

Once he had driven away, and those puzzled eyes had ceased leaning on her, she felt bad about the way she had treated him. He was a good friend, an old friend. He deserved better.

There's something wrong with me.

It was a thought that was never very far away. Some crack in her nature made her dissatisfied, where a normal person would have been satisfied. Most of the girls she knew locally regarded Simon Shuttleworth as a major catch. This mysterious fault both disturbed and excited her. She had taken to calling it her devil. Her devil made her do things for no reason. Why had she told Mr Jenks to scratch her back? Why had she made Simon take her to the Riverside?

Her body burned with a terrible restlessness. At the same time she felt as if she were tied down by fine cords. The cords tugged at her, cut into her.

Am I a bad person?

She thought then of how she had told the art teacher about her great love affair. It was only a dream as yet, but she knew it would come true. And she knew something more. Her lover, when at last he stepped out of the shadows to claim her, would look deep into her heart and would see the devil in her, and he would still love her. He would love her even if she was bad. He would take her in his arms and say, 'You're wild and wicked and wonderful,' and for that she would love him for ever. For ever and ever.

When her stepfather came home that evening, Pamela tackled him on the subject of her future.

'Why can't I go to art school?' she said. 'You went to art school.'

'But it was all a waste of time,' Larry Cornford said. 'I was never really good enough. Someone should have told me that from the beginning.'

'But you liked it, didn't you?'

'Yes, I liked it. But that's not the only reason for doing something.'

'What other reasons are there?'

'Well, I needed to earn a living, for a start.'

'Yes, but you're a man. I'll get married.'

'And anyway, this isn't the time to start at art school. You start in the autumn.'

'I could do a course.'

'Oh, Pammy, darling. You know what it is you really want. You want to go to London and have fun.'

'Is that wrong?'

'No, not wrong. But it can lead to things going wrong.'

'You mean I'll be seduced by some heartless man about town and have my life ruined for ever.'

'Something like that.'

'Larry, darling.' She leaned her lovely head against his arm. 'Doesn't everyone have to be ruined, just a little bit?'

Larry sighed.

'I'll talk to Kitty.'

'Mummy won't want me to be ruined. She'll want me to stay unruined till I'm long past anyone wanting to ruin me.'

'I'll talk to her.'

Larry had an idea for a compromise solution, which he put to Kitty.

'Why don't we ask Hugo if he'll have her to stay? Harriet's still not getting any better, and I know they have quite a time of it getting Emily to school and back. Pammy could stay with them and help them out in exchange for bed and board, and Hugo could keep a bit of an eye on her.'

Hugo and Larry's wine business had flourished. Caulder & Avenell now had premises in St James.

'Do you think Hugo would want that?'

'To be honest, I think he finds Harriet's illness quite a trial. Pammy would bring a bit of life into the house. And he's certainly got enough room.'

'What would she do all day?'

'I'm sure I could sort something out for her at Camberwell. There's a couple of people still there from my time.'

He went up to find Pamela in her room. She was lying on her bed, smoking, drawing circles in the air with her cigarette. He told her his plan. She jumped up and threw her arms round his neck and kissed him.

'Thank you, thank you, thank you. Does Mummy really not mind?'

'She feels better about it knowing Hugo will be keeping an eye on you.'

'Has Hugo said yes?'

'I haven't asked him yet. But I don't see why he shouldn't. You will be good and sensible if we do this, won't you, Pammy?'

'I'll be so good and sensible. I truly will.' She unwrapped herself from him and tapped the ash from her cigarette into an overflowing ashtray. 'You don't think I'm a bad person, do you, Larry?'

'Why on earth should you be a bad person?'

'Sometimes I think I've got a devil in me.'

'What form does this devil take?' said Larry, smiling.

'Oh, you know. It makes me do things I shouldn't.'

'Things you like doing?'

'Oh, yes.'

'Then I shouldn't worry,' said Larry. 'But I do think you smoke too much.'

12

'Darling,' said Hugo Caulder to his wife Harriet, as she lay in her reclining chair in the darkened front room, 'I do hope you'll be feeling better by Thursday.'

'Thursday?' She was using her special voice, the low sweet voice that had so enchanted him when they fell in love. 'I'll do my best. I know it's such a bore for you.'

'It's just that we have our buyers' tasting on Thursday evening. And you know Emily has a dance class.'

Emily, seven years old, dutiful and silent, sat by her mother's side reading *School Friend*. Mother and daughter were very close.

'She may have to miss it,' said Harriet. 'Do you mind terribly, darling?'

She stroked her daughter's long ash-blonde hair with gentle fingers.

'You know I hate dance class,' said Emily.

'Yes, darling, but everyone has to learn to dance.'

There was no reproach in her voice. It was well understood in their little family that they preferred evenings at home to noisy parties.

'I don't suppose you've had a chance to do anything about supper,' said Hugo.

'Emily's had a soft-boiled egg,' said his wife. 'I don't want anything at all. You know how it is on my quiet days.'

Harriet's 'quiet days' were times of silent suffering. She would lie in her chair, her head pulsing with pain, overwhelmed by an unexplained fatigue. Doctors had been consulted, but no physical cause discovered. It was suggested that she had never got over the stillbirth of her second child, six years ago now.

Hugo retreated to the kitchen and made himself scrambled egg on toast. He ate alone, reading the sports pages of the newspaper, lingering attentively over the cricket.

Hugo Caulder thought of himself as a straightforward, uncomplicated, decent sort of person, not unduly clever, but well up to doing what was required of him. He knew he would never be a captain of industry like his father, but he was proud of the success of his wine business, and proud of his delicately pretty wife. It was her yielding softness he had fallen in love with, the way that she made him feel strong and protective. She had taught him that their marriage was made special by a shared sensitivity. 'Hugo and I can read each other's thoughts,' she liked to say, 'because we always think the same way.'

The chief virtue in their household was 'quietness'. The chief vice was 'noisiness'. How, Hugo wondered, would Pamela Avenell fit in?

So far he had not found the right opportunity to broach the plan to Harriet. It had been easy to say to Larry, his friend and partner, 'Yes, of course we'll have Pammy to stay. We'd love it.' He was also aware that the prospect rather cheered him. He had known Pammy almost all her life, he was fond of her, and she was extremely pretty. Harriet, however, might see things differently.

When he had finished his solitary supper, he returned to the darkened front room.

'I really am the most useless wife in the world,' whispered Harriet from her low chair.

'You know it's not your fault,' said Hugo loyally, 'and so do I. What's so rotten about it is the way it makes you feel guilty. I should think you hate that.'

'I do, darling. How well you know me.'

'You know what?' He spoke as if the idea had just come to him. 'What we need is some help in the house. Not full-time, just for those occasions when you're having a quiet day and I'm tied up at work.'

'I don't see how,' said Harriet. 'Emily, sweetheart, don't strain your eyes.'

Hugo then floated the Pamela plan. Harriet, who had thought they were talking in general terms, was caught off-guard by such a specific proposal.

'But we're so happy here,' she said, 'just being us. It's all my fault for being so silly and feeble.'

'There you go again, blaming yourself.' Hugo spoke with loving firmness. 'You're not silly and feeble, you're ill. You need rest, and you need help.'

'Do you think so?' Harriet found herself puzzled as to how to counter this argument.

'And if we don't like having her, she can be sent away again.'

In this way Hugo gained his point, and it was agreed that Pamela would come, and occupy the spare room beside the room called 'John's room', after the baby who had not lived to use it.

From the moment Pamela entered the house it was as if a bright light had been switched on. She was excited, and lovely, and determined to please.

'What a pretty house! Oh, aren't you lucky to live in London! Is that your cat? I adore cats. Oh, isn't it dark in here! That is such a beautiful portrait, he's really caught your delicate beauty, hasn't he? And you must be Emily. I'm Pamela. I've brought you a little present, nothing really. It's a doll who has all these different outfits she can wear. Oh, look at your garden! Do you sit out in it all summer long?'

Both Harriet and Emily reeled a little under the impact of Pamela's enthusiasm, but on the whole she was a success.

'You can't imagine how happy I am to be here,' she said to Hugo, sitting with him later. Emily and Harriet had both gone to bed. 'Your wife is so lovely.'

'I think so too,' said Hugo, smiling.

'Is it all right to smoke?'

'Yes, of course.'

'If you don't mind me asking,' said Pamela, lighting up a cigarette, 'what is it she suffers from?'

'We don't really know,' said Hugo. 'She gets tired very easily. In some ways perhaps she's oversensitive. Also we had a loss in the family, a child. She's never really got over it.'

'That is so sad.'

'He was stillborn, six years ago. You may hear her speak of him. We called him John.'

'Six years ago!'

'Harriet feels things very deeply.'

Pamela gazed at him, and he could see that she didn't really understand. The odd thing was that under the impact of her sceptical smoke-blurred gaze he found he didn't really understand either.

'Well, anyway,' said Pamela, settling down in Harriet's reclining chair, curling her legs beneath her. 'Now that I'm here you must tell me what I can do to help.'

Hugo thought how amazingly unlike Harriet she was. Where Harriet was muted and shadowed, Pamela was bright. Where Harriet was droopy, Pamela was coiled, full of energy, as if she was ready to spring up at any moment. She looked so like her mother, but she was also entirely herself. The child he had watched grow up was now a self-possessed, almost frightening, young woman. And she was so beautiful.

'It's mostly things to do with Emily,' he said. 'For example, we need someone to take her to her dance class tomorrow evening.'

'Oh, bother,' said Pamela. 'Tomorrow's no good. I fixed to go out with my friend Susie.'

13

'So are you going to say it?' said Rupert Blundell.

'Say what?' said Mountbatten.

'The thing you can't say.'

'Oh, that. Yes, I shall say that. That's the whole point, isn't it?'

A cluster of senior officials strode down Horse Guards Parade from the Cabinet Office to the Old Admiralty Building, on this cool and overcast spring afternoon. They were the members of the group set up at Mountbatten's request, known after some juggling with word order as the Joint Inter-Services Group for the Study of All-Out War, or JIGSAW. The group included senior scientific adviser Sir Solly Zuckerman, representatives of all three services, the Department of Defence and the Home Office, and lesser advisers, of whom Rupert Blundell was one. Today they were convening in the Admiralty cinema to brief a much larger assembly of ministers and civil servants on current defence plans.

The cinema audience was addressed by the Cabinet Secretary, Sir Norman Brook; by the Minister of Defence, Harold Watkinson; and by the Chief of the Defence Staff. It fell to Mountbatten to paint a word picture of the threat the nation faced. He took as his example the city of Birmingham.

'Let us suppose,' he said, 'a single bomb of one megaton strength is detonated at an altitude of 2,500 metres above the city. The impact would be as follows. First, an intense flash of light, accompanied by a pulse of X-rays that would kill everyone within two miles, and a pulse of heat that would set fire to everything combustible within ten miles. Then a fireball would form above Birmingham that would be so bright it would blind people up to fifty miles away. Then the blast wave would ripple outwards, flattening everything within one mile, and all non-reinforced buildings for five miles. Then hurricane-force winds would be generated out from the explosion, followed a few seconds later by an inward suction of tornado force, over a three-mile area, pulling people and objects into the heart of the inferno. The multiple fires ignited by the flash would burn up all available oxygen. One-third of the inhabitants would die instantly; another third would be seriously injured; the survivors would be contaminated by poisonous radiation. All the city's hospitals would be destroyed. All rescue services that survived would be overwhelmed. There would be no water, no electricity, no phones. Birmingham would have ceased to exist. And all this with one relatively modest thermonuclear device.'

The audience in the Admiralty cinema listened in silence.

'We are therefore obliged to conclude,' said Mountbatten, 'that if there is ever a full exchange of nuclear weapons this nation will cease to exist.'

Harold Watkinson took over the podium to explain the current government's policy on defence.

'Broadly speaking, the policy remains as laid down by Churchill in '54. The conclusion reached then was that effective civil defence, bunkers and so forth, was not practical. A facility does exist, and has recently become operational, to house the government in the event of a nuclear attack. To do the same for the whole population is out of the question. HMG's policy therefore rests on the threat of retaliation by our own nuclear forces. In short, our policy is to deter nuclear attack, not to survive it.'

In the space allocated for questions, a civil servant in the audience raised the issue of the American nuclear forces stationed in Britain.

'What would happen,' he asked, 'if the Soviets had reason to believe the Americans were planning to attack them? Would they not move to destroy the American weapons in Britain first, since they represent the closest threat?'

'Undoubtedly,' said Mountbatten. 'If nuclear war were ever to break out, Britain would be in the front line.'

'In which case,' pursued the questioner, 'what powers do we have to restrain the United States from provoking a nuclear exchange?'

'We have hope,' said Mountbatten, 'and we have prayer.'

Sir Norman Brook protested.

'Please,' he said. 'Let's show more respect to our allies. They are as aware as we are of the catastrophic consequences of a nuclear war. We have excellent relations with the Kennedy administration. As for our own vulnerability, we rely, as the Chief of Defence Staff has made clear, on the effectiveness of our deterrent force. As of the Defence Committee meeting of early March, later approved by Downing Street, and established as the basis of Bomber Command's strategic policy, we have a guaranteed second-strike capability to destroy fifteen of Russia's largest cities. We believe that constitutes an unacceptable level of risk to the Soviet Union.'

Mountbatten now returned to the podium.

'You will understand, gentlemen,' he said, 'that we are in the land of faith. We must have faith that no commander, British, Russian, or American, would ever seek to be the first to launch a nuclear strike. As Chief of the Defence Staff I tell you plainly: Britain can never win a nuclear war. Our country is too small, and the bombs are too big.'

After the briefing was over Harold Watkinson showed some irritation with Mountbatten.

'I must say, Dickie, was it necessary to be so strong on the doom? I really don't see how it helps.'

'I'm not a politician, Harold,' said Mountbatten. 'I don't have to tell lies.'

Later, in his office with Rupert Blundell and his personal secretary Ronnie Brockman, he said, 'Well?'

'Not bad,' said Rupert.

'What else should I have said?'

'That our possession of nuclear weapons makes us less, not more, safe.'

'Well, damn it! I came pretty bloody close! I said we were in the front line.'

'But not that we should give up nuclear weapons altogether.'

Mountbatten sighed.

'Oh, Rupert. You know the game as well as I do. There's no going back now.'

'You know what Oppenheimer called the first atom bomb test? Trinity. And you know what the Western church and the Eastern church fought over so badly, back in the eleventh century, that they split for ever? The Trinity. It's a theological conflict.'

'I don't know that that follows, you know.'

'That was the start of nine hundred years of schism. Nine hundred years of not understanding each other. Russia is steeped in Eastern Orthodoxy. They don't think the way we think.'

'Even so, Rupert, I don't see what's to be done about it.'

'All we ever talk about,' said Rupert, 'is the hardware. It just frustrates me that no one ever asks the big questions.'

'The big questions?' Mountbatten turned to Ronnie Brockman.

'Dig out my "Aim for the West" memo, Ronnie. Get Rupert a copy. How long ago did I write that?'

'Must be three or four years, sir. When you were still at the Admiralty.'

'Only a few thoughts that don't get very far,' said Mountbatten to Rupert. 'Went down like a lead balloon, of course. But it might interest you.'

As Rupert left Whitehall at the end of that afternoon, his mind continued to tug away at the conundrum of deterrence. The committee members of JIGSAW argued over scenarios of war and survivability, but he was becoming increasingly convinced that the real question was philosophical, even religious. In Henry Kissinger's book on nuclear weapons policy he had underlined a sentence that read: *Our feeling of guilt with respect to power has caused us to transform all wars into crusades.* Mountbatten had said it himself: 'We are in the land of faith.'

These thoughts were playing in his mind as he walked across St James's Park, briefcase in one hand and a rolled umbrella in the other. He rarely thought of the image he presented to idle onlookers, but had he done so he would have accepted that he was the very model of a mid-ranking civil servant. Balding, bespectacled, besuited and middle-aged; wrapped up in his work, even if unable to explain exactly what that work amounted to; shy, unremarkable and unremarked.

He followed the path alongside the lake, past a crowd of ducks round an old lady who was scattering bread, and so approached the bridge over the narrow waist of the lake. By the bridge, sitting on a park bench, was a young woman wearing a headscarf. Ordinarily Rupert would not have paid any attention to a stranger in a park, but as he came near she happened to look up and meet his eyes. He was struck by the simple perfection of her face, a face so pale and unadorned that it seemed to come from an earlier age. But it was the look in those wide brown eyes that stopped him in his tracks. It was a look of pure unhappiness. Only a moment, but in that moment he saw, or believed he saw, her undefended and truthful self. This look penetrated the private world of his thoughts, and found an echo within him. It was no cry for help, he understood that: it was a glimpse of a resigned but despairing spirit.

She looked down again at once, frowning a little, perhaps annoyed with herself for having given so much away. She wore a long grey woollen coat buttoned to the chin, and sat with gloved hands clasped. Her face was now hidden from him again, blinkered by the headscarf. It was quite clear to him that he had caught her unawares, that she had had no intention of letting him see so deep into her. But for that fraction of a second she had met his eyes without the expectation of any human contact, like a lost soul.

Rupert continued over the bridge, pondering what he had seen. The girl on the bench, or woman – she must have been twenty-five at least – had succeeded in touching a buried part of himself. Who was she? What was the cause of her sorrow? A boyfriend or husband who had abandoned her? A job lost? She had the look of one who had been sitting in the park for a long time.

As he traced his familiar route home across busy Victoria Street, down drab Rochester Row, he pondered the meaning of that pale staring face. There were many lost souls in the city. Why should this one concern him? No doubt because she was young and, in an old-fashioned way, good-looking. But there were far more beautiful women on the streets of London every day, and he barely gave them a second glance. The girl on the bench had possessed something unusual that had made a strong impression.

Beyond the despair there lay innocence.

A face glimpsed for a moment: ridiculous to presume to know so much. He told himself he was projecting his own fantasies onto that blank screen. A lost soul, innocence transfigured by suffering: it was all of his own making. It was, comically, his own secret picture of himself.

So, saved by self-awareness, mocking his moment of romance, he crossed Vauxhall Bridge Road and turned into the street with the Italian market where he had his lodgings.

There was a letter waiting for him, hand-delivered. He knew from the writing on the envelope it was from his sister Geraldine. His heart sank.

Please come and see me at once. I have a proposal to discuss with you. I will be in all this evening.

He phoned her.

'I'll come at the weekend,' he said.

But of course she was having none of that.

'Come now, Rupert. You must.'

So he ate a hasty supper, and set off to Victoria tube station. As always in the evening the trains were slow to come. From High Street Kensington it was a short walk to Campden Grove, and the big empty house where his sister lived.

Geraldine greeted him at the door, immaculately groomed, elegant as ever. She showed no signs of panic. This was a relief. After the failure of her marriage she had suffered a serious breakdown, from which she had never fully recovered.

'Rupert, darling. Sweet of you to come.'

He followed her into the gloomy drawing room. The house had belonged to her husband, Larry Cornford, and to his widowed father before him. Geraldine had changed very little in the furnishings and decoration. It remained a masculine house.

'So what's the big crisis?' he said.

'Oh, no crisis at all! What a silly idea. Why should there be a crisis?'

She was putting on her playful kittenish voice, which Rupert found so trying.

'It all sounded rather urgent.'

'Tell me how you are first. How is the great Earl Louis?'

'Same as ever.'

'And your beastly little digs in Pimlico?'

'I'm very happy in Pimlico.'

'You can't be, Rupert. No one can be happy in Pimlico. I was talking to Mummy about it and we agreed. You only live there out of masochism.'

'We don't all have houses in Kensington,' said Rupert.

'That's what I want to talk to you about, actually.'

'Don't tell me you've finally decided to move.'

Rupert had been trying to persuade her to sell the house ever since the divorce.

'Have you seen anything of Larry?' Geraldine said.

'I bumped into him a few weeks ago, I suppose.'

'How is he?'

'Same as ever.'

'And what about her?'

This meant Kitty, Larry Cornford's second wife.

'I haven't seen her for ages.'

'I feel so sorry for her.'

Geraldine had convinced herself that Larry had been trapped by Kitty, and would leave her and return to his true wife, who was herself. Rupert had heard this many times, and was weary of it.

'Kitty and Larry are fine, Geraldine. And so are their boys.'

'The children, yes. That's how she did it. Now poor Larry's caught. But they're growing up. Soon he'll be able to break free. If she doesn't kill him first.'

'Oh, for God's sake.'

'She killed her first husband. Everyone knows. She made him so miserable he jumped off a cliff.'

'Geraldine, please. You know this is all nonsense.'

'Well, never mind. Time will tell. God moves in mysterious ways.' She gave him a knowing look. 'Let's talk about the house.'

'Yes, the house. It's far more than you need.'

'That's perfectly true.'

'And it's not good for you. It keeps you stuck in the past. I've been saying this for ages.'

'The house is my marriage, Rupert. This is where Larry and I live. I can't possibly leave here. I'm keeping it for Larry's return.'

'The marriage is over, Geraldine. You're divorced. Larry's not coming back.'

'The law may say the marriage is over.' Again that arch look. 'Does God say the marriage is over? I don't think so. And I think I must take God's word over the law's.'

This was the sort of talk that drove Rupert to distraction.

'Please, Geraldine. Just tell me why I'm here.'

'Well, I've had this wonderful idea. As you say, the house is more than I need. It's so obvious really. You must come and live here with me.'

'But Geraldine—'

'No, let me explain. You could be quite independent. You could have the side door as your own entrance. We would convert the second floor into a self-contained apartment for you. There's already a bathroom up there, and a dressing room. You know it's where Larry's father lived. It would be the easiest thing in the world.'

'It wouldn't work.'

'I expect you're thinking, what will happen when Larry comes back? But you see, you're only renting your flat now, aren't you? You save on the rent for all the months you're living here. And then you go back to renting.'

He looked at her sadly. Her pale face was shining with eagerness.

'It just wouldn't work, I'm afraid.'

'But why not? We wouldn't even need to see each other, except when we wanted to. And you know, Rupert, really you and I are very alike. We both find we're called on, for now at least, to live our lives alone.'

She could have added, 'and we're both unloved.' Rupert shook his head, doing his best to control his mounting anger. This always happened when he visited his sister. She presented him with a reflection of himself as he might be, as perhaps one day he would be: lonely, bitter, half-unhinged by unhappiness. In panic flight from this future, he was capable of small cruelties.

'I'm not going to live here, Geraldine,' he said. 'I don't want to, so stop asking me.'

She looked away, and gave a small lift of her shoulders.

'Well, I don't know what I'm supposed to do in this great big house all on my own.'

'You know what I think. I think you should sell the house.'

'I couldn't do that. Not unless Larry wanted to sell it.'

'Geraldine, it's your house. He gave it to you.'

'And have you ever asked yourself why, Rupert? He gave me the house to keep it in trust. This house is our house.'

'Well, I'm sorry. I don't want to have anything to do with it.'

'You think about it,' she said. 'I'm sure you'll see I'm right. It's so silly, both of us moping about alone. And Mummy agrees with me. She thinks you need bringing out of yourself.'

She caught a flush of anger on Rupert's face.

'Don't be unkind, Rupert,' she said, touching his arm. 'You shouldn't blame me for asking. I do sometimes get a tiny bit lonely, you know.'

'Yes, well,' said Rupert. 'We all have our cross to bear.'

As always when visiting Geraldine, he left more disturbed than when he had arrived. He decided to walk back, through Knightsbridge and Chelsea and then along the river. It was a long walk, but he wanted to wear himself out so that he would sleep.

He was ashamed of himself, because he knew he was running away from his sister's unhappiness. He feared contamination. There was a kind of madness in the way she clung to the memory of her husband, and refused to believe that he had abandoned her.

But am I any better? What foolish dream do I cling to, against all the evidence of my life? The dream that I won't be alone for ever. The dream that one day I'll be loved.

Regaining the safety of his digs at last, he rediscovered, as if it had been waiting for him, the memory of the girl on the park bench. The memory was of her pale face, and of the feeling it had triggered within him.

She saw me, he thought. She knew me.

14

The coffee bar was on Queensway, and was called the Brush and Palette. Susie was already at a table, in the company of a youngish man with sandy hair called Logan. Susie jumped up and waved eagerly as Pamela entered, and then made a quick twirl so that Pamela could take in the smart new dress she was wearing. Susie was short and round and pink-cheeked, with the kind of looks that made older men say, 'You look good enough to eat.'

'It's heavenly,' said Pamela, immediately aware that her own frock looked dowdy in comparison.

'This is Logan,' Susie said, presenting the youngish man with the same proud ownership as she displayed the dress. 'He's a sort of a cousin.'

'Hello, sort of cousin,' said Pamela, shaking Logan's hand.

He held her hand a fraction longer than necessary, and his gaze lingered over her for a moment before he spoke, so that Pamela understood he found her attractive.

'Hello, Susie's school friend,' he said.

As she sat down at the small table, Pamela looked round and took in for the first time what was going on. At every table the customers were at work with sketch pads and pencils, and they were all intently drawing the same subject. In the middle of the café, raised up on a small platform, sitting on a bentwood chair, was a nude model.

'Good lord!' exclaimed Pamela.

'Isn't it fun?' said Susie. 'You can draw her too if you want.'

Pamela looked round the tables. All the artists bent over their sketch pads were men. She and Susie and the naked model were the only females in the café. She wanted to laugh out loud, but the atmosphere was rather serious; so instead she gazed at the naked model. She was sitting demurely, legs crossed, one arm draped over the seat back, head a little to one side, gazing in a bored away into the distance. Her breasts were heavy and hung down almost to her stomach, which bulged a little over her raised thigh. Not a beauty, but there was something powerfully physical about her appearance. Certainly the male artists were gripped.

'Logan thinks art's a waste of time,' said Susie, glancing at Logan and smiling.

'Well, bloody hell,' said Logan amiably, 'when a girl takes off her clothes I can think of better things to do.'

'You behave yourself,' said Susie. 'You'll shock Pamela.'

Pamela turned her gaze onto Logan. Susie smiled all the time, so Pamela chose not to smile.

'Yes, you will,' she said.

Logan stopped grinning and went a little pink.

'I hope you don't really think art's a waste of time,' said Pamela. 'That would be so stupid.'

'Oh, well, you know,' said Logan. 'Not my kind of thing and all that.'

'Logan likes fast cars,' said Susie.

Logan now produced a packet of cigarettes and they all took one. The waitress came up and they ordered coffee. Pamela let Logan light her cigarette. The not-smiling was having a notice-able effect on him. Most girls simpered and giggled like puppy dogs asking to be petted. Pamela was experimenting with a different approach.

'So what do you think of the model?' she said.

This was the first time in her life she had seen a grown woman fully naked, but she made her voice sound bored, as if she appraised models all the time.

'I wouldn't strip off if I looked like her,' said Susie.

'Bloody hell,' said Logan. 'I should hope not.'

'Pammy's going to study art.'

'Ah.' Logan turned apologetic eyes on Pamela. 'I'm not really such a philistine as I sound. But I expect you've already made up your mind that I'm a bit of an ass.'

'Naturally,' said Pamela; and still she didn't smile.

'I really envy you,' said Susie. 'I have to go to this wildly boring secretarial college and do typing all day. I know I'll die before I learn to touch-type. But Mummy says I have to have a skill to fall back on.'

'I don't see why,' said Logan. 'That's what girls' bottoms are for.'

He gave a great hoot of laughter. Susie laughed too. Then they both looked at Pamela.

'I don't want a skill,' said Pamela. 'I want an experience.'

Susie giggled a little and fell silent.

'Good for you,' said Logan.

'How old are you, Logan?' said Pamela.

'Me? How old?' For a moment he seemed at a loss. 'I'm twenty-six.' He turned to Susie. 'Am I?'

'Twenty-six,' Susie confirmed.

'And you're Susie's cousin?'

'Well, in a manner of speaking,' he said. 'There is a family connection somewhere.'

'Lucky Susie,' said Pamela, speaking still in the neutral tone she was trying out. Her withholding of approval was having a gratifying effect on Logan. He could now hardly bring himself to meet her eyes.

'So what are we going to do tonight?' said Susie, clapping her hands together like a teacher calling a class to order. 'Pammy, you're the new girl in town. You choose.'

Pamela allowed her gaze to float over the artists at their tables, intersecting here and there with their furtive looks. She watched the naked model rearrange her bored limbs.

'Dinner?' said Susie. 'A show? Both?'

'I want to go,' said Pamela slowly, 'to the place where the very smartest people in London go.'

'Quite right!' cried Logan. 'Good for you!'

'Where the film stars go,' said Pamela, 'and the millionaires.'

'Crikey!' said Susie. 'I've no idea. What do you think, Logan?'

'Well, bloody hell,' said Logan, 'I have heard of a place. But it's a bit on the fast side.'

Pamela gave him her unsmiling stare.

'I think you'll find I can keep up,' she said.

Just saying this gave her a secret thrill, but seeing Logan believe her, seeing him almost in awe of her, was blissful.

'The place I'm thinking of,' said Logan, 'they have showgirls and so forth. They say Princess Margaret goes there. The only snag is, I think maybe you have to be a member.'

At this point the man at the next table turned round. He was tall and slim, with a sweep of thick brown hair above a face that was both middle-aged and boyish.

'That would be Murray's, I think.'

'Yes,' said Logan.

'You do indeed need to be a member,' said the stranger. 'Pops Murray has a very strict door policy.'

'Oh,' said Logan.

But the stranger wasn't looking at Logan, he was looking at Pamela. He now held out a business card.

'Show that,' he said. 'They'll let you in.'

'I say,' said Logan. 'That's awfully decent of you.'

Pamela had now had time to take in the stranger and the sketch he had been working on. She found herself doubly surprised. The drawing was extremely good; and it was of the model's face alone.

'You've just done her face!' she exclaimed.

'Of course,' he said with a smile. 'I love to draw people's faces. I'd like to draw yours.'

Pamela blushed deep red. Her pose of sophisticated indifference collapsed in the face of the stranger's smile. It was such a direct smile, and so overwhelmingly confident.

Logan was struggling with a different kind of worry.

'So this club,' he said, 'is it a bit steep?'

'They'll sting you for a guinea on the door,' said the stranger. 'After that, it all depends on how much you eat and drink.'

He was getting up, packing away his sketchbook and pencils, lighting himself a Senior Service from the stub of the last one, pulling on a pair of dark glasses.

'Give it a go,' he said. 'It's fun.'

Then he went on his way.

'Crikey!' said Susie. 'Do you think he was trying to pick us up?'

'If he was,' said Pamela, 'he didn't try very hard.'

'A guinea on the door,' said Logan, scratching his head.

'Oh come on, darling,' said Susie. 'It's Pammy's big night on the town.'

Logan looked up at Pamela. Now, at last, she unleashed her smile. He brightened under its impact. He sat up straighter. He laughed.

'Bloody hell,' he said. 'Why not?'

15

Murray's Cabaret Club was in a basement on Beak Street. As they entered, and were led to a small table near the back, a show was under way on the dance floor. Three elaborately costumed dancers were gyrating to the sounds of a small band. But it wasn't the dancers who held Pamela's attention. Behind them, in variegated poses, wearing enormous feathered head-dresses, stood twelve motionless showgirls. They were tall, slim, beautiful, and almost entirely naked.

Pamela threw quick glances at the wealthy patrons with bottles of champagne on their tables, and it seemed to her that none of them were staring at the naked girls. And yet their presence changed everything. Beneath the cheerful beat of the band, and the chatter of voices, and the clink of glasses, throbbed the deep noiseless pulse of sexual desire.

'Better keep this to ourselves,' said Susie, bright-eyed and gaping.

'It's all tremendously respectable,' said Logan, waving for a waiter. 'The showgirls aren't allowed to move.'

'Why not?' said Pamela.

'That's the law,' said Logan. 'I suppose so long as they don't move they're statues, and statues are art.'

The dancers performing on the dance floor now began to

turn cartwheels. It seemed an odd sort of display to Pamela, given that even she could turn a cartwheel. Then she caught sight of a man's staring gaze and realised that as the girls turned, their skirts fell back and exposed their knickers. So this was all about sex too.

The male patrons had female guests with them, their wives or girlfriends, presumably. How did they feel about it all? Did they mind their husbands or boyfriends looking at naked show-girls? Did it make them feel inferior by comparison? What was it men liked?

She studied the showgirls more critically. Unlike the model in the café they all had slender waists and full firm breasts. Pamela imagined herself standing there, naked, with all the men's eyes on her. The thought of it made her shiver with excitement.

'Have you seen anyone famous yet?' said Susie.

'I'm not even looking,' said Pamela.

'I think the man at the table by the pillar is Mel Ferrer. Oh no, it isn't.'

'What do you think of the girls, Logan?' said Pamela.

'Very pretty,' said Logan.

'I wonder what they get paid. It's not exactly difficult, is it, just standing there?'

'Why,' said Susie, 'do you want to have a go?'

'No,' said Pamela. 'Not really. Maybe just once, for fun.'

Logan ordered champagne.

'Let me know when you do it,' he said. 'I'll be in the front row.'

The atmosphere of the club was having its effect on Susie too. She leaned closer to Logan, and drew his arm round her bare shoulders, as if to stop him from straying. Even as she did so Logan's eyes were on Pamela. But Pamela was no longer interested in exciting Logan's admiration. He seemed to her to be very young and callow alongside the men at the surrounding tables. They were older, richer and more sophisticated; they were men who belonged in this club, men who . . . but here she ran up against the limits of her knowledge. She blushed at her inexperience. What did these men do? Whatever it was, it was more than getting married and living happily ever after.

The cabaret show now came to an end. The dancers took their bow and filed off. The curtain was drawn across the statue-like showgirls. The band started to play dance tunes. A few couples took to the floor.

'Want to take a turn?' said Logan to Susie.

'Do you mind, Pammy?'

'Of course not,' said Pamela.

She lit herself a cigarette and smoked and watched them dance for a few moments, then let her eyes stray to the tables. It seemed to her that there were faces she recognised. Then she realised that some of the showgirls, now dressed, had come out and were being bought drinks by male patrons. She watched their pretty smiling faces, and saw the way the men leaned in close to them, and spoke low, and touched their hands. Only a few minutes earlier these same men had been lingering over every detail of the girls' naked bodies.

Pamela sat very still and upright, and she shivered all over. She smoked her cigarette to the end and stubbed it out on the silver ashtray. Then she was aware a man was sitting down at her table.

'Do you mind?'

It was the stranger from the café, only now he was in a dinner jacket and looked impossibly glamorous.

'No, no,' said Pamela.

'I'm so pleased you came.' He offered her one of his own cigarettes. 'How do you like it?'

'Very much,' said Pamela.

'Quite a mixed crowd,' he said. 'You see the two over there?

They're very successful criminals. And there . . . Oh, she's gone. Jean Harlow was in earlier.'

'But no Princess Margaret.'

'Not tonight.' He gave her his hand. 'Stephen Ward.'

'Pamela Avenell.'

'As it happens, I've met Princess Margaret,' he said. 'I've done her portrait. She has the hardest face to draw I've ever attempted. Something about the nose.'

'Is that what you do?' said Pamela. 'Are you an artist?'

'Not really. That's more of a sideline. I'm an osteopath. I sort out people's backs and knees and so on.' Seeing the surprise on her face he added, 'Yes, I know, it does seem improbable. It just turned out I was good at it. I did Churchill's back once, and I've also done Gandhi's. Churchill asked me if I'd twisted Gandhi's neck the way I was twisting his. I told him yes, I had. Too little, he grunted, too late.'

Pamela burst into laughter. Ward flashed her a bright smile.

'You really are delightful,' he said. 'Do let me draw you.'

The combination of easy humour and famous names was more intoxicating to Pamela than the champagne.

'I don't think I should agree to anything at all,' she said. 'I'm quite sure a girl could get into a lot of trouble here.'

'Oh, it's all very innocent really,' said Ward. 'Just bored people looking for fun, and a few lonely people looking for love.'

'Which are you?'

'I like making new friends,' he said. 'I find it exciting.'

'Me too,' said Pamela.

'So will you let me draw you?'

'I'm not sure,' said Pamela. 'What if you abducted me?'

'Well, I suppose I could.' He narrowed his eyes and expelled cigarette smoke, seeming to consider the pros and cons of the idea. 'But it would be much more fun if you came of your own free will.'

'Came where?'

'I rent a cottage on the Cliveden estate. Lord Astor's a good friend. I go there for most weekends. It's not very comfortable, but it's very pretty, and right by the river. I usually have an amusing crowd of friends along. Do you know Philip de Zulueta, Macmillan's private secretary? He's got one of the other cottages on the estate. Macmillan shows up from time to time. So you never know, you could be having tea on the lawn with the prime minister.'

It was all too much for Pamela. Lord Astor. The prime minister. It didn't have the ring of the white slave trade.

Susie and Logan returned. Ward rose, pressing his card on Pamela as he did so.

'By the way,' he said to Logan, 'don't worry about the bill. I've seen to it.'

He returned to his own group of guests. He was sitting with two extremely pretty girls.

'What an amazing chap!' exclaimed Logan. 'Who is he?'

'He's an osteopath,' said Pamela. 'He wants to do my portrait.'

'Do take care, Pammy,' said Susie.

'It's all right,' said Pamela. 'He's done Princess Margaret.'

16

'Consider this scenario,' said Ted Lovell. 'A CIA spyplane is shot down over the Urals.'

'Another Gary Powers.' Ian Shaw, the War Office man, spoke languidly, without looking up from doodling on his pad. Nothing ever surprised Shaw.

'It's happened once,' said Lovell, irritated. 'It can happen again.'

The Joint Inter-Service Group for the Study of All-Out War was in session in Room 302 of the Old Admiralty Building. This was a meeting of advisers, not chiefs. Rupert Blundell stood by the window looking out over Horse Guards Parade, only half paying attention.

'A spyplane is shot down,' Lovell repeated. 'The Russians have gone on record saying the next time they'll not only shoot the intruder down, they'll destroy the base from which the flight originated.'

He looked to Jim Shipman, the Foreign Office man, for confirmation.

'More sabre-rattling than policy,' Shipman said.

'In my scenario,' said Lovell, 'the sabre does more than rattle. The Soviets hit Eielson Air Force base in Alaska. How do the Americans respond? Do they go like for like, and hit Pevek or Anadyr? Or do they activate SIOP?'

Ah, thought Rupert by the window. How the committee loved this sacred monster: SIOP, the Single Integrated Operational Plan, the ultimate blitzkrieg. 'Wagnerian!' his friend John Grimsdale called it. He too was on the JIGSAW committee, representing the Joint Intelligence Council.

None of them wanted SIOP, of course. No sane person could want it. But it excited them. They loved to dwell on its awesome horror.

There must be something lacking in me, Rupert thought. All it represents to me is the appetite for bullying writ large. Isn't there enough misery in the world already?

He recalled the look in the eyes of the girl on the park bench. So much loss, so much loneliness.

'In my scenario,' said Ted Lovell, 'the Americans go for the big one. It's their only option. Here's why.'

Lovell proceeded to spell out the familiar chain of thinking that underlay all current nuclear strategy. The Americans have massive nuclear superiority. Therefore they have the greater chance of victory with a first strike. The Soviets, knowing this, can only survive by getting their strike in earlier: what might be called first-first. Therefore it was imperative that the US anticipated the moment of crisis and 'retaliated in advance': first-first-first.

The logic works, if not the grammar.

'In my hypothetical scenario,' went on Lovell, 'the US has been attacked. Only a limited attack, but nonetheless they *must* respond. Not to respond is to show weakness. We're talking about national prestige here. What range of response is open to them? At this point they ask themselves, what are the Soviets thinking?'

What indeed are the Soviets thinking? thought Rupert. It plays out so very like a game between lovers. Does she love me? Is she cheating on me? Why doesn't she answer my calls?

It amused Rupert to think this way. In the game of love the West played the feminine role, the Soviets the masculine role. The Russians so impenetrable, so crude, so frightening. Please show us love. Please hug us in your bear-like arms.

'Here's what the Soviets are thinking. They're thinking, we're now in an actual state of conflict. It's started. The top brass of Strategic Air Command all want SIOP. They may not go right to it, but it's coming. Better get our strike in first. That's what the Russians are thinking. And the Americans know they're thinking it. So you're the president. What do you do?'

'This is all standard war-game stuff, Ted,' said Shaw. 'This just takes us back into relative survivability calculations.'

Rupert watched the people and the cars passing down Horse Guards Road and thought of the lonely girl on the bench. Why, when human beings have the capacity to bring each other happiness, do they wreak such untold destruction?

'I'm not done yet,' said Lovell. 'This is where it gets interesting. In my scenario, the Soviets have prepared for just such a moment. Their missiles are widely dispersed and well protected. Their leadership is safe in a bunker deep in the Urals. So – the Americans launch SIOP. It devastates the Russian homeland. But, crucially, it leaves a small part of the Soviet nuclear force intact. Give me a number, Geoffrey.'

'Two hundred missiles,' says Geoffrey Unwin, the hardware man.

That's the JIGSAW game, thought Rupert. Dress up a fantasy with hard numbers and people start to believe it.

'Now,' said Lovell, becoming animated. 'Here's the twist. Everyone assumes the Soviets will retaliate with everything they've got. They don't. They launch only half their surviving armoury. A hundred missiles. They destroy a hundred American cities. The United States is crippled. Its days as a major power are over.'

'Ditto the Soviet Union,' interjected Shipman. 'Russia's a wasteland.'

'A wasteland,' said Lovell, 'with a hundred nuclear missiles in hand. And what do they do with them? They target the rich West. They demand aid for Russia, and refuse aid to the stricken US. Under threat of annihilation, the West rebuilds Russia. Within thirty years, the Soviet Union dominates the planet. The United States is history.'

'And the UK?' said John Grimsdale, smiling because he knew the answer.

'Wiped out.' Ted Lovell made a contemptuous gesture with one hand. 'To the Soviets we're just another American missile base. We're the first to go.'

No one dissented. It was one of the curiosities of JIGSAW that they all took for granted their own nation's impotence and irrelevance.

'Not bad, Ted,' said Edgar Anstey, the Home Office psychologist. 'I think you may have come up with an original wrinkle.'

At this point the tea trolley came clinking into the conference room. A polite scuffle ensued over the chocolate Bourbons. Alan McDonald poured the tea. Ted Lovell looked pleased with himself.

'What do you think, Rupert?' he said.

Rupert spoke the least on the committee, but was known to have Mountbatten's ear. It was also understood that Rupert had retained the ability to see the wood for the trees.

'There's only one part of your scenario that interests me,' he said.

'The partial retaliation trick?'

'I'm interested in your assumption that any attack must be answered by a similar or greater attack. You say not to respond is to show weakness. If you're right, the rest follows, and we're all doomed. But I don't believe you are right.'

'You think the West can afford to appear weak?'

'To whom?' said Rupert. 'Who is this display of power designed to impress? Khrushchev already knows how many bombs we've got.'

'But does he know,' said Grimsdale, 'that we've got the balls to use them?'

'Or that we've got the balls not to use them,' said Rupert.

'Come on, Rupert,' said Shaw. 'We're all highly educated products of generations of soft living. Khrushchev is a peasant who's clawed his way to the top. He'll do whatever he has to do to win.'

'But what does it mean to Khrushchev to win?' said Rupert.

'World domination,' said Grimsdale.

'Not that old chestnut!' exclaimed Rupert.

Suddenly he remembered the young Russian officer in the Great Hall at Cliveden, earnestly telling him, 'We want much the same as you.' What was it he had itemised? Eating. Dancing. Talking late into the night.

'No, you listen to me,' Grimsdale was saying, nettled. 'That's not some right-wing crankery. The Soviet Union is explicitly committed to the global triumph of Communism.'

'You know perfectly well—'

'Don't tell me what I know. Our enemy is a millenarian cult. Do you deny it?'

'Of course I deny it! It's utter nonsense!'

'These are people who believe the ends justify the means,' said Grimsdale, now pink in the face. 'These are people who believe history is on their side.'

'They're just whistling in the dark,' said Rupert, 'to keep their spirits up.'

'These are people,' retorted Grimsdale, 'who have not hesitated to sacrifice millions of lives in what they conceive to be their cause. It's our absolute duty to assume they will not shrink from sacrificing us. To think anything else is irresponsible.'

'Sacrificing us!' said Rupert. 'I know it excites you to play end-of-the-world games. But this is all a paranoid fantasy.'

'Paranoid fantasy!'

Grimsdale started to splutter.

'Can't you see?' Rupert pressed on. 'Assume the worst and you make it happen! Jesus, why can't you see that?'

In his mind's eye he saw three young men on the terrace at Cliveden, the Russian, the American and himself, their hands clasped in shared hope. 'No more wars.'

Where was that dream now?

He gave an awkward shrug. He was aware that he had allowed himself to become emotional.

'Sorry,' he said.

'I don't understand what it is you're arguing for, Rupert,' said Ted Lovell, speaking in reasonable tones. 'Are you suggesting that if we showed weakness, it would somehow benefit us?'

'I'm saying strategies based on worst fears can never make us secure.'

'So what can?'

'We have to change the terms of the debate. The threat facing us isn't an attack by an enemy, but the outbreak of war itself. Our allies are as potentially dangerous to us as our opponents. If there's a war, we all lose together. That's never happened before in history. We simply can't go on thinking in the old adversarial terms.'

'So what exactly are we to think, Rupert?' said Grimsdale.

'I'm working on that.'

It was all very frustrating. He felt so close to seeing the answer, but it eluded him. He was convinced that the way forward lay in the manipulation of ideas, not stockpiles of weapons. In its way a nuclear bomb was only an idea. To be effective, the weapon required the intention to arm and use it.

Are you suggesting that if we showed weakness, it would some-how benefit us?

A fair question.

What if the answer is yes? How could a display of weakness deliver a benefit?

It could reduce fear.

He could hear the objection coming back loud and clear. Weakness invites aggression: the lesson of Munich. The dread of appeasement hangs over us all. But surely that lesson has been overlearned.

Imagine you're the Soviet Union. What do you really want? You've recently endured the most devastating war in history, in which twenty million of your people perished. What you want is security. You want invulnerable borders. You want to know it can't ever happen again.

He pulled out a sheet of paper and jotted down his thoughts in note order.

1. Each side has reason to fear the other.
2. In the pursuit of invulnerability, both sides increase their stockpile of weapons.
3. The more we arm, the more fear we create.
4. The pursuit of invulnerability thus renders both sides more vulnerable.
5. Therefore we must accept some level of vulnerability.

He stared at the page. How do you sell that to an electorate in a democracy? All it takes is some new demagogue whipping up the people's fears, and you're back in maximum-aggression mode.

Fear is a ghost. How do you fight a ghost?

With a spirit.

Rupert felt a prickling of his skin, the sensation that for him was always the prelude to an intellectual breakthrough. Maybe there was a way to reframe the debate after all.

6. The Cold War can be understood as a spiritual conflict. Communism makes messianic claims. America is the self-proclaimed crusader, the defender of freedom.
7. In a spiritual conflict, there is a higher goal than victory on the field of battle.
8. The nuclear arms race threatens the destruction of the world.
9. Our higher goal is to save the world.

Rupert stared at the sheet of paper. Here was a way to combine national prestige with military restraint. There's only one game that trumps fighting and winning a war. And that's playing God.

Great power allied to infinite mercy. The Christian revolution.

Ronnie Brockman came in waving a sheet of paper.

'Dickie's memo,' he said.

'What?'

'"Aim for the West". He asked me to get you a copy.'

Rupert had entirely forgotten.

'What is it?'

'Oh, typical Dickie stuff. Very big picture. Let's all find something to believe in, and so on.'

Rupert took the paper and read its first sentence.

The basic thing which seems to put the West at a demonstrable disadvantage with the East is the absence of a philosophy, a policy, an ideal, or an aim.

'Was this circulated?'

'Only to immediate staff.'

'Was there any response?'

'Not really. What can you say?'

Ronnie Brockman left him to his musings. He read further.

The East have, of course, Communism and the creed of Karl Marx, which has undoubtedly helped them to make up their minds on policy, and in their determination to see things through.

   Can we not find an aim for the West?

The memo then discussed four options: Religion, Western Democracy, Way of Life and Anti-Communism. It dismissed each in turn. The last line ran:

Can we not find some common rallying cry to give us some common purpose?

17

Walking briskly across the park on his way home, Rupert found himself looking out for the girl on the bench. There was no reason why she should be there. Just because she had chosen to sit in the park at this time of day on one occasion did not mean that it was her regular habit. Coming in view of the bridge, his first impression was that she was not there, because there were three people by the bench. They were nuns, dressed in black habits. Then as he came closer he saw that only two were nuns, both standing, and between them, seated on the bench as before, was the young woman in the grey coat and the headscarf.

It seemed the nuns were speaking sharply to her. She had her head down, her hands clasped.

Nearer now, Rupert could make out the voices.

'Come along now, Mary. That's enough of this foolishness. You know you can't sit all day in the park.'

As he approached, the young woman looked up and saw him. In the same instant, she recognised him. Her frightened eyes transmitted to him a mute appeal.

'Didn't I tell you?' she said to the nuns, speaking with a strong Irish accent. 'Here's my cousin Frankie come to meet me.'

Rupert came to a stop. Both nuns turned round to stare at him in surprise.

'Your cousin Frankie?'

Rupert looked back in silence. He was suddenly aware that this was one of those moments on which lives turn.

'Yes,' he said. 'That's me.'

Then, to the young woman on the bench, 'Hello, Mary. Sorry I'm late. I got held up at work.'

The young woman called Mary kept a perfectly straight face.

'You promised you'd take me to Fortnum & Mason,' she said.

'And so I will,' Rupert heard himself say. 'We'll have to hurry, or they'll be closed.'

Mary jumped up from the bench. Rupert gave her his arm. The nuns stared.

'You'll not be late, Mary,' said the older one. 'Supper at seven.'

'Yes, Mother,' said Mary, giving a half-bob of a curtsy. 'Come along, Frankie.'

Off they went across the park towards the Mall. Rupert, trembling, amazed at himself, said nothing. The young woman called Mary had created this situation. He would let her explain.

They walked briskly. She turned once, to look back and satisfy herself that the nuns were out of earshot. Then she let go of Rupert's arm.

'Well!' she said. 'Aren't you the knight in shining armour!'

'How did you know I'd play along?'

'I didn't.'

'You have seen me before. Do you remember?'

'Of course,' she said. Then, 'I suppose you think I'm a poor mad woman.'

'Possibly,' said Rupert. 'I shall reserve judgement.'

'They watch me like cats. I shouldn't be surprised if they follow us to Fortnum's.'

'Oh, are we really going to Fortnum's?'

'Cousin Frankie!' Her voice rose in mock surprise. 'You promised!'

Crossing the Mall they looked back into the park once more.

'They're not following us,' Rupert said.

He looked round and there she was, gazing up at him, half laughing, half desperate. She had the most perfect face he had ever seen. White skin, faintly freckled. Green-brown eyes. Pale lips. A tilted chin.

'I can't explain,' she said. 'So don't ask.'

'All right,' said Rupert.

'You were the best.'

'I'm afraid I couldn't do the Irish accent.'

'There really is a cousin Frankie,' she said, 'but he's got ginger hair and lives in Dublin.'

'And he never promised to take you to Fortnum's.'

'No. That was me. Only I've no money.'

'Then I'd better pay, hadn't I?'

He spoke lightly, but his heart was hammering. The mystery, the secrecy, the childlike quality of her trust in him, the sweetness of her face, the charm of helping one who was so evidently in need of help, all combined to astonish and delight him.

'Why do you want to go to Fortnum's?'

'To have a Knickerbocker Glory, of course,' she replied. 'Isn't that why everyone goes there?'

'Yes, I suppose it is.'

So they made their way to the Jermyn Street entrance of the soda fountain at Fortnum & Mason, and sat side by side on high stools at the bar, and Rupert ordered her a Knickerbocker Glory. She didn't remove her shapeless grey coat, or her headscarf.

'Aren't you going to have anything?' she said.

'I'll have the pleasure of watching you,' he said.

'Is it horribly expensive?'

'Yes,' he said.

It arrived in a tall glass, all pink and white and creamy, with a straw and a long-handled spoon. Mary gazed at it in a kind of ecstasy.

'You can't imagine,' she said.

She sucked on the straw and closed her eyes.

'Heaven,' she said.

He let her drink in silence. Then when she had finished, 'You must feel ill now, surely?'

'Only a little.'

She gave him a smile that was so filled with gratitude that he blushed and looked away. In her presence he felt old and undeserving.

'So what's your name?' she said.

'Rupert. Rupert Blundell.'

'I'm Mary Brennan.'

She held out her hand and he shook it. Her hand was cold.

'Are you training to be a nun?' he said.

This was the furthest he had got in solving the puzzle she presented.

'No,' she said. 'I just live with them, at the convent in Queen Anne's Gate. They're very good to me. They give me a little room of my own, and all my meals.'

'But you don't like living with them?'

'I've nowhere else to go,' she said simply.

'Are you a fallen woman?'

'A fallen woman? Oh!' She blushed as she understood, then she laughed. 'No,' she said. 'If I was a fallen woman I'd have some money, wouldn't I? From the falling.'

Rupert watched her, entranced; but she said no more.

'You're not going to tell me, are you?'

'No, I can't. Which is such ingratitude, after all you've done for me.'

'Is there anything more I can do for you?' he said.

'Oh, no. I mean, why should you?'

Impossible to answer. Why was he helping her? Because she amazed him. Because in her presence his life was transformed. But for her benefit, he gave a more sober reason.

'I'm a civil servant,' he said. 'I work for the Ministry of Defence. My area of expertise, as they say, is the risk of nuclear war. When you live with the knowledge that the world may end any day, it makes you more willing to help people.'

She gave him a long keen look.

'So it does,' she said softly.

'I can't offer you a room in my flat,' he said. 'That would be open to misunderstanding. But I might be able to help you find somewhere else.'

'I told you,' she said. 'I've no money.'

He thought of his sister's big house in Kensington, and Geraldine's loneliness. Empty rooms there and to spare. But he thought it only to dismiss it. There were other options.

'How about a room in a family house in exchange for help with childcare?'

He had in mind his former brother-in-law's business partner, Hugo Caulder. Hugo had a family house with many rooms, and a wife who was often poorly, and a child. Of course, Rupert knew nothing about this Mary Brennan, but presumably the nuns would vouch for her.

She was astonished by his suggestion.

'Why would anyone take a stranger into their home?'

'We all start out as strangers,' he said. 'I have a family in mind. They're good people. Shall I ask them?'

'To tell you the truth,' she said slowly, 'I'd go anywhere that would have me, if I could get out of the convent.'

'I take it you can't go home.'

'No.'

146

A pregnancy? An abortion? The Irish took all that sort of thing far more to heart.

'Let me have a number where I can reach you,' he said. 'I'll have a word with the family.'

'No,' she said. 'I'll phone you.'

He gave her his home number and told her what time in the evening was best to find him in. Before they parted she offered him her hand again.

'Thank you, Mr Blundell. I don't know why you're helping me. But as they say, beggars can't be choosers.'

'I'll do what I can, Mary.'

'And thank you also,' she said, looking at him very gravely, 'for the Knickerbocker Glory. It was a glory. You should have had one too.'

'We all come short of the glory of God,' he said.

She stared for a moment, and then realising he was teasing her, she smiled a sweet warm smile.

'Can it be that you're a papist too?' she said.

'I was once.'

'I might have known. The way you lied with a straight face.'

'Does that mean you tell lies?'

'You know as well as I do,' she said. 'When you're raised our way you're filled to the brim with stories that aren't exactly true and aren't exactly lies. Isn't that what's called faith?'

With this she made him a little curtsy, as she had done to the nuns, and headed back across the park. Rupert watched her go in wonder.

She may be lost and unhappy, he thought, but she's certainly no fool.

18

Pamela told Hugo that she was spending that Saturday afternoon with her friend Susie in Cadogan Square. It was a sunny day in June, and she had put on her prettiest summer frock, cornflower-blue edged in white. She left the house in Brook Green and headed in the direction of Hammersmith Broadway. Long before she got to the tube station she stopped beside a tobacconist's shop. Here, pulled up at the kerb, was a white Jaguar sports car with Stephen Ward at the wheel.

He jumped out and opened the passenger door for her.

'I'd just decided you weren't going to come,' he said.

'I said I'd come,' said Pamela. 'I always do what I say.'

This was not true at all, but it came to her in the moment as a fine thing to say, and she was pleased by the sound of it. She meant Stephen Ward to know from the start that she was no wide-eyed child.

He pulled the Jaguar out onto the main road and drove round the Broadway onto the Great West Road. He never looked at her once as he drove, and seemed to take her presence for granted. Pamela was both relieved and a little disconcerted. What for her was an extraordinary adventure seemed to be for him an everyday occurrence. She tried to guess his age. Forty at least, more than twice as old as she was.

'There should be a few other people turning up,' he said as they bowled down the straight road past the airport. 'Quite a mixed bunch.'

Pamela wanted very much to know if any of them were famous, without giving away that she had never in her life been in the company of famous people.

'I hoped it was to be just you,' she said. 'I do find crowds boring.'

'Oh, I don't think you'll be bored.'

After a while they turned off the main road and headed down a narrower road between trees. Then they passed through some grand gates, down a long private drive.

'This is Bill Astor's place,' said Ward, gesturing at the woodland on either side. 'The big house is up that way. We go down here.'

He made a sharp turn to the left, and they drove deeper into the woods. In a little while the trees ended, and there was the river with a pleasure boat cruising slowly by. On its deck lounged two pretty young women drinking what might have been champagne. Both were wearing dark glasses and gazing impenetrably at the river bank as they churned by. Seeing them Pamela wished she had brought a pair of dark glasses.

The Jaguar followed the track by the river for a little way, and pulled up at last beside a large cottage with steep roofs and high chimneys and leaded windows. Between the cottage and the river was a sloping garden bright with roses and irises.

'Oh, it's so pretty!' Pamela exclaimed.

'My hideaway,' said Stephen Ward, escorting her to the door. 'I love it here.'

His hideaway. A romantic nook where he brought his women. He took her arm as he led her inside, and there was something about the pressure of his hand that told her he knew just what to do with women. He was slim and muscular and moved with grace. She wondered if he would try to kiss her, and what she would do if he did. Many boys and some men had made lunges at her in her young life so far, and she had become adept at evasion. One day, of course, she would not get away. She would be caught and kissed properly, and all the rest of it.

The interior of the cottage was not glamorous. It was basically furnished, with worn and non-matching chairs. The rooms were heated by oil stoves. There was no phone or fridge. The kitchen seemed to be bare of food.

'Everyone just mucks in here, as you see,' said Ward, dropping his jacket on a chair. 'What can I get you? Tea? Coffee? I can usually scrounge up a cup of coffee.'

Saying this, he produced a sketch pad and a tin of pencils. Pamela realised with a shock that what she had taken as a ruse was in fact genuine. He was going to draw her portrait.

He sat her outside on a low wall of rocks by a little stream that tumbled past bright blue campanulas to the river. The afternoon sun shone warm on her face as she posed, two hands crossed obediently in her lap. He worked quickly, squinting his eyes in concentration, looking from her face to his pad and back. She felt the unceasing intensity of his gaze but was unable to tell from it what he was thinking about her, if anything. She found this provoking.

'So what have I done to deserve the honour of this invitation?' she said.

'Nothing at all,' he replied.

'That's not very gallant. You make it sound as if you picked me out at random.'

'On impulse, let's say.'

He went on sketching. Pamela began to feel restless. She wondered what would be done about lunch.

'When can I have a fag?'

'Any time you like.'

'When are all these other people coming?'

'Later,' he said.

'Will they be fun? What if I don't like them?'

'My dear,' he said, 'if you feel yourself becoming bored, you have only to say the word and I'll run you back to Hammersmith.'

He was so relaxed about her presence that it bordered on indifference. Pamela thought that perhaps she was bored already. Perhaps she would ask him to take her home as soon as he was done with his sketching.

'So do you have a boyfriend?'

'No,' she said. 'Do you have a wife?'

'Not anymore. I like my freedom too much.'

'Oh, your freedom.'

She meant her tone of voice to imply that she knew just what men meant by 'freedom'.

'I like to come and go as I please. I like to see who I please. Really I'm a collector of people. I love to meet people, and get to know them, and bring them together.'

'Have you collected me?'

'Of course. Here you are.'

Pamela pouted at that. She didn't want to be just another specimen in his collection.

'You're very beautiful.' His voice was matter-of-fact. 'Play your cards right and you could have any man you wanted.'

'My cards?'

'There are ways of doing these things. I can introduce you to some real prospects. What sort of chap are you looking for?'

'Who said I was looking for anyone?'

'Oh, come on,' he said. 'What's the point of a pretty girl if she doesn't let some lucky fellow love her?'

'I'm sure you know a great deal better than me.'

He laid down his pencil and smiled at her, crinkling up his brown eyes.

'Don't be cross with me,' he said. 'I'm on your side.'

Before the portrait was done the other guests began rolling up. A small, very pretty, girl called Christine, who kissed Ward on the lips and called him 'darling'. A broad-faced smiling man with a broken nose called Eugene, who Ward introduced as 'our Russian spy.' And a slender man called André, who was either Belgian or Dutch and had a sad but beautiful face. All the newcomers arrived with provisions of one sort or another. Eugene brought bottles of vodka. André brought wine. Christine had an entire shopping bag, out of which came fruit and vegetables, bread and pickles and chocolate.

'Stephen never has anything in the house,' she said. 'If nobody feeds him, he just doesn't eat.'

They clustered round and admired Pamela's portrait, taking her presence in the cottage for granted. Pamela now looked at the sketch herself. She saw the head and shoulders of a haughty sophisticated beauty who looked like a fashion model.

'Good Lord!' she exclaimed. 'Is that what I look like?'

'Not one of my best efforts,' said Stephen.

Christine made decisions about who was to sleep in which bedroom.

'Eugene, you'd better share the front room with André. Pamela can go in the little back room. Pamela, is there anyone in particular you'd like to sleep with?'

Until this moment Pamela had not known she was staying the night.

'Could I have Sean Connery, please?'

This went down gratifyingly well.

'I think I'd better share Stephen's bed,' said Christine. 'He's very well-behaved, unlike some.'

'So you've decided to stay?' Stephen said to Pamela.

'I might,' she said. 'And I might not.'

But she was starting to enjoy herself. Both of the new men were paying her attention, in their different ways. Eugene, the Russian spy, was open in his admiration.

'Lovely, lovely,' he said, pouring her a glass of vodka. 'Stephen, how is it you know so many beautiful girls?'

'Beautiful girls are the same as everyone else,' said Stephen. 'They want to make new friends. They want to have adventures.'

'We have very beautiful girls in Russia,' Eugene said.

He then proposed a toast to his country.

'The greatest country in the world, and the future of the world.'

André smiled and shook his head.

'Except you have to build a wall to keep your people in.'

'Oh, the wall, the wall,' said Eugene. 'I don't like walls. Don't talk to me about the wall.'

They sat together on the river front and watched the Saturday cruisers go by and smoked and drank Eugene's vodka. André gazed at Pamela from time to time, but he did not speak to her. When he himself was speaking she watched his face, and caught the sadness in his limpid grey eyes, and wondered what he thought of her, and whether he found Christine more attractive. Christine was curled up with her head in Stephen's lap, which implied that she belonged to Stephen.

Eugene was boasting about the Soviet Union.

'By 1970 we will be richer than the United States. That is a fact.'

'Not the way you spend money,' said Stephen.

'Me! I am a man of modest means.'

'You get your suits at Harrods.'

'Of course!' said Eugene. 'I represent my country. I must dress well. Shirts and shoes from Barkers, suits and ties from Harrods, cologne from Christian Dior. But when we are victorious, when we have built true Communism, all this will wither away.'

'I've been meaning to ask you, Eugene,' said Stephen. 'Do you actually believe the tosh you talk?'

Eugene leapt to his feet.

'I am Yevgeny Mikhailovich Ivanov, Captain Second Rank, descended on my mother's side from the family Golenishchev-Kutuzov. My ancestor Mikhail Ilarionovich Kutuzov defeated the Grande Armée of Napoleon in 1812. I am Russian and patriot, and if you insult me I will break your nose, as my nose was broken when I was middleweight squadron champion of the Pacific fleet!'

He gave a mighty salute, and they all cheered. He sat down again, grinning, and poured everyone more vodka.

'You'll never build true Communism,' said André. 'America will never allow it. They'll destroy Russia first.'

'My friend,' said Eugene, 'that would be tragedy. All men of goodwill must combine to prevent. I tell my friend Stephen here, if the Germans gain access to nuclear weapons, the world is in great danger. The Americans must not supply nuclear warheads for their Pershing missiles in Germany.'

Christine was up on her feet now.

'Come on, Pamela,' she said. 'The men are going to be boring. Let's take a walk.'

They strolled together up and down the towpath, aware that the men's eyes were following them. Pamela asked Christine how she came to know Stephen, and so learned that she had once worked as a showgirl at Murray's club.

'Were you a dancer?'

'Oh, no, I can't dance,' said Christine. 'I was one of the girls who just stands there. I can do standing still.'

Standing still naked, thought Pamela. All the men's eyes lingering over your body.

'Did you like it?'

'It was all right. It gets boring very quickly, I can tell you. Perce pays well, nine pounds a week. But really it's a chance to meet people, isn't it?'

A chance to meet people. What she meant was that men stared at your naked body and desired you, and later you went out with them.

'Is Stephen your boyfriend?'

'Oh, no,' said Christine. 'Stephen's no bother at all in that way.'

'Oh,' said Pamela.

She wondered if this meant that Stephen was homosexual. Christine evidently followed her thoughts.

'He's not queer or anything,' she said. 'He has this great story about when he was young and visiting Mexico. He and a friend went to a brothel and they picked a girl each, and Stephen went off into one of the rooms with his girl. Then she came running out to bang on all the other girls' doors, shouting out, "Come and see Stephen's *pinga grande*!"'

'Good heavens!'

'It's perfectly true,' said Christine. 'He's got a whopper.'

Pamela smiled, as if such talk were familiar to her, but everything about Christine was a revelation. She was presumably what is referred to as a 'loose woman', but there was nothing sordid about her. She was pretty and friendly, funny and honest. It was quite plain that all the men adored her.

'So do you have a boyfriend?' Pamela asked her.

'I think I've got several,' said Christine. 'Or maybe none. How about you?'

'Definitely none.'

A car drove up bringing a chauffeur with a note from Bill Astor.

'Who's for a swim?' said Stephen. 'Bill says I'm to bring some amusing people up to his pool.'

They piled into the cars and drove through the woods to the biggest house Pamela had ever seen. The car deposited them by a door in a high brick wall, to the right of the palace. Here, set in a walled garden between lines of dark-green hedge, was a blue swimming pool. Conical yew trees stood at each corner, and at the far end there was a pillared circular pavilion.

Pamela had not come prepared with a costume, and so assumed she would be among those who watched from the side. But all the others stripped to their underwear and jumped in.

For a while she stood on the side feeling like a child who couldn't swim, which wasn't fair because she was a good swimmer. So when Christine called to her, 'Come on in, it's not cold!' she slipped off her dress and joined them.

The water was cold, at first at least, and rather shocked her. Then Eugene came up behind her and clasped his powerful arms round her and lifted her up out of the water. She screamed and he dropped her. André emerged from the water before her, sleek as a seal, and gazed at her for a moment. Then he slipped underwater again.

A group of men in dinner jackets appeared on the poolside. Pamela failed to catch who any of them were, except for the stout figure of their host, Lord Astor. They were all middle-aged or older. They gazed with smiling longing at herself and Christine. Christine climbed out of the pool in her brassiere and knickers and talked to them as unselfconsciously as if she was fully dressed. Pamela too got out, and found a towel to drape round her shoulders, but it covered very little. One of the men from the big house party engaged her in conversation, speaking with a faint middle-European accident.

'I envy you,' he said. 'I'd love a dip.'

'Why don't you?'

'I'm too old for that sort of thing. And then it would get into the papers, and there'd be a fuss.'

'Are you someone famous, then?' said Pamela, letting the towel slip open a little more.

'No,' he said. 'But once, before the war, I was a king. Now I am an ex-king. I would like to see you privately. Will you give me your phone number?'

'I'm afraid I don't have one,' Pamela said.

'If I was still king,' he said sadly, 'you would have a phone number.'

Later they put their clothes back on and drove back to the cottage by the river. Night had now fallen. They all had another vodka and Stephen proposed a game of Ghosts.

'It's very easy. We spread out in the trees. Then you have to creep up on someone and give them a fright.'

There was very little light between the trees, and the game quickly became genuinely scary. Pamela moved about, looking to all sides, and thought she saw someone, and then lost them again. So after a very short time she came to a stop by a big tree and stood and waited, trembling.

All her senses were in a state of heightened alert. She felt she had never lived until now. She longed for someone to creep up on her and . . . and what?

A sharp scream sounded from elsewhere in the woods, followed by soft laughter. Then came the crashing of running feet. She moved cautiously around the trunk of her protecting tree. Then she sensed there was someone behind her.

'Beautiful ghost,' said a voice.

She turned round. It was André.

He gazed at her, not moving. In the darkness it seemed possible to remain like this, looking, not speaking, caught in an intense stillness. She could barely make out his face.

Then Eugene burst out of the trees, bellowing.

'Boo! Boo!'

Stephen could be heard calling them. And so the game ended, and one by one the guests made their way back to the cottage.

Pamela hardly slept that night. She was on fire with excitement. She felt as if she had stepped out of one life and into another, a life that was more brightly lit, more intensely lived. In this new life, she possessed power.

Of course in the end it was all about sex. Pamela was not a fool. She understood that this was what all men wanted. But she herself had never had sex, nor had she yet felt anything she could identify as sexual desire, so the physical aspects remained remote to her. And yet her body trembled. Her skin glowed. She loved the sensation of men's gaze on her body. She desired desire.

Christine fascinated her. She imagined her standing naked in Murray's club accepting the lustful gaze of strangers. What did that feel like? Pamela wriggled in her bed as she imagined herself on that stage. In her fantasy there was no sequinned G-string. She was entirely naked, and she was able to move. She strutted past the tables at which the rich, sophisticated men sat in silence, and their eyes devoured her, but not one of them was permitted to reach out and touch.

Their eyes implored her, as André's had done. What could she tell them? What were they to do for her? She had no answer. As yet she had too little experience, no experience at all. She knew only that some man, somehow, someday, would wake her from her trance of youth.

'Make me love you,' she said to her unknown lover. 'Make me want to die for love.'

In the morning she came down late to find only Stephen up. He had made a pot of coffee, and was sitting in a silk bathrobe in the open doorway, drinking coffee and looking out at the river.

'How is Miss Pamela this morning?' he said.

'Half awake,' she said. 'I wasn't planning on staying the night. I didn't bring any overnight things.'

'So did you have to sleep in your birthday suit?'

'Well, in my knickers.'

'Don't,' he said. 'I shall get overexcited.'

But he didn't sound excited. He sounded languid. She poured herself a mug of coffee, pulled up a chair beside him, and lit herself a cigarette. She was realising what Christine had meant when she said Stephen was very well behaved. He was safe; for all his *pinga grande*.

'Glad you came?' he said.

'Very.'

'They're not a bad crowd.'

'I feel quite out of my depth,' said Pamela. 'I know it's all just fun. But does it ever get serious?'

'Oh, yes,' said Stephen. 'I brought Bronwen here when she was still modelling. Now she's married to Billy Astor.'

Pamela found this confusing. In the other world, the world of her parents, male desire was channelled into marriage. But here, in this riverside Garden of Eden, men and women were naked and unashamed.

'To be honest,' said Stephen, 'I'm not sure I did Bronwen any favours there. It's not easy being Lady Astor. And he is twenty-three years older than her.'

'What about Christine?' said Pamela.

'Oh, Christine. She's virtually uneducated, you know? But she knows more than any girl I've ever met.'

'What do you mean? Knows what?'

'How men work. How to get what she wants. But she's no gold-digger. She wants to have fun, and she wants to be looked after, but she's as likely to sleep with a roadsweeper as a duke.'

Pamela was mystified.

'Why? What is it she wants?'

'You'll have to ask her that.'

Christine herself now appeared, bleary-eyed, wearing only a long man's shirt. She stroked Stephen's shoulder.

'Morning, darling.'

'Pamela wants to know what it is you want.'

'Coffee,' Christine said.

Then Eugene appeared, and the room was filled with noise and laughter.

'Stephen, my friend. I have been thinking. You must introduce me to Lord Mountbatten. He is Chief of Defence Staff. He can tell me many things.'

'I don't know him, old chum.'

'What nonsense is this! You know everybody!'

'I believe he did hear about me, when I was working as an osteo in the Army in India. He was a great help, actually. But I never met him.'

'So arrange to meet! I must be his friend.'

'What kind of spy do you call yourself?' Stephen appealed to the others. 'Aren't spies meant to operate undercover? You can't just go up to the enemy and say you want to be his friend.'

'Why not? We must love one another or die!'

'Oh, Eugene! You're quoting Auden.'

'Am I?'

> 'I and the public know
> What all schoolchildren learn,
> Those to whom evil is done
> Do evil in return.'

Eugene embraced Stephen, kissing him on both cheeks.

'That is beautiful, Stephen, and it is true.'

Pamela asked Stephen to drive her home. It was now past eleven on Sunday morning, and it had finally occurred to her that Hugo and Harriet would be worried about her. She made her goodbyes to the others. André was still not up.

In the car heading into town they talked about Christine.

'I never knew girls could be like that,' said Pamela.

'Ah, Christine is special,' said Stephen. 'No one owns Christine.'

'But she has boyfriends?'

'Certainly. Men fight over her. But she doesn't care.'

'How can she not care?'

'She's not the possessive type. Sex doesn't really interest her. But then, a lot of girls are like that. The bed part of it does nothing for them. Not very surprising when you think how useless most men are in that department.'

'So why does she do it?'

'It's how she gets by. Before she started at Murray's she was working in a dress shop. She got bored, she wanted more. More fun, more pretty things. You can't blame her.'

'Oh, no. I don't blame her.'

Pamela's thoughts went all the other way. It seemed to her that Christine had got too little, not too much. This power that Christine possessed seemed to Pamela to be like a weapon of limitless force. So armed, the world lay at your feet.

Stephen said, 'I wouldn't follow Christine's example, if I were you.'

'What do you think I should do?'

'Have a little fun. Break a few hearts. Then find yourself a good man to love, and settle down with him.'

'And then what?'

'After marriage? There is no life after marriage. That's the happy ending.'

Pamela thought then of André. Eerily, Stephen read her thoughts.

'I think you made quite a hit with André.'

'But who is André?' said Pamela. 'He hardly said a word.'

'André Tillemans. He inherited a large part of a large fortune. Steel, I believe. His passion is art, eighteenth-century miniatures in particular. He's recently bought a house in Mayfair. He isn't married.'

'I wonder why not.'

'He's never had what you might call a lady friend, as long as I've known him. Plenty of girls have had a shot at him, but no one's got him.'

This had the effect of raising his status even higher in Pamela's eyes.

'By all means enjoy his company,' said Stephen. 'Just don't expect too much.'

'I don't expect anything,' said Pamela.

'He's planning a party for his new house. Would you like to go?'

'What sort of a party?'

'There's only one sort of party, isn't there? Lots of guests. Lots of drink. Beautiful people in beautiful clothes.'

'I'm not sure I have anything to wear.'

'My dear, you could wear a sack and you'd be the most heavenly creature in the room.'

'Oh, Stephen. You are sweet.'

'I shall arrange it. I'll tell André you accept.'

He dropped her off on Hammersmith Road and she walked back up Brook Green to the Caulder house. It was early afternoon on Sunday and all the family were at home. She let herself in with the key she had been given. Hugo came rushing wild-eyed into the hall.

'Where in God's name have you been?'

'At Susie's. I told you.'

'Not all night! You never said all night!'

'We got talking. It was late.'

'And you never thought of phoning? My God, Pamela!'

'I am eighteen, you know.'

Harriet called from the front room.

'Is it Pamela? Is she all right?'

'Yes. She's fine.'

'I don't see why you have to get so worked up,' said Pamela, simulating anger to cover her guilt. 'I don't see why you have to treat me like a child.'

Hugo gave her an agonised look.

'I know you're not a child, Pamela.'

Pamela stared back, and as she looked at his exhausted features she understood. Hugo, her father's business partner, who had known her almost all her life, was staring at her as André had stared at her, with a kind of hunger in his eyes.

She relaxed. There was no need to make excuses, or to apologise. He didn't want courtesy from her. He wanted so much more.

She reached out one hand as she had seen Christine do, and smiled, and lightly stroked his arm. He softened. He smiled back.

'Never mind,' he said. 'Good to have you home.'

19

Junior naval attaché Yevgeny Mikhailovich Ivanov, Captain 2nd Rank, was at his office desk in the Russian embassy by nine o'clock on Monday morning. His first task was to prepare his report on his weekend activities. General Pavlov, the GRU *rezident*, looked in on him as he himself arrived for the day.

'Well, Zhenya? How was the weekend?'

'I am planting seeds, Anatoly Alexandrovich,' said Ivanov. 'I am watering soil.'

'Judging by your requisition slips for vodka,' said Pavlov, 'you must be watering the soil with your piss.'

'That too, General,' said Ivanov.

He and the *rezident* got on famously, which was just as well, since his immediate boss, naval attaché Sukhoruchkin, Captain 1st Rank, was a bumpkin. As Ivanov complained daily to his great friend Tolya Belousov, Sukhoruchkin wouldn't have been allowed through the doors of the London clubs where he, Ivanov, was a familiar figure.

'I've had Moscow Centre on my back again,' said Pavlov. 'They want to know if you've got anywhere with Mountbatten.'

'These things take time, Anatoly Alexandrovich.'

General Pavlov wagged a warning finger at Ivanov, and retired into his own much grander office. Ivanov completed his report, listing the guests at the cottage, and also those at the big house he'd been able to identify round the pool. The Cliveden connection was his great coup, and much was expected of it. Lord Astor's circle included members of the royal family such as Mountbatten, several ministers of the Crown and a wide range of foreign leaders. Ivanov had been present at one gathering that included Ayub Khan of Pakistan, Nubar Gulbenkian and Lord Hailsham. For all this, his social connections had yielded nothing of concrete value to the service so far.

Scratching his head, he pondered whether to bother to list the newcomer to the group, the pretty girl called Pamela. As far as he could tell she was of no interest. But you never could be sure. Some important man might take a fancy to her; in which case it would be useful to have the record show that he, Ivanov, had spotted her first.

Also present at Spring Cottage, Cliveden, he typed, a young woman associate of Stephen Ward, name Pamela. Second name to follow. Young, very attractive. Ward claims he picked her up in a café.

Ivanov had noted André's interest in the new girl, but André had no professional value for him. A wealthy young man with artistic interests, he was just the type of dilettante that did not exist under socialism; as Ivanov told him regularly, over a glass of his excellent claret.

Christine Keeler present, he typed. Confirmed that all is over between her and Profumo, as I reported 11.11.61. She has refused to move out of Ward's flat.

Ivanov did not add that he suspected he himself was the cause of this development. John Profumo didn't like him, and especially didn't like coming across him in Ward's flat. Ivanov was philosophical about this. Profumo was Minister for War; he had political considerations to worry about. They were all playing a game that required them, from time to time, to do disagreeable things. After all, there had been a few heady weeks when Moscow Centre, excited by Ivanov's reports, had planned an operation to entrap Profumo. Ivanov had told them that it was pointless, that such affairs as Profumo's with Christine Keeler were tolerated in the British establishment, and that anyway it had been of very brief duration. Better by far to demonstrate discretion, and so make a lifelong friend. But intelligence services the world over are infatuated with entrapment.

'Remember, Stephen,' Ivanov had said laughingly to Ward, 'it is my duty to my country to entrap you if I can, and it is your duty to try to entrap me.'

'I wouldn't know how to,' said Stephen.

'D-Branch will tell you what to do. You find something out about me that compromises me.'

'What on earth could compromise you, Eugene? Everyone knows you work for the Russians.'

'Ah, perhaps you can discover I am a secret capitalist. Then I will be shot!'

Ivanov understood very well that it was just this combination of intrigue and openness that made him a success in London's clubs and dinner parties. Also, a little to his surprise, they admired his patriotism, and his vigorous and well-informed defence of socialism. That and the fact that he played a good hand of bridge.

His boss Sukhoruchkin came in and slapped some papers on his desk. He mumbled some idiotic suggestion about a trip to Holy Loch in Scotland.

'Grigory Vasilovich,' said Ivanov, 'if you order me to hide in a Scotch bush and count submarines I will of course obey. But that is a job anyone can do. I must ask you to confirm with the *rezident* that he considers it the best use of my time.'

As usual, that was the end of that.

Ivanov had lunch with Tolya Belousov in the Italian bistro by

Notting Hill Gate. Belousov, an easy-going fellow whose only failing was that he had no idea how to dress, was the junior Air Force attaché at the embassy.

'Men like Grigory Vasilovich,' Ivanov said to Tolya over his plate of spaghetti, 'think that only secrets have value. They think that what is learned through deception is worth more than what is openly shared. I'm beginning to think this is non-sense. Why don't we stop trying to trick each other, and try to learn about each other?'

'Ah, Zhenya,' said his friend, 'you say that because you're a warm-hearted fellow and you want to love everyone.'

'No, listen to me. Isn't it true that what we need more than spies and secrets is friends we can trust? Friends who will tell us what the other side is actually thinking?'

'Why should they tell us? Information is power.'

'Accurate information is power. It's more than power, Tolya, it's reality. It's the ground beneath our feet. But you see' – he raised his voice in his eagerness to persuade his friend, confident that as they were speaking Russian they would not be under-stood by the other diners – 'we all share the same need, which is to make decisions based on reality. Not on false information, or fantasy, or paranoia. So why not speak openly?'

This was Ivanov's big idea. He had talked it over with his wife Maya, and she agreed with him, though she had cautioned him to be careful who he discussed it with. Her father, Alex-ander Fedorovich Gorkin, had been secretary of the Presidium, and Maya was no fool.

'Of course you're right, Zhenya,' she said, 'but there are many careers built on the control of information.'

'Information is part of a nation's assets,' said Ivanov. 'Under true socialism it will be shared by all.'

At that Maya rolled her eyes, as she always did when he spoke of true socialism.

'You're not at one of your London dinner parties now,' she said.

And yet, for all the cynicism that came as standard issue in their set, Ivanov did truly believe in socialism. He knew it had not been achieved yet; but he believed it was coming. This was one of the reasons for his success. He did all he did with a whole heart. His childhood hero had been the Baltic seaman Artyom Balashov in the film *We Are From Kronstadt*, who cried so famously and so rousingly, 'Well, who else will rise for the Soviet Union?'

'What we need,' he told Tolya over the spaghetti, 'is bridges. We stand on opposite sides of a great chasm, and we live in fear of each other, because we believe, socialists and capitalists both, that our enemy seeks to destroy us. Do you believe that?'

'Do I believe the Americans seek to destroy us?' said Tolya.

'Yes. Do you genuinely believe that if they could they would destroy the Soviet Union and all its people?'

'Unprovoked?'

'Yes. Unprovoked.'

'No. I don't believe that,' said Tolya.

'There! You're a fine fellow!' Ivanov was pleased. 'And would we destroy the United States if we could, without provocation?'

'No. Of course not.'

'So you see! That is what we must tell each other! That is real information! It's not secret, but nor is it official. Khrushchev can't say to Kennedy, "Don't worry, Jack, we'll never attack you," because it would make the Soviet Union look weak. But you know it's true, and I know it's true. So you see, we need bridges.'

'Well, maybe you're right,' said Belousov, 'but if I were you I'd take care not to do anything without permission. You need cover, just in case it goes wrong.'

'Oh, Tolya! Doesn't it break your heart? None of us can make a move without some kind of official permission. Our system is so constipated we can't even shit without a signed order. In capitalism, initiative is rewarded. We should learn from that.'

'Even so. Talk to Pavlov.'

At the end of the afternoon Ivanov joined in a volleyball game on the court behind 10 Kensington Palace Gardens, an informal game between the *rezidenturas* of the GRU, which was Army Intelligence, and the KGB, the state intelligence apparatus. Ivanov, even now at the age of thirty-seven, was the stand-out player, and the GRU team trounced their opponents 30–5. General Pavlov did not conceal his delight. The KGB had a way of looking down on the GRU, because their budget was so much greater.

'Zhenya,' said Pavlov, coming alongside him in the men's room and undoing his flies, 'let's give our best to the Lubyanka.'

They then pissed together on the KGB.

Pavlov put his arm round Ivanov's shoulders as they walked back together to his office.

'Now we drink a toast.'

There would never be a more suitable opportunity. As they drank together, Ivanov outlined his 'bridge' plan to his *rezident*. Pavlov listened attentively.

'What you're describing,' he said, 'is a back channel. A means of communicating between governments that doesn't commit them, and is subsequently deniable.'

Ivanov knew all about back channels. He had meant something far more significant, amounting to a shift of emphasis away from paranoia towards trust. However, he understood that it would be wise to proceed one step at a time.

'Of course, Anatoly Alexandrovich,' he replied. 'You may describe it as a back channel.'

'What do you have in mind?'

'I would like to establish a bridge of trust,' said Ivanov, 'based on honour and friendship. A chain of trust, perhaps I should say.' The metaphor shifted as he began to construct the reality. 'The first link would be my friend Stephen Ward. I believe that through him I can gain access to the very highest levels of the British government. Through myself, and through yourself, Anatoly Alexandrovich, we would then build a bridge, a chain, from Downing Street to the Kremlin.'

General Pavlov lifted his bushy eyebrows and gazed into the distance. Ivanov could tell that his boss was silently calculating whether or not such a move would be to his advantage.

'Do nothing for now, Zhenya,' he said at last. 'I will make enquiries.'

That night, at home in Bayswater in his modest flat with Maya, Ivanov permitted himself a little self-congratulation.

'Maybe your dolt of a husband, whose father was a peasant from Mytishchi, will turn out to be one of the men who change the world.'

'Just make sure you change it for the better,' Maya replied.

'Trust,' said Ivanov. 'Honour. Friendship. That's how to make a better world.'

20

Rupert Blundell put his proposal to Hugo Caulder over the telephone, only to learn he was a month too late. Pamela was already installed in their spare room. However, barely an hour later Hugo called back, having thought more on the matter.

'This Irish girl,' he said. 'Would she be wanting to go out on the town every night?'

'Not at all,' said Rupert. 'She's much too shy.'

'Not got crowds of smart friends?'

'None whatsoever.'

'Pammy's wonderful, of course. But she's not quite turning out the way we expected. I mean, we love having her and so forth. But we don't actually see all that much of her.'

'Mary needs a home. I think you'll find she'll make herself really useful.'

They met by prior arrangement on the steps of the National Gallery, as if they were running away together. It was Mary who insisted on this conspiratorial manner of leaving the convent.

'They'd never let me go if they knew.'

Even here she glanced round from time to time, afraid she had been followed. She held tight to a small cheap suitcase, and looked mostly at the ground, like a child who believes that if she can't see then she can't be seen. Only when they were in a taxi and heading west, and had left Knightsbridge and Kensington behind them, did she look up and give Rupert a small nervous smile.

'I hope they live a hundred miles away.'

Harriet and Hugo came out onto the steps of the tall house in Brook Green to welcome her. Emily, even shyer than Mary, hid behind her mother. However, the child was already prejudiced in Mary's favour. She had been taken to see *The Sound of Music* at the Palace Theatre not so long ago, and understood perfectly how it could be that Mary had been living in a convent, but was not yet a nun.

'She wants to be a nun, Mummy,' she explained to Harriet, 'but she's always singing when she shouldn't be.'

Mary's drab garments and gentle demeanour pleased Harriet from the start. Here, unlike Pamela, was someone who understood the virtue of quietness.

'Come on in, Mary. Rupert's told us all about you.'

She showed Mary to the room that was to be hers, on the third floor, an attic room with a small dormer window that looked out onto a tree in the street outside.

'It's not very much,' said Harriet apologetically, 'and you'll have to go down two floors to use the bathroom. But we have the daughter of some friends staying at present, and the other room is John's, which we like to keep it as it was.'

The attic room was the largest space Mary had had to herself in all her life.

Left alone, she unpacked her few belongings. She placed her statue of Our Lady of Fatima on the chest of drawers with her rosary at its feet. Then she knelt down and prayed.

'Holy Mother, watch over Mam and Eamonn and Bridie, and keep them safe. Teach me how to serve these good people who have taken me in, a stranger in their home. Show me God's will for me and give me the strength to follow it.'

Rupert Blundell stayed long enough to be sure she was safely settled, and then said he must go. Mary's face filled with alarm.

'Come and see me off, Mary,' he said.

She came with him out into the warm evening street.

'May I give you a word of advice?'

'Of course.'

'Take off the headscarf.'

'Oh.'

She reached up at once and drew it off. Her hair beneath was dark, cut short like a boy's.

'That's a convent haircut, is it?'

'I hate it,' Mary said.

'As a matter of fact,' Rupert said, 'it suits you.'

The short dark hair framed her pale face, changing the look of her. She seemed less fragile.

'And the coat?' he added gently.

She took off the long grey woollen coat to reveal a long brown woollen dress. It was not quite a nun's habit, but in its determination to conceal all and flatter nothing it might as well have been. She saw the look on his face and tugged awkwardly at the sleeves as if to improve its fit.

'Same colour as your eyes,' he said with a smile.

He said this because he felt her embarrassment and wanted her to know it didn't matter. But evidently she wasn't used to such attentions. She blushed deeply.

He looked away.

'I'd better be on my way.'

'You'll come back and see me?' she said.

'Of course I will. But you'll be fine here. They're good people.'

'When will you come?'

'On Sunday,' he said.

He pointed to the church at the bottom of the road.

'That's Holy Trinity. Go to Mass there on Sunday and I'll meet you afterwards.'

'Won't you come to Mass yourself?'

'No, Mary. That's all over for me.'

He shook her small firm hand and strode away towards Hammersmith Road. She watched him out of sight.

Mary understood that her duty now, and her only means of repayment, was to make herself useful to the family who had offered her sanctuary. Lonely and frightened as she was, she set herself to learn as much as possible about her new home. She kept silent at mealtimes, and watched and listened, and so very quickly came to know the cause of the sadness she had sensed in the house from the start. There had been a child who had died.

'John would be old enough to go to school now,' Harriet said. 'I would never have sent him away to school.' Or, when Emily wouldn't eat up her greens, 'Think what a bad example that would be to John.' To Harriet, and to Emily, John was a real and constant presence. Hugo was another matter. When they talked of John, he remained silent.

Mary asked if she might see John's room, and Harriet took her there herself. The room was clean and bright, with wallpaper of pretty white clouds sailing across a blue sky. There was a white painted wooden cot with a little bed made up in it, and a woolly lion lying by the pillow. On a tall chest of drawers there was a nappy-changing mat, with a stack of fleecy folded nappies beside it, and a tub of zinc ointment. The curtains, which hung in generous swags across the window, were printed with circus clowns and seals balancing balls on their noses.

Mary gazed at the room, which looked exactly as if it had been newly furnished a few days ago, and then looked at Harriet. What she saw on her face was not grief at all, but a kind of expectant happiness.

'How old was he when he died?' Mary asked.

'No age at all,' said Harriet. 'He was stillborn.'

'How long ago?'

'Six years,' said Harriet.

But her face told a different story. Something in her had stopped at the time of the fateful birth, and time was suspended. She had gone back to the day before, or perhaps even the hour before. Her baby had not yet been born. She was still waiting.

Harriet for her part found that she was soothed by Mary's undemanding presence. The day following Mary's arrival proved to be one of her 'quiet days', when she took to her bed with a crippling pain in her temples. Mary brought her painkillers and cups of tea, and sat with her and listened to her tell how she was feeling: a story everyone else had tired of long ago.

'I can always feel it coming long before it comes,' Harriet whispered in the darkened room. 'Nobody can know the horror of that feeling. You sense the pain is on its way, and there's nothing you can do to stop it. Sometimes I wish there was a wound, and bleeding, so everyone could see how much it hurts. Hugo is very sweet, but I'm sure he thinks I'm making a lot of fuss over nothing. Thank you, Mary, I'll have that cup of tea now. You see? I can barely lift my arm.'

'Does the pain last very long?' said Mary.

'It comes and goes,' said Harriet. 'It comes in waves. It gets worse and worse until you think you can't take any more, then it starts to fade. Then you have a little time of peace. Then it comes back.'

Mary was shocked.

'And do these waves go on all day?'

'Not all the day,' said Harriet, gratified. 'Perhaps half the day, or three-quarters. And then after the pain is gone, I have this overwhelming weakness. I can't get out of bed. I can hardly speak. I can't bear loud noises or bright lights. Really I am a quite useless person.'

'You're called to suffer,' said Mary.

'I suppose it's just my bad luck,' said Harriet.

'Oh, no,' said Mary. 'These are the trials the good Lord sends us.'

Harriet had only the most conventional religious faith herself, but she liked Mary's version of her condition. She was being tested. There was courage in her suffering.

'I like her very much,' she told Hugo. 'I'm so glad she's come to live with us.'

Pamela was out of the house, and did not return until after Mary had gone to bed in her attic room. Her initial reaction to the newcomer was suspicion.

'Does Rupert know anything at all about her? What does he think she's supposed to be doing here?'

'She can help out with Emily,' said Hugo.

'I thought I was supposed to be doing that.'

'Yes, but you have so many other things you have to do. And anyway, it's an act of charity, taking her in. And you never know, you may get an art course sorted out and we'll be glad to have her.'

'So you don't want me to go?'

'Of course not. You're like family.'

This was all the reassurance Pamela needed.

'You're so sweet to me, Hugo.'

It soon became apparent that Mary would undertake all the chores that it had been supposed Pamela would do; and better still, would do them willingly. This gave Pamela increased freedom to come and go as she pleased. She withdrew her hostility to Mary and even became, in idle moments, a little curious about her. Like Rupert, she suspected that behind Mary's homeless condition there was trouble with some man.

'Were you ever married, Mary?' she asked her.

'Oh, no,' said Mary, blushing.

'Rupert said you were living in a convent, but that you're not actually a nun.'

'I was living in a convent, yes,' said Mary.

'So you must be very religious.'

'We're all religious in Ireland,' said Mary.

'Where do you come from in Ireland, Mary?'

'From a little village nobody ever heard of,' she replied.

Pamela concluded that Mary was concealing some mystery. When Rupert came round she was open about it.

'I know there's a secret there. What's she doing alone in London? Why did she want to leave her convent?'

'You'll have to ask her.'

'Don't you want to know?'

'Yes. But she doesn't want to tell.'

'Do you think she's pretty?'

'Yes, I think I do. Don't you?'

'I think she could be pretty,' said Pamela, exercising a judicious and semi-professional judgement. 'But I think she doesn't want to be. She looks so washed out. A little make-up would do wonders for her. And that dress!'

'I think she's happy to stay as she is.'

'Don't you believe it,' said Pamela. 'She wants a man, like everyone else.'

'Some people are happy to be alone,' said Rupert.

At this point Hugo came in.

'Rupert's telling me there are people who want to be alone,' Pamela said to him. 'But it's all nonsense, isn't it?'

'That's Rupert's philosophy of life,' said Hugo. 'He's told me before. We're all alone, whether we know it or not.'

'What, always?' said Pamela.

'Deep down,' said Rupert.

'What about love? When you fall in love you're not alone any more.'

'Have you ever fallen in love?'

'No.' Pamela blushed a little. 'But I can imagine what it must be like.'

'I'm afraid I'm the wrong person to ask about falling in love,' said Rupert. 'My own view is that the very act of falling in love blinds you to the reality of the one you love. So yes, you're still alone.'

'I don't believe it,' said Pamela.

'Come on, Rupert,' said Hugo. 'Just because it's never happened to you.'

'I didn't say it had never happened to me,' said Rupert.

'Oh, well,' exclaimed Pamela. 'So you've fallen in love and it hasn't worked out. That's just sour grapes.'

'Maybe it is,' said Rupert.

He was untroubled by her disapproval. This provoked her.

'You're not that old,' she said. 'You should make more effort.'

'I'm forty-four,' he said. 'I'm not love's young dream. I'm not rich. I think it's quite wise of me to make the most of my quiet bachelor life, don't you?'

'Actually,' said Hugo, 'Rupert moves in far higher circles than the rest of us. You know he works for Mountbatten?'

'Mountbatten?' said Pamela, greatly surprised. 'Do you actually know him?'

'Very well,' said Rupert. 'I see him every day.'

'Golly!'

Mary said little and saw much. She saw how Rupert, unlike Hugo, was immune to Pamela's charms. It wasn't that he was unaware of how attractive she was, more that it never occurred to him that her charm was anything to do with him. Blinking through his spectacles, smiling when she smiled, but still speaking his own awkward truth, he enjoyed her radiance without seeking to possess it; as one might turn one's face to the sun. Mary recognised in him the virtue of humility, and she too respected him the more for it.

Hugo was another matter. Hugo looked at Pamela as if it hurt him to look but he couldn't stop himself. Pamela sometimes touched him, carelessly and in passing, and when she did so he went still all over. He was plainly troubled by her unexplained comings and goings, but lacked the authority to control her.

'Who are these new friends you go off to meet?' Hugo asked her one day at dinner. 'I feel we should know more about them.'

'Just friends,' said Pamela.

'Yes, but what sort of people? Would your parents approve?'

'I've no idea,' said Pamela. 'They're very well connected, if that's what you mean.'

'Well connected?'

'They're just people,' said Pamela irritably. 'I don't see that it's anyone's business but mine.'

'You live here,' said Hugo. A plaintive note had crept into his voice. 'I should have thought I have a right to know something about the people you're meeting.'

'There's Stephen, who does portraits, and has done Princess Margaret. And Eugene, who's a diplomat. And André, who's an art collector. There. Now you know.'

Mary could never have spoken to anyone the way Pamela did, but she didn't judge her for that. She didn't have a high enough opinion of herself to judge anyone. She just watched and wondered what it was that Pamela wanted, never doubting that whatever it was she possessed the power to get it.

Mary had arrived in Brook Green at the start of the last week of the school summer term. For those few days she took Emily to school in the morning, and was waiting outside the school gates to walk home with her at the end of the day. She also sat with her over her homework, and watched with her the allocation of television viewing she was permitted. Mary had seen almost no television in her life, and was repeatedly astonished by the happenings on screen.

'Oh, no!' she cried, covering her face with her hands. 'The poor child!'

This while watching *Emergency Ward 10*. Emily was entirely won over by Mary's terrors before the television.

'Look, Mary, that's her mother. She doesn't know her child's been in the accident. She's got a nasty shock coming.'

'Please! I can't look!'

So the first week went by, and Mary was accepted into the family, and the mystery surrounding her arrival receded into the past.

21

Rupert was crossing the park as he did at the end of each day when he saw the two nuns again. He knew from far off that they were waiting for him. As he approached he felt their eyes on him. One was tall and stern, with thick eyebrows. The other was smaller and more timid.

He stopped before them.

'Can I help you?'

'I hope so,' said the stern one. 'We're concerned about Sister Mary.'

'Sister Mary?'

'Your cousin,' said the other nun.

Rupert felt himself go red.

'Whether or not she is your cousin is beside the point,' said the first nun. 'Eight days ago she disappeared, leaving no word of where she had gone and when she would return.'

'She's safe,' said Rupert. 'She's well.'

'So she's with you.'

The stern nun's voice vibrated with angry suspicion.

'No, not with me,' said Rupert. 'She's staying with a family I know.'

'Why has she not informed us of this?'

'I think she's afraid.'

'Afraid of those who love and protect her? Afraid of her own family in God?'

'Sir,' said the smaller shyer nun, 'we've been so worried about her. She shouldn't be out in the big city alone.'

'I'm sorry she didn't leave any forwarding information,' said Rupert. 'But I do assure you, she left of her own free will.'

'Without a word,' said the stern nun, her voice trembling. Rupert realised she was more hurt than angry.

'Will you be seeing her, sir?' said the smaller nun.

'Yes,' said Rupert. 'I'll be seeing her after Mass on Sunday.'

'Oh,' said the tall nun bitterly. 'So she still goes to Mass.'

'Please tell her you saw us, sir. I'm Sister Cecily. Please tell Mary we love her and miss her.'

'And tell her—'

'No, Mother. That's all she needs to know.'

The tall nun bowed her head in silence.

'I'll tell her,' said Rupert.

When Sunday came, Rupert was waiting outside Holy Trinity Church as Mass ended. Mary came out, wearing her headscarf, looking round to see if he was there. When she saw him, her face lit up.

'I wasn't sure you'd come!'

She took off her headscarf and shook her short hair.

'How are you today?' he said. 'Sister Mary.'

'Why do call me that?'

'Because that's what Sister Cecily called you. And the other one, the one with the eyebrows.'

'Oh, Jesus,' she said softly.

Instead of returning directly up Brook Green to the house, they walked down one of the adjoining residential streets.

'I was going home across the park on Friday,' he told her, 'and they were waiting for me.'

'I knew it.'

Her face had gone white.

'Don't worry. I didn't tell them where you are.'

'They'll find me out in the end.'

'Sister Cecily asked me to tell you that they love you and miss you.'

'Oh, Blessed Jesus!'

She was becoming more and more distressed.

'Mary, it's none of my business. But if you were in a convent, and then you decided to leave, that's your right.'

'You don't know how it is.'

'I know you're frightened. What is it you're afraid of?'

'They'll make me go back,' she said very low.

'How can they make you go back? Do they use force on you?'

'They've no need of force,' said Mary. 'They've ways and means.'

'But you don't want to go back?'

She shook her head vigorously.

'This last week I feel like I've been free for the first time in my life.'

They walked on past the quiet windows of the terraced houses, shuttered in Sunday calm.

'How long have you lived in the convent?'

'That one and others, fifteen years.'

'Fifteen years!'

'Since I was fourteen years old.'

'But surely,' said Rupert, 'that's too young.'

'I was only there for my own good. For my protection.'

'Protection from what?'

'It doesn't matter,' she said. 'They meant well. Everybody meant well.'

'I don't understand,' said Rupert. 'Have you been kept as some kind of prisoner?'

'No,' she said. 'Whatever I've done, I've done of my own free will. There's no one to blame but myself.'

She came to a stop and covered her face with her hands.

'I thought I could get away,' she said. 'But there's nowhere. Even you, you've been so kind to me. But you're doing it too.'

'Doing what?' he said.

'Making me tell.'

Rupert was silent, mortified. But if he didn't know what it was she feared, how could he help her?

They started to walk again.

'I'm such a little fool,' she said, seemingly speaking to herself. 'There's no running away. They always find you in the end.'

'The nuns?'

'All of them.'

Rupert thought about that. He didn't know what it was she was running away from, but he did know that running away wasn't the answer.

'If they're going to find you in the end,' he said, 'they might as well find you now.'

She stared at him.

'What you mean?'

'Go back to the convent. Tell them you want to live your own life.'

'My own life?'

'If that's what you want.'

'They'll make me stay. You don't know them.'

'They can't make you stay if you don't want to.'

'That's what you don't know,' she said. 'You think it's all simple. You want this, you don't want that. But it's not simple at all. That's how they get you.'

'They make you want to stay?'

'They do.'

By now they'd walked all the way down the road to the back

of the great exhibition hall at Olympia. They turned about and retraced their steps. Rupert glanced at her from time to time as they went, as if to reassure himself that she was not in too much distress. It angered him that she should be so bullied by the nuns.

'They should accept that you're never coming back.'

'They will never accept that.'

'They would if I told them so.'

'You?'

'I could come with you to talk to them. I'm not afraid of them.'

'Would you do that?'

'Yes. I would.'

She was silent for a few moments. Then she looked up at him and he was ready, waiting for her look. She saw in his face that he meant what he said.

'Would you promise not to let them take me away?'

'Yes. I would.'

'When would we go?'

'We could go now.'

'Now!'

Her eyes widened with fear.

'Then it'll be over,' he said.

The convent was a Victorian red-brick building, its windows and doors topped with pointed arches. The windows were frosted glass, giving the building a blind air. There was no name on the black-painted door, but there was a bell-push.

Mary had her headscarf tightly tied, and her hands clasped. She was trembling. Rupert pressed the bell.

The door was opened by an elderly nun in a grey habit.

'Mary!' she said. Then seeing Rupert beside her she became confused, and stepped back.

'May I come in?' said Rupert.

The elderly nun seemed too awed to answer.

'There is a visiting room,' said Mary.

They were in a dark hallway, with plain wooden stairs rising ahead. There was a faint smell of disinfectant.

'Yes, the visiting room,' said the elderly nun. 'I'll fetch Mother Martina.'

The visiting room was square and empty but for a number of upright chairs placed round its walls. There was an empty fireplace, and a window, its frosted glass throwing bright grey light across the polished wood floor. On the facing wall hung a large crucifix.

'I'm not surprised you wanted to get away,' said Rupert.

'The chapel's pretty,' murmured Mary.

Mother Martina swept into the room. It was the tall nun Rupert had met in the park. Here on her own ground she seemed even taller and more formidable.

'Sister Mary!' she exclaimed, rapidly crossing herself. 'God be praised.'

'Mother.'

Mary gave a little bobbing curtsy.

'I'm obliged to you, sir,' the nun said to Rupert.

'She wanted to explain her decision herself,' Rupert said.

'Please sit down.'

Mother Martina indicated the chairs round the walls. Rupert and Mary sat down side by side. Mother Martina drew a chair into the middle of the room where she could sit facing them.

'What is this decision, Mary?' she said.

Mary looked down at her hands. She spoke in a whisper.

'I want to leave, Mother.'

'You want to leave what, Mary? Our house? Your faith? Your God?'

'I don't want to live here, Mother.'

'You are free to come and go as you wish, Mary. You know that.'

'Yes, Mother.'

'Have we ever asked you to do anything against your will?'

'No, Mother.'

'And was it not you who came to me, begging to be allowed to enter our house, and live with us?'

'Yes, Mother.'

'And now you tell me you want to leave. Why is that, Mary?'

'I want,' whispered Mary, faltering, 'I want a life of my own.'

'A life of your own? Do you mean to live by yourself on a desert island? Or in a wild forest? Or on a mountain-top?'

'No, Mother.'

'You mean to live among people, then, Mary?'

'Yes, Mother.'

'And who are these people?'

'I don't know, Mother.'

'You mean to live among strangers rather than with your own sisters, here in the family God has given you?'

Mary was silent.

'It seems to me you don't clearly know what it is you want, Mary. Have you thought to ask yourself what God wants? Have you prayed about this?'

'Yes, Mother.'

'If you've turned to God with a truly humble heart, he will have heard you. He will be guiding you now. Do you think God is asking you to go out into the big city, among strangers, where they know nothing of the gifts God has given you, where you can be of no use other than to feed their own evil purposes, where you will be flattered and deceived and used and discarded? Do you think that is what God wants for you, his chosen beloved child?'

Rupert could endure no more.

'Forgive me, Mother. This is nonsense.'

'Oh?' The nun raised her eyes to Rupert with the look of one who is accustomed to being obeyed. 'What business is this of yours?'

'Mary has asked for my help. That makes it my business.'

'Mary,' said Mother Martina, rising. 'Come with me. I need to speak with you alone.'

Mary rose at once. Rupert caught her by one hand.

'No,' he said. 'Whatever you have to say to her can be said in front of me.'

'I think not, sir,' said the nun. 'I need to speak to Mary on a private matter.'

'You mean to warn her against me,' said Rupert. 'You mean to tell her I'm not to be trusted. That men can't be trusted with vulnerable young women. That my intention can only be to seduce her and then abandon her. Because why else would I take the time and trouble to befriend her?'

'I would not be doing my duty if I didn't warn her,' said Mother Martina with dignity. 'I stand in the place of her own mother.'

'Now I've warned her myself,' said Rupert. 'You can sit down again.'

Mother Martina sat down again, gathering her long skirts about her.

'Just because he speaks openly about such matters, Mary,' she said, 'does not mean he can be trusted.'

'Are all men not to be trusted, Mother?' said Mary.

'No, not all. There are good men in the world. But I think the good men do not make a habit of picking up young women in parks. I believe this gentleman, if gentleman he is, had seen you before, and was looking out for you.'

'Were you?' said Mary to Rupert.

'It's true that I'd seen you before in the park,' said Rupert. 'I remembered you. Yes, I was looking out for you.'

'There, now,' said Mother Martina grimly. 'We come to the truth at last.'

'You were looking out for me?' said Mary.

'And what was it that so piqued your interest?' said Mother Martina. 'Why, I wonder, would a middle-aged man stare at a pretty young girl?'

'She looked unhappy,' said Rupert. 'That's what I remembered. She looked lost, and unhappy.'

'So I was,' said Mary.

'I've felt those feelings myself,' said Rupert. 'I think that's what made me want to help her.'

The nun frowned at this.

'I'm sorry to hear you were lost and unhappy, my dear,' she said. 'I wish you had told me.'

'I couldn't tell you,' said Mary. 'It seemed so ungrateful.'

'You were so unhappy with us, you preferred to trust yourself to strangers?'

'To this stranger, Mother.'

The nun turned accusing eyes on Rupert.

'If you have harmed this child,' she said, 'in thought, word or deed, may Almighty God strike you dead. May you suffer the torments of Hell for all eternity.'

'Mother!'

'If this man is pure in heart he has no need to fear God's judgement.'

'Do you not fear God's judgement, Mother?' said Rupert.

'What has that to do with the matter?'

'We all come short of the glory of God.'

Mother Martina turned to meet Mary's eyes, her eyebrows raised.

'He was brought up in the faith,' said Mary.

'He's a Catholic!'

Rupert bowed his head, accepting the charge.

'I was educated by the Benedictines, at Downside Abbey.'

'Well, now. Why didn't you say so in the first place? Not that there aren't plenty of rotten apples in our own orchard.'

'You seem to me to have a remarkably bleak view of humanity, Mother,' said Rupert. 'There is virtue beyond the convent walls.'

Mother Martina allowed herself to look at Rupert properly for the first time.

'If I seem overprotective,' she said, 'it's because this child is precious to me, and to God. She has a special destiny, and I have been charged with the duty of keeping her safe to carry it out.'

'This special destiny is God's work?'

'It most certainly is.'

'And you don't trust God to protect her in his own work?'

The nun stared back at Rupert in silence.

'She's not a child any more,' said Rupert. 'She has her own life to live. And if God has plans for her, that's between her and God.'

'Do you rebuke me, sir?'

'I do,' said Rupert. 'I think you care less for her than for your own power and glory.'

A slow flush crept up Mother Martina's sallow cheeks.

'No one has ever spoken to me like that in all my life.'

'I don't know the truth in your heart, Mother,' said Rupert. 'But you do. This young woman has told you she does not want to live here any more. Why do you keep her?'

'I keep no one! Every soul in my charge is free!'

'Then you'll let her go, with your blessing.'

Deeply hurt, Mother Martina turned to Mary.

'I don't know how we've failed you, Mary,' she said. 'I wish you had told me sooner. Is it really true you want to leave us?'

'Yes, Mother.'

'And do you want my blessing?'

'Yes, Mother.'

'Then you have it. Our door is always open to you. May God watch over you. We will pray for you.'

With that she rose and left the room. Mary stayed on her chair, head bowed, trembling.

'There,' said Rupert. 'It's over.'

Outside, the sun was shining. They walked up the road and into the park. There, as if safe at last, Mary lifted her arms and whirled round and round. Rupert smiled to see her so happy. Then they set off together, sauntering across the park.

'You were amazing, you know?' Mary said.

'Mother Martina's right to warn you. I could be planning to seduce you and abandon you.'

'I don't think so,' she said.

'Why not?'

'You don't strike me as the seducing type.'

'From your vast experience of men.'

'No, Rupert, don't mock me.' Her sweet face laughed at him. 'I admit I know nothing at all, but I'm not a fool.'

'Not at all. You have a special destiny.'

'Oh, phooey,' she said.

'Phooey?'

'I don't want to hear any more about that.'

'Just tell me one thing. Are you a nun or aren't you?'

'I never took vows. I lived with the nuns as what they call a postulant.'

'For fifteen years?'

'Don't ask me any more, Rupert. Please.'

She slipped her arm through his and leaned a little against him as they walked.

'What you've done today,' she said, 'I'll never be able to

repay you. But if there's ever anything you want, you only have to ask.'

'I don't want anything from you, Mary.'

'I've never known a man like you.'

'I don't think you've known many men at all.'

'A person, then. All the others want something from me. They don't see me at all. They see something they think I've got, that they need. But you're different.'

He supposed she meant that men wanted her in the way that men want women. He wondered whether he was different from the rest after all.

Back in his own flat in Pimlico, Rupert settled down to work on the paper he was preparing for Mountbatten on his 'Aim for the West'. He found himself unable to concentrate. Instead, he kept recalling Mary's face, and the direct gaze of her eyes. He wondered about the unexplained facts of her life in the convent, and her mysterious special destiny. There was so much about her he didn't know.

Other people are unknowable. Why then this urge to learn secrets, to dig deeper? There's no end to the mystery of the human soul.

Into his mind jumped one of the philosophical topics proposed by the appropriately named John Wisdom, his teacher at Cambridge.

Other minds are, and are not, like a fire on the horizon.

John Wisdom, keeper of the flame of his master Ludwig Wittgenstein, loved to provoke his students with ambiguous images. This one had stayed with Rupert, perhaps because it held out the promise of shared warmth.

A fire on the horizon. The remote possibility of love.

He could see Mary's sweet unadorned face looking up at him, her brow wrinkling, trying to make him out, just as he was trying to make her out. He saw in her face, as he had seen the first time, as he had seen again when she sat trembling in the convent's visiting room, a look that contained all the sorrows of the world. Such a look should make the observer turn away, fearful of contamination, but he had not wanted to turn away. Her look had spoken to him saying: I know sorrow, but I also know love, and love is greater.

He laughed softly at that, alone in his room. He mocked his own pompous thought, capitalising the nouns. Sorrow and Love, and the greatest of these is Love. Oh yes? What was this capitalised Love that was supposed to trump the misery of existence? It sounded dubiously close to the Love of God, that God with whom he had parted company years ago. No God means no Love. All that is left is little love, without the capital letter. Something personal and short lived, based on need and illusion.

Even so, he thought, I look forward to seeing her next Sunday. The days will pass quickly. How different the world looks when you have hope in your heart.

PART THREE

Mutually Assured Destruction

July – September 1962

22

Operation Anadyr, named after a river in Siberia, was launched with the utmost secrecy. In order to disguise its true purpose, the soldiers and engineers allocated to the troopships were issued fur hats, fleece-lined parkas, felt boots and skis. The rocket teams were given to understand that their destination was Novaya Zemlya, in the Arctic. The dockworkers who loaded the ships worked in fenced compounds guarded by the KGB. The ships' captains were instructed to open their sealed orders revealing their route only once they were well out to sea.

The first ship in the armada, the *Maria Ulyanova*, sailed out of a Soviet port on July 5 1962. Eighty-five merchant ships followed, carrying everything needed for a nuclear army. The big weapons were the twenty-four R-12 missiles, and the sixteen R-14s, each designed to carry a one-megaton nuclear warhead. In support, the Army sent two tank battalions equipped with the new T-55s, a MiG-21 fighter wing, forty-two Il-28 light bombers, four motorised regiments, two cruise missile regiments and twelve SA-2 surface-to-air missile units. The Navy sent two cruisers, four destroyers and twelve Komar ships. Future plans called for a submarine base to be built on Cuba that would house a squadron of eleven submarines. To service this massive deployment the Soviet merchant ships also transported three 200-bed hospitals, seven food warehouses, a bakery, twenty prefab barracks, ten prefab houses, ten cranes, twenty bulldozers and two thousand tons of cement. In all, Operation Anadyr carried over forty thousand Soviet personnel across the ocean.

To avoid surveillance from the air the troops remained mostly below deck. Soldiers sailing on the *Khabarovsk*, caught by a NATO plane, improvised a spontaneous party on deck, dancing with the female nurses, to dispel any hint of military purpose. On arrival in Cuba they were issued with plaid shirts and ordered to blend in with the local population.

To Khrushchev's great relief, virtually the entire *maskirovka* fleet reached Cuba undetected. To protect his bold plan he instructed Anatoly Dobrynin, his ambassador in Washington, to repeat his assurances to the American president that he would never deploy offensive weapons on Cuba. This deception was vital to the success of Operation Anadyr. The cause was great. What did he value more highly, his own personal honour or the survival of socialism?

'Diplomacy is a game,' he told his friend and adviser Oleg Troyanovsky. 'No one takes the words of a diplomat literally. We look for the truth between the words.'

'Might that not also be true for Kennedy?' said Troyanovsky.

'Of course,' said Khrushchev, troubled.

After some thought, he determined to send a second message through a very different channel. His son-in-law Alexei Adzhubei had a friend called Georgi Bolshakov, who was a junior cultural attaché in the Soviet embassy in Washington. Bolshakov had an American friend, a journalist called Frank Holeman. Holeman in turn was friendly with Ed Guthman, Robert Kennedy's press secretary. Through this chain of contacts Bolshakov had achieved several face-to-face meetings with the president's brother. Both Kennedy and Khrushchev trusted information passed down this back channel precisely because it was unofficial, and permitted questions to be asked and positions to be presented that could never be admitted in public.

Georgi Bolshakov was an officer in the GRU, the intelligence section of the Red Army. He was considered to be 100 per cent loyal to the Party. Even so, he was not entrusted with the secret of Operation Anadyr. He was told to repeat the assurance that the only weapons the Soviets would ever send to Cuba were for defensive purposes.

'He will convey our message more convincingly if he believes it,' said Khrushchev. He then told Troyanovsky his favourite anecdote about the two old Jews on a train.

'The first old Jew says to the second, "So where are you going?" The second Jew answers, "I'm going to Zhitomir." The first Jew nods and smiles and thinks to himself, "That sly old fox doesn't fool me. He tells me he's going to Zhitomir so I'll think he's going to Zhmerinka. So now I know he's really going to Zhitomir."'

Now that the armada had sailed, Khrushchev turned his attention to the next stage in the deception. The unloading and deploying of the nuclear missiles within Cuba had to be achieved in as complete secrecy as the loading. All local people within two kilometres of the new bases were forced to leave their homes and crops. Only Russians were permitted inside the bases. The new concrete launch pads began to be built behind high fences, screened by palm trees.

One window remained open wide. Neither the Cubans nor the Russians could fence in the sky.

Marshall Malinowsky warned Khrushchev that sooner or later the missiles would be detected by the high-flying US reconnaissance planes. The U2s flew at seventy thousand feet, out of range of Cuban anti-aircraft batteries. The Soviet SA-2s could bring down a U2, and had already done so, over Soviet airspace in 1960. Khrushchev therefore ordered that the SA-2 units be deployed first, before the huge R-12s and R-14s became operational. At the same time he began to put pressure on the Americans to cease their surveillance flights. He spoke out publicly against the U2s that flew over international waters, and most of all over the island of Cuba, calling them harassment and warmongering.

Troyanovsky, who thought privately that the missile deployment was bound to be discovered, nevertheless did what he could to minimise the risks.

'The Americans don't respond well to name-calling,' he said. 'What they understand is making deals.'

'What do you mean, deals?'

'If you want something from them, offer them something they want in exchange.'

'What do they want?'

'Ask them.'

Khrushchev reflected on this advice. Then he sent a message, through Bolshakov, that in order to get the U2s grounded he was willing to trade.

The record player in the little gym by the White House pool was pumping out Hank Williams. Jack Kennedy, groaning in time to the music, was going through his round of stretch exercises to ease the pain in his back. Mac Bundy sat on the edge of the massage couch, watching him through his clear-plastic-frame glasses.

'This damn bomb,' said Kennedy between pulls. 'Can't stop thinking about it.'

'Hell of a thing,' said Bundy.

'Your dad knew Henry Stimson pretty well, right?'

Mac Bundy nodded. He had known Truman's Secretary for War pretty well himself. As a young man he had ghost-written

Stimson's memoirs. He had more or less authored Stimson's famous *Harper's* article in 1947 that proved once and for all the president had had no choice but to drop the bomb.

'Was it Truman's decision in the end?' said Kennedy. 'Or was it the military?'

'The chiefs were all against it,' said Bundy. 'Eisenhower, MacArthur, all of them. It was Truman's decision, all right.'

'And Stimson's.'

'You want to know something, Mr President. Henry never forgave himself for that. By September of '45 he knew he'd started an arms race we'd never be able to stop.'

'We sure as hell got that.'

Kennedy climbed to his feet and mopped the sweat off his face with a towel. Hank Williams started singing 'I'm So Lonesome I Could Cry'.

'Turn it off, will you?'

Bundy shut down the music.

'You know, Mac, the chiefs tell me, "You just give the order, Mr President, and we'll deal with the rest." Like I'm not to worry my silly little head with the details. Like it's just another war.'

'Lauris Norstad says it's only a matter of time,' said Bundy.

'They scare me,' said Kennedy. 'They royally screwed me over the Bay of Pigs. They knew that dumb operation was going to fail. They just assumed I'd never be able to take the humiliation, and I'd send in the Marines. So I end up with the fucking humiliation.'

He stripped off and ran a shower. Taking showers helped with the back pain too. Sometimes he had five showers a day.

Out of the shower, towelling, dressing, he reverted to his fascination with the momentous decision made at Potsdam.

'Sometimes I wonder how it would be if we hadn't dropped the bomb.'

'It'd still exist,' said Bundy. 'The Russians would have built their bomb.'

'Yeah, I know. There's no going back. But seeing what that first bomb did to Hiroshima – you can't really believe it till you see it. That's what changes history.'

They walked back to the Oval Office together.

'You know Henry Stimson's whole idea about the atom bomb,' said Bundy. 'His idea was that it was so terrible it would make war impossible. It was the ultimate peace weapon.'

'And here we are, relying on it for our first line of defence. Hell, what do we do if they roll their tanks into West Berlin?'

Both men knew the Soviets had eighty divisions at the gates of Berlin. Only nuclear missiles could defend that embattled island of freedom.

'You think I want to go down in history as the president who started a nuclear war?'

In the Oval Office they found Bobby Kennedy pacing up and down, looking agitated.

'I've just had a visit from Bolshakov,' he said. 'You know how Khrushchev's been getting all worked up over violations of Cuban air space? Looks like he wants to do a deal.'

'Jesus! Fucking Cuba!' exclaimed the president. 'Why does everyone go on about Cuba?'

'Cuba's Khrushchev's Berlin,' said Bundy.

'So what's this deal, Bobby?'

'According to Bolshakov,' said Bobby Kennedy, 'he wants to know our price for grounding the U2s.'

'Do we believe this?'

'We believe he wants something. And when a guy wants something, there's usually business to be done.'

Kennedy was under pressure on multiple fronts. His prime objective at this point was to make it to the mid-term elections without any nasty surprises.

'What's bugging him about Cuba?' he said to Bobby.

'He's stuffing Cuba with guns.'

'And we let him do that?'

'You want another Bay of Pigs?'

'I've got that prick Keating on my back day and night, acting like if I don't force regime change in Cuba I'm exposing the country to – to what? Is Castro supposed to scare us?'

'I say forget Cuba,' said Bobby. 'Cuba's a pimple on our backside. But if we can use it as a bargaining chip, hey, why not?'

'To get what?'

Bobby shrugged.

'Berlin. We tell him, you leave Berlin alone, we'll leave Cuba alone. At least until after the mid-terms.'

The president nodded. He turned to Bundy.

'How does that look to you, Mac?'

'Looks pretty good, Mr President,' said Bundy. 'If we think we can trust him.'

'I don't trust him to keep his word. But I do trust him to do what's in his interests. Ask yourself what it is Khrushchev wants. He wants to look good on the world stage. He wants his people to see him as a successful leader. Kind of like I do.'

The others laughed.

'Except he doesn't have to win a popularity contest every two years.'

'So what do I tell Bolshakov?' said Bobby.

'Try your trade on him. Tell him if Khrushchev guarantees to lay off Berlin until after the elections, I'll ground the U2s.'

The message passed back to Khrushchev through the Bolshakov channel was that Kennedy wanted Berlin put 'on ice'. Khrushchev hadn't met this expression before. When Troyanovsky explained it to him, he liked it a lot.

'Let's put their balls on ice,' he said.

The Presidium authorised Bolshakov to tell President Kennedy that his offer was acceptable. Kennedy ordered the U2s to be grounded.

The window in the sky was closed.

23

The taxi pulled up outside a house in Mayfair. There was nothing to distinguish the address: the same blank house front, the same three steps rising to a front door. The tall windows either side of the front door were shuttered on the inside.

André took out a ring of keys and unlocked the door. He stood there in his perfectly tailored dove-grey suit, his silky hair brushed back on his head, his handsome high-cheeked profile towards her, and smiled as if he was about to reveal a mystery.

'This is where it's all going to happen.'

He opened the door and ushered Pamela in ahead of him. A wide empty hall faced her, from which rose a handsome staircase. The house seemed much bigger inside than outside. Doors to left and right stood open.

'Go ahead. Look round.'

The rooms were immense, and entirely empty. She stood gazing at the expanse of polished boards, the high plastered walls rising to ornate cornices.

'There's nothing here.'

'Almost nothing.' He was watching her closely, expectantly, seeing if she could guess. 'Space,' he said. 'The house is full of space.'

She moved from empty room to empty room, and there was nothing, not a chair, not a rug, not a lamp. And yet for all its emptiness the house didn't feel abandoned. The paintwork on the walls was pristine. The brass door-plates and door handles gleamed. The floors had been polished to a golden glow.

'Is this how it was when you bought it?' she asked.

'Lord, no!' he exclaimed. 'It's taken a lot of work and a lot of money to make this emptiness. The rooms were full of junk. Most of the plasterwork has had to be stripped and replaced. There were internal walls in this room. There was a narrow passage right where you're standing. They had four rooms in here. It was used as offices for an insurance company.'

She looked round in wonder.

'You've made it so beautiful. It's not like a house at all. It's like a different world.'

'All parties should happen in a different world.'

'Yes, of course. The party.'

He led her back into the hall.

'Go on up the stairs,' he said.

She climbed the stairs. At the top there was a wide landing, with closed double doors facing her.

'Open the doors.'

She opened the doors, and found herself standing on a platform or stage. Wide steps descended a short distance from this stage to a great room, a ballroom, lit by tall windows on either side. Like the rooms below, this too was empty.

'I bought the house for this room,' André said.

It was the width of the entire house, and deeper than it was wide. Supporting columns ran down either side, between the windows. The ceiling was arched, with a long glazed lantern down the centre through which sunlight was streaming.

How rich do you have to be, thought Pamela, to buy a house so you can hold a party?

'This is where my guests will make their entrée,' he said, sweeping one arm from the double doors over the raised plat-form.

'Make their entrée?'

'For a party like this, people go to a lot of trouble over their appearance. They deserve their moment.'

'Like coming on stage.'

'Everyone a star.'

Pamela stood just inside the entrance doors and imagined the moment.

'How will you decorate the room?'

'With beautiful people,' he said, smiling.

She turned to him, about to ask a question, and then looked away again.

'What is it?'

'I suppose your party will be very smart,' she said.

'My guests are a very mixed crowd,' he said. 'I hope my party will be beautiful, and surprising, and joyful.'

She said nothing.

'I think you're concerned about what to wear.'

'How did you know?' she said, amazed.

'I could tell you that whatever you wear you will be the most beautiful of all. But instead I will make myself useful. Will you allow me the pleasure of buying a dress for you?'

Even as he spoke in this quaintly formal way, his gaze was moving over her like a caress. He combined perfect manners with something quite different: the wordless impression that he was used to getting what he wanted. Because he never raised his voice, and because his face habitually wore an expression of sadness, as if he lived with the memory of some great loss, she had at first taken him to be weak-willed. Then she had come to realise that he was simply lazy, with the golden laziness of the privileged. Great wealth and natural beauty had made exertion unnecessary.

207

'Please let me. You know I can afford it.'

'Have you always been rich?'

'Yes, always.' Then as they descended the stairs, 'Never be born rich. Desire puts down roots in stony soil.'

Did that mean he desired her, or that he wanted to desire her and couldn't? As yet she had no idea how to respond to him. She didn't believe herself to be in love with him. All she knew was that everything in her life was transformed by his attentions, and she didn't want them to stop.

She was also a little frightened. She was afraid he would discover her ignorance, and so spoke very little. She was afraid he would grow bored with her, and so cultivated an air of being bored with him.

'Don't you find shopping rather tiresome?' she said.

'Shopping for oneself is a melancholy business, like eating alone. But shopping for someone else is joyful.'

It was the second time he'd used this word. Joyful.

The following day they met by arrangement at the showroom of a designer Pamela had never heard of. It was in a smartly converted stable-block on Pavilion Road, just off Sloane Street, and was called Bellville Sassoon. The main floor was a cross between a shop and a dressmaker's, with ready-to-wear gowns on display, and dressmaker's dummies wearing half-made garments that bristled with pins.

A small intense-looking man greeted André as an old friend.

'André! It's been too long!'

'Hello, David. How's Belinda?'

'Very well, very well.' He stood back to scrutinise Pamela. 'Who do we have here?'

André introduced them.

'David Sassoon. A magician.'

'So what do we have in mind?' said Sassoon, diplomatically

including both in his gaze.

'An evening gown,' said Pamela. 'André's having a grand party.'

'Long, simple, pure,' said André. 'None of your Oscar de la Renta feathers and frills.'

David Sassoon pulled a face that said, But of course.

'Have you seen the new line from Valentino Garavani?'

'Too much red,' said André.

Sassoon now turned his full attention to Pamela. She felt that he was seeing through her clothes to her naked body beneath.

'What would you like, Miss Pamela?'

Pamela had an answer, but she wasn't sure if it was the right kind of thing to say.

'Just a suggestion,' she said.

'Please.'

'I'd like to look like Audrey Hepburn at the beginning of *Breakfast at Tiffany's*.'

'Just so,' said André, approving. 'Long and black.'

'Hubert de Givenchy,' said Sassoon. 'But what I do for you will be better.'

He drew out a tape measure and flicked it round her with quick practised movements.

'I don't want to look like anyone else at the party,' said Pamela.

'Every one of my dresses is unique,' said Sassoon.

He finished measuring, and stood back to appraise her as he might a model.

'You have an excellent figure,' he said. 'Are you shy?'

'I don't think so,' said Pamela.

Sassoon went to the rails and drew out a long black sleeveless gown. On the hanger it was impossible to judge. He held it up.

'High neck. Close-fitted waist. Full skirt. You would wear it with black gloves above the elbow, black patent leather shoes, high heels.'

'High neck?' said André.

'Ah, but do you see the material?'

Sassoon slid his hand inside the dress.

'Silk chiffon.'

It was transparent.

'And underneath?' said André.

'Here. A black silk slip. Low neckline, high hem. Two inches above the knee.'

André turned to Pamela.

'What do you think?'

'How does she know?' said Sassoon. 'Try it on. If she likes it, I can alter it to fit.'

He took the dress and the slip to a small changing room at the back. Pamela undressed. The slip fitted well. She drew it up until the straps were over her bare shoulders. Then she stepped carefully into the chiffon dress.

Sassoon was waiting outside to button up the back.

'Not so far off, actually,' he said, pinching the fabric.

Pamela presented herself for André's inspection; then turned to look into a long mirror on the side wall. The gauzy chiffon clung close to her upper body, and then fell away in full gathers to the floor. It was revealing, showing her upper chest and her legs from the knees down, but it shadowed what it revealed. The result was simultaneously formal and sexy.

'Is it all right?' she said, turning nervously to André.

'Of course it's all right,' said Sassoon. 'You can see for yourself.'

'Yes,' said Pamela. 'It's beautiful.'

'I told you,' said André. 'He's a magician.'

'Work still to be done,' said Sassoon, taking out his pins. 'Stand still, my dear.'

He proceeded to tuck and pin the fabric.

'Of course someone will have to see to her hair,' he said, his mouth full of pins. 'Take her to Annette.'

Pamela said nothing. She wanted to cry with happiness.

'When can you have it, David?' said André.

'Tomorrow.'

As they came out onto Pavilion Road André said, 'Will that do?'

'Oh, André. I don't know how to thank you.'

'I'll be well repaid,' he said, 'when I see you enter my party. Now where can I drop you?'

'Take me to Stephen's,' she said. 'I don't want to go home yet.'

He drove her to Wimpole Mews, where Stephen Ward had his flat. She offered André her cheek.

'You've been such a darling,' she said.

'Entirely selfish,' he replied.

She rang the bell on the flat door, and no one answered. She rang again. At last she heard a patter on the stairs within, and the door opened to reveal a sleepy Christine in pyjamas.

'You can't still be asleep,' said Pamela.

'I'm not, am I?' said Christine.

Stephen was out, in his consulting rooms, as Pamela had assumed. It was Christine she wanted to see.

'André's buying me a dress for his party.'

Christine's eyes opened wide.

'Good work, Pammy!'

'It's going to be so amazing!'

Now she allowed all the accumulated excitement to pour out of her. She described the new dress in detail. Christine listened with sleepy pleasure.

'Looks like you hit the jackpot there, girl.'

'He's so polite, Christine. And he knows so much. He knows exactly what I'm thinking. It's almost scary.'

'But you like him?'

'Oh, yes! Don't you think he's beautiful?'

'So have you slept with him yet?'

'No,' said Pamela, trying to sound nonchalant, as if this was merely a tactical decision.

'Good for you,' said Christine. 'Make them wait. They're much nicer to you before than after.'

'What are you going to wear on Saturday, Christine?'

'I'll show you if you like.'

Christine went into the room that was still known as 'Christine's room', even though she had her own flat in Dolphin Square. She brought out a garment on a hanger that looked like a bright red plastic bag. Pamela stared in disbelief.

'What is it?'

'It's a mac. I got it from Bazaar, in the King's Road. Cost a bloody fortune.'

'What do you wear it with?'

'Not a lot,' said Christine. 'It comes down to here.'

She indicated a point about halfway down her thigh.

'You'll look as if you're undressed!'

'André's parties are like that,' said Christine. 'Anything goes.'

Pamela pictured Christine making her entrée in the shiny short red mac, her shapely legs bare beneath. She would be the sensation of the party. Her own elegant floor-length black chiffon would look middle-aged by comparison. Unless – she had a sudden idea that made her laugh out loud.

Do I dare?

They heard the sound of a key in the front door, and hastily put away the party clothes. It was Stephen, returning with Eugene.

'Lovely ladies!' cried Eugene, and kissed their hands.

'Pamela's been to a dressmaker with André,' said Christine. 'He's buying her the most gorgeous frock for his party.'

'These parties of André's,' said Eugene to Pamela, 'they are without rules. You must be prepared.'

'He's shown me where it's happening,' said Pamela. 'He's got an empty house in Mayfair.'

'You and I, Stephen,' said Ivanov, 'we must protect little Pamela, on Saturday.'

'Do I need protection?' said Pamela.

'It is the gentleman's duty to protect the ladies,' said Ivanov.

'Do shut up, Eugene,' said Christine. 'Since when did you have gentlemen in Russia?'

'You must be kind to Eugene,' said Stephen. 'He's in despair over Berlin.'

'Too many speeches!' said Eugene. 'Why must they all make speeches? For every speech, two audiences. Your own people, and your enemy. Your people cheers, your enemy fears.'

'That's rather good, Eugene.'

'No more speeches. Our leaders must talk in private. Then we can arrange everything.'

'I have a friend who knows Mountbatten,' said Pamela.

Eugene turned to her in astonishment. The change in his manner was gratifying.

'Who is this friend?'

'He works for Mountbatten. He's some kind of adviser.'

'I must meet him! Can you introduce me?'

Pamela suddenly felt unsure of her ground. After all, Eugene was known to them all as the 'Russian spy'.

'I'm not sure,' she said. 'I don't want to get him into trouble.'

'There will be no trouble. I hide nothing. I am naval attaché at the Russian Embassy. If he doesn't want to talk to me, good. I say no more.'

'Eugene believes dialogue helps,' said Stephen. 'So do I.'

'Well, I suppose it's all right,' said Pamela. 'I'll see what I can do.'

24

Rupert pulled off his spectacles and wiped them with his pocket handkerchief.

'Are you really steaming up your glasses?' said John Grimsdale, amused.

'Why not?' said Rupert. 'I'm excited.'

He was testing his latest thinking on his friend and sparring partner from Intelligence.

'Why me?' said Grimsdale. 'What have I done to deserve this honour?'

'I know you have no principles of any kind,' said Rupert. 'So if what I'm thinking makes sense to you, then maybe I'm on the right track.'

Rupert did not reveal to his friend the extent of his secret ambition. He was only a lowly adviser. But he did have the ear of the Chief of Defence Staff, and it was said that there was nothing so powerful as an idea whose time had come.

'The heart of the Cold War,' he explained, 'is not weapons, but intentions. The fear isn't generated by the bombs and the missiles. It's generated by the presumed intention to use them. Manage the intentions and we reduce the fear. Reduce the fear and we reduce the danger.'

John Grimsdale was unimpressed.

'Manage our enemy's intentions?' he said, peering at the writings on Rupert's walls. 'I'm all for that. Let's manage him so he gives up all this Communist nonsense and goes shopping.'

'Of course I know intentions are complex,' said Rupert, too eager to pursue his line of thought to respond to his friend's mockery. 'In fact, that's part of my idea. If you take a power like the Soviet Union, you have to deal with three forms of intention. You've got its true intention, whatever that is. You've got its presented intention, which is what it wants us to believe it'll do. And you've got its perceived intention, which is what we think it'll do. These can all be different. And that's where it gets dangerous.'

'Look, Rupert,' said Grimsdale. 'It's not difficult. We don't know for sure what the bastards might do, and we're never going to know. So we plan for the worst possible scenario.'

'There!' cried Rupert, banging his hands on his desk. 'Exactly! You've said it!'

'So I'm right?'

'No! You're so wrong!'

'I rather thought I might be.'

'Your way of thinking creates a spiral of fear. My way of thinking creates a spiral of trust.'

'Oh, well. Let's by all means have a spiral of trust. I think your spectacles are steaming up again.'

'All I'm saying,' said Rupert, 'is that instead of putting all our intelligence effort into counting their missiles we should focus on understanding what's going on inside their heads.'

'It's a whole lot easier to count missiles.'

'Come on, John. Take me seriously here.'

'All right,' said Grimsdale. 'I'll take you seriously. Yes, we do need to understand Soviet intentions. And what tools do we have for reading their minds? We have their words, and we have their deeds. We listen to their rhetoric. "Communism will bury

215

capitalism," says Khrushchev. They arm our enemies in South East Asia. In the Congo. In Cuba. What are we supposed to think they're up to?'

'This is all business as usual. This is standard big power rivalry. We've been dealing with this sort of jostling for the last three hundred years. But SIOP? Three thousand two hundred and sixty-seven warheads? That's the end of the world. Is that really what we want? Do we really believe it's what they want?'

'No,' said Grimsdale. 'Of course not.'

'Then what on earth is going on?'

Grimsdale looked at his watch. He'd lingered too long.

'All right, Rupert. I take your point. But it's not me you need to convince. What does Dickie say to all this?'

'I haven't tried it on him yet. And anyway, I know what he'd say. He'd say, "Tell the Americans. Don't talk to the monkey, talk to the organ-grinder."'

Grimsdale chuckled at that.

'Nobody does national humiliation quite as well as we do,' he said, and headed off down the corridor.

The other problem with Mountbatten, Rupert reflected, was that he had difficulty with ideas. He was a practical man above all, a details man. At the monthly meeting of the Defence Ministry chiefs, which was attended by the Cabinet Secretary, all he could talk about was retaliation procedures.

'Who has the sole authority to launch a nuclear retaliation, should we be attacked? The prime minister, advised by myself, as Chief of Defence Staff. What arrangements are there for contacts to be established with the prime minister or myself at the critical period, when every minute will count? None! In the event of a bolt out of the blue attack I'm told we will receive four minutes' warning, and that only when Fylingdales becomes operational sometime next year. This is madness!'

Norman Brook did his best to calm him down.

'The JIC takes the view that an unprovoked strike by the Soviets is highly unlikely. And since as you say, Dickie, we'd have no warning of a missile strike at all, not until the early warning system is up and running – well, really there's not a lot of point worrying about it, is there?'

'Please, Norman,' said Mountbatten, gripping the Cabinet Secretary by the arm, 'let's not be too relaxed about this. In the event of a strike taking out the PM and myself, there must be an agreed procedure for the authorisation, or not, of our retaliation.'

'But it's not really there to be used. It's there to deter.'

'Suppose Harold's dead. Suppose I'm dead. Can anyone else push the button?'

'Well, there has to be a chain of command. You know that.'

'It's Bomber Command, isn't it? It's bloody Bing Cross.'

'These are very extreme hypotheses,' said Brook.

'In my extreme hypothesis,' said Mountbatten, 'a Soviet attack on London causes a military officer, an unelected leader, to retaliate against Russia, and so trigger a global nuclear holocaust. That is simply not acceptable.'

Norman Brook turned to Frank Mottershead, the Deputy Secretary concerned with such matters at the Ministry of Defence.

'Frank?'

'I'm inclined to think there is a cause for concern here,' said Mottershead. 'As matters stand, C-in-C Bomber Command does have the delegated authority, under exceptional circumstances, to use his own judgement.'

'And what counts as exceptional circumstances?' said Mountbatten.

'If the PM can't be reached. If an attack is understood to have been launched.'

'If the PM can't be reached! So if Harold takes a nap, Bing Cross can scramble the V-force!'

'I wouldn't go that far, sir.'

'What arrangements do we currently have for communicating with the PM when he's out of his office?'

'Well, by phone, sir.'

'And when he's in his car?'

'The PM's car has a radio which can receive messages via the AA's radio network.'

'Scrambled messages?'

'No, sir.'

'So anyone can hear them?'

'The radio message would be no more than an alert to the driver to proceed at once to the nearest phone box.'

'And put four pennies in the slot, and press Button A?'

Mottershead looked at his hands.

'I suppose so, sir.'

'Ronnie. Make a note. All the PM's drivers are to be issued with four pennies forthwith.'

'For heaven's sake!' exclaimed Norman Brook impatiently. 'The driver can reverse the charges! You dial one hundred, and the operator asks the person at the other end to accept payment.'

'Excellent!' cried Mountbatten. 'After all, he does have a whole *four minutes* before the bombs go off!'

A silence fell.

'All right, Dickie,' said Norman Brook at last. 'You've made your point. We'll look into it.'

After the meeting, alone with Ronnie and Rupert, Mountbatten said, 'I'm not just being an old woman, am I?'

'No, sir,' said Rupert. 'I remain convinced that the greatest threat of nuclear holocaust lies in human error.'

'By God, yes! Have you read *The Guns of August*?'

'Not yet,' said Rupert.

'It should be required reading. The First World War wouldn't have happened but for the mobilisation plans. One side began to mobilise, the other side had to follow suit. The fear of attack mounted to the point where the momentum was unstoppable. Once that machine started rolling, there was nothing anyone could do. Apparently the Kaiser had tears in his eyes. He begged his General Staff. But they told him it was too late. That's what I dread. Kenneth Cross launches his bombers because if he leaves them on the ground they're vulnerable. So off they go, each with their target in the Soviet Union. Who calls them back?'

'You have to be at the MoD by five, sir,' said Ronnie.

'Oh, damn! What's that about?'

'The CENTO meeting in Karachi.'

Mountbatten sighed.

'What can I do about Pakistan? They're convinced we're in the pockets of the Indians. Then India goes and buys fighter jets from Russia.'

He started gathering up his papers.

'That memo of yours, sir,' said Rupert. '"Aim for the West". I've been doing some thinking.'

'Thought you would. Rather up your street, I should say.'

'I think it's important, actually.'

'Then you're about the only person who does.'

'I've become convinced the solution is ideological, not military.'

'That's very interesting, Rupert. I want to have this discussion properly. Have you written your thoughts down?'

'I'm doing so, sir.'

'You know who'd understand this? Edwina.'

Edwina Mountbatten had died two years earlier.

'I remember her well,' said Rupert. 'You're right. She saw things clearly.'

'She made me the man I am. I miss her terribly.' He sighed. 'I shall have to be off.'

'I'll finish my paper.'

'You know what they'll say, of course? Too abstract. Too emotional and humanitarian. Too many airy-fairy ideas.'

'It's ideas that will destroy the world,' said Rupert.

'By God, you're right there.'

He paused, frowning, considering a new thought.

'When am I in Ireland, Ronnie?'

'Last week of September, sir.'

'I have a house in Ireland,' Mountbatten said to Rupert. 'Miles from anywhere, right on the coast. Most glorious scenery you ever saw. It's the only place I can get away to think. I have this bloody paper to write on the reorganisation of defence, which, let me tell you, is proving a great deal tougher than fighting a world war. Why don't you join me? Then we can really talk.'

'Thank you, sir. I'd be glad to.'

'Put Rupert on the list for Classiebawn, Ronnie.' He picked up his worn briefcase. 'Yes, I'm on my way.' And to Rupert as he left the room, 'I'm glad you knew Edwina.'

25

That evening Rupert sat in the armchair in his living room, writing in longhand on a lined pad. The little room was filled with music, flowing from the record player by the side of the empty fireplace. Music was one of Rupert's great loves. Tonight he was playing a recording of *Tristan und Isolde*. As Wagner's themes wove their patterns in the air around him, he filled his pad with the ever-evolving chain of ideas that in his secret heart, in his wildest dreams, he believed might just save the world.

The flat in Tachbrook Street consisted of this front room with its window onto the street, an even smaller bedroom at the back that looked out on the backs of other houses, a galley kitchen, and a bathroom across the stairs. He rented it for £4 a week from the building's owner, a solicitor who lived in Surrey. The furnishings belonged to Rupert. He was responsible for the utilities and the rates. The reward for this modest style of living was that he owed no money to anyone, and had been able to save on his income for many years. He invested his savings prudently, for his old age. He expected to live alone until his death.

At times like this, when his brain was racing, he felt his solitude as a source of power. He felt that he was on the brink of a major achievement, of the kind that only came after prolonged unbroken concentration.

Let us explore the concept of *intention*. What reality can it be said to have? What validity? If I say I intend you no harm, what will cause you to act as if this statement has force?

This brings us to the *roots of trust*.

Trust is not the same thing as expectation. If I can see that you're bound hand and foot, I may have the reasonable expectation that you won't harm me. But I may still not trust you. Nor is trust a matter of assurances given. Trust can only be earned. Each act of trust is conditional, but with each successful transaction, trust grows—

The phone rang. After eight on a Thursday evening: an unusual occurrence. Irritated, he laid down his pad, lifted the needle from the record, and picked up the receiver.

It was Hugo.

'Sorry to bother you at this hour. It's just that something's come up with Mary. We don't quite know what to do.'

'What is it?'

'It looks like there's been a theft.'

Hugo let Rupert in to the house in Brook Green, and took him through to the drawing room, where Harriet was sitting.

'So good of you to come, Rupert.'

Mary was upstairs, in Emily's bedroom. After reading her her bedtime story, it had become her habit to sit by the bed in the gathering darkness until the child was soundly asleep.

'Mary knows nothing at all about this.'

They spoke in low voices. Rupert listened as they told the story. Hugo did the telling, appealing constantly to Harriet for corroboration. Harriet seemed quite distressed.

Hugo had been at work. Harriet had also been out, and had stopped at the bank, and drawn out ten pounds. The money had been given her as one £5 note and five £1 notes. She had bought some fish at the fishmonger's on the way home, for this evening's dinner, using one of the £1 notes, and receiving change. She had put down her handbag where it always rested on the little table in the hall by the phone. She made herself a cup of tea and sat down here, in the drawing room, to drink it. Going out had tired her. She may have dozed a little.

Mary and Emily came home after school. Harriet didn't hear them come in.

'Mary is wonderful with Emily, Rupert,' Harriet said. 'She makes such a difference to me.'

The window cleaner came, and clattered about with his ladder. Then he rang the bell to be paid, and Harriet went to her handbag for half a crown. She found she had only the four £1 notes, and some coins. The £5 note had gone missing.

She paid the window cleaner, and returned to her handbag for a more thorough search. She tried the pockets of the coat she'd been wearing. Nothing.

Then Pamela came downstairs. She'd been asleep most of the day. Harriet told her what had happened. Pamela couldn't help, of course. She went to the kitchen to make herself a cup of coffee. Then she came out again to say, 'Is Mary home?'

Yes, Mary was home.

Pamela then told Harriet that she had been lying on her bed in her bedroom when she'd been roused by running footsteps. Somebody, presumably Mary, had run up to the attic above, and then, a moment later, run down again.

That was all.

Hugo and Harriet gazed at Rupert in unhappy perplexity.

'What are we to think?'

'You think Mary took the money?' said Rupert.

'Someone took it,' said Hugo.

Rupert's immediate reaction was one of anger. Of course Mary hadn't taken the money. It was inconceivable. But then he obliged himself to think more objectively. All he knew about Mary was that she had lived for years in a convent. He also knew that she had no money.

'Harriet says it can't have been Mary,' said Hugo, 'but really, as Pamela says, there is something odd about her. Why is she homeless and friendless in London? What's she done to end up like this?'

'All I know,' said Harriet, 'is that she's an absolute treasure to me, and I don't want to lose her.'

'But if she's stealing from you, darling.'

'I won't believe it.'

'No, please. It just won't do, you know. We can't have this sort of thing going on.'

Rupert said, 'And you've said nothing at all to Mary?'

'Not yet,' said Hugo.

'I won't have her accused of being a thief,' said Harriet.

'All I was going to do,' said Hugo, 'was ask her if she had any idea what had happened to the money.'

'What do you expect her to say?'

'I don't know. But we have to find out.'

'I said to call you,' Harriet said to Rupert. 'You know her better than we do.'

'I hardly know her at all,' said Rupert. 'But I certainly don't think she's a thief.'

'There's something fishy about her,' said Hugo.

'Would you like me to talk to her?'

'Oh, would you, Rupert? You'd do it so much better.' Harriet looked pathetically grateful. Evidently this was why he'd been sent for. 'But you won't say we suspect her, will you? Just say we can't think where the money's gone.'

Hugo gave a sardonic snort. But he too was happy to pass the awkward business over to Rupert.

After a little while Mary came down from Emily's bedroom. Her face lit up at the sight of Rupert.

'Just a friendly visit,' he said. 'How are you getting on?'

'I've just been seeing Emily off to sleep,' said Mary. 'She doesn't like to go to sleep on her own.'

'You give in to her too much, Mary,' said Hugo. 'She has to learn.'

'Oh, but she's only a child.'

Harriet smiled at Mary, understanding and approving.

'It's still a lovely evening,' said Rupert to Mary. 'How would you like to join me for a stroll?'

They walked up Brook Green, crossing onto the grass between the trees.

'Oh, Rupert,' she said, 'I just love it here.'

'Anything's better than the convent, eh?'

'I've been thinking about Harriet, and her little boy who died,' Mary said. 'Would it be wrong to talk to her about it?'

'No,' said Rupert. 'Why should it be?'

'I'm thinking it's time she let the child rest in peace.'

'Ah, I see. I'm sure you're right. No harm in trying.'

As they walked and talked Rupert was only aware of how happy it made him to be in her company. He was entirely convinced that she could not have been robbing her hosts only a few hours ago. But the matter had to be raised.

'Harriet was telling me something odd happened to her today,' he said. 'Somehow she lost a five-pound note from her purse.'

'Five pounds! That's a terrible lot of money. Was it while she was shopping?'

'No. It was after she'd come home.'

'Home? But that's impossible. There've been people in the house all the time.'

'She can't understand it. It looks like it happened in the late afternoon.'

'She said nothing to me when we came in from school.'

'No. It happened after that.'

Mary came to a stop and went a deep red.

'Does she think I took it?'

'No, Mary, she doesn't.' Rupert was able to say this with a clear conscience. 'But she's very puzzled.'

'I would never steal, not from anyone! Not from those as have taken me in off the streets.'

'Of course you wouldn't. I know that.'

But Mary's agitation was growing, despite his assurances.

'Of course they'd think it was me. A stranger with no home to go to. Who else could it be?'

'No, Mary! Please!'

'I must leave their house. I must leave at once.'

'That's the last thing Harriet wants. And Emily. Please. Don't get so worked up about this. Of course it's nothing to do with you.'

She looked at him, biting her lower lip, on the point of tears.

'You don't know that,' she said. 'You don't know anything about me.'

'That's because you won't tell me.'

'I can't,' she said.

'I know you're not a thief, Mary.'

'How do you know?'

'Because I know you could never tell a lie.'

'It's true,' she said. 'Not to save my life.'

'So why don't we go back, and you can tell them what you told me.'

'What if they don't believe me?'

'Then you'll have to leave.'

'Yes, I will.' She looked down, and spoke very low. 'I'll have to go home. God help me.'

'We'll see about that.'

He was sure now that there was something or someone she

feared at home. She had been fourteen when she left: not too young to have been abused, perhaps by some member of her family. You heard about such things from time to time. The thought angered him. He wanted to protect her, without knowing what had harmed her, and to avenge her, without knowing who had done the harm.

They returned to the house. Mary did not hesitate.

'I'm sorry about the money, and I know you must think it was me that took it, but I swear on the Mother of God that I didn't, and I never would. I beg you to search my room, and anywhere else, to make sure I'm telling you the truth. But the Lord knows I'm no thief, and nor would I be so ungrateful to you after all your kindness to me.'

Having said this, she burst into tears. Harriet took her in her arms.

'Of course you didn't, Mary,' she said. 'No one thinks you did.'

Hugo frowned and looked at Pamela, who had now appeared in the kitchen doorway.

'You know when you ran up to your room?' he said to Mary. 'After you came in?'

'No,' said Mary, dabbing at her eyes. 'I've not been up to my room since we came home.'

Pamela gave a shrug of her shoulders.

'I expect I was dreaming,' she said.

Emily came downstairs in her pyjamas, blinking sleepy eyes.

'Why's Mary crying?'

'It's nothing, darling,' said Hugo. 'You're supposed to be asleep. Go back to bed.'

'Rupert,' said Pamela, 'there's something I want to ask you before you go.'

'I can't go to sleep without Mary,' said Emily.

So Mary went upstairs with Emily, giving Rupert one grateful backward glance, and Harriet went to the medicine cupboard in the kitchen for an aspirin.

'Thanks,' said Hugo to Rupert. 'Though I've no idea where that leaves us.'

'It's not her,' said Rupert simply.

'Fivers don't fly about all on their own.'

Pamela came up to Rupert in the hall as he was leaving.

'I've made a friend who's a Russian spy,' she said. 'I told him you work for Mountbatten. Was that very wrong of me?'

'A Russian spy?' said Rupert, smiling. 'Does he wear a badge saying so?'

'He works at the Russian embassy. And he's Russian. He wants to meet you.'

'So he can spy on me?'

'I think really he wants to spy on Mountbatten.'

'Is that what he told you?'

'No, not exactly,' said Pamela. 'He says our leaders should talk to each other in private. He doesn't like all the speeches. Your people cheers and your enemy fears.'

She recited this as if it was a well-known saying. Rupert was intrigued.

'I'm rather inclined to agree.'

'So will you let him spy on you? He's awfully nice.'

'I don't mind meeting him. What's his name?'

'Eugene. I don't know the rest.'

Rupert returned home, and remained awake late into the night. He was not thinking about his paper for Mountbatten any more, or about Pamela's friend the Russian spy. He was thinking about Mary. Whatever it was in her home in Ireland that frightened her would have to be faced one day. Whatever this 'special destiny' the nuns spoke of, one day it must come to pass.

He was now more convinced than ever that somehow she must break the chains of her mysterious secret and be set free.

At one level his analytical mind conceived of Mary's freedom in the abstract, as if it had nothing to do with him. He sought the solution to the puzzle she presented in much the same way that he sought a solution to the puzzle posed by nuclear weapons. Rupert supposed himself to be a rational being, who reached his conclusions by a process of rational argument. But he was not entirely lacking in self-awareness. He knew there was a second process going on, in the shadowed depths of his mind. This was the realm of hopes and fears, of dreams and nightmares. Out of it, all unsought, there burst from time to time flashes of brilliant light that transformed his carefully constructed chains of reasoning. The image of Mary's face would spring into his mind: hardly an argument, or even an insight. And yet by its light everything was changed.

26

On the evening of André Tillemans' party Pamela joined Stephen Ward and his friends for dinner at the Dorchester. She looked dazzling and sophisticated in her new dress, her hair swept back and held with a clip. They were seven at table: Stephen and Pamela; Eugene Ivanov; Christine Keeler accompanied by a good-looking man called Michael Lambton, who seemed to be her boyfriend; a friend of Christine's, a kitten-faced blonde called Mandy; and Mandy's boyfriend, a short round balding man called Peter. The men were all in evening dress, apart from Eugene, who wore full dress naval uniform, complete with decorations. Christine and Mandy wore identical apple-green dresses, sleeveless, unadorned, and very short. They made a comical pair: Christine slight and dark-haired, Mandy sweet and blonde, deliberately underdressed for such a grand party, but unforgettable.

Pamela was nervous, and began smoking as soon as they were settled at their table. She had no idea what she wanted to eat, and let Stephen order for her. He ordered noisettes of lamb, but she barely touched her plate. Stephen himself ate sparingly and, as ever, drank no alcohol at all. Pamela drank whatever was poured into her glass.

She heard the chatter and laughter of the others but took nothing in. She was in a strange heightened state, in which sounds seemed sharper and colours brighter, but nothing conveyed any meaning. This, for her, was the *time before*. The wild idea she had conceived in Stephen's flat was about to become a reality.

Mandy laughed all through the meal. Christine's friend Michael was silent. Eugene and Peter got into an argument about a town in Poland, or Ukraine, called Lvov, which was Peter's birthplace. According to Peter the Russians had stolen Lvov after the war.

'Lvov was liberated,' said Eugene. 'The people of Lvov welcomed the Red Army with open arms.'

'What you call an army,' said Peter, 'was no better than a mob of butchers and rapists.'

Eugene's face darkened.

'The Red Army,' he said, 'saved the world from fascism. If it weren't for the sacrifices of my people, your precious Lvov would even now be ruled by the Third Reich.'

'My precious Lvov,' said Peter. 'My poor Lvov. But that's all in the past, eh? How do you like the wine? Have another glass.'

Peter seemed to regard himself as the host. At the end of the dinner he produced a fat roll of notes and peeled off enough to pay for them all.

'You're most generous, Peter,' said Stephen.

'Have to be,' grunted Peter. 'That's my charm.'

'He's a sweetheart really,' said Mandy, pinching his cheek.

Pamela was drunk by now, drunk enough to carry out the next stage in her plan. She paid a visit to the Ladies, and there made some adjustments to her dress. She emerged wearing her light summer coat over her dress, for the short walk to the party.

Mandy and Christine led the way, bags swinging in their hands, whispering and laughing to each other. Eugene followed, walking with Michael. Stephen, Pamela and Peter brought up the rear.

'I don't know why we're walking,' complained Peter. 'I've got the Roller here, sitting doing nothing.'

'Come on, Peter,' said Stephen. 'It's good for you.'

Darkness had long fallen, but London was still warm. As they turned into South Audley Street they could see the crowd of guests gathered round the entrance to the party. Taxis were lined up along the kerb, their doors opening and closing, spilling out men in black and women in exotic colours. Pamela stumbled, unused to her new high-heeled shoes. Stephen took her arm.

'Easy there.'

As they approached André's house, Christine and Mandy opened their bags and took out identical short red macs. The plasticised fabric shone in the light of the street lamps. They put on the macs and held hands and capered about, laughing.

'What do you call that?' said Peter. 'Is it raining?'

'It's the new look, darling,' said Mandy. 'Don't you think it's the sexiest thing you ever saw?'

'Crazy,' said Peter. 'Crazy.'

The hallway of the house was crowded. Stephen smiled and nodded, seeming to know everybody. Young men in white shirts stood on either side, waiting to take coats, but Christine and Mandy kept their shiny macs on, and Pamela kept her coat. The crowd moved slowly up the stairs. From the top came the sound of band music, and the low roar of a packed room. Michael and Peter escorted the girls in red, Stephen and Eugene escorted Pamela.

At the top of the stairs the guests were backed up on the landing, as the ones ahead made their entrée. There was no major-domo shouting out names, as at a society ball; but each new group of guests paused before entering, to be greeted by their host and noted by the crowd already in the great room. The more striking of the new arrivals were acknowledged with cheers.

Pamela let herself be swept slowly up the wide stairs in this tide of glamorous people, taking in almost nothing. She was dazed by alcohol and excitement. She had shared her plan with no one, but already, caught in the crush on the stairs, she was past the point of no return. As she reached the top of the stairs she started to shake, overwhelmed with sensations she was unable to control, that alternated between terror and ecstasy. To conceal this she held her head high and drew her coat tight around her, and pinched her fingernails into the flesh of her hands so that it hurt.

Christine and Mandy made their entrée together, posing hand in hand on the platform in their shiny red coats. André, elegant in a perfectly fitting dinner jacket, silently raised his arms above them as if offering his guests a rare treat. The crowd cheered. Christine and Mandy then skipped down the steps, followed by Michael and Peter.

Pamela, coming immediately behind, now caught her first sight of the great shadowy ballroom packed with André's guests. Tall lamps threw pools of light up onto the arching ceiling, and illuminated the band at the far end on their specially built stage. Apart from that, the beautiful people swarmed in a velvety and flattering half-light. André himself, tall, slender, elegant, turned his grey eyes onto Pamela with silent enquiry.

'My dear.'

He held out one hand, so that she would come forward onto the platform. Pamela slipped off her coat and reached it out to Stephen, who was just behind her.

'Would you mind, Stephen?'

She stepped forward to stand by André's side. André gazed at her in silence. Then he smiled. In the same moment, the crowd in the room saw, and from end to end there came a rippling gasp.

Pamela's face was turned towards André as if she was unaware of the sensation she was causing. André raised her hand to his lips and kissed it.

'*Étonnant!*' he murmured.

The beautiful black chiffon dress covered her from neck to ankle, but concealed nothing. Beneath the gauzy silk, shadowed but visible to all, she was naked but for a black lace brassiere, and black lace panties. She wore black gloves high above the elbows and black high-heeled shoes, but no black silk slip. The effect was electrifying: her body made available and yet withheld. There was not a man in the room who didn't stare and stare. Pamela made her entrée to the party as every man's dream of sexual desire made flesh.

After the intake of breath came the applause. Carried on a wave of admiration and longing, Pamela slowly descended the steps and entered the space made for her by the crowd. She looked at no one, and she didn't smile. Moving with small steps, almost gliding, her lovely head held high, she passed among them like a princess, offering them the priceless gift of her presence. The guests gaped, and clapped, and made way for her. A waiter approached, bearing a tray of glasses of champagne. She took one and turned, raised it to André up on the platform where the guests were still arriving, and drank it all in one go. The crowd round her cheered once more.

Pamela felt immortal. She could do no wrong. Her every gesture was necessary and beautiful. Her triumph was so complete that it now seemed to her to have been inevitable. On every face turned towards her she saw something more than admiration. It was awe.

Stephen now caught up with her.

'By God, Pamela! You're a killer!'

Christine and Mandy crowded round. They had shed their red macs and were now in their identical bright-green short frocks.

'Pammy! What a sneaky sneak you are! Why didn't you tell?'

'Did you see André's eyes? He almost passed out!'

They felt the fabric of her dress and inspected the underwear beneath, with professional interest.

'Where did you get the smalls?'

'Marshall & Snelgrove,' said Pamela. 'They're Kayser.'

'Peter just about had a heart attack,' said Mandy.

It was all Pamela had ever hoped for and more. She floated through the party, barely taking in any of the other guests. Men and women both let their eyes linger over her body, and she turned this way and that before them, permitting the intimate exploration while remaining beyond their reach. When her glass was empty she held it out to the nearest man, and off he went to find her a refill. When a cigarette burned down, a dozen hands reached out to offer her a fresh cigarette, and lighters rasped into flame all round her.

André sought her out in the midst of his hostly duties.

'I have to be everywhere,' he said. 'But I only want to be with you.'

She held his eyes, but did not speak.

'You're magnificent,' he said. 'Don't leave without seeing me again. I have something to ask you.'

He was drawn back into the throng. Pamela moved on, alone, entranced. She was performing the part she believed she had been born to play: the beautiful woman who knows effortlessly what to do, who is desired by all but owned by none. It was only an act, but in the night world of this great party it had for a time become real. If this were a fairy story, on the stroke of midnight she would find herself back in rags, by the dying kitchen fire. But it was no story, and midnight was long past.

People were dancing in the space before the band. She danced a little, with Eugene, who spun her about too fast, and with Stephen, who danced slowly and beautifully. Then she allowed herself to be drawn into drifting conversations with men she didn't know, saying little herself, moving on without apology or explanation. She passed men and women whom she half recognised, most likely because they were famous, and saw their eyes invite her to talk to them, and pretended she didn't see.

One man leaned close as she passed and murmured, 'Darling, you're sensational! Do you fuck?'

She barely missed a beat, concealing her momentary tremor of shock.

'Of course, darling,' she replied. 'But only my friends.'

She went in search of the Ladies. There she found Christine and Mandy, sharing a cubicle, smoking, gossiping about the guests. Christine beckoned her in.

'Come in, Pammy! We're having our own party.'

The light was brighter here. Pamela blinked and felt strange. Mandy moved to sit on the toilet seat, and Christine sat on the floor. She patted the space on the other side.

'Plenty of room.'

Pamela realised that her legs felt wobbly, and would no longer support her. She slid down onto the floor of the cubicle.

'I don't think I'll ever get up again,' she said.

'Everyone wants to know who you are,' said Christine.

'You know what, Pammy,' said Mandy. 'If you wanted, you could make a fortune.'

'Don't be daft,' said Christine. 'She's a lady, isn't she?'

'Oh, I don't care about that,' said Pamela. 'I just want . . .'

But she found she didn't know any more what it was she wanted. It had seemed so clear not so long ago.

'You want a rich husband,' said Mandy.

'I want someone to love,' said Pamela.

'Take it from me,' said Mandy. 'Rich helps.'

'Look who's talking!' said Christine. 'You don't love Peter. You just love it that he's got so much money.'

Pamela thought of Peter, small and fat, unpeeling banknotes in the Dorchester.

'Do you have to do it with him?' she said.

'I don't have to,' said Mandy. 'But I do.'

'She does it sitting on top of him, with her back to him,' said Christine, giggling.

'Her back to him?'

Pamela couldn't work this out at all.

'Doesn't take long,' said Mandy. 'And you know what? I've got a real soft spot for Peter. He's a sweet, kind man.'

'You're in there now with André,' said Christine, poking Pamela with her toe. 'He's got even more money than Peter.'

'We've all had a crack,' said Mandy. 'No one's got him yet.'

'Why not?' said Pamela.

'I thought maybe he was queer,' said Mandy. 'But seeing the way he was looking at you, he's up for it all right.'

'Just make sure you're fixed up,' said Christine.

Pamela realised now that this was what she had come for. She was drunk enough to tell the truth.

'I don't know how to,' she said.

'You'd better find out,' said Mandy. 'You can't trust men.'

'No,' said Pamela, 'what I mean is, I've never done it.'

'What, not ever?'

'Not ever.'

'Crikey! I started when I was thirteen.'

'Yes, well, we all know about you,' said Christine.

'I don't really know anything,' said Pamela.

'You know the basics,' said Mandy. 'Everyone knows that.'

'Yes. I suppose so.'

'You don't sound at all sure, girl.'

'Well, I suppose I'm assuming the man will know what to do, and I just . . .'

She let the thought tail away.

'Don't tell me,' said Mandy. 'You just lie there.'

'Well, yes.'

'Don't go on at her,' said Christine. 'She's not wrong. That's how it is for most girls.'

'But she wants it to be fun, right? For him too.'

'Yes,' said Pamela. 'I do.'

'You want some tips?'

Pamela didn't know how to say she wanted more than tips, she wanted basic information. She wanted a step-by-step illustrated guide. But all she did was nod her head.

'Just listen to us!' said Christine. 'Like a pair of old witches.'

'Make him go slow,' said Mandy. 'They're always in such a tearing hurry. That's my tip.'

'My tip is get him talking. About what you're doing, I mean. Men like that. They think they can't say things. But they want to. And they want you to.'

'What things?' said Pamela.

Christine lowered her voice to a whisper.

'Fuck,' she said. 'Cock. Cunt.'

'I've got another tip,' said Mandy. 'Jelly.'

'Jelly?'

'You squeeze it out of the tube. Slippery stuff. Really helps. Most of all if you're taking it up the bum.'

'Oh, God.' Pamela put her head in her hands. She was beginning to feel sick.

'Don't tell her that!' chided Christine.

'She might as well know,' said Mandy.

'Seriously, Pammy,' said Christine, 'there's only one thing you have to do, and that's get yourself fixed up.'

'How do I do that?'

'You go to Teddy Sugden in Half Moon Street. Tell him you're a friend of mine, he'll do you a good price.'

'How much?'

'No more than a fiver.'

'I don't have it,' said Pamela. 'I spent all I had on the underwear.'

'Get it off André,' said Mandy.

'You zombie!' said Christine, smacking Mandy's leg. 'She can't get it off André. She hasn't done it with him yet.'

'She got the dress, didn't she?'

'Go to Stephen,' Christine said to Pamela. 'He'll help you. God knows, he's helped me enough times.'

Some other women came into the Ladies, and the little group in the cubicle broke up, laughing. Pamela went back into the big room, in search of a cigarette, still feeling queasy. Eugene loomed into view before her, red in the face, his uniform jacket unbuttoned.

'Pamela! I look for you everywhere! Good party, no?'

'What time is it?'

'I don't know. Three, four? Soon the sun come up.'

'Do you have a fag, Eugene?'

He produced a cigarette, and lit it for her.

'When do I meet your friend?'

'What friend?'

'The one who works for Mountbatten.'

'Oh, Rupert. Yes, that's all okay. I'll fix it up.'

'I adore you. I worship you.'

'Go away now, Eugene.'

He went away. Pamela crossed the great room, which was much emptier now. The waiters were still in place, offering glasses of champagne, but she didn't want to drink any more. She made her way out through double doors to an open-air terrace, and stood there, finishing her cigarette, watching the light of the approaching dawn steal up into the sky over the roofs of London.

Here André found her. He had undone his bow tie and the top button of his shirt, but he still looked elegant.

'I thought you'd gone.'

'Not without seeing you.'

He took her in his arms, and they kissed. She had expected this kiss, and wanted it, but now she was tired and had drunk too much, and she found she felt nothing at all. She liked the feel of his arms round her, and she liked his smell. But she felt nothing that she could call desire.

After a few moments she leant her head on his shoulder.

'You should go to bed,' he said.

'Has your party been joyful, André?'

'Yes. Come along, now. I'm going to put you in a taxi.'

They walked back through the house, arm-in-arm. He found her coat for her and put it on her. They went out into the street, and round the side of the Dorchester, where there were taxis waiting.

'My family has a house in the country,' he said. 'Will you let me show it to you?'

'Yes,' she said.

'Will you join me there, next weekend?'

'Yes,' she said.

He told the taxi driver where to drive her, and paid him more than the fare could possibly amount to.

'See her safe into the house,' he said.

By the time the taxi was rounding a deserted Hyde Park Corner, Pamela was asleep.

27

Every three months or so the firm of Caulder & Avenell, wine shippers of St James, held a tasting for buyers in the trade, and for their more serious private clients. The event took place in the large room they called the boardroom, above the shop. The wines were lined up on a long table covered with a white tablecloth, and served by junior members of staff; along with cubes of white bread to cleanse the palate, and black olives, and fragments of Cheddar cheese. The managing partners, Hugo Caulder and Larry Cornford, moved among their guests discussing the merits of the wines, but drinking nothing themselves.

The handsome panelled room was candlelit for these events. This was Larry's idea. The firm was not yet twenty years old, but clients liked to believe it had been founded at least a century ago.

'People associate good wine with venerable age,' said Larry. 'It's nonsense, of course. Most wine is at its best after four or five years. But the image of the musty cellar persists.'

So everything about the appearance of Caulder & Avenell was designed to look long-established. Even the lettering of the firm's name above its shop window had been copied from a Victorian font book and reverse-painted on glass, with gold-leaf accents. The partners and their staff dressed in dark suits and ties, and spoke in low voices, as if in attendance at a church service.

'How are you finding the Pauillac? Give it a few more years and it'll be really special, don't you think?'

Pamela arrived early, and gave her stepfather Larry a hug, and promised not to get in the way. Larry studied her with smiling admiration.

'You look lovely, Pammy, darling. So is London suiting you?'

'I just adore it,' said Pamela.

'Hugo tells me he hardly ever sees you.'

'I do help out whenever they ask me. Really I do. But now they've got a live-in help, an Irish girl, so there's not so much for me to do.'

'We'll talk later, darling.'

One of the firm's main buyers had just come in.

'Richard! Great that you could make it.'

Pamela hovered near the stairs, looking out for her own invitees. Rupert Blundell was the first of them to arrive.

'Rupert! I wasn't sure you'd come.'

'It's all very cloak-and-dagger, this,' said Rupert. 'Is it really necessary?'

'My friend hasn't arrived yet. Let's get ourselves something to drink. Hugo says I'm only to have the Beaujolais.'

'Beaujolais's good enough for me.'

Pamela got them a glass each, making the young man with the bottle fill up the glasses to the brim.

'There,' she said, handing a glass to Rupert. 'Everyone else gets a teaspoonful.'

'How's Mary?'

'Oh, she's fine. That fuss has all blown over.'

'I really don't think she had anything to do with it,' said Rupert.

'That's because she's your pet.'

The room slowly filled with serious-looking men in dark suits.

'Wine experts don't look as if they have much fun, do they?' Pamela whispered. 'Oh, good. He's come.'

Eugene Ivanov, also wearing a dark suit, walked into the candlelit room as if into his own home. He looked round until he found Pamela, gave a wave of greeting, and stopped to sample the wines. Pamela and Rupert watched from across the room as he sniffed and sipped and spat and asked for more.

'That's your Russian spy?' said Rupert.

'Yes,' said Pamela.

'I see he feels it's his duty to explore capitalist luxury in all its forms.'

Ivanov joined them, and was introduced. Pamela identified Rupert by the comical formula that always amused her.

'Rupert's the brother of the first wife of my mother's second husband.'

'That's Larry over there,' said Rupert, pointing to their host.

'And you work for Lord Louis Mountbatten?'

'I'm one of his advisers,' said Rupert.

'As you know,' said Ivanov, 'I am second naval attaché at the Russian embassy. I make no secret.'

'Pamela has told me.'

'You must make secrets of some things, Eugene,' said Pamela. 'You can't do your spying in public.'

Ivanov smiled.

'This is a joke in our set,' he explained to Rupert. 'I am the Russian spy.'

'Are you not?' said Rupert.

'My job here is to learn all I can about British military capability and intentions,' said Ivanov. 'Why else would I be here? To drink this excellent claret? I think not. So you may call me a spy if you wish. I call myself a channel of information. What is

243

more, Mr Blundell, I believe that the more information my country has about your country the safer we will all be.'

'Very interesting,' said Rupert.

'That means he doesn't trust you,' said Pamela to Ivanov.

'Captain Ivanov will understand my caution,' said Rupert. 'I'm afraid I'll prove to be a disappointment as a source of information.'

'I understand, of course,' said Ivanov. 'But would you not like to be a recipient of information?'

'Information that my government is not able to obtain through the usual channels?'

'The usual channels are nothing but posturing and lies. Do you have any idea what Chairman Khrushchev is really thinking?'

'Do you?'

'Of course!'

At this point Larry joined them.

'Don't tell Hugo I said so, but get some of the Puligny-Montrachet before it disappears. Hello, Rupert. How's life?'

'Ticking along much as ever.'

'Isn't it wonderful having Pamela in town?'

'She certainly seems to be making the most of it,' said Rupert.

'I'm not sure how she manages it. Kitty keeps her on a very tight allowance.'

'A lady should never have to pay,' said Ivanov.

Pamela introduced Ivanov to Larry.

'Even so,' said Larry, 'there are things a girl needs beyond dinners and restaurants. Five pounds a month can't go very far.'

As he said this Pamela looked up quickly at Rupert, and Rupert caught the look, and a new idea entered his head.

'Don't worry about me, Larry,' she said. 'Everyone is so kind.'

'We pay tribute to beauty,' said Ivanov, giving a small bow.

Larry moved off to greet a new buyer who had just entered. Ivanov turned back to Rupert, serious once more.

'I do not believe in secrets, Mr Blundell. I believe secrecy breeds fear, and fear breeds aggression.'

Rupert nodded his head, and sipped his wine.

'An open flow of information, however,' said Ivanov, 'breeds trust, and trust breeds security for all.'

Rupert turned to Pamela.

'This spy of yours, Pamela,' he said, 'talks remarkably good sense.'

'Of course!' cried Ivanov. 'And you know why? Because I am only second naval attaché. Because I am not official spokesman. Because I am little fellow of no importance.' Here he seized Rupert by the arm. 'Don't you see? It's only we little fellows who can tell each other the truth!'

He went to the window and pointed out into the street.

'You see the car there? Those are British Secret Service agents. They follow me.'

Pamela was intrigued.

'What, everywhere?'

Ivanov shrugged.

'I always tell them where I'm going. Then they come. That's their job. But it's not secret.'

'Don't you do any real spying?' said Pamela. 'Don't you even have a secret spy camera?'

'Yes, yes, I have all that,' said Ivanov, waving one hand dismissively. 'My bosses are as stupid as Mr Blundell's bosses. They believe that information obtained by covert operations is more valuable than information that is freely given. That is stupidity.'

'Is it?' said Rupert. 'Your bosses would love to know our military capability, but we're not likely to give you that information freely.'

'Why not?' said Ivanov.

Rupert gazed at him, half smiling.

'If I keep a dog to frighten away thieves,' said Ivanov, 'why would I shut my dog in a kennel? No, let him out, where all can hear him bark!'

He looked once more out of the window.

'My friends are waiting. I must go.' He held out his hand to Rupert. 'Shall we meet again, Mr Blundell, more privately?'

'Yes, Captain,' said Rupert. 'I would like that.'

Ivanov produced a card.

'I am at your disposal.'

He left. Rupert and Pamela remained by the window. They saw Ivanov come out onto the street, and stride away towards Piccadilly. After a moment the car followed.

'He's quite a character,' said Pamela.

'Oddly enough, some of the things he said are pretty much what I've started to think myself.'

'Most people think he's a bit of a joke. But I like him.'

'I don't think your Captain Ivanov is a joke at all. I think he's a clever man. The question is, just how clever is he?'

'That's rather a mean thing to say,' said Pamela. 'Surely the question is, is he sincere?'

'You're quite right.'

'Shall we have some of Hugo's posh white wine? He insists on serving it at room temperature.'

Rupert laid one hand on her arm to detain her. He spoke softly.

'About Mary,' he said.

Pamela looked down.

'It was you, wasn't it?'

She didn't answer.

'Oh, Pamela. Can't you see? I'm not trying to get at you. What you do is your own business. But you know it's been torture for Mary.'

'I never said it was Mary.'

She was still avoiding his eyes. He waited.

'What will you do?' she said.

'I'd like Mary to know the truth.'

'And the others?'

'That's up to you.'

'It's not the way you think,' she said.

'Of course not. Nothing is ever the way we think.'

'So why dig it all up again?'

'I just want Mary's mind put at rest,' he said. 'Will you tell her, or shall I?'

'I will.'

'She won't blame you, or judge you. She's not like that.'

Pamela looked up, and said with a trace of bitterness, 'You think very well of Mary, don't you?'

'Yes,' he said.

It was almost nine o'clock. The wine tasting was coming to an end. Most of the clients had left. Hugo finally felt free to attend to his friends.

'It's always a bit hectic for a while,' he said.

'How's it gone?' said Rupert.

'Well, I think. The new Rhônes were a big hit.' He smiled at Pamela. 'If your father were here, he'd be amazed. In his day we wouldn't have dreamed of offering wines at these sorts of prices. But those *vins de pays* he came up with, they were fun to drink. And that's what it's all about in the end.'

Pamela said nothing. Hugo thought perhaps his reference to her father had been tactless.

'Pamela's a terrific hit, you know,' he said to Rupert. 'We all love her.'

Larry came in the taxi with Hugo and Pamela back to Brook Green, where he was staying the night. They found Harriet in the drawing-room with Mary sitting beside her, reading to her aloud. They were reading a Georgette Heyer novel called *A Civil Contract*.

'My eyes get so tired,' said Harriet. 'And Mary has such a lovely voice.'

Hugo kissed her.

'How's the book?' he said. 'Don't tell me. There's one heroine who's plain but worthy, and another who's beautiful but worthless.'

Mary laughed, and then gave Harriet an apologetic look.

'Hello, Larry,' said Harriet. 'Did your evening go well?'

'Very well,' said Larry. 'I have no complaints.'

Pamela excused herself and went up to her room. There she sat in the armchair by the window and smoked a cigarette and thought what best to do.

She felt cross with Rupert. As she saw it, the whole fuss over the money had died down, and no real harm had been done. She felt no guilt about taking it. The money was Hugo's, and Hugo and her stepfather were partners. It was like taking money from her own parents. She would have asked for it openly, except she could never have made them understand why she needed it. She knew with absolute clarity that the two worlds did not intersect: the world of her family, and the world of André's party. What made sense in one world was nonsense in the other. How could she have made even Hugo, who indulged her in all things, comprehend the absolute necessity of buying expensive black underwear? Under such circumstances she had taken the only path open to her, and had been proved right a hundredfold. She had no regrets.

Pamela had wanted her triumph so intensely that it had come to seem to her to be worth whatever price she might have to pay. The taking of the money had become an act of courage – it had taken courage – in the pursuit of a noble cause. She had not anticipated that Mary would fall under suspicion. Even now she couldn't stop herself from feeling that Mary was the most to blame, for making her life such a secret that she appeared to be the likely culprit.

Pamela was also irritated with Rupert because of his fondness for Mary. This wasn't jealousy. Pamela had no interest in Rupert for herself. It was more that Rupert's preference for Mary seemed wilfully perverse. Of course one never said such things aloud, but Mary was the sort that you pitied, the humble kind who had learned to be content with a humble life. It was all horribly unfair, but what could she do about that? So it was annoying of Rupert to treat Mary as if she had the same claims to consideration as the rest of them. Pamela suspected it was some sort of moralism aimed at her, a punishment for her good looks. Rupert was, after all, a man. Men desired her. Why should Rupert be any different? So desiring her, and knowing she was beyond his reach, he looked for a means to punish her. He singled out Mary for his attentions. And when the occasion arose, he forced her into a position where she had to humiliate herself in front of Mary.

So reasoned Pamela, sitting by her window, wishing the whole ridiculous little mess would just go away.

She heard footsteps coming up the stairs, and on up the attic stairs. Mary going to her room. With a cross little shake of her head, Pamela stubbed out her cigarette and rose to go after her.

She tapped on the attic bedroom door.

'May I come in?'

Mary was surprised, and a little ashamed. The room was very plainly furnished.

'Yes, of course,' she said. 'I'm afraid there's nowhere to sit.'

'We can sit on the bed.'

So they sat on the bed, side by side.

'There's something I have to tell you,' said Pamela, wanting to get it over as quickly as possible. 'You'll be terribly cross with me.'

'Oh, I'm sure I shan't.'

Her soft Irish lilt grated on Pamela's ear. Now Mary would be Christian and forgiving. But it had to be done.

'You know that money that was taken? It was me.'

'You!'

'I should have owned up. I never knew they'd suspect you. I was going to give the money back, as soon as I could. Then it all turned into such a fuss, I just got scared.'

'Oh, Pamela.'

'I can't tell you why I needed the money. But I did.'

'How awful for you!'

This was harder than Pamela had expected. She had no wish to be pitied by Mary.

'I'd rather you didn't say anything to Harriet or Hugo.'

'No, of course I won't.'

'If it comes up again I'll tell them that I'm perfectly sure it wasn't you. They won't blame you, I promise.'

'I think,' said Mary hesitantly, 'that Hugo still believes it was me took the money.'

'I'll tell him he's wrong. I'll tell him you and I have talked about it, and there's no doubt in my mind.'

'Won't he ask you how you can be so sure?'

Pamela understood this to mean she should confess the truth to Hugo. This caused her irritation to surface.

'Really, Mary, you've only yourself to blame. Why do you have to make such a mystery out of your life?'

'I'm sorry,' said Mary.

'I don't know what sort of a mess you've got yourself into, but I'm sure everyone would understand if you told us. Everyone makes mistakes.'

'So they do.'

'Unless you've done a murder or something.'

'Oh, no! Nothing like that!'

'Well, I've told you about a bad thing I did. So you're one up on me now. But you're still keeping your secrets.'

'I'm sorry. Truly I am.'

'You know the worst thing about secrets? People start imagining things. And what they imagine is far worse than the truth.'

Mary hung her head in silence. Pamela knew she shouldn't press her any more, but the devil in her was driving her on, saying to her, 'She's no better than you are. She's got something to hide too.'

'You know, Mary, we don't even know where you come from. What if something were to happen to you? What if you fell ill? What if you were dying?'

'I don't mind dying.'

She sounded so lost, and so unhappy. Pamela felt exasperated.

'So you wouldn't want your family told?'

Mary was silent. Some instinct told Pamela to remain silent too, and let Mary's conscience do the work.

After some moments, Mary said, 'County Donegal. Kilnacarry.'

'That's where you come from?'

Mary nodded.

'So if anything happens to you, that's where we send word?'

She nodded again. Her face had gone very pale.

'All right. We'd better go to bed now.'

She got up off the bed.

'I'm sorry about the money.'

Mary gave a shake of her head that said, That's all over.

'Just our secret,' said Pamela.

A mute nod.

Pamela left, closing the attic door behind her. Back in her own room she took out paper and pencil and wrote down what Mary had said, so she wouldn't forget it.

Donegal. Kilnacarry.

28

The increase in the number of Soviet freighters docking in Cuban ports in August was noted by the CIA. Interviews with Cuban refugees in Miami revealed that the cargoes were being unloaded under conditions of maximum security. Trucks were being lowered by crane into the holds of ships, and lifted out again with the payloads covered by tarpaulins.

'So what's going on, John?' Bobby Kennedy said to John McCone, the Director of the CIA.

They were gathered in the Oval Office, the close-knit group round the president. Mac Bundy had his glasses off and was polishing the lenses, frowning at the news. Kennedy himself was sitting sprawled across one of the armchairs, his legs dangling.

'Well, it's weapons, that's for sure,' said McCone. 'The question is, what weapons? What if it's nukes?'

'Are you telling us the Soviets are putting nukes on Cuba?' said Bundy, sceptical.

'We've no hard evidence of that,' said McCone. 'But my hunch is they will.'

Bob McNamara shook his head, irritated.

'Khrushchev would be insane to put nukes on Cuba.'

'Maybe so,' said McCone. 'But the intelligence shows that

Soviet military aid to Cuba is increasing all the time. Even if they're not bringing in nukes, they're arming Castro to the point where we'll never get him out of there. And so long as Castro controls Cuba, the Soviets have got themselves a launch pad right by Florida.'

The president listened, swinging his legs, saying nothing. He turned his gaze on his Secretary of State, inviting his views.

'We can't launch an unprovoked attack on a sovereign nation,' said Dean Rusk, 'because of something they might do to us in the future.'

'Fine,' said McCone. 'Don't say I didn't warn you.'

'I hear you, John,' said the president. 'I don't like this arms build-up any more than you do. But if we make a move against Cuba they're going to retaliate. They'll take Berlin. We can't risk that.'

'Can we risk letting them put nukes on Cuba?'

'No. That would be unacceptable. But let's be damn sure they're doing it first.'

'Then send the U2s out again, sir.'

Mac Bundy shook his head.

'You do that, they'll shoot 'em down.'

'Can they do that?' said Kennedy.

'It's a risk,' said McCone. 'We believe they have at least eight SAMs at operational level.'

Kennedy blinked at him. Slowly he pulled himself upright and rose from the chair.

'You're telling me there are operational Soviet missiles on Cuba?'

He was imagining the newspaper headlines.

'Anti-aircraft missiles,' said McNamara. 'Defensive, not offensive.'

'This thing is moving too damn fast,' muttered Kennedy. He crossed to his desk, grimacing at the pain in his back.

'Send in the U2s,' said McCone. 'Then we'll know what's going on.'

'And have a SAM knock one of our boys out of the sky?' said Bundy.

Kennedy was looking over his desk diary.

'Aren't you supposed to be getting married, John?' he said to McCone.

'August 30th, sir. We've planned a honeymoon on the French Riviera.'

'Can I come?'

Everyone laughed.

'So what do we do?' said Kennedy.

'Maybe we should fire some kind of warning shot,' said Bundy.

'I'm with you there,' said Bobby Kennedy. 'We need to slow these fuckers down.'

The president nodded.

'Draft a statement. Show 'em we know what's going on. Show 'em where we draw the line.'

On September 4 the president's press secretary, Pierre Salinger, released a statement to the press.

Information has reached this Government in the last four days from a variety of sources which establishes without a doubt that the Soviets have provided the Cuban government with a number of anti-aircraft defense missiles. Further information will be made available as fast as it is obtained and verified. The gravest issues would arise if Soviet military bases are found on the island, or offensive ground-to-ground missiles, or any other significant offensive capability.

Oleg Troyanovsky was with Khrushchev at the chairman's dacha on the Black Sea when the statement came through.

He read it out as he translated it, doing his best to speak in neutral unemphatic tones. Even so, he could hear from Khrushchev's laboured breathing as he listened that the chairman was rattled.

'They've discovered Operation Anadyr,' Khrushchev said, smacking at his head, rubbing his brow.

'There's nothing in the statement to suggest that, Comrade Chairman,' Troyanovsky murmured.

'Read it to me again.'

On the second hearing Khrushchev's nervous panic receded. He realised that Kennedy knew nothing for certain.

'He's banging sticks in the forest in case there are wolves.'

Still, that one phrase worried him: *the gravest issues would arise.* Soon now Kennedy would learn the truth. What would he do?

'When will the R-12s and the R-14s come into full operation?'

'Mid-October,' said Troyanovsky.

'Five weeks.' He looked up at his adviser. 'Do you think they'll find them in that time?'

'We have to be prepared for that possibility, Comrade Chairman.'

'And if they do, will they invade?'

This was precisely what Troyanovsky and others had feared all along. But Khrushchev would not thank him for saying 'I told you so.'

'We have to be prepared for that possibility also.'

'Prepared how?' Khrushchev jumped up and began to gesticulate. 'You think the Cuban Army can fight off an American invasion?'

'Perhaps Comrade Castro could make them a speech,' said Troyanovsky.

Khrushchev burst into laughter. Castro's interminable speeches were one of the jokes of the socialist world.

'But seriously, Oleg Alexandrovich,' said the chairman, 'is it possible that we could lose Cuba?'

'We have to be prepared—'

'Yes, yes, yes. You and your have-to-be-prepared! Well, I'm not prepared to be fucked in the ass!'

Khrushchev summoned Marshal Malinowsky.

'We must defend Cuba,' he said. 'If the Americans attack, will it be by air or by sea?'

'Both,' said Malinowsky. 'First they'll bomb the coastal defences. Then amphibious landings.'

'Can they be stopped?'

'Not by conventional means, Nikita Sergeyevich.'

'Then by what means?'

'Lunas. FKRs.'

'These are nuclear weapons?'

'Small battlefield nuclear missiles, Nikita Sergeyevich. The Luna has a range of thirty miles, and carries a two-kiloton warhead. The blast would wipe out a battalion and leave a crater over a hundred feet deep. The FKR is a nuclear-tipped cruise missile with enough power to destroy an aircraft carrier.'

'How fast can you get such weapons over there?'

Malinowsky referred this question to the logistics experts in the Ministry of Defence in Moscow. Khrushchev, meanwhile, had a courtesy visit to make.

The eminent poet Robert Frost was in the Soviet Union, on a cultural exchange. He had let it be known that he would welcome a meeting with the leader of the socialist world. Khrushchev had not been inclined to interrupt his vacation, but now it seemed to him there was value in the meeting. The 88-year-old poet was even now resting in a hotel nearby.

'Let us show the world that our intentions are peaceful. Does this poet write poems in praise of peace? Most of them do.'

Out of respect for his fame and his venerable age, Khrushchev called on Frost in his hotel room, accompanied by Oleg Troyanovsky.

The poet was lying on his bed. He sat up when Khrushchev entered, and extended a wrinkled hand.

'This is an honour, Mr Chairman.'

'The honour is mine,' said Khrushchev.

Their exchange, passing back and forth through Troyanovsky, was a model of goodwill. The old poet had thought long and hard about the rivalry of the two superpowers, and had concluded that for the sake of world peace there must be mutual respect.

'Both countries must trust each other and speak honestly to each other,' he urged Khrushchev. 'Let there be rivalry, but let it be truthful, honourable rivalry. No deception, no propaganda, no name-calling. You hold great power in your hand. You have a duty to the world to use it responsibly.'

Khrushchev listened politely, nodding his head. These were the kinds of sentiments out of which most Soviet homilies were built. He was happy to agree with every word.

'You have the soul of a poet,' he told the old man.

Robert Frost was elated. He had achieved his goal. He had told the leader of the Communist world, face to face, without beating about the bush, what had to be done for the sake of the world, and Khrushchev had agreed with him.

'You're a great man,' he told Khrushchev, exhausted by his efforts.

Khrushchev returned to Pitsunda. There waiting for him was Mikoyan with a hand-delivered package from the Ministry of Defence listing the battlefield nuclear weapons that could be shipped to Cuba. The recommendation was that two divisions of Luna missiles be sent, and one FKR brigade, accompanied by a squadron of Il-28 light bombers equipped with twelvekiloton nuclear bombs of the type known as Tatyanas. This range of weapons was small enough to move into place quickly, but potent enough to destroy a beachhead in the event of invasion.

'Can they go by plane?'

'The Ministry recommends sending the warheads by sea. The *Indigirka* is ready to leave right away.'

Khrushchev signed the secret authorisation that day. The Soviet freighter *Indigirka* was loaded in total secrecy with eighteen battlefield warheads, thirty-six cruise missile nuclear warheads, and forty-five one-megaton warheads for the medium-range ballistic missiles that had already reached Cuba.

'These weapons are not to be used,' Khrushchev instructed, 'without my direct order.'

'What if communications to Moscow are cut, Nikita Sergeyevich?' said Mikoyan. 'What if an invasion is under way, but General Pliyev can't reach you?'

'Then he must use his own judgement,' said Khrushchev. 'I will not allow Cuba to fall.'

The *Indigirka* sailed for the Caribbean on September 15, with an expected journey time of twenty days. It was carrying over twenty times the explosive power of all the bombs dropped on Germany in the entire Second World War.

While the *Indigirka* was at sea, a CIA agent in Cuba reported suspicious activity in the area round San Cristobal. Soviet soldiers were guarding a fifty-mile stretch of the main road from Havana to Pinar del Rio. Local people told stories of large trailer trucks carrying tarpaulin-covered cargoes that were knocking down telegraph poles as they negotiated tight corners in village streets. At the same time, Senator Keating had renewed his attacks on President Kennedy for allowing the Soviet arming of Cuba.

In the light of the latest information, the Executive Committee agreed that they had no choice but to resume high-level reconnaissance flights. There was a real risk that a U2 pilot would be shot down over Cuba, but it had become vital to gain accurate information about developments on the ground. The president authorised the Committee on Overhead Reconnaissance to resume U2 flights, with special attention to the San Cristobal area.

A successful mission required clear visibility from the ground all the way up to the U2's flying ceiling of seventy thousand feet. It was now hurricane season in the Caribbean. For the next few days the skies were overcast.

29

Dr Edward Sugden's waiting room in Half Moon Street, Mayfair, was strange and a little frightening. The walls were lined
with glass cases containing snakes and lizards. At first Pamela
thought they were stuffed. Then one of the lizards opened a
yellow eye and stared at her, giving her a small silent shock. She
told herself that the lizard could not have any opinion of her,
but she felt the cold chill of its indifference.

There was one other woman in the room. She was expen-
sively dressed, in her thirties, inattentively reading a copy of
Vogue. She was called before Pamela, by a male voice through a
half-open door. Within five minutes she was out again.

'Miss Avenell?'

The man at the consulting-room door was older than she had
expected, and balding, with wavy curls of white hair on the
back of his head. His face was puffy and lined.

'Come in, come in. Tell me what I can do for you. Tell me
how you heard of me.'

He indicated that Pamela should sit down on an upright
wooden chair, while he took his place behind a wide desk, and
opened up a new file. She told him that Christine Keeler had
recommended him, and that she needed to be 'fixed up'.

'Quite right,' he said. 'Doesn't do for young girls to be having babies they don't want. One day the government will wake up, and you'll be able to do this on the National Health. Lovely girl, Christine. How is she?'

'She's fine,' said Pamela, thinking how odd it was that this old man should know all Christine's intimate details. And her own, soon enough.

'So let's take a look at you.'

Following his instructions, she partially undressed and lay down on the examination couch, a blanket over her lower body.

'If you're a friend of Christine's,' he said, 'I don't expect you're shy. Flex your thighs, please.'

He eased a pillow beneath her buttocks.

'I'm going to conduct a simple examination. One finger, that's all.'

She closed her eyes and tried not to think about what was happening. She felt his probing finger. For what seemed like a long time, his finger moved inside her, but he didn't speak.

'Is everything all right?' she said.

She had no idea what she meant by this question, except that suddenly it seemed important to know.

'Yes,' he said. Then, with a faint note of surprise, 'Not sexually active yet?'

'No,' she said.

'A wise virgin, I see. Not many of those about these days. I wish all girls were as sensible as you.'

His finger continued to probe.

'You're in luck,' he said. 'Not much in the way of a hymen.'

'Is that normal?'

'Perfectly normal.'

He withdrew his finger.

'You'd be surprised how many girls ask me that. "Am I normal down there?"'

He laughed as if this were amusing. But Pamela realised this was exactly what she wanted to know.

'Here's something that should help you,' he said. 'A lot of girls don't realise how their body's put together. Give me your hand.'

He took her right hand and guided it beneath the blanket.

'Vagina is Latin for sheath, you know? Like the sheath for a sword. So which direction do you think it goes inside your body?'

Pamela had never in her life asked herself this question.

'I expect you think it goes upwards.'

'I don't know,' said Pamela.

'Well, feel for yourself.' He guided her finger. 'Do you feel it? It goes front to back. That's worth knowing. Not up and down at all, but front to back. Can you feel that?'

'Yes,' said Pamela.

'Have a good rummage around. Get to know the lie of the land.'

He moved away from her. She heard clicking and clattering noises.

'This is what you've come for,' he said. 'I'm going to fit you with something called a diaphragm. It's an awkward little bugger, but you'll get used to it.'

He returned to her side. Pamela opened her eyes. Teddy Sugden was holding up a large saucer of beige-coloured rubber.

'You may have heard of it as a Dutch cap. Basically it just sits inside you and puts a stopper on the whole works. Very simple, and very effective. You can put it in up to eight hours before, if you want.'

It seemed to Pamela's alarmed gaze to be far too big.

'I'll show you first,' he said. 'Then you have a go.'

He squeezed the saucer in his hand and the sides bent inwards, turning it into a narrow scoop.

'A little blob to help' – he added something from a tube – 'not Vaseline or anything made of petroleum jelly, because it rots the rubber. This is a spermicide, and it does half the work.'

She felt his warm hand between her legs. Then there came a brief cramp of pain. Then it was in.

'Can you feel it?'

'Not really.'

'Good. Now see if you can get it out and put it in again yourself.'

Pamela fumbled with her right hand. It wasn't at all easy. She got hold of it, but it wouldn't come out.

'You have to squeeze it,' said Teddy Sugden.

She squeezed it, and managed to get it out, but as soon as it was free the sides sprang open, and it jumped out of her hand to the floor.

'Don't worry,' he said, retrieving it. 'You'll be chasing it all over the bedroom often enough. Just give it a clean.' He wiped the cap and gave it back to her. 'Now see if you can get it in.'

It was quite a struggle. She managed in the end, but the effort left her tense and trembling.

'There has to be a better way,' she said.

'There's condoms. But not all girls trust their boyfriends on that front.'

After several attempts she found she could insert the cap, and remove it, but the whole process dismayed her. It was not at all sexy. Very much the opposite. To add to the burdensome nature of the process, she had to take in details of spermicidal jelly, and what to do if her lover had multiple orgasms, and how many hours to leave the cap in place afterwards, and how to wash her hands every time she touched it, and how to clean it every time it jumped onto the floor.

Then he asked her for ten guineas, and she burst into tears.

It wasn't just the money. It was the passing of the dream.

She knew very little about lovemaking, but she had imagined it as a more intimate, more thrilling version of kissing, which in turn was the physical expression of mutual desire. Scenes in books and films had led her to expect a mysterious and uncontrollable crescendo of excitement, in which beautiful bodies, lost in a trance of passion, experienced sensations of bliss. There was no bliss, no passion, in this clumsy precalculated jelly-slicked act of self-protection. In her dreams of lovemaking there had been no physical details. What was to happen *down there* was to take place spontaneously, urgently, in obedience to natural instincts. Now, for the first time, she was faced with a very different reality. Sex was dangerous, and embarrassing, and expensive.

Christine didn't much like sex, Stephen had said. A lot of women don't, he had said. Mandy did it with Peter with her back to him, as if she couldn't bear to look at him. Why? Why did any woman do it? Because it's what men wanted, presumably. Sex was the price women paid for love.

'Here,' said Teddy Sugden, giving her a tissue. 'Dry your eyes. Tell me how much you can afford.'

'I've got five pounds,' whispered Pamela. 'Christine said that would be enough. I haven't told my parents.'

'Yes, yes, I understand. We'll call it five pounds, then, shall we? Better that than you coming back to me in a few months' time with a far bigger problem.'

She put her clothes back on and gave him the five pounds she had borrowed from Stephen Ward. He packed up the cap in its box together with a tube of cream, and gave it all to her in a brown paper bundle.

'You'll get the hang of it,' he said. 'Come back in a couple of months, so we can be sure we've got the right fit. Give my love to Christine.'

30

That same afternoon Rupert was meeting Ivanov by arrangement at Stephen Ward's flat in Wimpole Mews. Stephen himself joined them, to act, as he said jokingly, as a neutral observer.

'I hope I'm not wasting your time, Captain,' said Rupert.

'Eugene, please. Call me Eugene.'

The walls of the living room were hung with Stephen Ward's portraits, mostly pencil sketches. Rupert studied them unseeingly as they talked.

'You do understand, I hope,' he said to Ivanov, 'I'm not in a position to pass you any information of any kind.'

'Mr Blundell,' said Ivanov. 'Rupert – may I call you Rupert? Stephen here knows me well. Stephen, tell Rupert what it is I want most in the world. What is it I say to you, many times?'

'Eugene wants peace,' said Stephen.

'You know what Chairman Khrushchev says?' said Ivanov. 'He says, "Communism is the best life for everyone. Why should we carry it to other countries on bayonets?"'

'Do the people of East Germany agree with that?' said Rupert.

'Some do, some don't.' Ivanov waved the issue aside with one hand. 'Socialism is young, the socialist countries are poor, capitalism offers many temptations. All we ask for is the chance to make our dream come true. For that we need peace.'

'No one is against peace,' said Rupert.

'Then why does General Curtis LeMay, who commands the United States Air Force, say in public that the Soviet Union should be bombed out of existence?'

Rupert gave a shrug of his shoulders and turned round to offer Ivanov his full attention.

'LeMay's a soldier. Soldiers think about winning battles. But I can assure you he takes his orders from his elected leader.'

'You do understand, Rupert, that we in the Soviet Union have reason to fear attack by the West? We are surrounded by nuclear missiles. In Germany, in Italy, in Turkey, and here in Britain.'

'Yes, I understand.'

'There are many regions of great tension. Most of all West Berlin.'

'Yes.'

'One day there will be a spark. A flash of fire.' He reached forward and tapped Rupert on the arm. 'On that day, how will war be averted? A war that will begin with two tanks, perhaps at Checkpoint Charlie, and will explode within days, within hours, into a global holocaust.'

He sat himself down in one of the armchairs, staring at Rupert, nodding his big handsome head.

'I can only hope,' said Rupert, 'that saner counsels will prevail.'

As if to show his willingness to achieve this end, he too sat down. He was realising that his first instincts had been right: he and the Russian had much in common.

'You think,' said Ivanov, 'there will be no temptation on either side to launch a pre-emptive first strike?'

'The temptation exists,' said Rupert. 'But I don't believe either our leaders or yours want a global holocaust.'

'You don't want it,' said Ivanov. 'We don't want it. But if you think we might do it, or if we think you might do it, then either of us might choose to do it first.'

'That's the problem of intention,' said Rupert. 'I've been doing a lot of thinking about that.'

'The problem of intention?'

'We base our assessments of our enemy's intentions on our worst fears, and so we're drawn into needless aggression.'

'That is so true!' exclaimed Ivanov. 'Stephen, this is a wise man! Tell him, he speaks like me!'

'Eugene believes,' said Stephen, 'and I agree with him, for what it's worth, that should a crisis occur the greatest danger is that the opposing leaders mistake each other's purposes. They don't speak each other's language. There's no direct phone link from Washington or London to Moscow. All communication is through layers of intermediaries. There will be distortions and misunderstandings.'

'And there will be misinformation,' said Ivanov. 'There are many who will seek to control the message. We too have generals like Curtis LeMay. This is what you call the problem of intention.'

'Exactly,' said Rupert. 'I believe the only way out of the present situation, which is essentially a balance of terror, is to transfer the intelligence effort from weapons to intentions. We must become far better informed about the minds of our opponents.'

'Yes!' cried Ivanov. 'Yes, and again yes! I am the man who can make this happen!'

'You?'

'I can have a report on Khrushchev's desk in twenty minutes.'

Rupert raised his eyebrows.

'That's quite a claim.'

'The Soviet system has many failings. One of its failings is a distrust of official channels. They are seen as forms of propaganda. A secret report from a second naval attaché who has formed his own private relationships in a foreign capital will be given more weight than an official communiqué from that capital's foreign minister.'

'I see.'

'I am not a rogue operator, Rupert. Everything I do is cleared with my superior at the embassy, and by him with his superior in Moscow. I am known to have friends in the British ruling circles. I have been authorised to build a private bridge between our leaders and yours. But bridges, you know, must not be too long, or the river will wash them away. I can offer you two arches. From me to my boss. From him to Khrushchev.'

'And you want a bridge from me to Mountbatten, and from Mountbatten to the prime minister.'

'And from Macmillan to Kennedy.'

'Yes. I can see that.'

Rupert sat in silence, pondering. Stephen went into the kitchen to make a pot of coffee.

'Tell me, Eugene,' said Rupert at last, 'isn't an initiative of this sort unusual for a man in your position?'

'I think so, yes.'

'You must be a very ambitious man.'

'Ah, I see. You think I do this for my own glory.' He turned and called to Stephen in the kitchen. 'Am I a vain man, Stephen?'

'Vain as a peacock,' Stephen called back.

Ivanov laughed.

'In my squadron,' he said, 'in the Black Sea fleet, I was graded the top of my artillery class. The number one. I was hand-picked to join the Academy of the Soviet Army. I received an honorary gold medal. So yes, I have a high opinion of myself. But let me also tell you about my father. He fought on the Valdai in '41. He was awarded the highest combat decorations,

268

the Order of Lenin, and the Order of the Red Banner. But he was very badly wounded, and sent back to us in Sverdlosk. I was fifteen years old. I saw how war had turned him into an old man. He died only a few years later. Because of that, even though I wear a uniform and am a patriotic citizen, I hate war. I fear war. And I will do all in my power to prevent it.'

Stephen came in with a tray of coffee.

'Wouldn't that be something?' he said. 'I can see the headlines now: "Men of Goodwill Save the World."'

'There'll be no headlines,' said Ivanov. 'The leaders will take the credit.'

'So describe to me,' said Rupert, 'the kind of traffic that will pass over this bridge of yours, that will save the world.'

'I will give you an example,' said Ivanov. 'A Soviet missile shoots down an American spyplane that enters Soviet airspace. The American public demands reprisals. The Soviet leadership threatens to attack the base of the spyplane. The American military pushes for a pre-emptive attack. The rhetoric on both sides becomes more belligerent. Through our bridge we communicate that the aggressive words are all for the maintenance of national prestige. There will be no attacks. The American president is able to restrain his generals. So the incident passes.'

'Well,' said Rupert after a pause. 'That's all very interesting.'

'We have a deal?'

At this point Pamela came in, carrying a brown paper package.

'Oh, hello, Rupert,' she said. 'Are you having your secret meeting?'

'Very secret,' said Ivanov, pointing out of the window. 'See? No car. I gave my escort the slip, as you say.'

'Is it all right if I go and lie down in Christine's room?' Pamela said to Stephen. 'I'm feeling really done in. I can't face slogging all the way out to Brook Green.'

'Go ahead,' said Stephen. 'I've no idea where Christine is.'

Pamela gave them all a faint wave and left. Rupert rose.

'Let's keep in touch,' he said, shaking Ivanov's hand. 'You interest me very much. Who knows what the future will bring?'

31

André arranged for Pamela to be driven down to his house in the country by a friend of his called Bobby Marchant. Bobby and Charlotte, his girlfriend or wife, were to be weekend guests too. Pamela had understood that the weekend was to be André and herself alone, and that in accepting the invitation she had tacitly agreed to sleep with him. Now she was not so sure. She was nervous about the prospect of her first sexual experience; both excited and apprehensive; but most of all she wanted it over and done with.

Bobby drove a Bentley convertible. He was big and handsome, with dark swept-back hair and a broad chest like a rugby forward, which it turned out he had been at school. Charlotte was small and blonde, and more or less asleep, curled up on the car's back seat.

'She had a very late night,' said Bobby, smiling, showing excellent white teeth. 'She'll be fine in an hour or two.'

Pamela got in the front seat beside Bobby, and he drove off through a maze of London streets, over Putney Bridge. As they went they talked about André.

'Cleverest chap I've ever met,' said Bobby. 'Best friend a man could have.'

'Were you at school with him?'

'Not school, no. We met at Oxford.'

'I'm in a terrible muddle about André's nationality. He's Belgian, isn't he?'

'Probably. I think his dad's Belgian. His mother's English, very top-drawer. She's Lady Tillemans, by the way. You'll meet her. Very unusual woman. She lives at Herriard.'

Herriard was their destination. Pamela had thought it was the name of a village. Now it sounded like a house.

'Are his parents divorced?'

'Not divorced, as far as I know. Detached, more like. But they have so many houses, and move about so much, I don't see how anyone could ever know.'

'Everyone seems to be so fearfully rich. It makes my head spin.'

'All the Tillemans are rich. I think they may be the richest family in Europe, I'm not sure. But André never flashes it about. I don't think he cares a rap about money. All he spends it on is art.'

He threw her a glance.

'I don't suppose you've seen his collection?'

'No.'

'Quite something.'

'I think André almost wishes he wasn't rich,' said Pamela.

'You could be right. But I'll tell you what, Herriard's a nice place. You'll see, you get well looked after there. It takes money to be a good host.'

'It takes money for most things,' said Pamela with a sigh.

'You don't need to worry,' said Bobby. 'A girl as gorgeous as you shouldn't need to pay for a thing. André's a lucky fellow to have you.'

Pamela wasn't at all sure that André did have her. Perhaps by the end of the weekend her status would be clearer.

'So where do your people come from?' said Bobby.

'Sussex.'

'Do you know the Egremonts?'

'No,' said Pamela. 'We're not at all grand. My stepfather sells wine.'

'Oh, really? Where?'

'It's called Caulder & Avenell, in St James.'

'I know the place. Good business, I shouldn't wonder.'

'What do you do, Bobby?'

'I work for a bank. I persuade people to buy things for more than they're worth, and sell things for less than they're worth.'

'Why would anybody do that?'

'Ignorance. Greed. Vanity.'

'But you don't have any of that?'

'I have all of it.'

He grinned at her. Pamela found herself liking him.

'So who's the girl asleep in the back?'

'The girl asleep in the back is my wife. We've been married four months.'

'Congratulations.'

Herriard turned out to be both a village and a house. The house was set in a park down a long winding drive. It was a classic early nineteenth-century gentleman's residence, free from the usual Victorian additions, set on a slight rise, overlooking grounds that, according to Bobby, had been laid out by Humphrey Repton.

André himself came out to greet them. He was wearing a jersey and casual trousers, but still looked stylishly elegant. While Bobby roused Charlotte from the back seat, André kissed Pamela chastely on one cheek.

'I'm so happy you've come,' he said.

Commonplace words, but he held her eyes as he said them, and spoke as if he meant it. He then led her into the house to meet his mother.

Lady Tillemans was in a back pantry, cutting the long stalks off a heap of dahlias. She was a tall woman with greying hair pinned up in a bun, and a gravely beautiful face like her son's. She wore a dark-green apron and wielded a pair of secateurs.

'Mummy, this is Pamela.'

'How good of you to come,' said Lady Tillemans, not pausing in her work. Her voice was low, almost masculine. 'Aren't we lucky with the weather?'

André then led Pamela upstairs and along a passage to her bedroom. The room was pretty and feminine, with pink toile de Jouy curtains. The wide bed had a quilted counterpane embroidered with roses. There was a tall wardrobe, and a dressing table with a mirror on the wall above it.

'You should be comfortable here. The bathroom's across the passage.'

'It's lovely,' said Pamela.

'I'll leave you to sort yourself out. Come downstairs when you're ready. No rush.'

Left alone, Pamela unpacked her overnight bag and puzzled over what to wear now, and what to wear for dinner, and what to expect later. Would André sleep with her tonight? And if so, where? He had shown her to a room of her own, not to his bedroom; but this was his mother's house, and presumably the decencies had to be observed. On the other hand, she could have misread the signals. Just because he moved in the same circles as Christine and Mandy did not mean he shared their appetite for promiscuity.

Then she remembered the man at the party who said to her, 'Do you fuck?' This was André's world. Her instincts, she was sure, were not deceiving her.

That left the question of when she should insert the Dutch cap. Not at the last minute. She shuddered at the picture of herself breaking away from an intimate embrace to struggle with the spring-lined rubber and the cream. It must be done ahead of time. Teddy Sugden had set a limit of eight hours. It was now coming up to five in the afternoon. She had no way of knowing how late they might stay up. Best to wait.

She put on a simple cotton frock, and hung up her blue silk for later.

She came down to find Lady Tillemans arranging her flowers in the big drawing room.

'I think they're playing tennis,' she said. 'I expect they're hoping you'll go and admire them.'

She gave Pamela a keen appraising look as she said this.

'Then I'd better not let them down,' Pamela said.

'Oh, no,' replied Lady Tillemans. 'We must never let the boys down.'

Pamela laughed, presuming this to be said jokingly, but Lady Tillemans did not laugh.

'You'll find the court beyond the stables,' she said.

Pamela went out by a side door and across an empty stable block. The late afternoon sun lay golden on the grey stone of the buildings. Beyond the stables was a tennis court surrounded by a high wire fence. André and Bobby, both in whites, were playing hard. Bobby was excellent, which Pamela would have expected. The surprise was André. He was slighter than Bobby, and his serves lacked Bobby's raw power, but he was fast and accurate. It became clear that he was winning.

As they changed ends they turned and briefly saluted her, raising their racquets. Then they resumed play with fierce concentration. Pamela sat in the warm sun and watched them. She made no attempt to follow the score. Instead she let her eyes linger over their leaping bodies, over their long bare legs and sweeping arms. André graceful and beautiful, Bobby muscular and very male. She had never seen a man entirely naked.

They came to the end of the set and stopped at last. Pamela clapped. André had won. Both were sweating and happy.

'I let him win,' said Bobby to Pamela. 'Never show a man up in front of his girl.'

Pamela liked Bobby for that.

'Quick hose down,' said André, 'then I'll show you the park.'

'I'll go and rouse Charlotte,' said Bobby. 'I swear that girl could sleep for England.'

André re-emerged in a white open-neck shirt and white linen trousers, in honour of the golden evening.

'You look fresh as a daisy,' said Pamela. Then, annoyed with herself for saying something so obvious, 'What is it that's so fresh about daisies anyway?'

They strolled arm-in-arm down a grassy walk between high beeches to what had once been a sunken garden. It had been allowed to grow wild, but in a discreetly managed way. The stone pavers and low walls were overrun with acanthus and ox-eye daisies and soft-pink rock roses. At one end there was an open-fronted pagoda. They stood in its shade and looked back up the handsome vista to the main house.

'It's a lovely place, André,' said Pamela.

He took her in his arms and kissed her briefly and lightly on her lips.

'I've never seen anyone as lovely as you,' he said. 'I can't take my eyes off you.'

'You don't have to,' she said, smiling prettily. 'I won't wear out.'

'How do you like Bobby?'

'I like Bobby very much. He seems to me to be very straight-forward.'

'More so than me?'

'Much more. You're not straightforward at all. You're' – she searched for a word – 'enigmatic.'

'I'm sorry,' he said. 'I don't mean to be.'

'Then tell me more about yourself.'

'What would you like to know? My age? My inside leg measurement?'

'Yes,' she said.

'I'm thirty-two. That also happens to be my inside leg measurement.'

'As you grow older will your legs grow longer?'

'We shall have to see,' he said.

'And you've never married?'

'Not so far.'

'Why is that?'

'My darling girl,' he said, 'surely you don't need to ask? I'm a spoilt child. You must blame my mother.'

'You don't seem like a child to me. You seem like the most grown-up person I know.'

'Ah. You've spotted my secret. Beneath this debonair appearance, I'm actually over a thousand years old.'

They walked back across the sunken garden, back up the beech avenue.

'As well as blaming your mother,' said Pamela, 'I hope you thank her for all she's given you.'

'Yes, of course,' he said. Then after a pause, 'But one can be given too much.'

'Money, perhaps,' said Pamela. 'I was meaning love.'

'One can be given too much love,' said André.

'I don't see how,' said Pamela. 'It seems to me that the more love anyone's given, the better.'

André said nothing to this. He seemed to be pondering the point.

To provoke him, Pamela said, 'But I expect, being a man, you don't believe in love.'

'On the contrary,' he replied. 'I believe in love, as you put

277

it. But my mother – does she love me? There's a kind of love that's more than love. She lives for me. My happiness is her happiness.'

Pamela hardly knew how to respond. She understood that André was confiding in her, but was he proud of this strange love or burdened by it?

'I have no secrets from her,' André continued. 'To her, nothing I do can ever be wrong. She never judges me. All she asks is that I never close the door between us.'

'But you do love her?'

'Can you love someone,' he replied, 'who's so close you can no longer see them?'

Then realising he'd become far too serious for this sunny afternoon, he threw up his hands in mock despair.

'Listen to me! That's what you get when you question a thousand-year-old man.'

'I must say,' said Pamela, 'you don't look your age.'

He laughed at that. For a moment, laughing, he was like a child after all.

Bobby and Charlotte joined them for drinks in the big room with its tall west-facing windows. They drank Martinis and watched the sun descend over Repton's park. Charlotte was very pretty, in the English doll-like fashion, and seemed to be entirely disconnected from her husband. Whenever he spoke she looked at him with wide eyes, incredulous, as if she hadn't known he was capable of speech.

'When will you show Pamela your collection?' Bobby said to André.

'After dinner,' said André.

'I remember when he bought his first miniature,' said Bobby. 'He told me the price, I don't remember what, and asked me if I thought it was worth it. I said, "Absolutely not, the chap saw you coming!" But he got it anyway.'

'It's worth ten times what I paid for it now.'

'What's the point of miniatures?' said Charlotte. 'Why not have proper-size paintings you can actually see?'

'You carry them around with you,' said Bobby. 'Portraits of your beloved.'

'Do you carry one round with you?'

'No, of course not.'

'And anyway,' said Charlotte, 'they're not André's beloveds. Or are they?'

'They are indeed,' said André. 'I love them all.'

'I suppose it's like snapshots,' said Pamela. 'People carry snaps of their loved ones round with them.'

'Bobby doesn't,' said Charlotte.

'Your image,' said André to Charlotte gallantly, 'is graven on his heart.'

Charlotte stared at him for a moment, and then burst into laughter.

After drinks they retired to change for dinner. Back up in her pretty pink room Pamela undressed, took out the zipped bag in which she kept her diaphragm, and began the exhausting battle to insert it. She had only done this before in Teddy Sugden's consulting room, and though she had memorised every step, she found it simply would not go where it was supposed to go. After several attempts she managed to get it far enough in, but then she realised she'd forgotten the spermicidal cream, and had to take it out and start again. A further protracted struggle followed. On the third go she decided she'd got it as well in as she was ever going to, and if she'd done it wrong it was too bad.

Dinner was formal, served by a woman who had not been in evidence before. Herriard had a resident staff of four, but Lady Tillemans liked to maintain the illusion that it was a simple family home. She was constantly thanking the staff, as if it were sheer kindness that motivated them.

'You are an angel, Betty. Yes, you can clear away the plates now.'

The wine was excellent and flowed freely. André and Bobby looked magnificent in their dinner jackets. Pamela wore her best silk frock, midnight-blue with a low neckline, which had been a present from her stepfather. Charlotte wore a loose-knit silk jumper, through which it looked as if you could see her breasts, but in fact you couldn't.

André turned his gaze again and again to Pamela, who was across the table from him. When she met his glance he smiled. She liked seeing him in these home surroundings. He seemed gentler, more serene. Bobby and Charlotte both drank too much. This made Bobby noisier, and Charlotte less inhibited.

'So how well do you know André?' said Charlotte to Pamela.

'How can I answer that?' said Pamela. 'How well does anyone ever know anyone?'

'Goodness gracious! What a question!'

'I have a friend,' said Pamela, thinking of Rupert, 'who believes people are unknowable.'

'Really?' said Charlotte. 'How about that? Bobby, I'm unknowable. So are you.'

'Okay with me,' said Bobby. 'Makes life more fun. Meeting new people's a great adventure.'

'An adventure?' said Charlotte. 'Do you mean like a safari?'

'Sure,' said Bobby. 'Why not?'

'Bobby's a hunter,' said Charlotte. 'Take care. He shoots things.'

Lady Tillemans' gravelly voice interjected here.

'I once shot a man in Scotland. We had to pick the pellets out of his legs.'

'Perhaps I should reassure your guests, Mummy,' said André. 'It was an accident.'

'Yes, that's perfectly true,' said Lady Tillemans. 'Still, he deserved it.'

At the end of dinner Lady Tillemans rose and nodded to Pamela and Charlotte.

'Shall we leave the gentlemen to their port?'

Pamela followed Lady Tillemans into the drawing room, where coffee was laid out waiting for them. Charlotte went off to powder her nose. Lady Tillemans poured coffee, and indicated with a slight gesture of one hand the inlaid wooden box containing cigarettes.

'You smoke, I believe.'

Gratefully, Pamela lit up a cigarette.

'That silly girl asked you how well you know my son.' She spoke abruptly in her deep voice, startling Pamela. 'But of course you don't know him at all.'

This was certainly direct enough. Alerted by her earlier conversation with André, Pamela understood that this was in the nature of a warning shot. The mother was laying claim to the son. Pamela was a guest in the house, and more or less out of her depth, but she had a fighting spirit of her own.

'At least I can presume he enjoys my company,' she said.

'Of course. You're pretty.' This in a dismissive tone. 'I was pretty in my day.'

'André tells me you and he are very close.'

Lady Tillemans smiled coldly.

'He's my son,' she said. And then, turning away, taking out and lighting a cigarette, 'He cares nothing for you.'

Pamela flushed with anger.

'And yet here I am,' she said.

'Yes. Here you are. I wonder if you know why.'

This was becoming unbearable. Before Pamela could respond, Charlotte rejoined them, greeting them with an enormous yawn.

'God, the countryside always makes me so sleepy.'

'How fortunate, then,' said Lady Tillemans, 'that the countryside comes furnished with bedrooms.'

'I don't want to see this collection of André's,' said Charlotte plaintively. 'I want to go to bed.'

'Oh, you must admire André's collection,' said his mother. 'He's so proud of it.'

Shortly after this she announced that she was retiring for the night.

Left alone with Charlotte, Pamela said, 'Have you met Lady Tillemans before?'

'No,' said Charlotte. 'Never.'

'She's quite unusual.'

'I expect she's off her rocker,' said Charlotte. 'A lot of these rich old women are.'

André and Bobby now entered. André was twirling a key on a chain.

'Mummy gone to bed?'

'Just gone up,' said Pamela.

'Right, then. Time for the tour.'

The miniatures were kept in a locked room to which only André had the key. Here they were displayed on sloping shelves in glass cases. Concealed lights in the frames of the cases came on at the touch of a switch.

'You have to view them in the right order,' said André. 'Start with the case on your right and work your way round the room.'

The miniatures were mostly painted enamel on bronze medallions. They showed ladies, some head only, most from the waist up. The subjects were all young, they were all pretty, and many of them were décolleté.

André indicated some of the best specimens.

'This is Boucher, of course. This is Charlier. This is Greuze.'

The pretty little portraits soon blurred into one, as the eye slipped from shelf to shelf. All wore the same simpering expression on their soft little faces, as if they were saying to their lovers, 'Aren't I just adorable?' Still tense from her encounter with André's mother, Pamela was in no mood for such pink-and-white vanities. She wanted to smack them. But she kept this to herself.

'Have you been to the Wallace Collection?' said André. 'They have a fine display of miniatures there. But I think you'll find mine is finer.'

'All these pretty girls,' said Bobby. 'What do you think became of them all?'

'They're dead,' said Charlotte.

'But here they live on,' said André.

'You do rather get the feeling they're all the same,' said Pamela, feeling mutinous.

'Not quite,' said André. 'Keep going.'

She moved on to the next case. Here she began to notice a change in the young ladies. They were exposing more of their bodies. By the time she got to the fourth case, they were naked from the waist up, and in many cases, their hands were playing with their bare breasts.

'Heavens, André,' she said. 'This is getting almost indecent.'

'Doesn't she just look like a Playmate of the Month?' said Bobby.

'Well, you're right,' said André. 'This is the erotica of the early nineteenth century.'

Pamela stopped being bored. She began to realise that the images on the painted medallions were becoming more openly erotic as she progressed round the room. There were six illuminated cases in all. By the fifth case the naked ladies had been joined by naked men. It was all very decorous, the men did no more than pinch the ladies' nipples between reaching fingers; but coming after the simpering portraits it was almost arousing. A further secret thought added to her excitement: André could not possibly have assembled such a collection without himself having a healthy sexual appetite. And in showing her his collection he was clearly advertising his intentions.

'Didn't you say you'd seen all this before, Bobby?' she said.

'Many times,' said Bobby.

'It's all new to me,' said Charlotte. 'My word! They are having fun.'

By the sixth case the little scenes had become fully pornographic. Some were medallions, but there were also snuff-boxes with images painted on the inside of the lid, and lockets, and hand-painted cards the size of playing cards. The men were now naked, and fully aroused. In some scenes the lady's hand caressed the man's erection, in others the lady was obligingly drawing back her voluminous skirts so that the man could penetrate her.

Pamela took in the meticulously painted details in silence. She had never seen such images in her life. Gazing upon them she understood what until now had been imprecise in her mind, which was exactly what happened in the act of intercourse. She found it astonishing: ungainly, comical, hypnotically fascinating, all at the same time. Her cheeks were tingling. She was breathing rapidly. It was those male parts – so tacked on, so out of keeping with the rest of the male body – and yet the focus of the ladies' attention, and the magnet to which her own eyes were irresistibly drawn.

'Makes you think, doesn't it?' said Bobby. 'They were at it even in the olden days.'

'Mankind never changes,' said André.

'Nor womankind,' said Charlotte.

'They do look as if they're enjoying it,' said Pamela. 'The ladies, I mean.'

'To be fair,' said André, 'these are all images produced for the pleasure of male patrons. They reflect the male desire for women to be wanton. That doesn't mean women in that time actually were wanton.'

'I don't see why they shouldn't have been,' said Charlotte.

No one seemed the slightest bit shocked by the pictures, so Pamela took good care to conceal her own astonishment. In one scene, painted on a playing card, the woman was crouching, her dress pulled over her head, while the man, naked from the waist down, stood above and behind her. It took Pamela a few moments to work out that this must be what Mandy had called 'taking it up the bum'.

As the first shock subsided, Pamela realised that the images had produced a strong physical reaction in her. This was quite independent of any opinion she might have. She had become sensitive to her body in a way that she had never been before. Even the heady moment of entering André's party and feeling the impact of so many men's eyes had not delivered this deep hot flush of physical awakening. Seeing these funny, beautiful, yearning embodiments of male desire flooded her with sensations she had never known before.

The male desire for women to be wanton.

Is it because I want to be desired? Or is it even more primitive than that? Do I want to be *fucked*?

She formed the word in her mind as a deliberate obscenity, but it no longer seemed obscene. They like to talk, Christine said. *Fuck, cock, cunt.* The words carried an entirely new meaning now, faced with these playful images. Not swear words at all, but terms of desire.

She realised André was watching her. She turned to him, smiling, making her voice sound as casual as she could.

'You like to surprise your guests.'

'I find the tour is more fun if you don't know what's coming.'

'How about you?' she said. 'Is the fun all used up?'

'The fun for me,' he said, 'is seeing others view my collection for the first time.'

'Aren't you afraid someone might take offence?'

'I choose my guests with care.'

'Then he sends us all off to bed,' said Bobby. 'I told you he was the perfect host.'

Nothing could be clearer. The erotic pictures were a prelude to the real thing.

The party broke up for the night. André gave Pamela another of his chaste little kisses on the cheek and murmured to her, 'I shall see you later.'

Pamela washed and cleaned her teeth and put on her night-dress and climbed into bed, all in a daze of anticipation. She turned out the light, and lay in the darkness, and waited. The house was full of noises. Footsteps came and went, padding up stairs and along corridors. Doors opened and closed. Then little by little the house fell silent.

Time passed. There was no question of sleep. Even so, a half-sleep crept over her, and she found herself slipping in and out of dreams. Then there were sounds again, soft footsteps passing her door. She waited for a tap-tap, but none came. She heard the creaks and groans of old timbers, and silence once more.

Then far away, a door opened. Again, the approach of a soft tread. The sounds stopped outside her door. She was fully awake now, tingling, ready. No tap-tap. Instead, the sound of the door being opened, very carefully. In the absolute darkness she felt him come into the room, but saw nothing. The door closed behind him. She heard his breathing as he stood still, lis-tening for her. She expected him to speak but he said nothing, so she too stayed silent.

Now he was crossing the room to the bed. He knew his way in the dark. A tug at the bedclothes, and he was slipping in beside her. She moved to give him room, felt the rush of cool air as the covers rose to admit him. Then his arm was over her, reaching for her, drawing her close against him.

Not André.

She pulled back, suddenly frightened.

'Bobby?'

'Hush,' he said. 'Don't make a noise.'

'Bobby! What are you doing?'

He took her hand and drew it beneath the bedclothes. She felt his erection, big and strong, just like in the pictures.

'No,' she said, whispering. 'We can't.'

His hands were on her body, stroking her, exciting her.

'Sure we can,' he said.

'Bobby, Bobby, stop. You mustn't.'

She tried to push his hands away but only succeeded in sending them further down, to between her legs. She knew she should get out of bed, leave the room, but she made no move. The same imperative that had made her conceal her shock at the pictures held her in its grip. She didn't want to appear naive.

Instead, she offered what seemed to her to be an insuperable objection.

'Bobby, I think André will come.'

'André won't come,' said Bobby.

'How do you know?'

'Trust me, I know.'

All the time his hands were moving over her body. Now he had hold of her nightdress. He was tugging it up over her thighs.

'But what about Charlotte?'

'Charlotte likes to sleep.'

He moved over her and found her face in the dark, and kissed her.

'I want you so much,' he said.

'No, Bobby. We can't. It's not right.'

How could she tell him it was her first time? How could she say she wanted her first time to be with someone she loved? Even as she struggled with these thoughts, her body was betraying her.

Her body liked Bobby's body. She could feel his erection pressing against her, long and hard, and it excited her whether she wanted it to or not.

She now realised he was fully naked. Had he come down the passage naked? She wanted to see him. She wanted to see a man's naked body, charged with desire.

Now he was pulling her nightdress up and over her head. She meant him to stop, she asked him to stop, but the words remained unspoken. Her body was speaking for her.

He kissed her breasts. She stiffened and shivered and turned her head from side to side.

'Can I see you?' he whispered. 'You're so beautiful. I want to see you.'

She said nothing, no longer trusting herself to speak. I'm not in control any more, she thought. I can't stop this.

He reached for the bedside lamp, turned it on. She closed her eyes against the sudden brightness.

She felt him draw down the covers, and run his hands over her body. Then he was still, and she knew he was just looking. Then she opened her eyes and looked too.

His body was beautiful. *It* was beautiful. He smiled for her, showing his fine white teeth.

'You're the loveliest girl in all the world,' he said.

'Oh, Bobby. What are we doing?'

'What we were made to do.'

He pointed to the mirror above the dressing table.

'There. Look at us.'

She looked, and it was like the erotic miniatures. There she lay, completely exposed, and beside her a strong young man with his cock standing out, stiff and proud.

'Go on looking,' he said.

He parted her legs, and before she could stop him he had moved down and his face was between her thighs. She jerked away, but he pinned her down with his arms. So she lay there and let him do what he wanted. Head turned to one side, she watched in the wide mirror.

His tongue was tickling her down there. For a moment she wanted to laugh. Then it stopped being tickly and became exciting. Then it was overwhelming. Without knowing she was doing it, she moved her hips under his mouth, pressing for closer contact. Shivers of pleasure began to course through her body. She closed her eyes and surrendered to the feelings.

Then he was moving back up her body, kissing her navel, her nipples, her lips.

'Shall we do it, Pamela?' he whispered. 'Do you want me to do it?'

She tried to shake her head even as he was kissing her, but already he was moving on top of her, and her treacherous body was preparing to receive him.

'Please, Bobby,' she said, making one last protest.

She could feel the head of his cock now, pushing against the place where his tongue had excited her so much. Her legs were wide apart, hungry for him to enter her, even as her lips were framing her final appeal.

'Think of André,' she said.

'Don't you understand?' he whispered. He moved his hips. His cock pushed into her. 'André asked me to come to you.'

Now he was inside her, filling her. Her body clung to him, holding him in her, craving him, even as her mind reeled in confusion.

'André asked you?'

'Hush! Hush!'

Now he was moving, drawing his cock almost out of her, then slowly driving it back in. As he did this he bent his head down and took one nipple in his mouth and tugged on it with his teeth. A cascade of sensation overpowered Pamela. She understood nothing. But Bobby's few words released her from whatever inhibitions remained. None of this was of her doing. She need feel no guilt, and no responsibility. Her body was awakening, and could not be sent back to sleep now. She had entered the secret world of desire.

She opened her eyes again and looked in the mirror. She could see Bobby's long body over hers, his hips rising and falling, the curve of his buttocks. At the same time she felt the mounting tempo of his thrusts, rocking her on the bed, and she wanted him to go on and on. She put her arms round him, she kissed his cheek, she whispered words she couldn't even hear herself. She gave him her body, all of it, wanting him to need her, have her, use her. She felt the rising tide once again, that had begun when he licked her. She closed her eyes and turned her head from side to side on the pillow.

Then suddenly he stopped. She felt a faint pulsing between her legs. Then nothing.

So that was it. It was over.

He gave a sigh, and rolled off her. She felt a warm trickle between her thighs. She didn't move. Slowly the storm of excitement within her abated.

What now?

'Bobby?'

'Mmm?'

'What did you mean? You said André asked you. Why did he do that?'

The answer came drowsily, as if it was something already known.

'The mirror,' he said. 'André likes to watch.'

The mirror over the dressing table. Not on a stand, as was usually the case. A mirror fixed to the wall.

Pamela felt cold and stupid. But how could she have known?

'Just his particular thing,' said Bobby. 'He's still a wonderful chap. And fun for you and me.'

'Yes,' said Pamela.

Bobby now roused himself. He pulled up his bath robe from the floor, where he had dropped it in the darkness, and climbed out of bed.

'Back to your wife,' said Pamela.

'Always observe the decencies, eh?'

He bent down to kiss her on the lips.

'That was delicious,' he said.

Pamela was staring at the mirror. Was he still there, silent on the other side?

'So it was all arranged.'

'You should know André by now. He arranges everything, down to the last detail.'

'Have you done this before?'

He reached out and stroked her cheek.

'How can a gentleman answer a question like that?'

She gave a little shrug of her bare shoulders. Then realising how cold she was, she pulled the covers up over her body.

'It was fun, wasn't it?'

'Yes,' she said.

'That's all that matters in the end.'

He left the room, treading softly. She heard his footsteps move down the corridor to his own room. She heard the bedroom door open and close after him.

My first time.

She reached out to turn off the bedside lamp. She cried a little, soundlessly. Then she went to sleep.

The next day it was as if it had all been a dream. Lady Tillemans did not appear, but André was sweet and attentive as before. Bobby was friendly and loud. There were no secret knowing looks between them. The only moment in which any reference was made to the events of the night was when she and André were briefly alone together after lunch, out on the terrace.

'Have you liked your visit?' he said.

'Not quite what I expected,' she replied.

'Would you like to come again sometime?'

'No,' she said. 'I don't think so.'

32

Only after she had left Herriard behind her, and returned to Brook Green, did Pamela allow herself to feel the true impact of shock and humiliation. Something of her distress must have been visible on her face, because after getting back and retreating to her room, there came a tap on the door. It was Hugo.

'I don't want to bother you,' he said. 'But is everything all right?'

'Yes, I'm fine,' she said.

Then, all unbidden, the tears started to flow. It was the sweet concern on Hugo's face, the simple decency in him, qualities she had never valued before, but which suddenly seemed to her to be infinitely precious.

'Pammy, Pammy,' he said, holding her in his arms. 'There, there. Don't cry.'

She let him soothe her, and slowly her crying ceased.

'Do you want to talk about it?'

She shook her head.

'Boyfriend trouble, I suppose.'

'I haven't got a boyfriend,' she said.

'Why don't you run yourself a nice hot bath, and then come downstairs and have a glass of sherry. That's what I do when I have a bad day.'

'Is it, Hugo?'

She smiled at him, touched.

'The bath has to be hot, mind. And the sherry has to be the best. I have a Very Old Reserve Oloroso downstairs.'

'Thank you, Hugo. I'll be all right. I'll come down soon.'

Hugo left her alone. She didn't have a bath, because she'd had a bath already, that morning at Herriard. She had scrubbed at her body as if to remove from it every trace of her night's shame.

Even now she didn't know what to think of it all. Had she been abused? And if so, who was to blame? André, or Bobby, or both? She hadn't been made to do anything against her will. And yet if she'd been asked in advance, she would have refused. Somehow, in the context of such a group of people, on such a night, it had seemed childish to make a fuss. So who was right? Perhaps her dream of being loved was naive, and in the circles in which André moved, where everyone could have whatever they wanted, all liaisons were fluid, marriage most of all. Bobby and Charlotte certainly behaved that way. Was it bourgeois and provincial to hope for love?

She thought about André's mother. What sort of mother knows her son's perverted tastes, as surely she must have known, and says nothing? 'She lives for me,' André had said. 'My happiness is her happiness.' For a moment, shuddering, Pamela had the sensation that she had been watched through that silent mirror by both of them, mother and son.

What kind of love is this?

She recalled Stephen Ward's words to her, in the basement club where the showgirls posed naked. 'Just bored people looking for fun,' he had said, 'and a few lonely people looking for love.' The world he had introduced her to offered everything she had dreamed of. On the night of André's party, making her sensational entrée to the grand room, she had felt as if she

294

belonged in this world, as if she had been born for it. How could she go back now? And back to what?

She went to the bathroom and washed her face and reapplied her make-up. Then she went downstairs and found Harriet alone in the kitchen, with a bottle of sherry.

'Hugo says you're to have some of this,' Harriet said, pouring the dark liquid into a small narrow glass. 'He's down in his wine store, arranging his bottles.'

'Arranging his bottles?'

'Oh, you know. Everyone has something they do, which no one else can see the point of. With Hugo it's his wine cellar.'

Harriet too had a sherry. They took their drinks into the drawing room. Pamela lit a cigarette.

'Hugo says your weekend has worn you out,' said Harriet.

'Yes, it has rather.'

'I can't cope with parties anymore. But of course, after you're married there isn't so much point in parties anyway.'

This practical view of the purpose of parties made Pamela smile. But then she thought of the other purpose to which she'd been introduced, and the smile faded.

'I met Hugo at a party,' Harriet said. 'It was a fund-raising dinner for our local MP. Hugo and I were the only people under fifty. He was very gallant, and talked to me. I knew right away he was the one.'

'You're lucky.'

'Hugo would say we're both lucky. Though I do often wonder why he puts up with me. My headaches and so on. But you know, we just adored each other from the start.'

Harriet spoke in a soft silky voice, as if she was stroking herself. Suddenly Pamela was overcome by the urge to shock her. She wanted to make her wake up and see that men were not to be trusted.

'Hugo's very open with his emotions,' she heard herself say.

'I was feeling rotten when I got in, and he just let me cry on his shoulder.'

'You cried on Hugo's shoulder?'

'It was so sweet of him. When he holds you, you feel so safe, don't you?'

'Yes,' said Harriet, pouring herself more sherry.

'He's so protective of me,' said Pamela. 'He's always warning me about men. One-track minds, he says.'

'Hugo says men have one-track minds?'

'You know. Getting their wicked way with you.'

'Well,' said Harriet, massaging her temples. 'What a lot you two talk about.'

'Mostly he talks about you, of course,' said Pamela.

'What does he say about me?'

'How rotten it is for you to have these headaches. How uncomplaining you are. How sorry he feels for you. He's just so amazingly sympathetic.'

'Yes,' said Harriet. 'I've always thought so.' She gave Pamela a faint smile. 'The awful truth is I can feel one of my headaches coming on now. I shall have to go upstairs. Bright lights make it so much worse. It's better for everyone if I cast my gloom alone.'

'I'm so sorry,' said Pamela. 'It must be the sherry.'

Harriet took herself up to her bedroom. Mary came downstairs. She'd read Emily her bedtime story, and now Emily was ready for her goodnight kiss. Pamela told her that Hugo was down in the cellar, and Harriet was up in her room with a headache.

'Oh, poor Harriet,' said Mary. 'Do you think there's anything I can do for her?'

'You could chuck a bucket of cold water over her,' Pamela said.

Mary burst into a guilty laugh.

'Oh, don't!'

'I bet you it'd work faster than aspirins.'

'I'll go and see if there's anything I can bring her.'

While Mary was upstairs, Hugo emerged from the cellar, brushing dust off his hands.

'How's the sherry?' he said. 'Has it done the trick?'

'I think so,' said Pamela.

'Where's Harriet?'

'Headache.'

He nodded as if he had known before he had asked. He poured himself a glass of sherry.

'I like it down there,' he said, nodding at the floor. 'It's cool and orderly, and stacked with fine bottles that are steadily getting finer. That's quite something, isn't it? A place where the future is guaranteed to be better than the past.'

'I hope that's true even above ground,' said Pamela.

'Me too,' said Hugo.

Then his eyes met Pamela's and they looked at each other and neither of them spoke.

The front doorbell rang. It was Rupert.

'I've come to say goodbye,' he said. 'I'm off to Ireland in the morning.'

'Stay and have a drink,' said Hugo. 'Stay for supper.'

Hugo and Pamela both knew it was Mary that Rupert had come to see. These days Pamela spoke openly of her belief that Rupert was in love with Mary. She said it not because she believed it, but because it displeased her. There was too much need on either side. It was all a little too pitiful for her liking.

Rupert declined supper. Hugo went up to Harriet, and Mary came down. Rupert told her that he was going to Mountbatten's summer home in County Donegal, on the west coast of Ireland. Pamela, hearing this, slipped upstairs to her room.

'And where would it be in Donegal?' said Mary.

'It's called Mullaghmore. A few miles north of Sligo.'

Mary said nothing to this.

'I'm told it rains all the time.'

'So it does,' she said.

'Promise me. No running away. I'll only be gone a week.'

After Rupert had said his goodbyes, and was walking briskly down the street towards the Broadway, Pamela came running after him. She pressed a folded piece of paper into his hand.

'I made her tell me where she's from. It's called Kilnacarry. In Donegal.'

33

Mountbatten's summer house in Ireland turned out to be a castle. Set on a low headland jutting out into the sea, its massive granite walls and pointed turrets dominated the landscape for miles around.

'Some people find it a bit grim,' said Mountbatten, walking Rupert round its roof terraces, gazing out over the iron-grey Atlantic. 'I love it. The worse the weather, the happier I am.'

Classiebawn Castle was a neo-Gothic fantasy, built by Lord Palmerston, the pugnacious Victorian statesman. Like most of his grand properties, Mountbatten had inherited it from Edwina.

'Mind you,' he said, 'after you've paid 80 per cent death duties, and handed over another 15 per cent to the girls, there's not much of the inheritance left.'

This was a working holiday, not a family holiday, so Mountbatten's daughters, sons-in-law and grandsons were not in residence. The great house was gloomy and silent. The party from London was four: Mountbatten, his defence adviser, his secretary and Rupert. The regime was strict. From breakfast to lunch, Mountbatten pored over the minutiae of the service departments, as he refined his proposal for a centralised command structure. Rupert, alone in a separate room, worked on his own paper. They came together for lunch in the long bleak dining room. Then, in the afternoon, they went mackerel fishing, or shrimping, or walking.

Rupert was undoubtedly surplus to requirements. He knew very little about the controversial defence reorganisation. He wondered why he'd been invited. Then on the second afternoon Mountbatten said to him, 'Come along, Rupert. I'll show you our beach.'

It was a grand blowy day. Mullaghmore beach stretched in a long crescent of brown sand almost all the way to Bundoran. Across the choppy water of Donegal Bay they could see St John's Point and Drumanoo Head.

'We come here every August,' said Mountbatten, striding into the wind. 'But it's not the same without Edwina. You never married, did you, Rupert?'

'No.'

'Why not? If you don't mind my asking.'

'I don't think I'm the marrying kind,' said Rupert. 'Bit of a loner.'

'A loner? I can't really imagine that. I hate being alone. Even when Edwina and I were fighting, and God knows there was enough of that, I'd rather be with her than on my own.'

Rupert said nothing. He understood that it was a comfort to Mountbatten to have someone to talk to about Edwina.

'Poor old bugger, banging on about his wife.'

'Not at all,' said Rupert. 'I envy you.'

'Don't bother. It's hell losing her. They told me on the phone, in the middle of the night. It was the governor of Borneo himself. Edwina was in Borneo for the St John Ambulance people. I didn't know what he was saying at first.'

They walked on over the sand.

'I still dream the phone's ringing, and I answer, and this voice is there, telling me she's dead.'

'But you wouldn't want never to have known her.'

'No. God, no. It's a funny business, though. I adored her, but I'm not sure she adored me. I never really felt good enough for her.'

'Maybe we expect too much,' said Rupert.

'How do you mean?'

'This idea of love. We expect the other person to love all of us. But I don't see how that's possible.'

'Oh, it is!' cried Mountbatten. 'Edwina could be foul, utterly foul, but I loved her even then. That's what happens when you truly love someone. You even love their faults. You love all of them.'

'Do you think you knew all of her?'

'Oh, yes.' But then he frowned and corrected himself. 'Though perhaps not. I didn't always understand her. Is that what you're getting at?'

'I'm not sure that people can ever fully know each other,' said Rupert. 'Did Edwina know all of you? In the way you know yourself?'

Mountbatten thought about that.

'No. Not like that.'

'But you didn't try to conceal part of yourself from her?'

'No. I don't think so. Not consciously, at any rate.'

'Then it must be that no one can ever know you as you know yourself. Because each one of us is simply too complicated. It's like someone saying, "Oh, I know France well, I adore France." The truth is he knows hardly anything of France at all.'

'Well, well.'

He came to a stop, and began scraping at the damp sand with the toe of one boot.

'It's not a lot of fun thinking the way you do, though, is it? A bit on the gloomy side.'

'It can be.'

'So you've given up on love, have you?'

'I've learned to be content on my own.'

As he said this Rupert thought of Mary Brennan.

'But you never know,' he added. 'There might be someone out there.'

'Someone you could love?'

'Someone I could be with, while still being on my own.'

'You're a hard man to please, Rupert,' he said. 'You're determined to suffer.'

His scraping away at the sand was taking the form of a circular ditch. He turned to look at the waves hissing into the shore.

'The tide's coming in. We could build a moat. Have you ever built a moat?'

'No.'

'It's really great fun. I'll show you. But we should get nearer to the water.'

He strode towards the waves, and picked a spot a pace or two from the highest current water-mark. Then throwing himself down on his knees, he began to burrow in the sand with his hands.

'Come on. We're building a castle with a moat.'

Rupert squatted down beside him and together they set about heaping sand into a mound, and hollowing out a surrounding channel.

'How are you getting along on my "Aim for the West"?'

'Very well,' said Rupert. 'Actually, I'm having a bit of a struggle stopping myself from getting carried away with it.'

'Get carried away. Why not?'

'You don't want a treatise on eschatology.'

'What's that?'

'Last things. Death, judgement, heaven, hell.'

'Do you think we need it?'

'I think the Cold War's about more than great power rivalry.

That's what makes it so scary. I think it's really a war of religion.'

'You call Communism a religion?'

'Actually, I think something a bit more involved than that. I think we in the West, and the Americans in particular, see Communism as a religion. That's why they're so afraid of it. America is a righteous nation, a land of believers. They hear the claims of Communism, about how they've got history on their side, and they understand that as a claim of faith. I'm not sure the Russians see it that way. But that's another matter.'

'So you think the Cold War is a religious war because that's the way Americans think?'

'Yes.'

'And that's bad?'

'Very bad. The worst wars are wars of religion. More atrocities are committed in religious conflicts than in battles for land or resources. Religious wars are about good and evil. You die before you surrender. Killing your enemy is a kind of purification of the world.'

'God help us!'

'If he's there.'

The sandcastle was growing. The moat round it was almost complete.

'Now,' said Mountbatten, 'we dig a channel to the sea. But we leave a wall between the channel and the moat.'

The digging progressed.

'So you see,' said Rupert, 'I've rather lost sight of your "Aim for the West".'

'I'm not so sure,' said Mountbatten. 'What you say gives me hope. I find myself thinking of our British way of doing things. We don't go in for ideology. We don't go in much for revolutions. We're reformers. We make the world a better place one step at a time. That way of thinking doesn't hold with religious wars.'

'Not at all. But it's not exactly a rallying cry, is it? Make the world a better place one step at a time.'

Mountbatten laughed. He stood up.

'Now, you see, the channel's almost there. Shall we make it longer, or wait for the tide?'

Rupert looked at what they'd built. The channel in the sand ran from the water's edge up the beach to the castle with its surrounding moat. As the tide came in it would find the channel and run down it to the castle.

'Let's make it longer,' he said.

'That's what my grandsons always answer. It's the lust for destruction.'

He knelt down once more and resumed scooping.

'So have you come up with an answer yet?' said Mountbatten.

'I'm getting there,' said Rupert. 'I see it in two stages. The first stage is all about managing the intentions of the other side. The second stage is about managing our own intentions. And whatever we do there has to take account of America's sense of manifest destiny. Somehow we have to take that drive to destroy the evil enemy, and redirect it into a mission to save the world.'

'A mission to save the world. Not bad.'

'If we can get all their generals and their missile launchers and their bomber crews to be prouder of not starting a war than of starting one, then maybe we can make it to the end of this century.'

Mountbatten was on his feet again.

'The next wave will find it,' he said.

They stood side by side in the wind coming off the Atlantic, and waited for the next big wave. It came at last, seething and boiling, sucking in on itself and breaking, then rushing in a sheet of spreading foam over the sand. The water entered the channel and swept down to the wall of sand that defended the moat.

'The third wave will break through,' said Mountbatten.

'Is that a prophecy?'

'No, that's hard intelligence. I've done this before.'

The second wave rolled in. The sand wall began to crumble.

'I like what you say, Rupert,' said Mountbatten.

'All the arguments about weapons deployment,' said Rupert, 'they're all irrelevant. The danger lies in the ideas behind the weapons.'

The third wave rushed in. The sand wall fell. The moat filled with seawater.

'Now,' said Mountbatten, 'if you were a seven-year-old boy you would jump on the castle and destroy it.'

'Plenty of seven-year-old boys in the world,' Rupert said.

Neither of them jumped on the sandcastle. They stood and watched as the swirling seawater caused it to crumble slowly away.

34

On the fourth day of his week at Classiebawn, Rupert borrowed one of the estate cars to drive to Kilnacarry. The car was pulled up in the narrow yard bounded by the castle walls, in front of the main entrance. Mountbatten, detail-obsessed as ever, came out to instruct Rupert.

'There's only one way to turn here. Hard right forward, then back, pulling hard with your left. Then forward again. Then back.'

Rupert attempted this manoeuvre, but not to Mountbatten's satisfaction.

'No, no! Not hard enough around!'

He leaned in the car window and seized the wheel himself. In this way the car was turned at last.

Rupert drove off, through Donegal and round the coast road to Killybegs, filled with amusement at how Mountbatten had controlled the car even when he wasn't in the driving seat. How frustrating, if you have the habit of leadership, to find you have only limited power after all, and the world refuses to do your bidding. But what self-confidence! As so often with Mountbatten, Rupert marvelled that the man who had been proved wrong by life so many times continued to overflow with the certainty that he was right. It was a kind of animal energy, the same drive that propelled his vanity. And yet alongside it lay the deep diffidence of a man who could say, 'I've never been much good with women.'

From Killybegs he followed the signs across the wild peninsula to Ardara, and so down a bumpy white road to Kilnacarry.

The village was a straggle of thatched whitewashed houses on the hillside leading to the sea. A small stone church stood a little apart, on the headland. Each house had its own plot of land, bounded by walls of loose stones. Tethered cows turned to gaze at him as he passed by. There was no sign of any people.

He pulled up where the road ended, and got out of the car. A cold wind came funnelling in between the headlands. He buttoned his coat up to his throat. A dog peered out from behind a house and barked at him.

There was a bar, and a shop with a sign advertising Carroll's No. 1. Rupert went into the shop, making the bell on the door clink. There was an old lady inside, buying tea and sugar. Behind the counter a thin woman with reddish hair, wearing a white apron, gave Rupert a nod. The old lady was slowly counting out coins.

Rupert's intention was to enquire after the Brennan family. Beyond that, he wasn't sure what he would do. He was trusting to the gossip of a small village. Whatever Mary was hiding, someone here would surely know something.

While he waited, he looked round the shop. It was small, and poorly stocked. Its most prominent feature was a wire rack displaying leaflets and postcards. The postcards showed different views of the same small bay. The leaflets had a black-and-white photograph of a girl on the front. The girl was gazing upwards into the sky. On her round face was a look of ecstatic surrender.

Rupert took out one of the leaflets. It was headed *The Visions of Kilnacarry*. Even as his eye travelled down the block of print he realised he knew the girl in the photograph.

On August 6, 1945 Mary Brennan, 12, was playing on the sandy
beach of Buckle Bay as the sun was setting over the sea . . .

The old lady was done at last. She bobbed a greeting at Rupert
as she made her way out. Rupert approached the shopkeeper.

'A soft old day,' said the shopkeeper. Then seeing the leaflet
in his hand, 'Are you here for the visions?'

'Yes,' said Rupert.

'You should've come in early August,' said the shopkeeper.
'There was a terrible crowd in the village then. The priest had a
service on the beach at sunset. Oh, it was something!'

'That's where this girl saw the visions?'

'Buckle Bay, yes. The next bay along.'

She nodded the direction with her head.

'And where is she now?'

'Oh, if you've come for Mary Brennan you're out of luck.
She's been in a convent these past ten years and more.'

'Do you know where?'

'I wouldn't know that. You'd have to be asking the priest.'

Rupert took out his purse to pay for the leaflet and for one of
the postcards of Buckle Bay.

'What do you make of these visions yourself?' he asked the
shopkeeper.

'I was there,' she replied, giving Rupert a significant look. 'I
saw it for myself.'

'You saw what?'

'The stillness. I was there, on the third evening, when Mary
received the warning. She prophesied all of it. You can believe
me or not, as you please.'

'What did she prophesy?'

'The bomb,' she said. 'The atom bomb on Hiroshima. Mary
saw it in her vision before it happened. She told the priest.'

'And there was a warning.'

'The great wind. Well! We all know what that is. That's the end of the world.'

'Yes,' said Rupert. 'Of course.'

'But Our Lord made Mary a promise. He told her, "When the time comes I will speak to you again."' She tapped the leaflet. 'It's all in here. Mary Brennan will come back to Kilnacarry. She'll walk on that beach again. And the Lord will speak to her again.'

'Yes,' said Rupert. 'I see.'

'Sure it's a consolation,' said the shopkeeper. 'The world can't end until Mary comes home.'

Rupert thanked her and went out into the cold wind. He sat in his car and read the leaflet. He read of the great crowd that had been present on the third evening, and read the testimony of those who had seen the 'stillness'. He read of the many signs of Our Lord's mercy that had been granted since, to visitors to the site of the visions. A woman from Wicklow had been cured of a disfiguring rash on her face. An American priest who had lost his faith found it again in the course of one of the August vigils on Buckle Bay. A deaf child began to hear.

The text of Mary Brennan's appeal to the world was laid out in the leaflet.

Our Father in heaven is saddened by the sinfulness of mankind. Why must you inflict such suffering on each other, he asks, when I made you to love each other? . . .

This time all living things will be destroyed by a great wind. When this great wind sweeps over the land, it will be made clean . . .

Yours is the generation that will perish . . .

He read of the simple shrine that had been built on the spot where Mary Brennan had seen her visions of Jesus, and of the explosion of devotion that had followed. Many thousands now made the pilgrimage to Kilnacarry each year. Father Dermot Flannery, parish priest of Kilnacarry, who had himself witnessed Mary Brennan as she had her visions, was raising money to build a chapel in the bay. All donations gratefully received.

So this was Mary's secret. Not some sordid affair, but something entirely innocent, and in its way moving. Rupert sat in his borrowed car and pictured the child she had been, her face shining with love, made bold by an unquestioning faith. It made him smile. Then he felt a surge of tenderness towards her; and along with the tenderness, a powerful sense of relief.

Is this all, Mary? Is this your shameful past?

Rupert had been brought up as a Catholic. He was familiar with the language of visionaries, with their promises and their threats. The recipients were always children, most commonly girls. Their usual fate was to spend the rest of their life in a nunnery. But Mary had run away.

No special destiny for you, Mary. So what is it you want?

He decided to seek out the priest.

Rupert crossed the village on foot, and entered the church. There he found a woman on her knees, scrubbing the stone floor. He asked where he could find the priest, and was directed to his house.

Father Dermot Flannery was grey-haired, with a pouchy sagging face and misty eyes. His cassock was stained with what looked like egg and ketchup. He showed no surprise at Rupert's appearance.

'Have you come about the visions? Sure you have. There's nothing else brings strangers to Kilnacarry.'

'I hope I'm not disturbing you, Father.'

'Well, as to that, a little disturbance is a healthy thing.'

310

He led Rupert into his parlour and offered to make a cup of tea. Rupert accepted.

'So what would be your particular interest?' he said as he bustled about with a teapot. 'All the way from England as you are.'

Rupert had no intention of giving away Mary's secret. He took refuge in a cover story, borrowed from the leaflet.

'I was born and raised a Catholic,' he said. 'But I've lost my faith. I heard about the shrine here.'

'So you've come for signs and wonders.'

The priest didn't seem as delighted about this as Rupert had expected.

'I don't really know why I've come.'

'But you know your Bible, I hope. You remember the words Our Lord spoke to Thomas. "Blessed are they that have not seen, and yet have believed."'

Rupert felt admonished. His respect for Father Flannery rose.

'Yes,' he said. 'I suppose so.'

The priest shot him a keen look.

'Ah, well,' he said. 'We're all frail vessels.'

'What about you, Father? Do you believe in these visions?'

'Yes, I do. I saw the child as she received the warning on the third evening. But that's not why I believe. I believe because the warning she has given us is in accordance with the teaching of the Church. And I believe because the shrine has been the saving of Kilnacarry.'

The kettle boiled. He poured steaming water into the pot.

'You mean saving as in souls?'

'That's as may be,' said the priest. 'I mean saving as in cash come into the village. There's not a family here but doesn't let out a room to the pilgrims. Every year the numbers grow. We shall have our chapel within three years, if not sooner.'

'Unless the world ends first.'

Father Flannery chuckled at that.

'I'll tell you this for nothing,' he said. 'When Mary Brennan comes back to receive the final warning, every house in the village will be full. There'll be caravans up the road as far as Rosbeg, and the pub will be drunk dry.'

'So she will come back?'

'Of course she'll come back. Isn't her old mother here, and her brother? Isn't this her own home?'

'The woman in the shop told me she was in a convent.'

'So she is.'

The tea was made. The priest handed Rupert a cup.

'Why did she leave Kilnacarry?' Rupert asked.

The priest gave him another sharp look.

'Will it give you back your faith to know what became of Mary Brennan?'

'No,' said Rupert. 'I'm just curious.'

'You wouldn't be a newspaperman, would you?'

'No,' said Rupert.

'But you are from London?'

'Yes.'

'I'll tell you why Mary Brennan left Kilnacarry if you'll tell me why you've come to Kilnacarry.'

Rupert reddened a little.

'I don't mean to deceive you,' he said. 'I'm just not sure where my duty lies.'

'Is that so?'

Father Flannery contemplated Rupert as he drank his tea.

'I don't like secrets,' he said after a moment. 'They do no good to anyone. You may tell me what you're up to or not, as you please. Mary Brennan left the village because she couldn't take it anymore. The pilgrims drove her away. They gave her no peace. Their hands out all the time, touching her, plucking at her. They came with little pairs of scissors, can you believe it? They cut off pieces of her dress, even her hair. Whatever she said, they wrote it down. She came to me, she said, "Father, I want to go." Poor child, she did her best. She said, "Does Jesus want me to stay, Father?" I told her no, Our Lord himself would have been on the first bus to Sligo. It was me that found a convent to take her in, and made the nuns swear not to give her away. I've never told a soul where she is, and I'll not tell you now.'

Rupert nodded and drank his tea.

'But I don't need to tell you, do I?'

Rupert looked up. There was the priest's grey head, canted to one side, the knowing look in his eyes.

'Because you know where Mary Brennan is, don't you?'

Still Rupert said nothing, and by his silence the priest knew he was right.

'We lost her,' he said. 'I'll admit it to you. I've been worried sick ever since the nuns called to tell me. So if you know where she is, maybe you'll be setting my mind at rest.'

Rupert shook his head.

'She's safe and well,' he said.

'You come all the way to Kilnacarry, but you won't tell me where she is?'

'Not without her permission.'

The priest pondered this in silence for a moment.

'Does she know you're here?'

'No.'

'Well, then. You say you don't know where your duty lies. I can tell you. Your duty is to go to Mary Brennan and tell her to come home. She needn't come for long, and she needn't show herself to the faithful. But she must let her mother see that she's safe and well, as you say.'

'Does her mother know she left the convent?'

'She does not. But she misses the child sorely.'

'All I can do is ask her.'

'You do that.'

The priest rose from his chair.

'Now I think you'll be wanting to take a look at Buckle Bay.'

They walked together over the bleak stone-littered hill and down the other side to the little cove.

'You have to understand,' said the priest, 'this is a child who had never been further than Rosbeg in all her life. It's a small world we live in here.'

The tide was out. They trod the sand as far as a small stone marker that had been placed halfway towards the water.

'This is where she stood, more or less. I got two of the village boys to build it here. At high tide it's surrounded by water, but you can still see it.'

He gestured all round, from the jagged rocks on the south side to the great granite hump on the north.

'On an August evening you'll not see an inch of sand here. Just people, shoulder-to-shoulder. I lay a white cloth on the stone and I say mass here, when the tide's out. And if the low tide comes at sunset, you should see those people! The faith is so strong in them you'd think the Lord was come again.'

Rupert looked out over the cold grey sea. It was heaving and rolling, flecked with foam.

'And do they see the stillness?'

'Ah, so you've heard of the stillness. Yes, some of them see it. I saw it myself, with Mary. You'll think I'm telling you a story, but it's God's own truth.'

'What was it like?'

'It was like a little piece of heaven. All the troubles of the world put to rest. You see it for a moment, and you say to yourself, This is how it's meant to be. Not all the hurrying and worrying. Like it says in the psalm, Be still and know that I am God.'

'It takes faith,' said Rupert, watching the rolling sea.

'It gives faith,' said the priest.

35

Harriet opened the door softly, as if what they were doing was secret, and beckoned Mary to follow her into the room. There were the blue walls with fluffy white clouds. The jolly curtains with their clowns. And in the middle of the room the white wooden cot, the woolly lion waiting on its pillow.

Harriet closed the door behind them. She stood still, looking round the room.

'I don't know what to do,' she said.

'Would you like to pray?' said Mary.

Harriet nodded. She knelt down by the side of the cot and pressed her brow against its white bars. Mary knelt beside her. For a few moments they were silent together.

'I thought I'd cry,' said Harriet. 'But I can't.'

'Do you want to talk to him?' said Mary.

Harriet threw her a frightened look.

'What would I say?'

'Tell him you love him. You miss him.'

For the moment Harriet was silent, her head against the bars of the cot. Then she spoke in a whisper.

'I love you, John. I miss you.'

'Tell him you know you'll see him again.'

'I'll see you again, John.'

'Now tell him goodbye.'

The whisper almost inaudible: 'Goodbye, my darling.'

She made a slight movement of her upper body. Mary opened her arms. Harriet came into her embrace, kneeling there by the cot.

Now the tears came. Mary rocked her weeping in her arms. Then slowly the crying ceased, and they parted. Harriet rose to her feet.

'I should do something about all these baby things,' she said, her voice unsteady. 'They're good as new.'

'I could help you.'

'Do you think anyone would want them?'

'I'm sure of it. The church I go to, they have a jumble sale coming up this Saturday.'

'We'll get new wallpaper. New curtains.' She turned to Mary. 'It could be your room.'

'I don't know how long I'll be staying,' said Mary.

'I want you to stay for ever. I was so lonely until you came.'

'But you've got Hugo,' said Mary.

'Yes. Darling Hugo. Where would I be without him?' She gave Mary an uncertain look, asking for reassurance. 'I know it might seem, with the headaches and everything . . . Pamela said he was sympathetic. Of course I do understand what she means, but even so . . .'

'Pamela's still young.'

'Yes, she is. She's just a child, really. It's not her fault that she's so pretty.'

They found some empty wine boxes in the wine store and packed away the baby things: the little quilt, the cot mattress, the never-used nappies, the woolly lion. The cot itself came apart into flat frames. They carried the boxes and the dismembered cot downstairs and stacked them in the front hall.

Harriet said, 'I never could have done that without you.'

When Hugo came home that evening he saw the boxes in the hall.

'What's all this?' he said.

'It's a new beginning,' said Harriet. 'I'm going to be so much stronger from now on.'

The next day Rupert called on them, back from Ireland.

'Just the man,' said Mary. 'You can help me carry these boxes down to the church hall.'

'The poor man's only just walked in the door,' said Harriet.

'Then he can walk out again,' said Mary. 'My mam always said you should never let a man sit down. Once down, they never get up.'

So Rupert took hold of the unwieldy cot frames, and Mary took one of the wine boxes, and they set off down the road.

'So how was Donegal?' said Mary once they were out of the house.

'Beautiful,' said Rupert. 'Sad.'

'It is that.'

'Mountbatten has a castle there, right on the sea. It's grand, but I wouldn't want to live there.'

'What does the man want for God's sake with a castle in Ireland?'

'It's his summer home. He goes there to relax.'

'So you were relaxing, were you?'

'And working,' said Rupert.

'I should hope so,' said Mary. 'If great men like you aren't working to make the world a better place, then what's the use of you?'

They carried the box and the cot frames into the church hall. A parish helper was there, sorting through the donations.

'Baby things! They'll go in a trice!'

They returned up the road to get the rest of the boxes. For a while they walked in silence. Then Mary spoke, very low.

'You went there, didn't you?'

'Yes,' said Rupert, not pretending he didn't understand.

'How did you know?'

'Pamela told me.'

'Yes. Of course she would.'

She was closing up against him. Running away again.

'Was I wrong to go there?'

'That's not for me to say.'

'I'll do whatever you want me to do, Mary.'

'I want you to forget you ever went there,' she said.

In the house again, by wordless agreement they said no more. But once out in the street, boxes in their arms, she began again.

'So now you'll be thinking I'm a mad woman.'

'Of course not,' she said. 'You were only a child.'

'A child making a holy show of herself. Telling stories she should be ashamed of.'

'Is that what you were doing?'

'That's what you're thinking I was doing.'

She was proud and angry.

'You don't know what I'm thinking,' he said.

'You don't believe in God,' she said. 'Why would you believe in my visions? So of course I made it all up. And that's what you think of me. I'm a story-teller and a liar.'

'Mary,' he said, 'I don't think you made it all up.'

'Then what do you think?'

'I think you saw what you say you saw. The sea went still, and Jesus came to you, walking on the water.'

'But you don't believe in Jesus.'

'I believe in you.'

They carried the boxes into the church hall. From there, instead of going back out into the street, they went into the church itself. It was empty. They walked down the centre aisle towards the altar. The stained-glass windows threw coloured light over the pews.

'The priest here's a fine deep man,' said Mary, 'with a fine deep voice.'

'The priest in Kilnacarry seemed to me to be a good man.'

'He is a good man,' she said.

She sat down in the front pew, and he sat down across the aisle from her.

'Now you'd better tell me the truth,' she said. 'None of your soapy English manners. What do you mean by what you say?'

She spoke sharply, as if she was offended by him. She wouldn't look at him.

Rupert found her question hard to answer. What exactly did he mean?

'I think you had a real experience,' he said, 'and you used the language you'd been given to make sense of it.'

'The language I'd been given?'

'Sinfulness. Suffering. Being made clean. And the figure of Jesus, of course.'

She listened in silence, frowning, looking down at her hands.

'But I do think the experience was real,' he said. 'I know it was real.'

'How do you know that?'

'Because others have had it. They all describe it in their own way, but it's obvious it's the same experience. The mystics talk of it as a kind of surrender. They call it a surrender to God. Others talk of a short precious moment when they escape the walls that shut us all in. Somehow they slip out, into something else. Into everything else. Even I've felt it, in a very small way. We have this constant awareness of how we're separate from everything that isn't ourselves. It's what we call loneliness. Then sometimes the walls disappear, and we know we're not alone after all.'

Mary said nothing. He could hear her soft rapid breathing.

'I'm sorry,' he said. 'You'll think I'm trying to explain it away. That's not what I meant at all.'

She looked up at last.

'You wouldn't lie to me? Not even out of kindness?'

'No,' he said.

'You really do believe me?'

'Many people believe you, Mary.'

'Oh, it's not me they believe!' She pulled a face at the thought. 'That's their own foolish fancies. They come looking for a cure for the toothache. They're after miracles and all sorts of nonsense. It's like they're playing the pools, they're all hoping for a big win. I could be a statue for all they care. But the way you talk, that's something else. Even the priest never said such things to me.'

'I'm only trying to make sense of it my way. I'm not telling you Jesus didn't appear to you. After all, he gave you a message. He spoke to you.'

She lowered her head and sat in silence.

'They're all waiting for your return,' he said. 'So they can be given the final message.'

'I'll never return.'

'You have to go back one day, Mary.'

'I can't.'

'If you told the priest ahead of time, I'm sure he'd do his best to manage things so you didn't get bothered by the pilgrims.'

She shook her head.

'If it were only that,' she said.

'Tell me what it is,' he said. 'Maybe I can help.'

'You?' She gave a low laugh. 'You're the last one can help.'

There was nothing more to say. She showed no sign of wanting to leave the church. So they sat there quietly, and time passed.

You're the last one can help.

He puzzled over this. What was it about him that so disqualified him? He watched her sitting there, hands clasped in her lap as they had been when he first saw her on the park bench. He recalled the look in her eyes then. It had been a look of despair.

Suddenly he understood.

'You don't believe in your visions any more,' he said.

He heard her give a sharp intake of breath.

'I'm right, aren't I? That's why you can't go back.'

'You're the devil, Rupert Blundell.'

'That's why you've run away.'

She kept her gaze lowered, avoiding his.

'What happened? Did you just wake up one day and think it was all a dream?'

Still she didn't answer. Head bowed, hands clasped, like one anticipating a coming storm, or punishment. Then, slowly, as if speaking to herself:

'I think I always knew. Right from the start. But they all believed me, and wanted it to be true. And I wanted it to be true. And there was the attention and all. I was such a little show-off. You wouldn't think it to see me now. But it all got too big, and the bishop came, and people said they saw what I'd seen, and these miracles started happening, and I was . . . I was caught. How could I tell them?'

'That you made it all up?'

'I never meant to make it up. It all came to me. But a whole lot of things came to me when I was a child. I used to talk to the fairies, and they'd talk back.'

'So seeing Jesus on the water, and his words to you – that all just came to you?'

'Yes.'

'As in a vision?'

'Yes.'

321

'So you did see a vision, Mary.'

'I thought I did.'

'You saw what you saw. No one can take that away from you.'

'I'll never forget it.'

She looked up at him shyly, and for a moment he saw there on her face a shadow of the shining glory that had been on the child's face, in the photograph.

'It was a glory,' she said.

'Tell me what you saw.'

'You won't laugh at me?'

'No.'

She turned away so she couldn't see his face while she spoke. The coloured light from the stained-glass window was now glowing red and gold on the aisle between them.

'I stood on the beach, and the sun was setting, and everything became still. Not a dead kind of stillness. A perfect stillness. It was just like you said, it was like I slipped out of myself. I was part of everything. Then seeing Jesus coming to me over the water – I don't know that I saw him – it was like there had to be a way to show how grand it was, how it was the grandest moment of my life. So I wanted Jesus to come to me, to make sense of the feeling.'

'And to speak to you.'

'That was to make sense of the feeling too.'

'What was this feeling?'

'How perfect the world was, and how fragile. How there was goodness at the heart of it. How easily the goodness could die. That was what I felt, more than anything. This fragile world, that was so still and so beautiful, and was going to die.'

'Yes,' said Rupert. 'I've felt that.'

She looked up quickly, eagerly.

'Have you? Have you? It's grand, isn't it? And it's a terrible fear comes over you. That's why I knew I had to tell everyone. To warn them. But what I said . . . I don't know where it came from.'

'You used the words you'd been given,' said Rupert. 'What else could you do?'

'I knew it was wrong. After the third evening I knew I was making it up. I could feel it. All those people, all watching me, all writing down everything I said. That goes to a girl's head, you know? I was the star. And after that, when I thought it would all go away, it got bigger and bigger. People came to see me, and I had to tell it all again. And they acted like I was holy, like I was a living saint. And Mam was so proud. And the priest was so good to me. So I couldn't tell them. I kept waiting for someone to pull my arm and say, "That's enough of all this foolishness, Mary Brennan." But they never did.'

'So you ran away.'

'Oh, after the longest time. I stayed as long as I could. They all expected me to live the rest of my life in a convent. Dear Lord, I expected it myself. It's terrible what a Catholic childhood does to you. A convent! Shut away with half a dozen miserable old women! If you want to know how Jesus suffered on the cross go into a convent, and you'll know for sure that God has abandoned you.'

'Is that what you felt? That God had abandoned you?'

'Of course. Hadn't I taken his name in vain? It was my punishment, living with the nuns. My punishment for all my terrible wickedness.'

'And you never told a soul?'

'What was I to tell them? That I was a wicked liar? There were all these other people who came to Buckle Bay and had visions and miracle cures and all sorts of wonders. That was me, started it all. If I was a liar, were they all liars?'

'You're not a liar, Mary.'

'But you see, Rupert, no one, in all my life, has ever said to me what you've said today. I thought my visions were either from God, or they were my own lies. But here you are, a man who doesn't believe in God, telling me I don't need God for my visions to be true.'

'That's exactly what I'm telling you, Mary.'

'Then God bless you!' she said with fervour. 'And even if you don't have a God, I've got a God, and my God blesses you.'

'And you know something else about your God?' said Rupert. 'God knows everything. God knows you better than you know yourself. So all along, God has known your secret. How you made it up, and never told anyone. You can't keep secrets from God.'

'You talk so like a priest, Rupert Blundell.'

'I was raised in the church. I can talk the talk.'

She jumped up out of the pew, suddenly filled with energy.

'Oh, dear Lord! I want to run about.'

'Run about, then. Run up and down the aisle.'

She raised her arms and did three rapid pirouettes, her eyes finding him on each turn. She looked radiant.

'I want to fly,' she said.

'Now that would impress me.'

'Darling Rupert. Can I hug you?'

He stood up and they shared a long hug in the aisle. Her joyous relief infected him too.

'You know why I'm so happy?' she said. 'I've escaped at last.'

'Almost,' he said.

'Why almost?'

'You have to go back to Kilnacarry first. You have to show them who you are. Then you'll be free.'

He felt quite sure of this, without entirely knowing why. Until she had returned, and let her mother and her brother and the priest and all the people of her childhood see and accept her as she was now, a part of her would be for ever held prisoner in Kilnacarry.

'I can't go back,' she said.

'There's a twelve-year-old girl there, Mary, waiting for you to come back and tell her she's done no wrong.'

'She told such stories.'

'There's more than one way for a story to be true.'

'I would die of shame if they ever knew.'

'Your God knows. Aren't you ashamed before him?'

'Oh, you Jesuit. What's it to you if I go back or not?'

'You're living your life in hiding, Mary. I want you to come out of your hiding place into the light, where I can see you.'

'Oh, do you? And what do you propose to do with me then?'

He looked at her, and then took off his glasses to clean them with his handkerchief. While he was occupied in this way, no longer seeing her, he spoke in a neutral reflective voice.

'I like the sound of this stillness. I thought I might ask you if you could try and show it to me.'

She hadn't expected that. She stared at his funny bumpy face, at his eyes no longer shielded by his spectacles, at his balding brow, and she couldn't speak, she was so moved.

'I'll go back to Kilnacarry if you'll go with me, Rupert Blundell.'

36

'It's so lovely to have you home again, darling. Why does it have to be raining?'

Pamela brushed the rain off her coat and hugged her mother. Everything at home was the way it had always been. She felt as if she had been away for a hundred years.

'I hope you don't mind, but I promised William I'd watch him in his match this afternoon.'

'Surely they don't play in weather like this?'

'It's rugger, darling. Nothing stops them.'

Pamela went up to her room carrying the small suitcase she'd brought from London. It was the bedroom of a child. This sensation, that she was no longer the person who had once inhabited this pretty room, swept over her so powerfully that she wanted to cry. It felt to her as if she had lost something that she cared about very much, in the short time since she had last slept in this narrow white bed.

'Well, darling,' she said aloud, mocking herself, 'you've lost your innocence, haven't you?'

She stood at her bedroom window, looking out at the distant hump of Mount Caburn, grey under the grey sky. The impulse to cry was still very strong, but she dug her fingernails into her palms and stopped herself. She went to the little washbasin in the corner and splashed her face with cold water, and brushed her hair hard with her old hairbrush, staring at herself in the mirror that was framed in pink seashells.

I'll show them.

Who they were, and what they were to be shown, was not clear to her. Only that she was hurt and angry. In the days that had passed since her weekend at Herriard, her feelings of shame had been overtaken by a growing anger. She was angry with André, and Bobby, and the world they came from, the world of Stephen and Christine. But this home world, to which she now fled, was no comfort to her. She felt that she belonged nowhere, and had no future.

I don't deserve this.

Here lay the core of her anger. She was owed a fine life, and she had been cheated. She was entitled to love, and no one loved her. Her mother loved her, of course, but that meant nothing. Everyone was loved by their mothers. Home love was as much a burden as a support, with its unasked questions and lingering looks. Her mother said things like 'So have you been having fun?' because she could see she was unhappy. What could you say to a question like that?

Pamela had retreated to Sussex not to be home but to be away from the scene of her humiliation. Now she was here she didn't know what to do. Her sister Elizabeth was at boarding school. Larry, her stepfather, was on a buying trip in France. Her mother was preoccupied with Edward, her younger half-brother, back from school for the weekend. And Edward, nine years old, knew nothing but the world of school, and his triumphs there.

'I'm the top arm-wrestler in my year! Put up your arm, I'll wrestle you!'

'I don't know how to arm-wrestle, Eddie.'

'It's easy. Put your elbow on the table. There. Now hold my hand.'

He forced her arm down in one quick pounce.

'Ow! You took me by surprise.'

'Do it again, then.'

They squared off again, sitting at the kitchen table, while their mother laid out lunch. Pamela pretended to resist as long as she could, and then let him win.

'You're rubbish,' said Edward, beaming.

'All right, Tarzan.'

'I'm the best horse fighter too.'

'My God,' said Pamela to her mother. 'He's turned into a monster.'

'That's boys for you,' said Kitty.

After lunch they drove over to Underhill and stood under umbrellas on the side of a playing field, watching small boys hurl themselves about in the mud. The parents on the sidelines were passionately engaged in the action on the pitch, calling out to the youthful players in angry voices.

'Get stuck in, Tom! Go, Peter, go, you can do it! Look where you're passing, Patrick! Come on, Underhill! Heave!'

The rain fell steadily, forming runnels of water trickling down the embankment at the edge of the playing field to the woods below. Somewhere in the haze the Downs loomed, lost in the sodden sky. Pamela clutched her umbrella and allowed her attention to wander. She had no interest in the match, even though it was against Underhill's great rival, Ashdown, and was, according to Edward, the most important match of the year.

'William's so proud to be in the team,' her mother said. 'I just have to be here.'

'I don't understand any of it,' said Pamela. 'I can't even see William.'

'He's in the second row. Look, there he is.'

A cluster of small, muddy eleven-year-old boys was forming a scrum, locking shoulders. William was somewhere in the middle.

'He's bound to hurt himself,' said Pamela.

'Don't! I dread it.'

Off they went again, scattering, chasing the odd-shaped ball that bounced in unpredictable ways.

'I think I'll go and take a look in the art room,' Pamela said.

'All right, darling. Team tea in the dining hall after the match.'

The art room, a hut on the far side of the school car park, was where Maurice Jenks worked on his own paintings at weekends. Pamela told herself that all she wanted was to get out of the rain.

She opened the door without knocking, and came upon him slumped in his canvas chair, apparently asleep.

'Whoever it is,' he said, not opening his eyes, 'go away.'

'It's me. Pamela.'

His eyes jerked open.

'The lovely Pamela?'

'Hello, Mr Jenks. How are you?'

'Nigh unto death. You've come just in time. My word, you're a sight for sore eyes.'

Pamela felt better at once. With a tiny twinge of shame she realised this was what she had come for.

'Still no further on with your great work.'

Maurice Jenks had been at work for as long as she'd known him on a large canvas he called his 'Last Judgement'. It was to be a contemporary take on the great heaven and hell scenes of Bosch and Michelangelo. He had never got beyond the sketching-in of a writhing mass of bodies.

'How's London?' he said, choosing not to speak of his own unachieved existence. 'Are you at art school?'

'Not yet,' she said. 'The new courses haven't started.'

'So much for art,' he said. 'I suppose you've chosen life.'

'Mind if I smoke?' She lit up as she asked. 'One of my brothers is in a rugger match. It's foul out there.'

'But in here we have warmth' – he gestured to the flickering blue flame of an oil heater – 'sustenance' – he raised a half-drunk mug of instant coffee – 'and beauty.' He inclined his craggy head towards her. 'Let the tempest rage.'

She drew on her cigarette, soothed by the nicotine.

'I hope you don't mind me bothering you.'

'It seems not.'

'I'll go as soon as the match is over.'

'I'm honoured to have you share my refuge. You can tell me tales of the city. Did you find your great love?'

'What great love?'

'I seem to remember you were going to have a great love affair.'

'Oh, that's all just stupid.'

'I'm sorry to hear that.'

Distant cries came through the falling rain from the playing fields.

'There are grown men out there,' she said, 'shouting at small boys to kick each other harder, as if it really matters.'

'Prep school dads,' said the art master. 'A special breed.'

'What I keep thinking,' said Pamela, 'is there must've been a time when they were young, and in love. And they went down on one knee or whatever, and asked the girl to marry them. And there was a wedding, and a honeymoon, and a baby, just like everyone dreams. Now there they are, bald and tubby, bellowing in the rain.'

Maurice Jenks squinted at her.

'Aren't you a bit young to be disillusioned?'

'I don't feel young.'

'Allow me to assure you, you look young.'

'I expect it's my fault,' said Pamela. 'I expect I'm just doing everything all wrong. But how are you supposed to know?'

'You don't know. You flounder about. You make mistakes. You learn.'

'Then what? Does it all come right in the end?'

'You're asking me?' he said. 'What do you expect me to say? I'm a prep school art master. That's one step down in social standing from the man who puts the jam in doughnuts.'

She smiled at him, and was gratified to see how he closed his eyes under the impact of her smile, and how his hand trembled.

'I think you're magnificent,' she said.

'You must want something from me.'

'No,' she said. 'Just to get out of the rain.'

She joined the after-match tea in better spirits. The junior team had won their match, and William, it turned out, was the hero of the day. Pink with pride, he accepted the praise that jostled him on all sides.

'Great try, Will! Quick thinking there, old chap!'

Pamela gave him a hug and told him she was proud of him. She remembered her half-brothers when they'd been little, chortling and toddling about her as she lay on the rug, catching at them with outreached arms. And here was William grown to be eleven years old, and a rugger star, and almost as tall as her.

'You never saw William's try,' her mother whispered to her, laughing.

'I wouldn't have seen it even if I'd seen it,' said Pamela.

'Me neither. The first I knew everyone was cheering and shouting his name. But he's so happy. Just look at him.'

'He'd better make the most of it,' said Pamela. 'This is as good as it gets.'

The school tea was a curious combination of sausages, mashed potato, sponge cake with butter icing, and ginger biscuits. Pamela ate it all. She caught several of the fathers sneaking looks at her. Edward came over at one point and whispered, giggling, 'David Davenport thinks you're sexy.'

'Which one's David Davenport?'

Edward pointed out a bold-looking thirteen-year-old with a thick shock of blond hair. He saw them looking at him and turned away abruptly, going red.

'Tell him to come back in five years.'

Edward loved that. He bounded off to relay the message. The double boost of nursery food and admiration restored Pamela's good temper.

That evening, alone with her mother, they curled up together on the sofa the way they used to do before she went away to school, and told each other secrets.

'So have you acquired any admirers in London?' Kitty said.

'There was someone I thought I might like,' she said, 'but he turned out to be no good.'

'Oh, darling. I'm so sorry. Was he a beast?'

'Just no good, really.'

'You have to be so careful with men. There aren't many good ones about.'

'How can you tell?' said Pamela. 'He seemed good. I mean, he was well-mannered, and generous, and clever. And actually quite grand and rich.'

She wanted her mother to know that she had attracted the attention, for a while at least, of someone of some distinction.

'Hugo said you'd been making some rather grand friends.'

'Funny old Hugo.'

'Don't laugh at him, darling. He's one of the good ones. I've no idea how he puts up with Harriet.'

Pamela put on a Harriet voice.

'We're having a quiet day.'

They both laughed.

'But I'm not laughing at Hugo, Mummy. He's a dear.'

'Do you remember how when you were little you were going to marry him?'

'Of course I do. What a fool he must have thought me.'

'No, of course he didn't. He's not like that. He's just completely decent and reliable and kind.' Then Kitty added after a pause, 'He was so patient with Ed.'

It wasn't often they talked about Pamela's father.

'Do you think,' said Pamela, 'if Daddy hadn't died, that I'd have grown up a different person?'

'How can we ever know? At least you had Larry.'

'I love Larry so much. But Daddy was Daddy.'

It was all so long ago, and truth to tell she had only confused memories of him. She remembered dancing with him, in the big room at Edenfield Place.

'You're like him in so many ways,' her mother said, tracing her cheekbones with one finger. 'I see him every time I look at you.'

Pamela had his photograph by her bed. He was impossibly handsome, and a war hero as well. He'd won the VC. How many men like that are there in the world?

'You're so lucky, Mummy. You had him, and now Larry.'

'There'll be someone for you, darling.'

'How can you tell?' she said again.

'When it happens, you just know. Although—'

Kitty stopped just as it seemed she was going to say more.

'Although what?'

'Actually, darling,' her mother said, 'I just realised how sometimes you think you know it's right, but you turn out to be wrong.'

'Because he turns out to be a beast?'

'Or just not the right one for you.'

'But there are a lot of beasts out there, aren't there? I mean, men who only want one thing.'

She was thinking of the man who whispered to her at André's party, 'Do you fuck?'

'Yes, darling, there are. You have to be careful.'

'I don't understand it. I mean, I do understand them wanting that, but wanting only that – as if it doesn't matter who you are at all.'

'Has someone been treating you badly, darling?'

'Oh, no. I'm fine. You know how it is. When you were young you must have had men buzzing round you. You were so pretty.'

'I think all girls do when they're young.'

Pamela knew about her father the war hero. But it had just occurred to her that she knew nothing about her mother's life before she was married. It was the war, of course, and everything was different.

'Was Daddy the first?'

She meant, first lover. Kitty understood her.

'Yes,' she said. 'He was my first everything.'

'And you were in love.'

'Terribly.'

'You're so lucky.'

'In some ways,' said her mother. 'Not in others.'

'Because he died young.'

He was thirty-two when he died. He had never seemed young to Pamela before. But now it struck her, he had been the same age as André.

Kitty was saying nothing.

'What is it, Mummy?'

She realised her mother was upset. She was biting her lip in that way she did when she didn't want to cry.

'I've always said to myself I'll wait till you're older,' she said. 'But you are older now.'

Pamela felt a coldness inside her.

'Is it about Daddy?' she said.

'Ed was a wonderful man, and a very troubled man. He found life hard, a lot of the time. He withdrew into himself. He was very unhappy.'

Pamela knew as she listened to her mother that she had always known. But there are things you don't choose to see in clear light.

'There came a time,' said Kitty, 'when he just didn't want to go on living anymore.'

His early death had been a tragic accident. But of course it wasn't an accident. He fell five hundred feet, from the top of Beachy Head. How could it have been an accident? My beautiful hero father wasn't the type to stray too near the edge by accident. He wasn't the type to fall by accident. She had always known this, even as a child. But she had never taken the next step. She had not strayed too near that cliff edge.

'Would you rather I didn't tell you this?'

'No,' said Pamela. 'Go on.'

'All he thought about at the end was you and Elizabeth and me.'

'Did he say so?'

'He left a letter.'

A letter. All these years there had been a letter.

'Can I read it?'

'Would you mind if I read it out to you? Some parts are very private.'

She went upstairs to her bedroom, where she kept her most precious things. Pamela stayed curled up on the sofa, feeling cold.

Kitty came back down holding a handwritten letter folded in four. She sat down on the sofa and opened it up and read it through silently. Then she read from it aloud.

Don't hate me for leaving you. Don't be angry. Just say he did his best, and when he could do no more he laid himself down to sleep. Kiss the girls from me. Tell them if there is a heaven after all, I'll be waiting for them. Tell them I go with my head held high, still storming that fatal beach, still the war hero. Tell them I'll love them for eternity. As I'll love you. If we meet again it'll be in a place where all things are known, and you'll forgive me.

She paused, trying not to cry. Pamela was already crying, noiselessly, not moving. Then Kitty cleared her throat, and continued to the end.

Goodnight, my darling. I shall fall asleep in your arms, and the hurting will be over.

She folded the letter up once more, and took Pamela in her arms. They wept together.

'He must have been so unhappy,' said Pamela, sobbing. 'Why was he so unhappy?'

'It was in him,' said her mother. 'I don't know why. It was in him from the beginning.'

'At least you had Larry.'

'Yes. Ed knew that.'

'He knew Larry loved you?'

'Yes.'

It was all so new to Pamela, and yet so long known. So much love, so much unhappiness.

'I should have told you before,' Kitty said. 'I think I've always been frightened of telling you.'

'I half knew,' said Pamela.

'What about Elizabeth? Should I tell her?'

'It's not the same for Elizabeth. She didn't really know him. She says she doesn't remember him.'

'Maybe when she's a bit older.'

'I need a drink. Do you need a drink?'

Pamela poured them both a shot of cognac.

'Brandy for shock,' she said.

'Is it a shock?'

'I'm fine now. Thanks, Mummy. I do love you.'

They drank the brandy, once more side-by-side on the sofa.

'It won't be the same for you, my darling. Everyone's life is different.'

That night, lying in bed unable to sleep, Pamela found it was a shock after all. A turbulent stream of emotions passed through her, stirring up long-dormant pools of loss and fear. Her own father had not been able to bear the pain of living. He had laid himself down to sleep. It was in him from the beginning.

What if it's in me? What if it's the devil in me?

Suddenly the world seemed to Pamela to be a frightening place. Where could she go to be safe? How could she ever be loved as her mother had been loved? A memory then jumped into her mind, from long ago, from before her father had died. She was standing in the hall, looking through the open kitchen door. In the kitchen, with his back to her, stood Hugo, with her mother in his arms. He was kissing her like a lover.

PART FOUR

Retaliation

October 1962

37

Mac Bundy was hosting a dinner party at his home when he got the call.

'Those things we've been worrying about in Cuba are there.'

'You're sure?'

'No question about it. We've got the pictures.'

Mac returned to his dinner guests and said nothing. The president had only just got back from campaigning in Niagara Falls and New York City and was worn out. Bundy made the decision to let him have a quiet night's sleep.

Next morning he went in to the White House to give the president the bad news. He rode the elevator to the private quarters, and entered to find the president in bed, sitting up reading the morning *New York Times*. The page one headline ran:

EISENHOWER CALLS PRESIDENT
WEAK ON FOREIGN POLICY

Bundy's style was to get to the point fast.

'They got the pictures back from the U2, Mr President. Not good.'

'What's this? Cuba?'

'They spotted two medium-range missiles and six missile transports, south-west of Havana.'

'Nuclear missiles?'

'Looks like it, sir.'

'That fucking Khrushchev! That fucking liar! He can't do that to me!'

Later, in the Oval Office, Kennedy was shown the photographs. The grainy images meant nothing to him. Amid the dots and blotches were labels and arrows: ERECTOR LAUNCH EQUIPMENT. MISSILE TRAILERS.

'They're what we designate as SS4s, sir,' said the CIA analyst. 'Range of 1,174 miles.'

'How do you know that's what they are?'

'The length, sir. Sixty-seven feet. Same as the SS4s paraded in Red Square.'

'Are they ready to fire?'

'Most likely not,' said Bob McNamara. 'Depends if they've got the warheads on site.'

'Warheads! Fuck!'

In a series of urgently called meetings, the president and his advisers debated what to do.

'The first thing I want,' said Kennedy, 'is secrecy. Fucking Khrushchev can keep a secret. So can I. I don't want the *New York Times* telling me what to do.'

The mystery was why Khrushchev had done it.

'Does he want a nuclear war? Is he insane?'

'If he wants war,' said Bobby Kennedy, 'let's do it. Get it over with. Take our losses.'

'If we attack Cuba,' said the president, 'the Soviets will attack Berlin. And if that happens, I have to push the button on the nukes. That's one hell of a decision.'

General Curtis LeMay saw the matter in clear and simple terms. As Air Force chief he was in overall charge of the missiles and bombers that between them would deliver the thousands of kilotons of destruction that was the Single Integrated Operational Plan.

'My boys can be ready to go in twenty-four hours, Mr President. The Cubans won't even know what hit 'em.'

'And lose Berlin?'

'Do nothing over Cuba, the Soviets will take Berlin. This is a test of will, sir. Back down now, you send a message of weakness.'

'So what are you advising, General?'

'Bomb Cuba to hell. No warning. No delay. You have all the justification right there.' He pointed his chewed cigar at the spyplane photographs. 'Right now we have overwhelming nuclear superiority over the Soviets. You think Khrushchev's going to risk war? We've got him in a trap. Let's take his leg off, right up to his testicles.'

'We don't know what risks Khrushchev might take,' said McNamara. 'He's an unpredictable guy. He might react emotionally.'

'No one wins a nuclear war,' said Rusk.

'The way I see it,' said General Tommy Power, Chief of Strategic Air Command, 'if there's two Americans and one Russian alive at the end of the war, we win.'

'Then I'm happy this isn't your decision,' said the president.

'Do nothing about this,' said LeMay, again angrily gesturing at the photographs, 'and it'll be bad as Munich.'

Bobby met his brother's eyes. Everyone knew their father Joe Kennedy had been accused of wanting to negotiate with Hitler. The president kept his temper.

'I'll do as I judge best, General.'

'Well, sir, I'd say you're in a pretty bad fix at the present time.'

'What did you say?'

'You're in a pretty bad fix.'

Kennedy stared at the pugnacious LeMay.

'Well, you're in there with me, General.'

After the meeting broke up, Kennedy said to Bundy, 'I don't want that man near me again.'

The question remained, how to respond? The options resolved into four. Hit the known missile sites from the air. Order a general air strike to take out all Cuba's defences. Order a full seaborne invasion. Or least provocatively, blockade the island to play for time, and prevent any more missiles being delivered.

The next day pictures produced by further U2 flights revealed that the situation was even more dangerous. The long-range cameras showed evidence of launch sites for SS5 missiles. With double the range of the SS4s, the SS5s could reach US bases in the Midwest, where much of the nuclear force was concentrated. The Soviets had given Cuba counterforce capability.

General Maxwell Taylor, head of the Joint Chiefs of Staff, explained the risk this posed.

'The Soviets know we outgun them. If it were ever to come to a global war, their only chance would be to even up the odds right off the bat. That means a first strike at our missile fields. They now have the capacity to do that.'

'But why?' Kennedy continued to struggle with the underlying mystery. 'Why would Khrushchev take such an insane risk?'

'You have to remember, sir, they don't think the way we do. Stalin held Stalingrad because he was willing to go on taking insane losses. One battle, over a million casualties.'

'But that was in defence of his homeland.'

In the light of the new information the Joint Chiefs were no longer confident that air strikes alone would eliminate all the missiles on Cuba.

'They've got bases popping up like measles.'

Taylor's recommendation now was that nothing short of a full invasion would do the job.

'This is our big opportunity. We destroy the Soviet missiles, and we destroy Castro along with them. There'll never be another chance like this.'

But still the president hesitated. He didn't want to appear weak, but he was more afraid of setting in motion a chain of events he couldn't control. He too had recently read *The Guns of August*. His instinct was to play for time.

Meanwhile, given that there was a high likelihood action would have to be taken, he ordered his military chiefs to formulate plans for armed intervention. At the same time he prepared a draft for a presidential address to the nation, should it become necessary.

'My fellow Americans,' the draft address began, 'with a heavy heart, and in necessary fulfilment of my oath of office, I have ordered, and the United States Air Force has now carried out, military operations to remove a major nuclear weapons build-up from the soil of Cuba . . .'

38

They took two rooms in the Nesbitt Arms Hotel in Ardara. Mary Brennan refused to go any nearer to Kilnacarry.

'You don't know what it's like, Rupert,' she said, trembling. 'Eamonn can bring Mam to see me here.'

Bridie no longer lived at home. She had found work in Dublin, and had been living there for the last many years.

Rupert drove the five miles to Kilnacarry by himself, and called first on the priest. He arrived just as Sunday Mass was ending.

The priest guessed as soon as he saw him.

'You've brought her back.'

'She won't come to the village. She just wants to see her mother.'

'Once Eileen Brennan knows she's here, the whole world will know,' said Father Flannery. 'Am I to see her myself?'

'Yes, Father. She'd like to see you.' Then he added, to prepare him, 'It's not just the crowds she's afraid of. She's very confused about what she thinks.'

'Why wouldn't she be?' said the priest. 'I've been confused all my life.'

'After all, she was only a child at the time.'

The priest returned with Rupert to Ardara, following behind in his own car. He entered the hotel by the back door, so as not to give rise to speculation.

'You think it's far enough away, but say *Dominus vobiscum* in Ardara and they're saying *Et cum spiritu tuo* in Kilnacarry.'

The hotel had a small wood-panelled meeting room behind the bar, with wallpaper the colour of wine. Here the priest settled down with a pot of tea and a plate of biscuits, while Rupert went to fetch Mary.

She came into the room with her eyes cast down. When she spoke, her voice was barely above a whisper.

'It's good of you to come, Father.'

'How're you keeping, Mary? Sit, sit. Have some tea.'

The priest eyed her keenly as she sat down at the table facing him.

'You've come home, Mary. That was the right thing to do.'

'I've come to see Mam, Father. I'll not go back to the village.'

'No, no. Nobody's going to make you do anything you don't want.'

'I'm sorry if I've let you down, Father.'

'You've not let anybody down, Mary. You have your own life to live, and why not?'

As she grew less afraid Mary's head rose, and she found herself looking properly at the priest. She was shocked to find him older than she had remembered. Father Flannery saw this at once.

'I'm an old man now, Mary.'

'No, Father! Not old.'

'Not so far off my seventieth birthday. Over forty years in the parish. There was a time when I'd have told you, if I'd been open with you, that my life was a waste of God's good creation, and that breathing in was not worth the effort when all that comes of it is breathing out. But I don't say that any more,

347

Mary. And that's because of you. What you saw on that beach, the day they dropped the bomb, has become my life's work. It's given hope, and faith, to thousands of lost and lonely souls. You should come to Mass of a summer Sunday, Mary. Weather permitting I say a Mass on the beach. We have a hundred and more come, and they go away with the love of the Lord alive in their hearts. That true faith, Mary. It's a rare and precious gift. I thank you for that.'

Mary looked unhappy. She appealed mutely to Rupert.

'It was all a long time ago, Father,' said Rupert.

'So it was, so it was. And the shrine has grown, and is growing still. We have the money raised to build a chapel, there's to be a window behind the altar that's one almighty sheet of glass, so the faithful can worship as the sun sets over the sea. You'll come when the chapel is built, Mary. You'll come home when the shrine is ready.'

'No, Father.'

'You can come on the quiet. There'll be no one to trouble you.'

'I shall trouble myself, Father.'

Rupert said, 'Tell Father Flannery how it is, Mary. He needs to know.'

Mary looked down, and said nothing.

'God bless you,' said the priest, 'I don't need to be told. The girl has parted company with her visions. And why wouldn't she, after all this time? The Lord picked out a child of twelve years old. That child is long gone.'

'I didn't know what I was doing,' said Mary, low.

'How could you know, child? You were doing the Lord's work.'

'It was like a game, Father. I didn't know how to stop.'

'So what you're telling me is that your visions weren't true visions, is that it, Mary?'

348

He spoke gently, and sounded neither shocked nor angry.

'Yes, Father. I'm sorry, Father.'

'So tell me this, Mary. How would the visions have been different if they were true?'

'I don't know, Father.'

'Suppose the Lord had wanted to send you a vision, and speak to you. He might have decided to play a child's game with you, mightn't he?'

'Are you wanting to tell me my visions were true after all, Father?'

'Not exactly, Mary. What I'm asking you is, does it really matter if they're true visions or not? Perhaps the Lord came to you. Perhaps you dreamed the Lord came to you. Perhaps you made it all up for a game so everyone would listen to you. What matters isn't how it all came about, but the truth of the message you delivered, and the faith that has grown from that. And your message was a good message, Mary, and a true one. And great faith has grown from it.'

Mary looked down again.

'Even if it was a foolish child playing a foolish game?'

'Why shouldn't the Lord use a foolish child for his great purposes?'

'But they believed me. They believed I saw Jesus walking on the water.'

'And did you not?'

'I don't know, Father. I think it was all just a fancy of mine, and a trick of the light.'

'Like a dream.'

'Yes, Father.'

'Do you remember when Monsignor McCloskey questioned you, and asked you if your vision might not have been a dream? You said to him, "If Jesus wanted to come to me it would never be ordinary. So it would have to be a dream."'

Mary nodded, remembering.

'You said to Monsignor McCloskey, "What does it matter what we call it?"'

Mary looked at Rupert.

'No one wins an argument with a priest.'

'Father Flannery has his reasons,' said Rupert. 'Your visions have become the main source of income for the village.'

'And I'm proud of that,' said the priest. 'And so should you be.'

'Father,' said Mary, 'I'm happy that good has come of it, and that you'll have your shrine and all, but I can't come back again. Not as the girl who saw the visions. It would be a lie.'

'I do see that, Mary.' He sighed. 'But they'll wait for you. They will. There's no stopping that.'

'You must tell them the visions are over. I'm not the little child I was.'

'I'll tell them, Mary. But they'll tell me that the Lord promised Mary Brennan he would appear to her one more time, to give the last warning. They say it to me every day. Depend upon it, "Father," they say, "she'll be back."'

'That's why I can never go back.'

'Well, well.' The priest sighed again. 'It's you that must decide.'

'So let me see Mam and Eamonn, and then I'll go away again.'

They made a plan. The priest would drive back to Kilnacarry to pick up Eileen Brennan and her son in his car. He would bring them to the hotel, and they would come in the back way, as he had done.

While they were waiting, Rupert asked Mary how she was bearing up.

'Better than I expected,' she said.

'Was I wrong to make you come back?'

'No, you were right. It feels better to have it out in the open. With the priest, at least.'

'He's an unusual man.'

'It's because he's not vain,' said Mary. 'He doesn't expect to be right.'

Rupert was struck by this perception. It linked up somewhere in his mind with other thoughts he had been pursuing, about the limits of certainty, and the grievous damage done by righteousness.

'Faith is a strange business, isn't it?' he said.

'How would I know? They put the faith into me with my mother's milk. I couldn't tell you what it is to save my life.'

She was making fun of herself; and, in her gentle teasing way, of him. Rupert found himself thinking that if he were God, she was just the sort he'd choose to appear to in a vision.

Mrs Brennan came, followed closely by her great man of a son. Mary burst into tears and threw herself into her mother's arms.

'I'm sorry, Mam. I'm sorry.'

'What have you got to be sorry about?' said Mrs Brennan, crying too.

Rupert withdrew, to leave them to their embraces and tears. He and Father Flannery stepped into the bar, and he bought the priest a whiskey, and himself a Mackeson's. It was lunchtime, and the bar slowly filled up as they sat there, conversing quietly.

'It's a good deed you've done today,' said the priest.

'I've done it for her,' said Rupert. 'She couldn't move on with her life so long as she was haunted by the past.'

'And what will that life be, when she moves on?'

'That's up to Mary.'

'Mary's a remarkable girl,' said the priest. 'She's not had much in the way of education, but she's smarter than all the rest of us.'

He was looking around the bar with a frown.

'Now this is something of a crowd. And not market day, either.'

He got up and walked over to the window.

'Will you look at that?'

Rupert looked out of the window. There was quite a crowd outside too, standing about in clusters, talking together.

'There's not usually so many lounging about the Diamond of a Sunday lunchtime in Ardara,' the priest said. 'Something's up.'

Rupert turned to watch the crowd in the bar. People were staring at him, and looking hastily away.

'I think it's us,' he said.

'I'm thinking the very same thing,' said the priest.

He went to the bar.

'Now then, Michael,' he said. 'What's going on?'

'You tell me, Father,' said the barman. 'The word is it's the end of the world.'

'What sort of godless nonsense is that?'

The barman lowered his voice.

'Is it true that Mary Brennan has returned?'

'Lord have mercy on me,' said the priest. 'I never knew a country like this for stirring the pot on other people's stoves.'

He beckoned to Rupert, and they returned to the wood-panelled room. Mary was sitting close beside her mother, their heads touching. Eamonn stood silent and awkward, screwing up his cap in his big hands.

'Someone split on us,' said the priest. 'There's a crowd out-side.'

Mary jumped up, alarmed.

'I must go!'

'No, Mary,' said the priest. 'You're not done here yet.' He turned to Rupert. 'Rupert here is going to tell you the same as me. There's no need for you to run away. This is something you must see through to the end and be done with, or it'll be hanging over you till the day you die. The people know you must come before them one last time. You can do that, Mary. And then you can go.'

Mary looked from the priest to Rupert.

'But what am I to say?'

'Say whatever you believe to be true.'

'That I made it all up?'

Eileen Brennan gasped.

'Yes,' said Rupert. 'If that's what you believe.'

'Whatever you say,' said the priest, 'they'll understand it as the last message.'

'But I haven't got a message.'

'Then tell them so,' said Rupert.

'Oh, Mary,' said Eileen Brennan, grasping her daughter's hand. 'You didn't make it all up, did you?'

'I was a child, Mam!'

'But I saw your face! I saw the light of heaven in your eyes.'

'Oh, Mam.' She kissed her mother. 'I felt as if heaven was in me that day. But I was just a wild and foolish child.'

'Are we now to be shamed before the neighbours?'

'No, no. It'll be all right.'

There was a tap on the door. Rupert opened it a crack. It was the hotel owner with a message for himself. A phone call had been received. Rupert took the piece of paper and closed the door. The message was from the office of the Chief of Defence Staff.

Return as soon as possible. Emergency.

Father Flannery now had Mary's hand in his.

'You can speak to them, Mary,' he was saying. 'You can tell them not to be afraid. You can tell them that each of us must find his own way through life. You can tell them how your visions brought a new spirit of faith to Kilnacarry, and how you're proud of that, and how it's up to all of them now to keep the spirit of Kilnacarry alive. Then you can go, with all our love, and live your life.'

Mary turned again to Rupert.

'He's right,' said Rupert.

'But I shall be so afraid.'

Eamonn Brennan now spoke up.

'It's only a bunch of eejits like myself,' he said. 'What's to be afraid of?'

'Oh, Eamonn! You're not an eejit.'

'I'm still in Kilnacarry, an't I?'

'Looking after his eejit of a mam,' said Eileen Brennan.

Mary shook her head, touched.

'Do you want me to do this, Mam?'

'If it's God's will,' said her mother. 'But if God could see his way to not letting Betty Clancy crow over me, I'd be well pleased.'

'Then I'll do as you ask, Father.'

Father Flannery proposed that Mary leave Ardara, now that word had got out, and stay with some good people he knew on the Killybegs road.

'You'll be out of the way of the crowds there,' he said. 'Meanwhile I'll announce that you'll be returning to Buckle Bay tomorrow at sunset. That'll give time for a good-sized crowd to gather. The bigger the crowd the better. There'll be so many wild rumours going about. Let them all see and hear the real Mary Brennan.'

He then went off to make the arrangements. Rupert sat down with Mary.

'Are you all right with this, Mary?'

She nodded.

'I've just received a phone message,' said Rupert. 'I have to go back to London.'

'Back to London! When?'

There was sudden panic in her voice.

'At once. This afternoon.'

'But how can I do it without you?'

'You don't need me. You don't even need the priest.'

'Do you have to go?'

'The message says it's an emergency.'

'What emergency?'

'I don't know.'

'I'm only here because of you.'

'That's not true, and you know it.'

But she looked at him so pitifully that he knew he couldn't abandon her.

'All right. I'll make a phone call. I'll try to find out what this emergency is. I'm sure they can manage without me.'

He went out into the bar. There was a phone in the passage, for the use of hotel residents. He put through a call to his office, but got no answer. Then he tried to call Ronnie Brockman at home, but the exchange misrouted his call, and then told him the number was not responding.

'Ach, it's a Sunday,' said the operator, as if this explained everything. 'I should try again tomorrow.'

He returned to Mary.

'I've not been able to get anyone on the phone.'

But she had had time to think, and her manner had changed.

'You go, Rupert. This is my home. These are my people. I'll come to no harm.'

She was no longer bending her head down, or speaking in that low fearful voice. She looked tired, but strong.

'What happened?' he said.

'Nothing.'

Father Flannery returned.

'All fixed,' he said. 'You'll not be bothered there.'

'No, Father,' said Mary. 'I shall go home to Mam.'

'You will?'

The priest stared at her in surprise.

'I was a child then. I'm not a child anymore.'

The priest turned to Rupert.

'You did this?'

'Not me,' said Rupert.

'Rupert has to go back to London,' said Mary. 'He has to go right away. It's an emergency. But I've no call to be going anywhere. There's no emergency for me. This is my home.'

She was so calm. Rupert was filled with wonder.

'Are you sure, Mary? I'll stay if you need me.'

'No, you must go. I was afraid at first, but then I thought to myself, what is it I'm afraid of? Am I afraid to be alone? Well, I've been alone before. So you go where you're needed, Rupert.'

'And I'll see you again in London?'

'Yes, of course. I'll stay with Mam and Eamonn for a few days. Then they'll be glad to see the back of me.'

It was all very unexpected. Now it was Rupert who found himself reluctant to leave. He told himself he was curious to see the crowd of pilgrims when Mary returned to the scene of her visions. But the summons from Mountbatten was not to be ignored.

That afternoon he drove back to Dublin and caught a late flight to London. He was shocked to discover how hard he found it to leave Mary, and how stubbornly the memory of her face lingered in his mind.

39

'I don't believe it!'

A cable late on Sunday night from David Ormsby-Gore, the British ambassador in Washington, had alerted London to the crisis.

'Bruce is on his way now,' said the prime minister.

'Nuclear missiles? On Cuba?'

Mountbatten could make no sense of it. He turned to Lord Home, the Foreign Secretary.

'Do you get this, Alec?'

'If it's true,' said Home, 'maybe it's to give him leverage over Berlin.'

David Bruce, the American ambassador, now arrived at Admiralty House, where the prime minister's offices were temporarily located during the refurbishment of 10 Downing Street. He was accompanied by a man from the CIA called Chet Cooper. Cooper showed copies of top-secret photographs taken by a U2 high-level reconnaissance flight. Macmillan barely glanced at the photographs.

'If the president tells me there's a meaningful offensive capability there,' he said, 'that's good enough for me.'

To the consternation of the two Americans, he seemed almost indifferent to the revelation.

'We've been living in the shadow of annihilation for the past many years,' he said, 'and we've somehow been able to lead more or less normal lives. Life goes on.'

Bruce spoke of the options open to the president, including the invasion of Cuba. Macmillan listened, frowning.

'And what if Khrushchev retaliates against Berlin, or against US bases abroad? Wouldn't it be better to deal with Khrushchev privately over this?'

'The president feels he must be seen to act,' said Bruce.

After the Americans had left, Philip de Zulueta raised the issue of public perception.

'A lot of people aren't going to believe it,' he said. 'They'll say it's a trumped-up excuse to get rid of Castro.'

'Nuclear missiles on Cuba!' said Mountbatten. 'I wouldn't call that trumped-up.'

'Philip's right,' said Home. 'We need to get the Americans to make the photographs public.'

'If you say so,' said Macmillan. 'I couldn't make out a thing.'

He turned to Mountbatten with a sigh.

'Brief the chiefs, Dickie. But tell them to play it down. I don't want anything in the newspapers. No panic moves.'

Back in his office in the Ministry of Defence, Mountbatten found Rupert Blundell at his desk.

'Thank God you're back, Rupert. Walk with me. Give me some perspective.'

They headed down the long corridor to the chiefs of staff briefing room. Mountbatten presented the crisis to Rupert in a few words.

'Strikes me as a clever move by Khrushchev,' he concluded. 'If Kennedy does nothing, he looks weak. If he launches an attack on Cuba, it gives Khrushchev the excuse to move on Berlin.'

'Maybe,' said Rupert.

'You don't think that's what it's all about?'

'I don't believe either Khrushchev or Kennedy wants to start a nuclear war.'

'No, of course not. It's about the achievement of limited objectives. Kennedy wants Castro out of Cuba. Khrushchev wants NATO out of West Berlin.'

'And we're the piggy in the middle,' said Rupert. 'I don't see that it matters very much what we say or do.'

'Oh, come on! That's a bit hard. We are a nuclear power in our own right.'

'Are we? We can't launch the Thors without American authorisation. In any nuclear exchange the Russians will target our Thors in the very first wave of attacks. If they're to be any use at all, we have to launch them before we're attacked, which we're never going to do. That makes them worse than useless: they're dangerous. You want perspective on this crisis? Offer to trade the Thors.'

'Trade the Thors!'

'Tell Khrushchev if he pulls his missiles out of Cuba, we'll dismantle the Thors. They're due to be phased out next year anyway.'

They had reached the briefing room. The heads of the services and their advisers were already there.

'Draw up a list of options as you see it, Rupert. Put the Thors on the list.'

Mountbatten went on into the big room. Rupert returned to his desk. He realised he was intensely excited. He took out a pencil and began to jot down the thoughts that were chasing round his head.

Why had Khrushchev taken such a giant risk?

In all his ponderings on the issue of nuclear weapons, Rupert had stopped short of considering an actual crisis. Each crisis came with its own set of specific circumstances, and had to be addressed in that light. Here now was a crisis.

The problem of intention loomed large. It was both critical to any solution, and unknowable. What did Khrushchev want? This deployment of nuclear missiles on Cuba achieved the exact opposite result to Rupert's hoped-for spiral of trust. It generated a spiral of fear.

Stay with the core conclusions. This is not a military crisis. Nuclear missiles are weapons designed not to be used. In this sense they are imaginary weapons. Understand the fear they are designed to allay, remove that fear, and the weapons become redundant.

But even now, Rupert knew, the Chiefs of Staff would be analysing the Russians' move in terms of the danger it posed to the West. They would be war-gaming every possible development of Soviet strategy in order to defend against it. In other words, they would be acting as if the Soviet intentions were wholly aggressive. That assumption generates fear. Fear leads to aggression.

So fear faces fear. Expectation of attack faces expectation of attack. Fingers begin to twitch on triggers. It would be a doomsday scenario but for one thing. Nobody wants to be the bad guy.

It's like the final gunfight in a Western. It's a moral stand-off.

The first and most crucial battle, Rupert wrote on his pad, *is the battle to make the other side shoot first.*

40

Pamela travelled back from Sussex to London on the afternoon of Monday, October 22. She found the Brook Green house empty. Hugo was at work. Harriet and Emily had gone to stay with Harriet's family in Lyme Regis for the week of half-term. Mary was in Ireland. Pamela was not sorry to have the house to herself. She was in a strange state of mind.

She phoned Susie and got no answer. Then after some hesitation she phoned Stephen Ward's flat, but no one answered there either. She wasn't sure what she wanted to say to Stephen. Had he known about André's tastes? Why had he not warned her?

Were all men incapable of love?

She went into the kitchen, and then into the larder, prowling for some source of gratification. She found a tin of Horlicks, and decided to have some. It was years since she had tasted Horlicks. She heated milk in a pan, and added the pale powder, and spent an annoying amount of time making it dissolve.

The hot sweet malty taste took her straight back to childhood. That brought memories of her father, pulling her over the snow on a sledge, turning back to smile for her. With a lurch she realised how much she had adored him. In her mind he was always some distance away from her, perhaps turning back to wave, but always leaving.

I hate you for leaving me.

The anger burst out of nowhere. *Still storming that fatal beach.* Why? The war was over, the medal won. What was there left to prove?

It was in him from the beginning.

And now it's in me.

This was what made Pamela walk about the empty house, unable to settle to anything. She was supposed to be calling the art college. Larry had made the contact, they were expecting her. But she could no longer imagine herself as an art student. It had been the picture she had built for herself once of the world she would enter that was beyond home, beyond school. But since then she had been introduced to a very different world, at Cliveden and Mayfair and Herriard, and by that bright light art school looked childish and provincial.

So what do I want now?

She felt hurt, and cheated. When her mother was her age war had come along, and swept her up and filled her days. She had been a driver, of all things. When she talked about it, which she did sometimes, she laughed, knowing it was a little ridiculous. But she had loved it. She was in control of her army staff car. She had known, day by day, what she was supposed to be doing. There had been days and nights off, and dancing in London clubs during the blackout, and boyfriends, but nothing serious. Then she had fallen in love.

The world is different now. Bored people looking for fun, lonely people looking for love.

Pamela thought back, asking herself when it was that she first saw a man look at her in that certain way. It was five years ago. They'd had a Christmas party at their house, just a drinks party, maybe thirty or forty local friends on one of the evenings leading up to Christmas. Her mother had said, 'Pammy, you can be our waitress. Take round the cheesy biscuits.' Edward had still been very small, so how old had she been? Twelve, thirteen. She had held up a plate before the local lord, George Holland, who was even older than her parents, and he had stared at her as if she were the only person in the room, and at the same time as if he didn't see her at all. Then he said, 'My word, Pammy, you are growing up.' She had understood then that he wanted her as a man wants a woman, and it had thrilled her. She had given him her special smile. This involved wrinkling up her nose and half shutting her eyes and giving a little lift of her shoulders, as if she and the person she was peeping at were sharing a secret that was funny and a bit rude. He had smiled back and said, 'You run along, you bad girl.' Later, remembering this, she had realised they had been flirting.

There had been a great deal more flirting since. Pamela adored flirting. She loved that moment when she caught a man's eye, and saw him struggling to conceal his response to her, and failing. She loved walking into a room and seeing every man there shift his posture to take account of her.

But flirting is only a prelude. The story has not yet begun.

In a sudden violent flood her mind filled with images of couples copulating, from André's collection. Women on their sides, one leg raised; on their hands and knees, bottoms in the air; astride their lover, head arched back; and always, in every pose, stabbing into them, the angry male weapon. This turned out to be the true story after all. This was what being pretty and flirting led towards. You were the only person in the room and they didn't even see you. It was so mean, it was such a swindle, it made her want to cry. Worse, it made her afraid. What if there was nothing after all? What if the years ahead held only loneliness and disappointment? What then?

You hear the hiss and suck of the waves rolling up the shingle beach, and they call to you, and you go.

The key scraped in the front door. Pamela ran into the hall. Hugo entered. The moment he saw her his face lit up.

'Pammy! You're back!'

His transparent joy at seeing her changed everything. She laughed and was light-hearted, skipped about making him a drink after his day's work, felt young and pretty again.

'Guess what I've been drinking? Horlicks!'

'My God! Is it drinkable?'

'Next I'll start wearing baggy cardigans and woolly slippers and keeping budgies.'

'I'm so glad you've come back. I thought perhaps you wouldn't. You know Harriet and Emily are away?'

'Yes, I know. I'm back for now, at least. If you'll have me.'

'You know you're always welcome here. You brighten up my drab life.'

'I don't see that it's so drab.'

'Actually, business is rather booming at present. Today I signed a deal to supply the new Hilton they're building on Park Lane.'

'Hurrah! Does that mean lots more money?'

'Some lots.'

'Then we should celebrate. Why don't we go out to dinner? There's only us, and I'm a rotten cook.'

'I say, shall we?'

His eyes shone with excitement.

'I shall dress up,' said Pamela, 'so that you won't be ashamed to be seen out with me.'

She put on her second-best frock, which was made of fine navy-blue jersey, and was very figure-hugging. There was nothing immodest about it, except for the closeness of the fit to her body. She brushed her hair back and wore it with an Alice band, aware that this showed her cheekbones to advantage.

'There,' she said, presenting herself with a demure curtsy. 'I'm practically a convent girl.'

'You're divine,' he said.

They hailed a taxi on Hammersmith Road, and he told the driver to take them to Franco's on Jermyn Street.

'You'll like Franco's,' he said to Pamela. 'Italian, but smart.'

In the taxi he asked after Kitty and the family, and quite suddenly Pamela found herself telling him about her father.

'Mummy told me what really happened,' she said. 'I'd never known.'

'Oh, Lord,' said Hugo.

'I'm glad she told me. You knew, I suppose.'

'Yes, I knew. A real tragedy.'

'Did you have any warning?'

'Not exactly,' said Hugo, sounding uncomfortable. 'I mean, there had been problems. But I never expected him to . . . '

His voice tailed off.

'Mummy says he just had this unhappiness in him.'

'Yes. I think it had been hard for Kitty for some time.'

'You were a good friend to her, Hugo.'

'I adored her,' said Hugo.

This simple statement pleased Pamela. It was so heartfelt.

The restaurant was bright and cheerful and reassuringly expensive. The maître d'hôtel clearly knew Hugo, and greeted him by name. They were given an excellent table. Hugo asked after the day's specials in the kitchen, and offered to order for Pamela, and studied the wine list with a frown of concentration on his boyish face, and quizzed the wine waiter before deciding. All this was a side of Hugo Pamela had not seen before: the successful man, comfortably in command of the good things in life.

'They have a truffle risotto, with fresh white truffles. We're in truffle season, so really we have no choice. And I've ordered a big bold Barolo. You'll like it. Oh, and how would you like a glass of Asti to start?'

As they sipped the fizzy wine, Pamela smiled at Hugo across the fresh linen and the sparkle of silver cutlery.

'What are you thinking?' he said.

'I'm thinking about you,' she said.

'What about me?'

'About how you were going to marry me and you promised to wait for me.'

He smiled, touched that she remembered.

'So I did.'

'But you didn't wait.'

'No. How fickle of me.'

'You married Harriet.'

'Yes. Apparently I did.'

'I wonder why.'

He raised his eyebrows at that, and didn't answer at once. Then he said, 'Is it so very surprising?'

'I don't know. She's just a different sort of person to you, I suppose.'

'Yes,' said Hugo, looking down. 'She is a different sort of person to me.'

'Of course,' said Pamela, 'she's not well.'

'No,' said Hugo.

He drank the rest of his Asti all at once.

'I'm not as good with her as I should be,' he said.

'Why do you say that?' said Pamela. 'Everyone knows you're the perfect husband. You're always so gentle with her. You really take care of her.'

'Like an invalid, you mean.'

'Well, she obviously has some sort of illness.'

'Not one the doctors can find,' said Hugo. 'So you see, I'm not really the perfect husband at all. I do what I can, of course I do. But it's not the way it was.'

Pamela said nothing. There was no need.

366

'When I first knew her, she was so adorable. She was so sweet to me, I couldn't help loving her. We used to play a game—' He stopped abruptly. 'Sorry. I've no idea why I'm telling you this.'

'No, go on. About the game.'

'It was Harriet's game. We'd hold hands and close our eyes and guess things about each other, just little things, like each other's favourite colour or the animal we'd be if we had to choose. The thing was, we both guessed right most of the time. Harriet used to say we were like one spirit in two bodies.'

'You were in love,' said Pamela.

'I thought so,' he said. 'Oh, God. I'm about to say something terrible. No, I won't say it.'

'About being in love?'

'No. Please. We mustn't.'

That *we* sent a thrill through Pamela.

'I don't want to be disloyal.'

'The last thing you are is disloyal, Hugo. You're the most dutiful husband in the world.'

'Well, duty, you know. That's a matter of upbringing. I know how to do the right thing, I hope.'

'Not everyone does,' said Pamela. 'Believe me.'

She spoke feelingly.

'Some chap been giving you the runaround?'

'You could say that.'

'Don't stand for it, Pammy!' He sounded almost angry. 'What right does any chap have to mistreat you? I hope you've told him where he can get off!'

'I don't see him any more.'

'I should think not!'

So Hugo was only doing his duty by Harriet.

Pamela thought then of what Stephen Ward had said to her. *There is no life after marriage. That's the happy ending.* He had spoken with such a bitter edge. She hadn't paid his words much attention then, and she didn't want to believe them now.

367

'I want to believe marriage can be more than duty,' she said. 'I suppose what I really mean is I want to believe people can fall in love and it can last.'

'I'm sure it happens,' said Hugo.

'Do you know any marriages like that?'

'Kitty and Larry.'

'But not my mother and my father.'

'Not Larry's first marriage, either.'

'So there you are,' said Pamela. 'Everyone should get their first marriage out of the way as quickly as possible, and then settle down to a happy second marriage.'

They ate the aromatic risotto and drank the rich red wine and shared the sensation of physical well-being that comes with a fine dinner. For their main course they had veal escalopes in Marsala sauce. Hugo's gaze rested on Pamela throughout the meal, and the expression on his face was often pensive. Pamela believed she knew what he was thinking. She too was allowing herself to play with thoughts she had not taken seriously before. She was meeting a different Hugo this evening: a Hugo who was more grown up than she had thought him to be. He was kind, and above all he was moral.

He had loved her mother. *I adored her*, he'd said. He had been much younger than her mother, of course. And he was much older than herself. She guessed at the age gap. Twenty years? Bronwen Pugh had married Billy Astor, who was twenty-three years older than her.

This train of thought caused her to smile. Hugo smiled back across the table at her.

'What?'

'Silly thoughts running in my head.'

He didn't ask her what silly thought she was having; which in itself was interesting.

'You have no idea what pleasure it gives me to be sitting here with you,' he said.

'Me too, Hugo.'

'Really? I should have thought you'd find me far too dull.'

'You're not dull at all.'

'I mean, after your smart friends.'

'They're not really my friends,' said Pamela. 'That's not my world. I'm much happier in my own world.'

'What's your own world?'

'People like us. People I've known all my life.'

He topped up her glass, and then his own. He raised his glass and she raised hers.

'Here's to people like us,' he said.

They clinked glasses.

Returning in a taxi Pamela had to restrain herself from snuggling up against him. Then as they entered the house, she realised she wanted Hugo to kiss her. She wanted him to kiss her as she had seen him kiss her mother.

He went ahead of her into the kitchen, saying, 'I'm going to drink a glass of water before going to bed. Always drink water after wine.'

She followed, and came to a stop just inside the kitchen doorway.

'That was a lovely evening, Hugo.'

'Wasn't it just?'

He drank his glass of water.

'You're a lovely girl, Pammy.'

'Come and say goodnight.'

The devil was in her. She felt her power. He came as she commanded.

'Kiss me goodnight.'

He took her in his arms, at first with his hands on the backs of her shoulders, as you might an old friend. She leaned in to him. His hands moved, to hold her more closely. His face came down to hers. He kissed her, a real kiss, on the mouth.

Pamela imagined herself as a child again, out in the hall, seeing through the kitchen door: two grown-ups locked in a kiss.

He moved back from her.

'Look,' he said, 'I shouldn't have done that. I think we'd better just pretend it never happened. I apologise. I just couldn't stop myself.'

'It does take two, you know.'

'I'm the responsible one here. I'm simply taking advantage of you, a guest in my house, the daughter of an old friend. My behaviour is unforgivable.'

'So is mine,' said Pamela.

'Don't, Pammy.' He waved a hand before his face, as if in doing so he could erase the effect she had on him. 'You mustn't encourage me. I'm no good for you. You could have any man you wanted. You're simply the most beautiful girl I've ever met.'

Helplessly, pitifully, his eyes implored her for mercy.

'Darling Hugo.'

'No, Pamela, don't look at me like that. I'm only flesh and blood.'

'I don't know how else to look at you,' she said.

'If it wasn't for Harriet, and Emily, God knows . . .'

He pushed his hands wildly through his hair.

'It's all right,' said Pamela. 'I understand. You have to look after Harriet.'

'You do see that, don't you? She needs me.'

'Of course. You're a sweet man, Hugo. I love you for that.'

She kissed him again, but this time chastely, on the cheek. Then she went up to her room.

41

On that Monday evening in Kilnacarry a soft drizzle filled the air, beneath an overcast sky. Mary Brennan, flanked by Father Flannery on one side and her brother Eamonn on the other, made her way down the hillside path to Buckle Bay. The beach was packed with silent pilgrims, for all the damp weather. They wore scarves over their heads, and hoods, and wool hats. They had been waiting patiently for an hour and more.

As Mary came in sight a rustling murmur passed through the crowd, and all eyes turned to see her. She was walking fast, her eyes cast down, her hair hidden beneath a scarf tied under her chin. Those in the crowd who remembered her from the time of the visions were shocked to see that she had become a handsome woman. Their voices murmured as she passed by.

'Will you look at her now? She's the Madonna herself!'

'God bless you, Mary Brennan.'

Some dropped to their knees, and all crossed themselves, their eyes tracking her across the beach, down the strip of wet sand that had been made for her to pass. It was like an aisle in a crowded church, and the stone marker was like the altar, and the sea and sky beyond was the great west window.

One or two of the pilgrims tried to reach out to touch her, but the priest and Eamonn brushed their hands away. When she got to the marker the crowd flowed back over the sand and the aisle disappeared. She was not a tall woman, and now surrounded on three sides she could barely be seen.

'Will you stand on the stone, Mary?' said her brother gently.

He helped her up with one strong arm. As the people in the crowd saw her pale face appear above them, against the fading light of the sky, they fell silent and waited for her to speak.

Mary had prepared what she wanted to say. But now, seeing that mass of humble faces gazing up at her, she didn't know how to begin. It was borne in on her for the first time that her own truth was of very little importance here. And yet she had nothing else to give them.

After the silence had gone on so long that she knew she must speak, she said, 'Well, I've come back.'

This was met by a wave of laughter. The laughter was affectionate. Voices called, 'Welcome home, Mary.' She waved as if she was on the deck of a ship coming into port. They all waved back. It was funny, and very touching.

'I've been away so long,' she said, 'because I didn't know what to say to you. And I don't know what to say now. All I know is, I'll not lie to you. The child who stood on this beach all those years ago is gone. She won't be coming back. Instead, all you've got is myself, and I'm just nobody at all.'

When she had been thinking about what she would say, Mary had been frightened at how the pilgrims might receive it. She thought they might be angry with her for letting them down. But now, looking round from one rocky slope to the other over this mass of listening faces, all she felt was love. She could hear the soft exclamations, saying, 'God bless you, Mary,' and 'I'm praying for you, Mary.' There were many she knew in that crowd, and many more she had never seen before. Father Flannery had told her there would be newspaper men there, and cameramen. They had been asked to show proper respect, and not to intrude on her return to Buckle Bay.

'If you're hoping I've come to see visions tonight,' she said, 'then I'm going to disappoint you. Whatever I saw all those years ago was meant for the eyes of a child. I've seen no visions since then. I've heard no voices. I don't even know anymore what it was I saw and heard back then. It's like a dream to me. So there's no need to listen to what I say any more, or to try to touch me. I'm just Mary Brennan from Kilnacarry, Eileen Brennan's little girl. My da died at sea the year I was born, there's many of you know that. My sister Bridie had the measles so bad it nearly killed her. My mam makes pinafores, or she did until the arthritis got to her fingers. I wasn't much of a student at school, though I did like it when Mr O'Donnell read us poems in that fine voice of his, and I'll never forget the taste of my first cigarette, given me by Brendan Flynn.'

A hand went up in the crowd.

'Oh, you're here, are you, Brendan?'

The crowd laughed. Mary felt as if she had now come home.

'So here I am, come to let you all take a good look at me, twenty-nine years old and neither married nor earning my own bread, and God help me, I'm not even a nun.'

The laughter rolled like waves over the twilight beach.

'You've no call to listen to me anymore. But I've not forgotten the words I spoke when I was a child. All I can do tonight is speak those words again. Love each other, and love our Father in heaven.'

She had no more to say. She looked down and saw Father Flannery smiling up at her and nodding. She reached out her hand for Eamonn to help her down. Then a voice called from the crowd.

'What about the warning, Mary?'

'I've no warning to give you,' she said.

'When will the great wind come?'

'I know nothing,' she said. 'I've come home because it was wrong of me to hide myself away. But I've no message for you.'

She then jumped down from the stone, and protected by Eamonn and the priest she made her way back across the beach. The newspaper men now came pushing forward, and asked her questions.

'You say you've no message, Mary. But why come back today?'

'No reason at all,' she said. 'One day is as good as another.'

'Will you be walking on the beach alone, Mary?'

'Little enough chance of that,' she said.

'You said time is running out. Do you think time has now run out?'

'What do I know about that?' she said.

They took pictures, the flashes dazzling her eyes. And so, slowly, the crowd dispersed.

The Brennans went back to the priest's house, where his housekeeper had prepared them a dinner.

'You did well, Mary,' said Father Flannery. 'You did well.'

'They'll be so disappointed, Father.'

'You were grand,' said Eamonn. 'I could sooner swim to America than I could stand on that stone and talk the way you did.'

'Will Betty Clancy crow over you, Mam?'

'No, no,' said Eileen Brennan. 'You did us proud.'

'I shall be interested to see what the pilgrims do now,' said the priest.

'They'll go home,' said Mary. 'It's over now.'

'I'm not so sure. I was hearing them as we came back. They're not done with you yet, Mary. They're saying God has brought you back to Kilnacarry for a reason.'

42

At 10 p.m. Moscow time on Monday evening Khrushchev was informed that Kennedy was to address the American people. He was scheduled to speak on all networks, both television and radio, in four hours' time. Khrushchev understood at once that the crisis was about to break.

'This could be war,' he said.

The missiles he had sent to Cuba were designed, by making the Soviet threat balance the American threat, to bring peace to the world. Now he faced a possible invasion of Cuba, and following that, a possible nuclear exchange.

'Two more weeks! That's all I needed.'

He summoned the members of the Presidium to the Kremlin. The Zil limousines sped through the night streets of Moscow, bringing Mikoyan and Koslov and Podgorni, Brezhnev, Voronov and Kosygin. Marshal Malinowsky attended, representing the armed forces.

'It's most likely a pre-election trick,' Malinowsky said of the upcoming television broadcast. But he knew as well as Khrushchev that his GRU had been reporting unusual US military activity in the Caribbean. A convoy of military planes had left for Puerto Rico. The number of bombers on duty in Strategic Air Command had increased. The US Navy was running an exercise round the island of Vieques code-named ORTSAC, which was CASTRO backwards.

'Ortsac!' snorted Khrushchev. 'That's not a code. It's a taunt.'

He told the Presidium members that he expected them to spend the night in the Kremlin. There were grave decisions to be made.

'We must face the possibility that Operation Anadyr has been discovered, and that action will be taken against Cuba.'

The first matter to establish was how many ships had reached Cuba and how many were still at sea. The three R-12 missile regiments were in place, as were the Lunas and the cruise missiles. The two R-14 regiments were still arriving. The *Yuri Gagarin* was two days away. The *Nikolaevsk*, carrying two thousand soldiers, and the *Divnogorsk*, were in mid-Atlantic. The freighter *Aleksandrovsk*, carrying twenty-four nuclear warheads for the R-14s, was still in international waters, half a day's sailing from Cuba.

'If they want to play games with us,' said Khrushchev grimly, 'they'll find we're ready. If they show their teeth, we'll show them our claws.'

'But we have no wish to go to war, Nikita Sergeyevich,' said Mikoyan.

'To avoid war, we threaten war,' said Khrushchev. 'The only thing the Americans respect is strength.'

The members of the Presidium settled in for the tense vigil. All they could do while waiting was make provisional decisions. How was the Soviet force on Cuba to defend itself in the event of an attack? They would be heavily outnumbered by an American invasion force.

'Do we sacrifice our assets on Cuba?'

The mood in the Presidium that night was grim but defiant. The twelve members voted to authorise General Pliyev, in command of Soviet forces on the island, to use tactical nuclear weapons in the event of a US landing. Marshal Malinowsky warned that this would give the Americans the pretext to use their own nuclear weapons. The order to Pliyev was held back until American intentions became clear.

Shortly after 1 a.m., an hour before President Kennedy was due to deliver his television address, an advance copy of his statement was cabled to the US Embassy in Moscow. Fifteen minutes later it was in Khrushchev's hands. He scanned the document at speed.

'No invasion,' he said.

The mood of the Presidium was transformed. They digested the details of Kennedy's ultimatum.

'Naval blockade. Demand that we remove the missiles. No bombing. No attack.'

Khrushchev looked round his colleagues' faces in triumph.

'The missiles scare them. We have saved Cuba.'

There followed a series of rapid decisions designed to convey simultaneously a proud defiance and a willingness to compromise.

'First,' said Khrushchev, 'we finish what we've started. I want as many of the missile sites as possible operational as soon as possible. Have them work through the night. Order the *Aleksandrovsk* to make for the nearest Cuban port at top speed. As for the other ships, order them to turn back.'

'Not without protest, Nikita Sergeyevich!'

'Of course we protest! This naval blockade is an outrageous demonstration of American imperialism! This is piratical aggression in international waters! This is a crude attempt to interfere in Cuban affairs! The USA is single-handedly preparing to unleash the Third World War!'

The Presidium note-takers busily followed the rush of words pouring from the chairman's lips.

'We must galvanise world opinion,' he said. 'Every action we take, every statement we release, must show the world these two simple truths: America is the aggressor, and the Soviet Union is now too strong to be pushed around.'

As the statements were being drafted by a team in the Foreign Ministry, Khrushchev requested his colleagues to remain in the Kremlin, to avoid revealing that they had gathered in emergency session. No more Zils roaring through the night. He himself settled down to sleep, fully dressed, on a sofa in the anteroom to his office.

'You remember the French minister who was caught with his pants down on the night of the Suez crisis?' he said to the faithful Troyanovsky. 'My pants will stay up.'

At 2 a.m. in Moscow, and 11 p.m. in Ireland, and 7 p.m. in Washington DC, President Kennedy made his broadcast from the Oval Office. He wore no make-up, and looked white-faced and grave. Alerted by a series of rumours in the press, Americans tuned in in record numbers, more than a hundred million of them. The address was carried over a network of Florida radio stations that could reach Cuba, Kennedy's words accompanied by a Spanish translation. The broadcast was also relayed live via the Telstar satellite to Europe.

'Good evening, my fellow citizens,' the president began. 'This government, as promised, has maintained the closest surveillance of the Soviet military build-up on the island of Cuba. Within the past week unmistakable evidence has established the fact that a series of offensive missile sites is now in preparation on that imprisoned island. The purpose of these bases can be none other than to provide a nuclear strike capability against the Western Hemisphere.'

The president told the shocked nation that the Cuban missiles could strike as far north as Hudson Bay, Canada, and as far south as Lima, Peru. He called them weapons of mass destruction.

'The 1930s,' he said, 'taught us a clear lesson: aggressive conduct, if allowed to go unchecked, ultimately leads to war. This nation is opposed to war. But now further action is required – and it is under way; and these actions may only be the beginning. We will not prematurely or unnecessarily risk the costs of worldwide nuclear war, in which even the fruits of victory would be ashes in our mouth. But neither will we shrink from that risk at any time it must be faced.'

He then laid out the steps he was taking: a naval quarantine to halt the build-up of weapons reaching Cuba, a demand that the missiles be removed, and a threat that any hostile move anywhere in the world would be met by whatever action was needed.

'The cost of freedom is always high,' he said, 'but Americans have always paid it. And one path we shall never choose: and that is the path of surrender or submission. Our goal is not the victory of might, but the vindication of right. God willing, that goal will be achieved.'

43

On Tuesday morning the people of Kilnacarry woke to the news of President Kennedy's speech. The pilgrims emerged from their bed-and-breakfast rooms and caravans to discover that the world was on the brink of nuclear war.

Mingled with the dread and horror at this prospect there was much nodding of heads, and an unmistakable air of satisfaction.

'You see it now,' they told each other. 'Mary Brennan comes home, and the very same night, what do they tell us? It's the end of the world, sure enough.'

'You'll not have forgotten our Mary's warning. The great wind, she said.'

By the time Mary herself was up, there was a crowd round the Brennan house, and Eamonn had bolted all the doors and closed the shutters.

'I knew nothing about it,' said Mary, frightened.

'They'll not believe that now,' said Eamonn. 'You're a prophet now.'

In London, in the corridors of the Foreign Office and the Department of Defence there was frantic activity. A series of overlapping meetings addressed the question of how Britain should respond. Sir Harold Caccia, Permanent Undersecretary at the Foreign Office, predicted that the Russians would enter West Berlin within hours. Sir Thomas Pike, Chief of the Air Staff, told his fellow chiefs of staff that they would have a maximum of forty-eight hours before the Americans launched an attack. Once the shooting began on the far side of the Atlantic, they must assume it would spread to Europe within hours, if not minutes.

The giant dish antenna of the Jodrell Bank telescope was requisitioned by the RAF to track incoming Soviet missiles. The sixty nuclear-tipped Thor missiles in their bases across East Anglia and Yorkshire were ordered to Readiness State Red, which required launch crews to take their missiles to Stage Two hold, erect on their pads, eight minutes from lift-off. American authorisation officers, required for the dual key authorisation of nuclear attack, were ordered to remain in the launch control trailer for their entire shift, without taking so much as a toilet break. At the V-bomber bases the Vulcans were loaded with thermonuclear weapons and held on Quick Reaction Alert, the crews eating and sleeping by their planes in full flight gear. On the Alert Alpha signal, which was the prelude to the final order, the bombers would take off and disperse to a wide spread of airfields, so that in the event of a missile attack some proportion of the force would survive.

At every meeting, up and down Whitehall, the central question was: why had Khrushchev done it? If his intentions were aggressive, if the Soviet Union's goal was the domination of the West by military power, then war was not only inevitable, it was desirable. The difficulty was that until the Russians made the next move, no one knew how much force would be needed to contain the threat. The United States had responded to the crisis with a holding manoeuvre, the naval blockade. This handed the initiative back to the Russians. The Russians must now decide whether to let their ships pass the quarantine line or not.

In the defence staff meeting which raged all morning Rupert kept returning to his core point.

'This is not a military stand-off, it's a moral stand-off. If this is going to be a shooting war, our goal must be to make them shoot first. Kennedy said it in plain words: "Not the victory of might, but the vindication of right". This is all about righteousness.'

'For God's sake, Rupert,' said Grimsdale. 'This isn't a philosophy seminar. The bloody balloon's about to go up.'

'And what are we sitting here doing? We're asking ourselves, Why has Khrushchev done this? What's he going to do next? That's what matters. Not how many warheads are going to survive a sneak attack.'

'So it's an intelligence matter. That's me. And I'm telling you, all our analysts are saying this isn't about Cuba at all. This is about Berlin. Cuba's a bargaining chip.'

'If this is really about Berlin,' said Mountbatten, 'we're in trouble. Berlin is non-negotiable.'

'Even when the other guy holds a card saying nuclear war?'

'He can't play that card.'

'How do you know that? Khrushchev's a gambler. Always has been.'

'He's a canny gambler,' said Rupert. 'He's not going to launch World War Three. He's going to try to push us to a place where *we* threaten nuclear war, where *we* strike first, and *we're* the villains of history.'

'So we let them blackmail us? We let them win?'

'We shouldn't be waiting for them to make the next move. We should be taking control of the debate. We should be in negotiations with the Russians right now, offering a reasonable deal to defuse the crisis. Then if they don't play, they're in the wrong.'

A babble of objecting voices rose up round the table.

'Yes, I know,' said Rupert, 'you all think it doesn't matter who's right and wrong, it only matters who wins. But you're wrong.'

This produced a laugh.

'What deal?' said Mountbatten.

'Trade the Soviet missiles on Cuba for our Thors.'

That reduced the meeting to silence. Rupert looked round the shocked faces of his colleagues.

'The Thors are no good to us. We all know it. We'll never use them. To hell with them. Let them go.'

Alan McDonald was going progressively redder in the face. Now his outrage burst from him in speech.

'You can go crawling to the Russians if you like! You can give in to threats! That's not my idea of being British. We're one of only three nuclear powers on the planet. Do you have any idea what that means? You want to be a second-rate power? This Cuban adventure is a test of our strength and will and you say, Roll over. Surrender.'

'So what do you say, Alan?' retorted Rupert. 'Fire the Thors? Scramble the Vulcans? Incinerate half Russia? That would show our strength and our will.'

'For heaven's sake! Can't we be a little grown-up about this?'

'Gentleman,' said Mountbatten, rapping the table. 'I must leave you. I'm lunching with Laurie Norstad.' General Norstad was CINCEUR, the commander of NATO forces in Europe. 'Please continue in my absence. I don't expect agreement. I'd appreciate a memorandum laying out the range of your suggestions.'

He rose to go.

'Rupert. A word.'

In his office, Mountbatten said to Rupert, 'We can't trade the Thors. It's too big a political hit. But what about the Jupiters in Turkey?'

'Wouldn't the Turks say that was too big a political hit for them?'

'Turkey's right on the Soviet border. Very like Cuba for the Americans. There's a symmetry to it. I'm going to try it on Laurie.'

'What's the PM saying?'

'Oh, you know Harold. He gives you that hooded look of his and says, "When in doubt, do nothing." It's driving the chiefs wild.'

The Campaign for Nuclear Disarmament announced a mass rally in Trafalgar Square in four days' time, on Saturday afternoon. The British Council of Churches met in Coventry and had an acrimonious debate over what statement to make about the crisis. The issue was whether to include the word 'truculence' in the sentence: 'The Council encourages Christian people to continue in prayer for the victory of moderation and statesmanship over pride, truculence and fear.'

The ageing philosopher Bertrand Russell declared, 'It seems likely that within a week we will all be dead to please American madmen.' He then sent a cable to President Kennedy.

Your action desperate. Threat to human survival. No conceivable justification. Civilised man condemns it. We will not have mass murder. Ultimatum means war. I do not speak for power but plead for civilised man. End this madness.

Kennedy's official reply ran: 'I think your attention might well be directed to the burglar rather than to those who caught the burglar.' Unofficially he said, 'He can go and soak his head.'

Russell also cabled Chairman Khrushchev:

I appeal to you not to be provoked by the unjustifiable action

of the United States in Cuba. The world will support caution.
Urge condemnation to be sought through United Nations.
Precipitous action could mean annihilation for mankind.

In the Russian Embassy in Kensington Palace Gardens, the GRU *rezident* General Anatoly Pavlov summoned Captain Ivanov.

'Zhenya,' he said, 'the time has come for you to build your bridge. Moscow wants this crisis settled.'

Ivanov put in a call at once to Rupert Blundell.

'Rupert, my friend,' he said. 'Our moment has come.'

They met that Tuesday evening at Mountbatten's house in Wilton Crescent. To start with Mountbatten was guarded and suspicious.

'You're very junior, Captain Ivanov.'

'I am disposable, your Excellency. I am, as we say, deniable. If our discussions are made public and cause embarrassment, my people wave their hands and say, "Who is this Ivanov? A junior naval attaché who has a fantasy that he is important. Forget him."'

'Yes. I do see that.'

'Eugene insists,' said Rupert, 'that Khrushchev has no aggressive intentions. What he wants now is to extricate himself from this mess.'

'No aggressive intentions? Nuclear missiles on Cuba?'

'May I ask, sir,' said Ivanov. 'Are your Thor missiles, which are targeted on Russian cities, a sign of aggressive intention?'

'One hundred per cent defensive,' said Mountbatten.

Then they all laughed.

'Still,' said Mountbatten, 'this whole thing could turn very nasty.'

'So we must make our bridge.'

'You're telling me you have the ear of Khrushchev?'

'Khrushchev will not listen to me,' said Ivanov. 'He will listen to you, and the British prime minister.'

Mountbatten turned to Rupert.

'Desperate times call for desperate measures, eh?'

'It's worth a shot, sir.'

'So we bodge up some sort of deal. I can tell you right off, the Jupiters can't be any part of it. I tried the idea on Laurie Norstad. He said it would break NATO if the Americans were seen to sacrifice Turkey's security for their own.'

'The Jupiters are junk,' said Ivanov.

Mountbatten looked at him in surprise.

'How do you know that?'

'I'm a military attaché. It's my job to know.'

'Well, they're not for sale. So what else have we got?'

'The deal will be hard to make,' said Ivanov. 'What will not be so hard is to get agreement on both sides that there must be a deal. We must remove the threat of war. I would propose that the British prime minister calls a top-level conference, here in London, to resolve the dispute.'

'Not the UN? Everyone's calling on U Thant to step in.'

'Who listens to the UN?' said Ivanov scornfully. 'No, the conference must be called by one of the nuclear powers.'

'What about the Americans? Would they go for it?'

'Not as things stand,' said Rupert. 'But if the Soviets turned the ships round, that could do it.'

'Even though that leaves the missiles on Cuba?'

'Of course the missiles will have to be withdrawn,' said Ivanov. 'But you understand that Chairman Khrushchev is very sensitive to world opinion. He is concerned for the prestige of socialism. He must make bold and angry speeches against the Americans. If your prime minister would offer a London conference today, he couldn't accept it. He would demand an American climb-down first.'

'So how are we to do it?'

'We establish in private that both sides would support a London conference. Then we discuss the moves that must be made before a conference is even spoken of. The two leaders then appear as statesmen, seeking peace. So no humiliation, please.'

Mountbatten looked at Rupert, and nodded.

'This is a sensible man.'

'And disposable,' said Rupert.

'Very well,' said Mountbatten. 'I'll sound a few people out.'

Rupert met Ivanov's eyes. Maybe they had a part to play after all.

44

Pamela was alone in the house on Wednesday morning when the phone rang. She answered, expecting to take a message for Harriet or Hugo, but the call was for her.

'Pamela? It's Bobby! Remember?'

'How did you get this number?'

'Don't be like that. Let me buy you lunch. I asked Stephen how to get hold of you.'

Stephen, who knew how to get hold of everyone.

'I can't.'

'Yes, you can. Whatever you're doing can wait. You know it can.'

He sounded so cheerfully untroubled. Pamela didn't know how to explain. This was the man who had witnessed her humiliation. More than witnessed. This was the man who had taken her virginity.

'What do you want, Bobby?'

'I want to give you lunch.'

'Why?'

'It's what chaps like to do with pretty girls. It cheers them up. The markets are falling off a cliff. I need cheering up. Be a pal. I can be with you in five minutes.'

'How can you be with me in five minutes? I'm in Hammer-smith.'

'So am I. I'm in a phone box by Olympia.'

She felt helpless. He was unstoppable.

'All right.'

She went up to the bathroom to brush her hair and touch up her lipstick. Gazing at herself in the mirror she wrinkled her brow, cross with herself that she had given in so easily. Then she realised that she wanted to see Bobby again. There was so much unfinished business. She wanted to know what André thought of her now, if he ever thought of her at all. She wanted someone to talk to about that night in Herriard. She wanted to know what she thought of it herself.

The doorbell rang. There on the steps was Bobby, big and beaming and handsome, with a wicker hamper in his arms.

'What's this?'

'Lunch.'

'I thought you were taking me out.'

He came into the house, looked round, found the kitchen.

'This will be far jollier,' he said.

He put the hamper down on the kitchen table and proceeded to unpack it. Out came pork pies, chocolate eclairs, and two bottles of wine.

'I take it you can rustle up a couple of wine glasses.'

Pamela looked on in bewilderment.

'How did you know I'd be alone?'

'There's enough for four here.'

'You're taking an awful lot for granted, it seems to me.'

Bobby moved about the kitchen finding plates and cutlery.

'Don't go all spinsterish on me, darling,' he said. 'It's only lunch. You do look ravishing.'

It seemed she had no choice. But she saw no need to pretend to be polite.

'And what about Charlotte?'

'Charlotte's fine. She sends her love.'

'And I suppose André sends his love too.'

'Absolutely.'

He drew the cork from one of the bottles. The wine glugged cheerfully into the glasses. He held out a full glass.

'Here! Bottoms up!'

'You don't think, I suppose, that someone owes me an apology.'

Even as she said it she realised she sounded what Bobby called spinsterish.

'Oh, come on!' said Bobby. 'Just a bit of fun.'

'Is that what you and André said afterwards? That you'd had a bit of fun?'

'Look, Pamela, no one died. No one got hurt. It happens all the time. Some people even like it, you know? André's a lovely man, he hasn't an unkind bone in his body. And anyone can see with one look that you're well able to take care of yourself.'

One look. She had so wanted them to believe she belonged in their world. But sometimes one look isn't enough.

He cut up the pork pie, and gave her some on a plate. Pamela struggled to express what had been to her a violation. In the end all she could say was,

'You should have asked me first.'

'Most people like surprises,' said Bobby. 'I know I do. That's how I got to know Charlotte.'

'What do you mean?'

'I was at Bovey for the weekend, the Hutchinsons' place, with Sally Milman, the girl I was with at the time, and Charlotte was there with some chap. Anyway, I was done in, so I went up to bed about midnight, and the others stayed up. An hour or so later this girl crept into my bed, and it wasn't Sally, it was Charlotte. Turned out they'd made this bet. Charlotte said men only recognised girls by smell, and that if she put on Sally's perfume I'd never know the difference. So Sally got out her perfume and Charlotte sprayed it all over. And away she went.'

'And you never guessed?'

'Of course I guessed. But I wasn't going to say no, was I?'

Pamela felt helpless. She was back in that other world, where other rules applied.

'But Bobby, when you do things like that, don't people ever get hurt?'

'I hope not,' he said. 'I wouldn't hurt a fly.'

'Didn't Sally mind?'

'Oh, she had her eye on the chap Charlotte had come with. That's why she cooked up the phoney bet.'

'And what about Charlotte when you were . . . when you were at André's?'

'At Herriard? Everyone knows what goes on at Herriard. You only have to take one look at André's collection to know. It's not exactly a state secret.'

'I didn't know.'

'You jolly well knew by the time you'd been given the tour.'

Even now Pamela found she was ashamed to admit her own naivety. The erotic miniatures had come as a shock, of course. But she had still expected the evening to take what one might call the traditional course. Did that make her stupid? Should she have expressed her disapproval then and there?'

But I didn't disapprove. I was excited.

'And what's more,' said Bobby, 'when we were in bed together, I got the distinct impression that you were all in favour.'

'It was just a surprise,' said Pamela. 'And it seems to me – I expect you'll think I'm being old-fashioned or something – but after all . . .'

She gazed helplessly at Bobby. He was happily consuming pork pie and taking good long gulps of red wine.

'It's not really love, is it?'

'Can be,' said Bobby. 'You'd be surprised.'

'I mean, you don't love me. André doesn't love me. So what's the point for me?'

'Fun,' said Bobby. 'It's fun or it's nothing.'

He looked up from his plate with a grin. It was quite clear that he felt no guilt.

'Love's the big one,' he said. 'But how often does love come round? So while we're waiting, in the long lonely days and weeks and months, we might as well have a bit of fun. Or am I missing something here?'

'I don't know, Bobby,' said Pamela. 'I feel so muddled.'

'But you're not eating! This is the best pork pie in London!'

'I'm not hungry.'

'Oh, you girls. Always watching your weight.'

He started on one of the chocolate eclairs. Pamela watched him. He was so very obviously enjoying his eclair. You couldn't stay cross with someone like Bobby.

'You don't really have a clue, do you?' she said.

'Probably not. Do you want me to?'

'André does.'

'Oh, yes. André's frightfully clever. But what good does being so brainy do him? All he wants to do is watch.'

'Did he say anything about me afterwards?'

'Don't think so. Just the usual.'

'What's the usual?'

'Oh, you know. Sweet girl. Lovely girl.'

He watched me in bed. He saw me naked with another man. He saw me making love with another man. And he calls me a sweet girl.

'I think he's sick.'

'Whoa! Slow down, gorgeous. That's my best friend you're talking about.'

'I think you're sick too.'

He stared at her, evidently baffled.

'Seriously?'

'Yes, Bobby. You're all sick.'

'Because we like pretty girls? That's a pretty common sickness, you know.'

'Because there's no love.'

'Oh, right!' Light seemed finally to dawn. 'I keep forgetting you're still young. You have this look about you, very cool and in control, like you know exactly what you're doing. It gives people the wrong idea.'

'I don't see what my age has to do with it.'

'It has everything to do with it! When you're young, girls especially, you still think you can have it all, in a single parcel, tied up with a bow. Love, fun, money, and happy ever after. Then after a few years you work it out. There is no single parcel. You get fun here and money there and love now and again. And that's if you're lucky. There's plenty of people in the world who don't get any of it, ever.'

Pamela reached for the bottle of wine, refilled her glass, drank.

'Are you listening to me?'

'Yes,' she said. 'You're not as stupid as I thought.'

'There you go!'

He seemed impossible to offend.

'And when you think,' he said, 'that the world may end tomorrow – well, hell, what are we waiting for?'

'Why should the world end tomorrow?'

'Pammy! What planet are you on? Don't you read the papers?'

'No.'

'There's going to be a nuclear war. Or there might be.'

'Why?'

'Oh, it's all about Cuba. Who cares? The point is, by the weekend we'll all be fried.'

'I don't believe you.'

'Is there a newspaper in this house?'

He cast around and found the day's *Times*. He scanned the main article on the news page, and read it out to her.

'"The choice now facing mankind," Lord Home went on, "was either to blow themselves to bits or to sit down round a table and negotiate."'

He found another headline.

'"Pope appeals to world leaders to spare the world the horrors of nuclear war."'

Pamela was shaken.

'But they'll negotiate, won't they?'

'Treasury stocks tumbling. War Loans have dropped a whole pound. There's a lot of fear out there.'

'What can we do, Bobby?'

'Nothing, sweetheart. Eat, drink and be merry, for tomorrow we die. Why do you think I'm here?'

'You should be with Charlotte.'

'I was with Charlotte this morning. I'll be with her this evening. But right now it's lunchtime, and I'm with you.'

He looked at his watch.

'I can't stay too much longer. I take it this house comes equipped with bedrooms.'

'Bobby!'

'It's not as if we haven't done it before.'

'What makes you think I want to do it again?'

'I don't think. All I can do is offer. Then you say yes or you say no. It's not so complicated, really.'

'I say no.'

'Fine. Shame, though. You're an absolute cracker in the sack.'

She was gratified in spite of herself.

'What a boy you are, Bobby.'

'Oh, go on, Pamela. Be a pal. It won't take long.'

The whole idea was insane, but somehow she had run out of objections.

'You promise me the world is going to end?'

'Very possibly after lunch.'

'All right, then.'

They went up the stairs to Pamela's second-floor bedroom like naughty children, leaving the picnic lunch scattered over the kitchen table. There was no time for the Dutch cap, but Bobby turned out to have come equipped with a condom.

'You are so vain!' She smacked him as they pulled off their clothes. 'You knew I'd say yes.'

'I was a Boy Scout,' he said. 'Be Prepared.'

He gave the scout salute, standing grinning in his underpants. They threw themselves onto Pamela's bed without turning back the covers. Pamela had abandoned all resistance. Suddenly his naked body was against hers, and she put her arms round him, and felt a surge of excitement.

He was strong and eager and everything seemed simple after all. Her body awoke under the assault of his body, and she wanted him and wanted to be wanted by him.

Then he was finished, and she wished he could have gone on longer.

Lying there in his arms, glistening with sweat, comfortable, expecting nothing, she thought about the world ending, and wondered if she cared. In Bobby's world you live for the moment, and then the moment passes. What then?

He gets up and leaves you and you're alone again, and the world doesn't end after all.

Bobby stirred beside her. He leaned over to check the bedside clock.

'Gotta go, girl.'

He jumped up, naked, and looked round.

'One floor down,' she said.

While Bobby was in the bathroom, she straightened up the bed covers that had been churned up by their lovemaking. Then she took her turn in the bathroom. By the time she was dressed and down in the kitchen, Bobby had cleared the kitchen table and packed all the leftovers of lunch back into the hamper.

'You're very house-trained.'

'I want to come again.'

'Absolutely not. Never.'

'Oh, well. You don't know till you ask.'

He gave her a lingering kiss on the mouth, and left.

Pamela moved slowly about the kitchen, erasing all the evidence of their unexpected lunch. She didn't think at all about what had taken place, because she didn't know how to think about it.

She went back up to her bedroom to make quite sure she and Bobby had left no tell-tale signs. Then coming down the stairs to the first floor, she opened the door to Hugo and Harriet's bedroom. As she looked round the pretty room she tried to imagine them in it: Harriet in a nightdress, Hugo in pyjamas, folding back the ivory-coloured quilted counterpane, climbing into bed beside her. She tried to imagine them making love, as she and Bobby had just done, but couldn't. Harriet would ask Hugo to turn out the light. She would sigh, to indicate that she was suffering from a headache but didn't want to trouble him with it. He would say something gentle and pitying like, 'Poor darling.' They would sleep without touching.

45

'Which ship is closest to the line?'

   'The *Kimovsk*, Mr President. Then the *Yuri Gagarin*.'

   'How soon before one of them crosses the line?'

   'Well, that's the thing. They may have turned round.'

   'May have? Don't we know?'

   'Not as exactly as we'd like, Mr President.'

The Office of National Intelligence tracked the movement of ships on the high seas by monitoring their radio messages. Transmissions picked up by land stations in Scotland, Maine and Florida were plotted on charts to give a current position. But transmissions were only occasional. Direction and speed of sailing took time to establish and were subject to error.

   'Why can't we send out planes to track them?'

   'That's a big ocean out there, Mr President.'

The *Kimovsk*, a lumber ship believed to be carrying SS5 medium-range ballistic missiles, was being hunted by an aircraft carrier group led by the USS *Essex*, with orders to stop and board. The ONI calculated the *Kimovsk* was close to the quarantine line, five hundred miles from the Cuban coast, and that the *Essex* would make contact very soon.

More accurate information reached ExComm mid-morning that Wednesday. CIA Director John McCone brought the news.

'Mr President, I have a note just handed to me that all six Soviet ships currently identified in Cuban waters have either stopped or reversed course.'

'What do you mean, Cuban waters?' said Dean Rusk.

'Dean, I don't know at the moment.'

'Did they cross the line?'

Then came more detail. The line had not been crossed. The Soviet ships had turned back.

'We're eyeball to eyeball,' said Dean Rusk, 'and the other fellow just blinked.'

'I like that,' said Bobby Kennedy.

But no one knew exactly what had happened, or why. It appeared the *Kimovsk* had received its order to turn back at least twenty-four hours earlier, because it was now reported to be eight hundred miles from the *Essex*, and steaming in the opposite direction.

The president wanted desperately not only to manage the crisis, but to be seen to manage it. He needed to show leadership and resolve. But how do you do that when you don't know what's going on? No one could tell him for sure what Soviet weapons there were on Cuba, or why Khrushchev had taken the risk of putting them there. He felt like a blind boxer, punching in the dark.

Meanwhile Khrushchev was sending out crazy statements attacking him as if he was the one who had put the whole world at risk, and all those fucking messages were piling up from self-appointed sages and holy men demanding that he choose peace over war.

'Shit, shit, shit!' muttered Kennedy to himself, hobbling on crutches across his private quarters, rooting out more pain-killers. 'I can hear the fucking guns of August.'

These endless meetings were half killing his back. He decided to take time out to soak in a tub.

'Then get the quack round to shoot me full of horse piss,' he told his secretary Mrs Lincoln.

As he lay in the tub in silence, away from the bickering voices of his advisers, he let the many strands of the crisis float through his mind. Maybe he was missing something.

Over in Europe they had this idea that it wasn't such a big deal. What was so different to the American missiles on Russia's borders? Everyone knew you couldn't use nuclear weapons. They were just there to show the world how big and strong you were. It was all just a big dick contest.

Try telling that to the American people. For ten years and more we've scared them shitless with the Red menace that's going to enslave the world. So now they can nuke us in our beds and we're supposed to do nothing?

Lying in the tub, feeling the hot water relax his muscles, he laughed quietly to himself. He got the big joke. All that Communist baloney about world domination was aimed at their own people, the Russians, to make them feel they were going through hard times for a purpose, that at the end of it all there was a bright and shining future. And all the Red scare baloney from McCarthy and Nixon and the rest was aimed at our own people, the Americans, to promote domestic political careers. We shout fire in our own backyard, but our voices carry across the ocean. Then the ones who truly believe there's a fire are ten thousand miles away, and by the time it reaches them it's lost its stink, and they don't know it's bullshit.

So this dickhead goes and puts nukes on Cuba! You had to admire his balls. It was an insane thing to do, to risk a nuclear war like that. Except there was no risk. How could the president of the United States set off a global holocaust for Cuba? Whichever way you looked at it, Khrushchev had played a blinder. He must know he'd have to take the missiles down. But he was going to extract a heavy price.

'It's all about fucking Berlin,' said the president to himself. 'That's the only way this makes any sense.'

After his bath Dr Max Jacobson did his voodoo with his needle, and Kennedy was ready to go back into the bear pit and show the requisite leadership and resolve. Tommy Power was there, all fired up to give him the unanimous opinion of the chiefs of staff.

'It's going to take a full-scale invasion to remove the threat now, Mr President. And we can't mount an operation that size overnight.'

'How long do you need, General?'

'Ready to go for Monday.'

Five days. A lot can happen in five days.

'Okay, Tommy. Set it up.' To Bobby he said, 'Try and get Bolshakov to tell us what's going on.'

'He fucked us over the U2s.'

'Who else have we got? Dobrynin knows fuck all about what's happening in Moscow. We've got five days to find a way out. Four days. We've got till Sunday.'

The 1st Armoured Division was ordered to begin the move to Florida. Fifteen thousand men had to be transported south in fleets of commercial airliners and thousands of railcars. Military aircraft began landing at Miami International Airport at the rate of one a minute. Off the Florida coast, on board the USS *Okinawa*, the 2nd Marine Division was practising boarding drills and studying landing maps. Operations Plan 316, the invasion of Cuba by 120,000 American troops, would be led by Marines landing on Tarara beach, east of Havana. First Armoured would land at Mariel to the west. The 101st and 82nd Airborne divisions would drop five thousand paratroopers behind enemy lines. Field hospitals were assembled to process a predicted eighteen thousand American casualties, and to repatriate the bodies of a predicted four thousand American dead.

Rupert Blundell sat in on the Chief of Defence Staff's meeting, where the chiefs were being briefed by Frank Mottershead on the complex interlocking nature of British and American nuclear weapons.

'You've got the B-47 bombers under SAC, and the F-101s under USAF. You've got the Polaris subs at Holy Loch. All these are under sole US control. The Thors are under dual control. The V-force is under our control, though for the planes to proceed past the Go/No Go line requires US authorisation.'

'So if the United States goes to war,' said Mountbatten, 'we go too.'

'We are allies, sir.'

'You think Cuba's worth a nuclear war?'

'It's not about Cuba,' said Sir Kenneth Cross.

'So what is it about? Freedom? Western civilisation? What is it we're defending by blowing up the world?'

'You know as well as I do,' said Cross. 'Resolve discourages aggression. They have to fear our power.'

'Well, we'll find out soon enough,' said Mountbatten. 'The Pentagon has set the invasion for Monday.'

'Bloody hell!'

'So what do we do?'

'We act on the prime minister's clear orders. No mobilisation. No dispersal of the bomber force. No unusual troop movements. No actions that might be construed as aggressive, or as preparations for aggression.'

'So we do nothing.'

'That is correct.'

Afterwards, when the chiefs had left, Mountbatten turned to Rupert.

'I spoke to Harold Caccia at the FO last night about your friend Ivanov's back channel idea. He cabled our man in Moscow, Frank Roberts. Roberts doesn't have much time for Ivanov.'

He showed Rupert the cable.

So far as I can judge the mood here is not desperate and
helpless as Ivanov suggests. Nor can I see why this junior
official in London should have complete and up-to-date
information on matters of highest policy outside his
competence and on a situation which has developed so
fast in the past forty-eight hours.

Rupert was irritated.

'Of course he's going to say that. He's the ambassador, he's supposed to be the channel between Khrushchev and Macmillan. The whole point is the official channels aren't working.'

'I just wanted you to see I've been doing what I can.'

'So what now?'

'We bypass the Foreign Office. I get this to the PM directly.'

Rupert was pleased.

'By the way,' said Mountbatten, 'I've put you on the list for Turnstile.'

'What's Turnstile?'

'It's the government bunker, somewhere in the Cotswolds. Highly restricted list. I'm only allowed twelve names. Consider it an honour.'

'Thank you, sir. Actually, if you don't mind, I'd rather take my chances here in town.'

'Me too. But someone has to be left to run the bloody country.'

46

By Thursday morning Rupert, along with all his colleagues, was feeling the strain of the prolonged period of heightened alert. Following the orders of the prime minister the headlines in the newspapers were concerned, but not alarmist. Life seemed to be continuing on the streets of London much as ever. This only added to the otherworldly nature of the crisis.

By Sunday it could all be over.

Rupert made a bet with John Grimsdale. He bet his friend the tension would be diffused by the end of tomorrow, Friday. He didn't tell Grimsdale about the back channel in which he was involved, only that he believed there would be a negotiated settlement. Grimsdale bet that it would turn into a shooting war by Monday.

'And after that?' said Rupert.

'Who knows?' said Grimsdale. 'I don't see why it has to be the end of the world. Why can't it just be another little war?'

'Because this isn't a proxy fight, like the Congo. This is the big boys in the ring.'

'You know your trouble, Rupert? You've philosophised your-self into a corner. You want this to be an epoch-defining experiment, don't you? Will mankind choose life or death?'

'How much?' said Rupert.

'Ten bob,' said Grimsdale.

A message came for Rupert that there was a lady at the Ministry of Defence outer gateway asking for him. For a single blinding moment he thought it was Mary, unexpectedly returned from Ireland. But surely she would have let him know? He ran down the stairs and out into the forecourt. There, on the street side of the gate, stood his sister Geraldine.

'For God's sake, Geraldine! What are you doing here?'

'I have to see you, Rupert.'

She sounded frantic.

'You can't come in. We're on top security alert.'

'You come out, then.'

'I can't.'

At that Geraldine burst into tears.

'All right,' said Rupert. 'Five minutes.'

He went out through the gate and his sister threw herself into his arms.

'I'm frightened,' she said. 'I heard it on the one o'clock news. I had to find you. There's something you have to do.'

She seized his hand and led him up Whitehall, past the Houses of Parliament.

'Where are we going, Geraldine? What do you want?'

'It's true, isn't it? There's going to be a war. I didn't really believe it, but I thought maybe I should go to confession, just in case. So I walked down to the Carmelite church. And Rupert, there was a queue!'

'For confession?'

'Three cubicles working at once. And there was still a long queue, all down the side of the nave. And that's not all.'

She led him across the green and into the big west doors of Westminster Abbey.

'Look!'

It took a moment for his eyes to adjust to the darkness. Then he saw that there were people scattered about, kneeling in the pews, praying. There was no service in progress. These were clearly people who had come in off the street to pray.

'Do you see?'

A lot of people, heads bowed, silent in prayer.

'They're praying,' whispered Geraldine.

'They're afraid,' said Rupert.

'Are they right to be afraid? Will this war really come?'

Rupert looked at his sister's flushed face, and saw that she wanted it to come. She wasn't afraid, she was exultant.

'It might,' he said.

'If it comes,' she said, 'all this, the Abbey, the Houses of Parliament, the streets, the houses, all London, will be swept away, won't it?'

'Yes, I suppose so.'

'No one will survive.'

'Very few.'

'Then don't you see?' She was whispering in her intensity. 'This changes everything. Larry must be told.'

'Larry must be told?'

'He has so little time. The news said it could be days. Hours, even.'

'Geraldine, if there is a nuclear war, I don't think it really matters who's been told what.'

'Will they drop a bomb on Sussex? Will *she* die?'

'If bombs are dropped on London, the whole south-east will be poisoned by radiation.'

'So she'll die later? Slowly?'

Rupert turned away.

'Stop this, please.'

'But there's no time! You must call Larry. Tell him to come. This is his last chance to come back and make everything right again, before the end. Rupert, you must do this! I have a right to die in my husband's arms.'

'I will not call Larry, Geraldine. Now I'm going back to work.'

She followed him out of the Abbey, running to keep up with his angry stride.

'You have to call him. He won't believe me. He'll believe you.'

'I'm not doing it.'

'But can't you see, Rupert? God is giving us one last chance. We've been given the warning. We must prepare our souls. Why do you think the churches are full?'

Rupert strode on in silence. She reached for his sleeve, pulled at him.

'Call Larry! Give him the chance to die with the woman he loves.'

'He loves Kitty,' said Rupert.

Geraldine let go of his sleeve and came to a stop.

'No,' she said. Then she screamed. 'No! No!'

Rupert was forced to turn back. Passers-by were staring.

'He doesn't love Kitty!' Geraldine howled. 'He loves me!'

The exultation was gone from her face. Tears were coursing down her cheeks. Her arms hung limp by her side.

This is my baby sister. We played together as children. I loved her once.

Rupert was overwhelmed with pity and sadness.

'Come here, sis.' He took in his arms. 'It'll be all right. There won't be any war. We'll all go on living.'

'I don't want to go on living,' she cried, sobbing in his arms. 'I want the world to end. I want it all to be over.'

'I know. I know.'

She calmed down slowly, her face pressed to his shoulder.

'We just have to struggle on somehow, don't we?' he said.

'It's too hard,' she said. 'Too hard.'

'I know.'

'What's wrong with us, Rupert? Why can't we be happy, like everyone else?'

'I don't think everyone else is all that happy. I think most people find it hard too.'

He hailed a cab for her.

'You go home now. Go home and rest. I have to go back to work.'

'Yes, I know. Men always have to work.'

Rupert gave the cabbie Geraldine's address. The taxi drove off. He walked slowly now, back to the Ministry.

I want the world to end.

An end to struggle and failure. An end to loneliness. What if those in charge of the nuclear buttons felt it too? Let all our sorrows be wiped away. Let the page turn and we can start afresh. A new story on a new sheet. The age-old seduction of the end of the world.

47

It was Father Flannery's idea to hold a prayer service that Thursday evening. The pilgrims weren't going away.

'We'll pray the rosary,' he said. 'We'll ask God for forgiveness.'

The rain was falling heavily, streaming down the tile roof of the church, overspilling the clogged gutters and running in streams between the gravestones. The pilgrims crowded into the church, shaking off their umbrellas, discreetly shuffling for a place in the whitewashed nave where they'd be close enough to hear.

Father Flannery and the Brennans and Patrick Dempsey, who had experience as a bouncer in the pubs of Sligo, were squeezed into the tiny vestry, waiting for the crowd to settle. The priest peeped through the crack of the door.

'That's a good crowd,' he said.

'Am I to say no flash photographs?' said Patrick Dempsey.

'No,' said Mary. 'Let them do as they wish.'

'They'll not come past the communion rail,' said the priest. 'Not in my church.'

'Will you speak to them, Mary?' said her brother.

'I've nothing more to say,' said Mary.

'We'll just pray,' said the priest. 'We'll pray together for the world.'

Then the priest stepped out of the vestry and spoke to the people packed into the church.

'I have Mary Brennan with me here,' he said. 'She's here to join us in prayer. She'll not be speaking to you herself.'

He beckoned Mary out, along with Eileen and Eamonn Brennan. There was a stir in the church as the people strained to see her.

'Now I'll ask you to kneel with me and pray to Our Father in heaven to show us his mercy and kindness in these troubled times.'

The people shuffled onto their knees, as did the Brennans by the altar. The priest made the sign of the cross and led them all in the prayers of the rosary.

'I believe in God, the Father almighty, creator of heaven and earth . . .'

The murmuring voices of the faithful filled the church, blurring into the sound of the rain on the roof. Mary spoke the familiar words of the creed by rote, no longer aware of any meaning.

'He descended into hell; the third day he rose again from the dead . . .'

She knew she should be thinking of the perilous state of the world, but she was not. She was thinking how small the church was, and the village, and how she wanted to get away from it. She was thinking how she had never had pretty clothes to wear, like Pamela, and how men had never looked at her the way they looked at Pamela.

Then she was remembering how Brendan Flynn had given her a cigarette to show him her weenie. And how she had flicked up her skirts to show the devil her bum.

Here I am, twenty-nine years old and never been kissed. All I've had is Jesus come to me over the water and say to me, 'Be my voice.'

I've done what you said, Lord. When's it my turn?

They were into the long chain of Hail Marys now.

'Hail Mary, full of grace, the Lord is with thee, blessed art thou among women . . .'

And I'm Mary too, and I'm blessed among women. Only nobody asked me and I don't want it.

'Holy Mary, Mother of God, pray for us sinners, now and at the hour of our death.'

Mother of God. Not wife of God. Not girlfriend of God. No fun and games for Mary, no making love, just a baby out of nowhere and a lifetime of sorrow and an eternity of being prayed at by keening women. Who'd be a Mary?

I'll go back to London tomorrow, she thought. First thing I'll be on the bus south, and catch an afternoon plane. Rupert will come to see me and I'll tell him all my wicked thoughts and he'll laugh at me. That's assuming the world hasn't ended after all.

She became aware of raised voices. Someone was shouting. There was a scuffle in the nave, and more raised voices.

'Save me, Mary! I don't want to die!'

A woman was pushing through the crowd towards the altar, her arms flailing. Her face was distorted with panic.

'Let me touch her! If I touch her I'll be saved!'

People were pulling the woman back, trying to get her on her knees again. From the sound of her voice she wasn't a local, Spanish perhaps, or Mexican. A lot of strangers had come to Kilnacarry in the last few days.

'The warning! Tell us the warning!'

This was a different voice, a younger woman, crying out from the back. At once a dozen other voices joined in.

'Mary! Speak to us! When's it to come, the great wind? The wind, Mary! Tell us!'

Mary turned towards them, not knowing what to do. The priest was on his feet, his hands raised in protest.

'That's enough now!'

But fear had taken hold of the pilgrims, and they were pushing forward, calling out.

'Take me with you, Mary! I don't want to die! Have pity on us! Tell us! Tell us!'

Now they were forcing their way past the communion rail, and Mary, frightened, was backing towards the altar. Eamonn and Patrick Dempsey stepped forward to protect her. The priest called out in vain.

'No! Go back! What are you doing? This is a disgrace!'

The woman who had first begun the calling out now broke free of those trying to restrain her and hurled herself forward onto the altar steps. She had black hair in a braid and big black frightened eyes. She lunged at Mary, hands outreached, and managed to seize hold of the hem of her coat.

'Take me with you!' she cried out. 'Take me with you to heaven!'

She had a mad desperate look about her. Mary shrank back in fear as Eamonn pushed the woman away. The woman held on so tight to Mary's coat that she was almost pulled over.

'Take her outside, Eamonn!' said the priest.

Everyone seemed to be shouting now, the whole crowd pushing forward to reach Mary. Eamonn took her by the arm and pulled her away to the vestry, while Patrick Dempsey blocked the rush of people. From the vestry Eamonn took her straight out into the night, into the falling rain, fumbling to open the umbrella he carried. Before he could get it open he saw there were pilgrims spilling out of the main door of the church, making their way between the gravestones of the churchyard towards them.

'Run, Mary! Don't mind getting wet!'

He kept hold of her hand, and they set off at a run up the road. The pilgrims caught sight of them and gave chase. It would have been comical if it hadn't been frightening.

Hot, panting, drenched, they ran all the way to their cottage. As soon as they were inside, Eamonn bolted the door. They stood there in the dark and listened as the chasing crowd caught up, and called to Mary, and beat on the door.

'Mary! Mary! Speak to us!'

Then they lit the lamp and took off their wet coats and dried their wet faces.

'It's madness out there,' said Mary.

'And it's cold and wet,' said Eamonn. 'They'll not stay long.'

Shortly there came a different voice at the door, the voice of the priest. He was outside with Eileen Brennan. They opened the door and let them in, closing it at once afterwards.

'That was a terrible disgrace!' said the priest. 'The shame of it in my church!'

He was very angry.

'It's the fear has got them,' said Eileen Brennan. 'They believe our Mary can save them.'

'I can't save them,' said Mary.

'It's the devil at work,' said the priest, brushing the rain off his coat. 'To riot like that in my church!'

Eamonn peeped out through the shutters.

'They're not going away.'

'I'll give them not going away,' said the priest. 'Open the door for me, Eamonn.'

Eamonn let the priest out and bolted the door after him. They heard him in the rain, raging at the pilgrims, ordering them back to their homes, threatening them with the police, and the bishop, and the wrath of God. The pilgrims listened in silence, but they did not go.

The priest came back into the house.

'They want you, Mary,' he said. 'They say you have a message for them.'

'I've no message at all, Father.' The pilgrims frightened her. 'I want to leave. I don't like this.'

'Of course you don't,' said her mother.

'Well, there'll be no leaving till the morning,' said Father Flannery. 'In the morning, they'll be gone. They'll not spend all night out there. Not in this weather.'

But they did. In the morning, when Eamonn looked out through the kitchen window, he reported that the rain had passed and the pilgrims were still out there. If anything the crowd had grown bigger.

The priest had spent the night on the wooden settle, and was in a foul mood.

'You'll have to tell them something, Mary,' he said. 'Just to get them to go away.'

'What can I say, Father?'

'They're wanting to be given a date for the end of the world. So give them a date. Tell them Wednesday fortnight.'

'Wednesday fortnight!'

'And for pity's sake someone brew me a mug of coffee.'

48

'Of course I want to do something,' said the prime minister testily. 'That is the bane of the politician's life, the urge to *do* something. And, need I add, to be seen to do something. But there are times when the right if inglorious decision is to do nothing.'

'We are not the principals in this affair,' said Lord Home. 'Our place is to support our allies.'

'Yes, but confound it!' said Mountbatten. 'How can we stand by and do nothing when we're on the brink of being dragged into an entirely unnecessary war? Today is Friday. On Monday the Marines go in. Kennedy doesn't want it. Khrushchev doesn't want it. But neither of them can back down. It's a matter of face. That's where we come in. We can broker a deal.'

'There's nothing I'd like better than to broker a deal,' said Macmillan. 'But are you quite sure this contact of yours isn't using you for some other purpose?'

Mountbatten sighed.

'Captain Ivanov is a member of the Soviet armed forces. His loyalties are to the Soviet Union. All he's saying is that the Soviet leadership wants a way out of this mess, but they can't say so in public because it would involve a loss of prestige, and so he offers to provide a back channel. Yes, he's using me. And we can use him.'

'And the proposal is that we call a summit conference in London?' said the Foreign Secretary.

'We propose that in private. If Khrushchev signals that he'd accept, we make the proposal to Kennedy, also in private. No one has to back down from a public position of strength. When agreement has been secured on both sides, we here in London make the public proposal, in the interests of world peace.'

Macmillan looked to his Foreign Secretary.

'What do you think, Alec?'

'I don't like it,' said Lord Home. 'This proposal comes from a junior Russian spy. I have to ask myself, to put it crudely, what's his game? None of these embassy boys makes a move without clearing it with Moscow.'

'Maybe his game,' said Mountbatten, 'is staying alive. If this thing goes up, we all go. Imminent global annihilation does tend to concentrate the mind.'

'Maybe,' said Home. 'But I think it's far more likely that this is part of a strategy to drive a wedge between ourselves and our allies.'

Macmillan nodded.

'I'm afraid I agree, Dickie. It's a Soviet ploy.'

'They play this game all the time,' said Home. 'Round up world opinion on some airy platform related to world peace in the hope of isolating the United States. The capitalist warmonger, and so on. If they could recruit us to their parade, it would be a major propaganda coup. This Ivanov of yours has been instructed to lay a bait for our vanity.'

'So you don't see any value at all in my back channel?'

'Let's stick with the usual sources, Dickie,' said the prime minister. 'Safer to leave it to the professionals.'

Back in the Ministry of Defence, Mountbatten told Rupert of the failure of their proposal.

'Leave it to the professionals,' exclaimed Rupert bitterly. 'Meaning the same bunch who got us into this mess.'

'I'm sorry. They're quite old school, you know. I think both Harold and Alec regard this back channel business as a touch ungentlemanly.'

'God save us from British gentlemen.'

Rupert was disappointed. But he had not given up yet.

'You know what?' he said. 'The back channel is based on a nod and a wink. Nothing in writing. Why don't I tell Ivanov to pass back the hint that London would be open to brokering peace, if given a strong enough nod from Moscow? Maybe if we start the ball rolling, the professionals can pick it up and run with it.'

'You're proposing to lie to Ivanov?'

'Is it a lie? Macmillan wants the conference. He gets to be the peacemaker, the wise elder statesman. He just doesn't want to initiate the proposal. But once we get it out there, once there are voices calling on him to step forward and save the world, don't you think he'd accept?'

'He'd think Christmas had come early,' said Mountbatten. 'I didn't have you down as a Machiavelli, Rupert.'

'I can go one step further,' said Rupert. 'You know nothing about this. Whatever I do, I do on my own initiative. As far as you're concerned, the matter was closed by your conversation with the PM today. This conversation has not taken place.'

'And still isn't taking place?'

'Even as we speak.'

'Then let me add this last thought. Harold's secret fear is that Britain's views no longer carry any weight in the United States. And his secret pride is that he has a fatherly influence on Jack Kennedy. They've spoken on the phone every evening, you know, since this crisis began. So if there were to be some sort of peace summit, he would see himself as the natural chairman.'

'Leave it with me,' said Rupert. 'I shall now go and not act on all that we haven't said.'

Rupert met Ivanov as before, in Stephen Ward's flat. Stephen Ward was present. A little to his annoyance, Rupert learned that Stephen had also been pursuing contacts for Ivanov.

'I've talked to Godfrey Nicholson,' he said. 'He sits on the backbenches, but he's highly respected. He's willing to get on to the Foreign Office for us. And I've been on to Lord Arran, who's a good friend, and he's willing to meet you.'

'Don't bother with the Foreign Office,' said Rupert. 'And actually, Stephen, I'm not sure that roping in Uncle Tom Cobley and all is going to do us much good.'

'I will meet anybody,' said Ivanov. 'The situation is critical.'

'Just doing what I always do, old chap,' said Stephen. 'Getting people together.'

'Listen, Eugene,' said Rupert. 'Mountbatten's had a word with the PM. Macmillan is definitely interested. But any proposal for a peace summit can't come from him. So you're going to have to deliver on two fronts. First, Moscow has to signal they want this to happen. Second, they have to prompt a third party to make the proposal.'

'Rupert! My friend! This is wonderful news!'

'Do you think you can deliver that?'

'Of course! All they're waiting for is the hint that the offer will be welcomed. You know, Rupert, great leaders of proud nations are like lovers. They don't wish to ask for a date until they know they will be accepted.'

He reached for his coat, and then, his coat on, he embraced Rupert.

'I go now, to save the world.'

From the window, they watched him stride away up the mews.

'Well done, Rupert,' said Stephen.

'We're not there yet,' said Rupert.

49

It was almost the end of Friday afternoon when Pamela arrived at the Kenya Coffee House on Marylebone High Street. She had suggested to Susie that they meet here, but had not told her friend that it was a favourite haunt of Stephen Ward's. Pamela wanted to see Stephen again, and to talk to him, but she didn't want him to know she wanted to see him.

Susie appeared, only a little late, wearing a fawn-coloured suit and too much make-up. She looked to Pamela like a middle-aged child.

'Darling Pammy, it's been ages! I've so much to tell you! What have you been doing? Where have you been hiding?'

She looked round the café as they settled down.

'No nude models here, as far as I can see.'

They both lit up cigarettes. Pamela was shocked by the experience of seeing Susie again. They had been such good friends at school. That now seemed as if it had been a hundred years ago.

'I've got something to tell you,' said Susie, lowering her voice to a whisper. 'Though I bet you've guessed already.'

'No,' said Pamela. 'Tell.'

Susie flashed her ring finger. A diamond winked.

'You're engaged!'

Susie nodded, bursting with pride.

'Who is it?'

'Logan, of course,' said Susie.

'I thought he was your cousin.'

'He's only a sort of a cousin. And anyway, you're allowed to marry your cousin.'

'Susie, how wonderful! Congratulations!'

Pamela did her best to come up with the appropriate ecstasy. In fact she was appalled. How could Susie be married? She knew nothing about anything. It was all a game to her.

'He's as thick as a brick, of course,' said Susie blithely, 'but he's an absolute sweetheart. I'm so lucky.'

'So tell me how it happened. When did he propose?'

'Actually on midsummer's day. It was so romantic. He got a ring and everything. He took me out to dinner, and to be honest I half-guessed. He ordered champagne! Then when we were clinking glasses, he pushed this little box across the table!'

'Oh, Susie! So what did he say?'

Pamela could picture the scene all too easily: pink-faced Logan, shiny-faced Susie, the champagne, the ring. The ritual gestures copied from a thousand magazine articles. She could even predict the words, some charming bumbling non-communication that only served to show how masculine he was.

'He said' – Susie covered her mouth and giggled – 'he said, "How about it, old girl?"'

She burst into laughter.

'Darling Logan. He's no poet. But he's a sweetheart. And Pammy, it's all your fault!'

'What did I do?'

'You made us go to that club, remember?' Once again she lowered her voice. 'With the showgirls.'

'I remember.'

'Logan got very amorous after that. In the car, after we dropped you off, it got quite steamy. He had his hands all over me. When it started to get a bit too much, I said, Little boys have to learn to wait for their treats.'

'You actually said that?'

'I said it. And he knew I was right. You know how boys are, Pammy. They have to have their noses smacked, like puppies, or they'll be forever jumping up at you.'

Pamela listened in awed silence.

'So have you or haven't you?' she said.

Susie giggled.

'Not all the way. But after he proposed I let him go a jolly sight further, I can tell you.'

'How far?'

Soundlessly, Susie mouthed, 'Knickers off.'

Pamela tried to picture this scene, and failed. She could get no further than a half memory from childhood of playing doctors and nurses.

'And you really love him?' she said.

'Madly. I can't wait for the wedding night.'

'But you will.'

'Oh, well, we might as well. It's not so long now. Then it can be special, the way it's meant to be.'

'Yes. Of course.'

She grasped Pamela's hands across the table, her over-made-up eyes shining.

'Now tell me all about you,' she said.

Pamela had no intention of doing any such thing.

'Oh, there's nothing much to tell,' she said. 'You're the one with the exciting news. So when's the big day?'

'We want it to be a spring wedding. We haven't quite settled on a date yet. Mummy thinks May.'

'My God! Can you wait that long?'

'Oh, there's masses to do. That's only six or seven months away. I don't know that we'll have enough time as it is.'

'No, I meant – is Logan happy with that?'

'Logan does as he's told. You have to start as you mean to carry on.'

Pamela could see the marriage stretching out before her, like a view of a landscape from a hilltop. The early excitement, the home-making, the babies. The boredom, the infidelity, the thickening waists.

At this moment Stephen Ward walked into the café. He saw Pamela at once and came over with a smile.

'Pamela! What a delight!'

'Hello, Stephen. You remember my friend Susie?'

Stephen smiled for Susie and pulled out a chair.

'May I?'

'Of course you may.'

Pamela was surprised to find how pleased she was by his arrival.

'Two lovely young ladies! Just the pick-me-up I need.'

'Are you hung-over, Stephen?'

'No, no. I don't drink. You know that. But I've just had an hour of Eugene ranting at me.' To Susie, with a smile, 'Eugene's a Russian friend of ours. He's full of some scheme of his that he swears will stop war breaking out.'

'War!' said Susie.

'It's this Cuba business. Eugene kept on telling me how strong and proud his people are. He's been telling me that if Kennedy invades Cuba, the sleeping bear will wake!'

He spoke the last words in a Russian accent.

'Is this the missiles row?' said Susie, trying to keep up.

'Yes,' said Stephen. 'Khrushchev's gone and put nuclear missiles on Cuba.'

'But they'll sort it out, surely? I mean, no one wants a nuclear war.'

'These things can happen by accident.'

'By accident?' Susie stared in bewilderment. 'A nuclear war?'

'All it takes is a ship to be fired on, or a plane to be shot down. Then the real shooting starts.'

'But a nuclear war!' repeated Susie. 'I mean, that means everyone gets killed.'

'It does rather.'

'And you think this might happen before my wedding?'

Pamela burst into laughter.

'I think you should tell Eugene,' she said to Stephen. 'Urgent message to Khrushchev. Delay end of world to after Susie's wedding.'

'Oh, Lord,' said Susie. 'I suppose you think I'm so silly. But it would be so jolly unfair.'

Stephen stayed with them long enough to down a double espresso. Then he got up, gave Susie a mock bow, and said to Pamela,

'If you're around at Sunday lunchtime – if, that is, the world hasn't ended – Bill's asked us to lunch. Do join us.'

'I don't know, Stephen.'

'Just give me a tinkle. I could swing by and pick you up.'

After he was gone Susie said, 'So who's Bill?'

'Just a friend of Stephen's.'

'You seem to have got some pretty rum friends, Pammy.'

'They're not really friends. You know how people appear in your life and then disappear again.'

'That's what so reassuring about Logan,' said Susie. 'I've known him for ever. He says he used to pull my pigtails, which is nonsense, because I never had pigtails. Just imagine, when I was seven he was twice my age!'

50

In Moscow, Khrushchev was maintaining his hard line in public. Privately, as Friday wore on, he began to be afraid that he had misjudged Kennedy. Might the still-inexperienced young president be so foolish as to risk war over Cuba after all?

This was the puzzle that kept Khrushchev awake at night. What was Kennedy thinking? Both Andrei Gromyko at the Foreign Ministry and Oleg Troyanovsky, his foreign affairs adviser, told him that Kennedy would never countenance a nuclear war.

'How do you know this?' said Khrushchev. 'Kennedy is a weak man. Weak men are dangerous.'

'All the assessments from our embassy in Washington reach this conclusion.'

'What do they know? They hear the official line. Of course Kennedy *says* he doesn't want nuclear war. Don't tell me what he *says*. Tell me what he's thinking.'

'How are we to know that, Nikita Sergeyevich?'

'That is what our intelligence services are for! No political leader reveals his true intentions in public. So we listen to the whispers and the murmurs, we look for the unguarded moments. A word spoken between friends is worth a year of public speeches.'

Khrushchev believed this because it was true of himself. At the same time he was aware that in moments of excitement or anger he could let his tongue slip. Secretly he regarded this as one of his most skilful strategies: the accidental outburst that could be excused later as a lapse in the heat of the moment, but which nevertheless conveyed a message.

In this spirit he arranged to meet an American businessman who was in Moscow to promote a deal. William E. Knox, president of Westinghouse International, found himself summoned to the Kremlin for a three-hour rant from Khrushchev. The Soviet leader defended his aid to Cuba, insisted on his desire for peace, and concluded with a threat.

'If the United States insists on war,' he said, 'we'll all meet in hell!'

Afterwards Troyanovsky asked Khrushchev why he had taken the trouble to say this to a businessman, who was no part of the American government.

'If I tell Dobrynin to say it,' replied Khrushchev, 'they won't believe it. When they hear it from an electrical goods salesman, they'll believe it.'

Later that day GRU headquarters in Moscow received an interesting report from a new back channel. A junior attaché at the London embassy had apparently succeeded in opening up a direct line to the British prime minister. His report was sent on to KGB headquarters in Dzerzhinsky Square in a purple folder. During the crisis all information received from abroad was coordinated by a special task force in the Lubyanka, reduced to manageable proportions and passed on to the chairman of the KGB, Vladimir Semichastny. The task force was encouraged to give priority to information not knowingly given.

In this light Captain 2nd Class Ivanov's proposal looked both promising and distinctly odd. Why were the chief of Britain's defence staff and the British prime minister in contact with such a junior official at all?

'Who is this Ivanov? Is he one of ours?'

Ivanov was GRU, Army Intelligence, not KGB. The task force was exclusively KGB.

'Surely the British are using him,' they said to each other. 'They may even have turned him already. He's either a dupe or a double agent.'

'This peace summit he proposes. This is London looking for a way to trick us into backing down.'

To give themselves political cover, the KGB passed the file to Oleg Troyanovsky in the chairman's office. Troyanovsky glanced at it, saw that it related to the British, not the Americans, and put it aside to read later.

Among the folders sent up by the KGB directly to Khrushchev's desk was one that gave prominence to two alarming reports. The first had come through KGB sources in Washington. A barman at the National Press Club called Johnny Prokov was serving drinks in the Tap Room when he overheard two *Herald Tribune* journalists. One of them, Warren Rogers, was telling the other, Robert Donovan, that he was due to fly south that same night, to cover the operation to capture Cuba. Prokov passed on this information to Anatoly Gorsky, TASS correspondent and KGB agent. The KGB team in Washington sent a second secretary from the embassy to hang around the parking lot behind the Willard Hotel, where Rogers kept his car. When Rogers showed up in the morning, the Russian fell into a 'chance' conversation with him, and asked if Kennedy was serious about attacking Cuba. Warren Rogers had no knowledge whatsoever of Kennedy's intentions, but he took it as his patriotic duty to assure the Russian that the American president was not a man who could be pushed around.

'He sure as hell is serious about Cuba,' said Rogers.

The report was transmitted to Moscow at once. At the same time the GRU office in the Washington Embassy, part of whose job was to track Pentagon radio signals, picked up an order from the joint chiefs of staff putting Strategic Air Command on DEFCON 2, an alert one stage short of war. A second intercepted signal ordered US hospitals to prepare to receive casualties.

This was the kind of information Khrushchev found convincing. None of it was meant for the ears of Moscow. Kennedy really was going to invade.

Khrushchev called Troyanovsky into his private office.

'Find me a speech of Lenin's that supports a tactical withdrawal.'

Then he summoned the members of the Presidium to the Kremlin. To their astonishment he announced a complete reversal of his tactics.

'The missiles have served their purpose,' he said. 'They have forced the Americans to accept that Socialist Cuba is a fact of life, and that the Soviet Union, as leader of the Socialist world, is committed to Cuba's defence. The time has now come to offer to withdraw the missiles in exchange for a cast-iron pledge from the Americans not to invade Cuba.'

The Presidium heard this in silence. They had not spoken up when Khrushchev had made the decision to send nuclear missiles to Cuba, and they did not speak up now. These were all men who had come of age politically under Stalin. They had looked on as colleagues had challenged the leader, and been charged with disloyalty. They had written on the guilty verdicts the one word, *da*: yes. They had signed their names. The guilty ones had then been shot. Such memories create the habit of absolute unquestioning obedience.

'Cuba will become a zone of peace,' said Khrushchev. 'These are correct and reasonable tactics. Lenin himself said, "To accept battle at a time when it is obviously advantageous to the enemy and not to us is a crime.'"

The Presidium voted unanimously to approve the new plan.

As more and more evidence poured in of American preparations to invade, Khrushchev brushed aside Gromyko, who was preparing a formal letter to President Kennedy, and began to dictate a letter of his own. Pacing up and down his office, striking the air with his hands, he hectored and pleaded, accused and flattered, and Troyanovsky wrote it all down.

'What would war give you?' he dictated. 'You are threatening us with war. But you will know that the very least which you would receive in reply would be that you would experience the same consequences as – as – as – those which you sent us.'

He stabbed a finger at Troyanovsky.

'You have that?'

'Yes, Nikita Sergeyevich.'

'It must all be very simple. Strong, but simple.'

He resumed pacing and dictating.

'I have participated in two wars, and know that war ends when it has rolled through cities and villages, everywhere sowing death and destruction. I don't know whether you can understand me and believe me, but I should like to have you believe in yourself and to agree that one cannot give way to passions. It is necessary to control them.'

He now spoke to Gromyko, who was listening in silence.

'There, you see. I address him as leader to leader. As man to man.'

He continued.

'Let us therefore show statesmanlike wisdom. I propose: we, for our part, will declare that our ships bound for Cuba will not carry any kind of armaments. You would declare that the United States will not invade Cuba. Then the necessity for the presence of our military specialists in Cuba would disappear.'

He stared at Gromyko. Gromyko nodded in silence.

'Mr President,' Khrushchev resumed, 'we and you ought not to pull on the ends of the rope in which you have tied the knot of war. The more the two of us pull, the tighter that knot will be tied. And a moment may come when that knot will be tied so tight that even he who tied it will not have the strength to untie it.'

He jerked his hands in the air, acting out the tightening of a knot.

'That's very clear, I think,' he said.

'The knot of war,' said Troyanovsky. 'A vivid image.'

'Consequently,' said Khrushchev, dictating again, pleased with his words, 'if there is no intention to tighten that knot and thereby to doom the world to the catastrophe of thermonuclear war, then let us not only relax the forces pulling on the ends of the rope, let us take measures to untie that knot.'

His hands moved in the air, untying the invisible knot.

Later that night, back at his own desk, Troyanovsky picked up the purple folder from the KGB. He was tired, and did not read it attentively, but it was clear to him that the KGB did not take this Ivanov seriously, and that whatever he was proposing was no longer of any immediate relevance. He wrote on it: *Not urgent. Apply standard procedures*. Then he added it to the pile of documents awaiting transfer to the archives.

Khrushchev's letter, translated, ciphered, cabled, and deciphered, reached Washington late on Friday evening. The president read it through once, and found himself unsure exactly what he'd read.

'Is he offering to take the missiles out of Cuba or not?'

He postponed any response until the following morning.

Over at the Pentagon, General Curtis LeMay also read Khrushchev's letter.

'What a lot of bullshit,' he declared. 'He must think we're a bunch of dumb shits if we swallow that syrup.'

51

Pamela had been more unsettled by Susie's prattle than she cared to admit. On the one hand she pitied her friend for the narrowness of the life she was choosing. To be married, at nineteen, to a braying fool who worked in the City. To think of sex as a treat for the boys. To choose to dress like her own mother. But at the same time, she envied her. Susie was moving on to the next stage of life, as ordained by her tribe. Marriage wouldn't bring happiness, but it would give her a place in the world, a function, a status. What else could a girl do but marry?

Let the world end, Pamela thought. What is there in the future to wait for?

Hugo had a business dinner that evening, so Pamela ate simply and alone. Tomorrow, Saturday, Harriet and Emily were due to return.

Quite suddenly, sitting by herself at the kitchen table, Pamela fell into a state of despair. It happened without cause, without warning. She had made herself some toasted cheese, and had cut it up, a little over-obsessively, into tidy rectangles. She was just lifting one rectangle on her fork, it was midway between the plate and her mouth, when her hand froze.

Why eat? We're all about to die.

The ground fell away beneath her, and she saw that she was resting over a dark void. The slightest movement could topple her into this void, and once falling, she knew she would fall for ever. Terror caused her muscles to tense and her heart to beat rapidly. The darkness came pressing in from all sides. She opened her mouth to cry out, but no sound came.

There's nothing after all, she said to herself. There's nothing.

It wasn't terror at death. To die you must first live. What Pamela felt was the horrified conviction of non-existence.

I am nothing. No past, no future. No meaning, no value. Only empty dark infinite space.

She fled from the kitchen, leaving her modest supper half eaten. She wanted to crawl deep into a hole, to close her eyes, to be safe. She went through her night-time ritual of undressing and washing, clinging to every familiar habit as if it would hold back the darkness; and little by little the terror abated. She had stopped trembling by the time she was curled up in bed. But she could not sleep.

What had happened? Was it Susie's engagement? Was it Eugene's warning that the Russian bear would wake? Or was it the unhappiness she had inherited from her father?

It was in him from the beginning.

Strange images passed through her mind. She saw herself standing naked on stage, and silent men staring at her. One of them was Stephen Ward, with his *pinga grande*. She was playing Ghosts in the night woods, and there were men in the trees, staring at her. The men were naked, and aroused. She saw Mary watching her, and didn't want Mary to look, shouted at her to look away. None of this felt like dreams. It was a parade of memories, with which she was helplessly tormenting herself.

She stood on the top step, looking into the great room, and all eyes turned to stare at her revealing costume. Those eyes undressed her. The silk chiffon fell away, the black lace under-wear fell away, and she was naked again.

Why am I always naked?

Do you fuck?

Only with friends.

I have no friends. *We're all alone, whether we know it or not.* Who said that? Oh yes, Rupert. Can he really be in love with Mary? They're all fools, all fooling themselves, Susie and Logan, Rupert and Mary, Bobby and Charlotte, all lost in the darkness. Bored people looking for fun, lonely people looking for love.

We must love one another or die. Say it out loud, in the blackness of night, and it reverses itself. We are already dead, and so cannot love one another. The mirror reverses the image. But André, looking through the mirror, sees truly. Desire puts down roots in stony soil.

I shall fall asleep in your arms and the hurting will be over. But in whose arms?

Later she heard Hugo come in, and climb the stairs to his bed-room. She could hear all his movements, the bathroom door opening and closing, the whoosh of the lavatory, the pad of his bare feet. Then the landing light went out and his bedroom door closed behind him.

She struggled against the impulse for as long as she could, but she was too afraid, too unhappy. So at last she got out of bed and went softly downstairs to the first floor, in the faint light falling through the landing window. She opened Hugo's bed-room door as quietly as she could, and crossed to his bedside. As her eyes adjusted, she saw that he was not asleep. He was lying in bed, his eyes open, gazing up at her.

'Please,' she whispered. 'I can't sleep.'

She drew back the covers and crept into the bed beside him. He put his arms round her and she pressed up close against him, feeling his warmth. Neither of them spoke. She heard his soft steady breathing, and knew that he was not going to sleep, just as she was not going to sleep. They lay wakeful in each other's arms, waiting.

Then his head bent down, and he kissed the side of her neck, by her shoulder. She stirred against him.

'I'm frightened,' she said. 'There's going to be a war.'

'Is there?'

'The world's going to end.'

'Tonight?'

'Or tomorrow.'

He kissed her again, and she moved against him, desiring his desire.

'Oh, Pammy,' he said. Then he turned his face away from her.

'I mustn't,' he said, his voice muffled in the pillow.

'Just let me stay with you,' she said. 'Just for tonight.'

'I don't think I can bear it.'

'Don't send me away.'

'Oh, Pammy.'

She stayed in his bed, in his arms, all through that night. They slept after a while and woke with the dawn. Hugo got up first, and went to look out through the curtains at the street outside.

'The world hasn't ended,' he said.

Pamela, waking slowly, stretched her cramped body. She saw him by the window, watching her.

'You all right?' he said.

'Mmm.'

'Nothing happened,' he said. 'Nobody needs to know.'

'Nobody needs to know that nothing happened?'

'That's right.'

'I was frightened. I wanted you to hold me.'

He left the window and came to the bed. He sat down beside her and stroked her cheek.

'Now you must go back to your room, and I'm going to make everything here be as if you never came. And we're going to forget all about it.'

'All about the nothing we did, that never happened.'

He bent down and kissed her cheek.

'There. Enough. No more.'

She got slowly out of his bed, and moved slowly across the room to the door. In the doorway she looked back at him and said, 'Thank you for not sending me away.'

He said nothing. She went out onto the landing.

I'd be safe with Hugo, she thought.

52

By Saturday morning, it was becoming clear in Moscow that the US attack on Cuba had not yet been launched. Khrushchev's mood changed again.

'You see,' he told his colleagues in the Kremlin. 'They were trying to force my hand. This has all been a trick to present us as the guilty ones. But I have stood firm. I have been reasonable. They have no excuse for the invasion they want.'

He was beginning to regret the tone of his overnight letter. In the cool light of day he saw that there was less to fear than he had thought. So far no answer had been received.

He reread his letter.

'There is nothing here to be ashamed of,' he said. 'I am on the side of peace. Who can dispute that? As for the missiles, well, there's no mention of them. I refer to our military specialists in Cuba. That can mean what I choose it to mean.'

'Are you proposing, Nikita Sergeyevich,' said Mikoyan, 'that the missiles remain in Cuba?'

'No, no,' said Khrushchev. 'We must not be obstinate. The missiles are a bargaining counter. We will take them out, but on our own terms. The world will see that we have given the Americans a taste of their own medicine, and as a result the Americans have been taught restraint.'

'I'm not following you, Nikita Sergeyevich.'

'I was standing on the shore of the Black Sea at Pitsunda when I had this idea,' said Khrushchev. 'I was gazing across the water at the American nuclear missiles in Turkey. We will offer to withdraw the missiles from Cuba if the Americans take their missiles out of Turkey.'

He turned to his colleagues and beamed at them.

'Simple. Fair. A victory for peace. Let us send a new letter at once. So you will see, comrades, that without a shot being fired, we will achieve a victory.'

Jack Kennedy sat sprawled across his chair, tapping his teeth with the end of a pencil. It was just after ten in the morning on Saturday, and ExComm had convened to decide how to respond to Khrushchev's rambling letter of the night before.

'There's nothing there that says Khrushchev's willing to take the missiles out,' said Rusk.

'Twelve pages of fluff,' said McNamara.

'He's playing for time,' said General Taylor. 'There's only one way we're going to get those nukes out, and that's we go in and take them out.'

'You could be right,' said Kennedy.

'Just say the word, Mr President. We're set to go, first light on Monday.'

Ted Sorenson came in with a ticker-tape transcript. He handed it to the president.

'New letter from Khrushchev. Just come over Moscow radio.'

'Another letter?'

Kennedy read the letter out loud. It was a revised deal. The Soviet chairman offered to withdraw the offensive missiles from Cuba if the United States withdrew its missiles from Turkey.

The ExComm members stared at each other.

'That wasn't in last night's letter, was it?' said Kennedy.

Rusk turned to an aide.

'Check this out. Is this part of last night's letter, or is this a new letter?'

'We have to ignore this,' said Mac Bundy. 'We can't trade away the missiles in Turkey.'

'Can't we?' said Kennedy.

'You want to blow NATO to hell? What's it going to look like, sacrificing our allies' security to look after ourselves?'

'What's it going to look like,' said Kennedy, 'making war on Cuba because they threaten us with missiles, while we're saying the Soviets shouldn't mind the nukes in Turkey?'

'Mac's right,' said Sorenson. 'You can't do this.'

'I don't see it either,' said Bobby. 'We can't ask the Turks to give up their defence system.'

'So what do we do?'

'We could just ignore the second letter,' said Bundy. 'Tell Khrushchev you want to deal with his interesting proposals of last night.'

'Can we do that?'

There was silence in the room. Bobby got up and went out.

'If you'll forgive me, sir,' said General Taylor. 'There's only one way this is going to end, and the longer we delay, the fewer options we have.'

'We haven't fully exhausted the possibility of negotiations, General.'

'Of course not, sir,' said Taylor. 'But we all know the boys in the Kremlin have read their Sun Tzu.'

'Meaning what?'

'Chinese. Fifth century BC.'

He pulled out a small notebook and read from it.

Speak in humble terms, continue preparations, and attack.
Pretend inferiority and encourage the enemy's arrogance.

The crux of military operations lies in the pretence of accommo-
dating to the designs of the enemy.'

He put his notebook away.

'Like I said, you're being played, Mr President.'

Kennedy stared back at Taylor, tapping his teeth with his
pencil.

Bobby came back into the room, brandishing a book.

'Remember this, Jack?'

'Another book,' said Kennedy. 'Great.'

'You read it last summer. *The American Senator*, by Anthony
Trollope.'

'Summer before,' said Kennedy.

Bobby had the book open at a marked passage.

'You told me about this back then. We called it the Trollope
ploy.'

'The Trollope ploy? What the fuck is this, Bobby?'

'Arabella Trefoil is desperate to get Lord Rufford to marry
her. They go for a ride in a carriage, they're alone together,
and they're flirting. He kisses her, but she can't get him to the
point.'

He read from the book.

'She flung herself onto his shoulder, and for a while she seemed
to faint. For a few minutes she lay there, and as she was lying
she calculated whether it would be better to try at this moment
to drive him to some clearer declaration, or to *make use of what he
had already said* without giving him an opportunity of protesting
that he had not meant to make her an offer of marriage.'

He looked up with a grin.

'You get the strategy? She hasn't received her proposal, but
she decides to act as if she has. When she gets home from the

437

carriage ride, she simply tells her mother that Lord Rufford has proposed. And he's caught.'

'Summer's over, guys,' said McNamara, impatient with this distraction. 'What do we say to Khrushchev?'

'We do like Mac suggested,' said Bobby. 'We answer the first letter, and act as if we never got the second letter.'

'Why would he buy that?'

'What choice has he got?'

'You know what?' said McNamara. 'I'm with the president on this one. Pull out the Jupiters. We all know they're a heap of junk.'

Lyndon Johnson snorted with disgust.

'I call that backing down,' he said. 'We've already got Soviet ships coming through the blockade. We're looking kind of old and tired and sick, I'd say.'

'Ships are not coming through the blockade,' said Bobby sharply.

'Start on the Jupiters,' said the vice president, 'and next thing you know you're pulling out your planes, and your technicians, and your fucking pants. Then you're standing there buck naked, and your dick don't look so big anymore.'

'So what do you propose?' said the president. 'We have to get those missiles out of Cuba.'

'Blast 'em out,' said General Taylor. 'The only language they understand is force.'

Kennedy nodded. Then he turned to his brother.

'Bobby: this Trollope ploy. Why don't you and Ted draft me something?'

'You got it.'

Bobby and Ted Sorenson left the Cabinet Room. An aide entered with a note for Bob McNamara. He scanned it rapidly.

'Looks like they shot down a U2.'

Sudden silence in the room.

438

'Is the pilot dead?'

'Major Rudy Anderson. Brought down by a Soviet SAM missile over Banes, east Cuba.'

'Fuck!'

'That's it, isn't it?' said Paul Nitze, assistant secretary of defence. 'They've fired the first shot.'

53

'Panic meeting,' shouted Macdonald, racing down the corridor outside Rupert's office. 'Get off your arses!'

Mountbatten was gathering the defence staff in the big conference room. Mountbatten himself sat grim-faced at the head of the long table as officers and advisers poured into the room.

'What the hell happened?' whispered Rupert to Shaw.

'Shooting over Cuba,' said Shaw.

Sir Kenneth Cross, chief of Bomber Command, was half shouting at Mountbatten.

'We need the go order now! We follow the drill. We use the BBC to call all personnel off leave.'

'No,' said Mountbatten, 'we do not use the BBC. We do not alert the press. The PM is adamant on this.'

'My bombers are sitting targets! I must give the signal to disperse! Damn it, Dickie, the rockets could start coming in any minute.'

'We're to take no overt measures.' Mountbatten looked round and saw that the room was now full. 'Ken, brief the room.'

Sir Kenneth Strong, director of the Joint Intelligence Bureau, spoke from a paper in his hand.

'Cuban anti-aircraft batteries have fired on US low-level reconnaissance planes. Ground-to-air missiles have fired at and hit a high-level reconnaissance plane. The plane is down, the pilot presumed dead.'

'They shot down a U2?' said Cross.

'Yes.'

'The Soviets or the Cubans?'

'We don't know.'

'The pressure on the United States to retaliate is now overwhelming,' said Mountbatten. 'We must plan for the likelihood of an American counter-strike, followed by an invasion of Cuba.'

Strong picked up again.

'Information coming out of Cuba shows their defence forces on invasion status. We have reports that Castro is demanding the Soviets launch a first strike.'

'A first nuclear strike?'

'What else?'

'There's no way Cuba can be defended by conventional weapons,' said Pike. 'From Castro's point of view, it's nukes or surrender.'

'Gentlemen,' said Mountbatten. 'There are two issues here. How we support our allies in the event of war. And how we defend the United Kingdom.'

'Right now we're at Alert Condition Two,' said Cross. 'I can have the V-force at Alert Condition Three in two hours.'

'I'm sorry,' said Rupert, 'but I'm not following this. The V-force carries nuclear bombs. How can we defend the United Kingdom with nuclear bombs?'

'We deter attack,' said Cross.

'When? Before the missiles come in, or after?'

'This isn't the time for this debate, Rupert,' said Mountbatten.

'Do we activate the Civil Defence?' said Hugh Stephenson. 'We have half a million trained volunteers across the country.'

'How about the Regional Government HQs?'

'Not yet,' said Mountbatten.

'Can I get this clear?' said Cross. 'We do nothing until the Soviet bombs actually hit us?'

'We do nothing,' said Mountbatten.

Rupert accompanied Mountbatten on the short walk to the Old Admiralty Building.

'For pity's sake!' said Rupert. 'Why won't Macmillan offer to mediate?'

'There's offers of mediation coming out of everyone's ears,' said Mountbatten. 'The UN, the pope, you name it. Khrushchev says yes to every one of them. Even to that chump Russell. As far as the Americans are concerned, it's just so much Soviet propaganda that allows them to keep working on getting their missiles combat ready. You want Harold to join that camp?'

'So we're heading for war.'

'Kennedy wants those missiles out. He won't believe anything Khrushchev says about peace until then.'

'This is madness.'

'The shooting's started now, Rupert. The best we can hope for is that it stops short of going nuclear.'

When they reached the prime minister's office Mountbatten went in alone. Rupert stayed in the outer office. After a while Philip de Zulueta came out, with a list of people for the PM's secretary to bring in for a meeting.

'I know it's the weekend, Monica. The PM says no one's to panic. Keep it calm.'

He saw Rupert sitting on the side of a desk, smoking.

'You up to date with the news?' he said with a thin smile. 'There's good and there's bad.'

'I heard they started shooting.'

'Khrushchev's put an offer on the table. He'll pull the nukes out of Cuba if the Americans pull theirs out of Turkey.'

'Well, Jesus!' exclaimed Rupert. 'That's a deal we can do. The Jupiters are coming out next summer anyway.'

'You're not a politician, are you?' said de Zulueta.

'So what's going to happen?'

De Zulueta shrugged.

'I wouldn't make any plans for the weekend.'

He went back into the meeting, closing the door behind him. Rupert lit another cigarette and smoked it in silence. He thought of Mary in Ireland. Maybe her great wind was coming after all. Maybe the sinful world was about to be swept away by the righteous anger of the Lord.

He felt frightened, and powerless, and stupid.

You do your job under the illusion that you have some influence, that your opinions matter. You scurry about gathering information, analysing it, producing conclusions. And all it achieves is precisely nothing.

I have a position without power, advising a military establishment without power, in a nation without power. Whether we live or die is outside our control. We could all go fishing. It would make no difference.

Suddenly Rupert had a vision of his entire life as if illumined by a brilliant white light. In this brutal glare he saw that all his efforts as adviser to the Chief of Defence Staff, which he had presumed applied reason, even wisdom, to the key decisions of the day, were in aid of something else entirely. It was all to foster in himself the belief that he was necessary. This was the true drive: not world peace, or national security, but the vital importance of the life and work of Rupert Blundell. It was almost comical once you saw it. The youthful dream, standing on the terrace at Cliveden, of putting an end to war. The moralistic huffing and puffing, all designed to say: look at me! I matter! I'm important, aren't I?

Because of course the truth is none of us matter. Not me. Not

Mountbatten. Not Macmillan. We're all spectators.

He thought of the attack plan in the event of war. The Vulcans would go first, and drop their bombs. Then the Thor missiles would be launched, to hit the same targets. The Vulcan crews knew they had little chance of making it back. Even now, the crews would be playing cards in the huts on the airfields, in full flight gear, on Quick Reaction Alert. What did they say to their wives and children as they left home this morning?

Beyond that door men who believed themselves to hold the fate of the nation in their hands were finding ever more elaborate ways of deciding to do nothing. In the bright light of his vision Rupert saw that they were all powerless, and their lives were of no significance. How are we to live with this knowledge?

He saw then how limited his own philosophical explorations had been. He had gone a little way, in understanding that each of us is fundamentally alone. That had seemed to him brutal enough. But he had hardly begun. We're not just alone. We're without meaning. Without value.

We are each of us a cluster of atoms, blown together by random winds, tugged about for a while by the balloon of our vanity. Perhaps this is why we stumble from war to war. Lacking any true purpose we breed ourselves enemies. Driven by fear, we wreak destruction. Those who survive call themselves victorious. Then the wind blows, and the atoms are dispersed again.

And yet here we are, courting the illusion that our lives matter. We have no choice but to live as if what we do makes a difference. So we live two lives at once. In one we are the lord of our little universe, and the wider world exists to serve us. In the other we are specks of dust.

'Hello, Rupert.'

A middle-aged woman stood before him. She wore a grey suit, and spectacles, and had her hair in a tight bun.

'It's Joyce. Joyce Wedderburn.'

'Joyce!'

He hadn't recognised her. The passing years had not been kind to her. She had thickened, in face and body, so that she looked now as if the old Joyce had been coated in layers of a putty-like substance.

'Still with Dickie?' she said.

'As ever. He's in there.'

He nodded at the closed door.

'I've gone back to work. I'm on the War Book, with Beryl Grimble.'

She deposited a file on Monica's desk.

'Bad show,' she said.

'Bad as it gets,' said Rupert.

'Funny to think that out there they have no idea, really.'

Rupert was recalling what he'd heard of Joyce's life since he'd last known her. Marriage. Children.

'How's the family?' he asked her.

'Blissfully ignorant,' she said.

She took out a snapshot and showed it to him. A drab-looking middle-aged man with a drab-faced girl beside him.

'That's Geoff. And that's our Sally.'

'I told you it would all work out for you, Joyce.'

'And for you, I hope, Rupert.'

'Well, no snapshot to show you, I'm afraid.'

'Really?' She seemed genuinely surprised. 'I was sure someone would have scooped you up by now.'

'I'm afraid not.'

'I should have come back for another shot.'

'What do you mean?'

'Well, do you remember our one date in Kandy? When you got cold feet and practically ran away?'

Rupert stared at her.

'What are you talking about?'

'At that Chinese restaurant in Kandy. We were chatting away, and our conversation got the tiniest bit personal, and I saw it on your face. You were terrified I was going to go all sweet on you. You just switched off, like a light going out.'

'No, Joyce. You've got it all wrong.'

'Oh, it doesn't matter now. It was awful at the time, but it's all years ago. I can laugh at myself now. You must have thought me such an ass.'

Rupert found himself in a state of agitation.

'Listen, Joyce. I have to get this right. Are you telling me that when we had that horrible Chinese meal in Kandy you were hoping it might lead to something more between us?'

'Of course I was. Why do you think I was there?'

'I don't know. Friendliness, I suppose.'

'Oh, Rupert! I'd been making eyes at you for months. But I never really expected it to go anywhere. I mean, let's face it, I'm no oil painting.'

Rupert found himself speechless.

'But you see, you're quite right. Geoff came along. I wouldn't say he's quite in your class, but he's made me very happy. And then there's Sally. She's fourteen now. Doing well at school. So all's well that ends well. Unless this war happens, of course.'

She darted forward and gave Rupert a peck on the cheek.

'For old times,' she said. 'Let's have a cup of coffee one of these days.'

She left. From the back, moving briskly, head held high, she looked like the old Joyce again.

'Old flame, eh?' said Monica.

'In a way,' said Rupert.

He was overwhelmed by the realisation of how his life could have been so different. The smallest alteration in the past, a different look, a different word, and he could have been married to

Joyce all these years. The change in her appearance which had so struck him would have taken place imperceptibly, day by day. He would be the man in the snapshot.

It was an impossible thought to take in. The actual life he had lived presented itself so strongly as the only possible life he could have lived. But it wasn't true. Even as he had been telling himself that he was no more than a helpless cluster of atoms borne hither and thither on the wind, Joyce had walked in to prove him wrong.

We make our own destiny. If I'm alone, then somehow, for some reason, that's the life I've chosen.

The meeting in the PM's office now broke up. The door opened and the Foreign Secretary came out, with Sir Thomas Pike, Chief of the Air Staff. Mountbatten followed, with Macmillan.

'Nothing that looks like mobilisation,' the prime minister was saying. 'Just keep it all as low-key as possible.'

Walking back with Rupert, Mountbatten said quietly, 'It's not looking good.'

'How soon?'

'Kennedy told Harold last night that if he doesn't receive the right assurances from Khrushchev in the next twenty-four hours, he's going in.'

'What do we do then?'

'It all depends on the Russians. If they retaliate against West Berlin, we're in the mess whether we like it or not. We have Operation Visitation on standby. There's a Cabinet meeting scheduled for tomorrow afternoon. If the PM hits the button then, we go to Precautionary Stage. That means helicopters on Horse Guards Parade, and we're all off to Turnstile.'

'Christ!'

'My only consolation is that once we're down in that god-awful quarry, Harold can't give the order for nuclear retaliation unless I put my code alongside his.'

Rupert didn't ask the obvious next question. What could the man say?

'There's not one officer in all our forces wants to drop the bomb,' said Mountbatten. 'Not even Bing Cross. The Americans are something else. They're the true believers. What was it you said, Rupert? The worst wars are the religious wars.'

54

By Saturday the tents had spread over the headlands on either side of Kilnacarry. What with all the rain over the last month and the ground being so boggy, every day there was another car with its wheels spinning in the mud.

The more panicky the news bulletins, the more the crowd grew in Buckle Bay. They were there in all weathers, singing and praying. One of the Hennessy brothers from the hardware shop in Donegal was selling candles and matches from the back of his van. When the sun went down the pilgrims lit their candles and it was like Christmas down there, until the wind blew the flames out again.

The crowd remained camped outside the Brennan house too, with Mary Brennan inside a virtual prisoner. Of course she was not a prisoner, as Eamonn told her. If she wanted she had only to say the word and he'd fetch his Massey Ferguson and drive her out of the village. Up on the high seat of the tractor the pilgrims would not be able to reach her.

Mary had come to hate and fear the pilgrims, with their reaching hands and their hungry eyes. But she knew it was not only their need that kept her a prisoner in Kilnacarry. She had begun something with her three nights of visions all those years ago, and it was up to her to finish it. The difficulty was, she didn't know how.

Penned in the little cottage, she felt unable to think clearly. At last she could stand it no more.

'Get me out of here, Eamonn.'

'I've not got enough fuel to take you to Dublin.'

'Not Dublin. Not yet. Just take me out onto the cliffs. Somewhere they can't follow.'

So Eamonn fetched his tractor and drove it to the back of the cottage, and Mary came out fast and climbed up with him, and they were away before the pilgrims knew what was happening.

Eamonn took the tractor off the road, over the dunes and out to Dawros Head, to the last spur of rocky land, where the ocean reached out before them to the far horizon. When the engine stopped its throbbing the world was silent. Then the sounds came, the wind and the waves and the seagulls.

Mary looked out over the sea and breathed in the salty air and felt the confusion slowly blow away. Eamonn said nothing. It struck her then how kind he was, and how undervalued.

'Sorry to cause so much trouble,' she said.

'Makes a change,' he said.

'You're a good brother, Eamonn. And a good son.'

'I don't know about that.'

'You are. Staying by Mam all these years.'

'Just the way it happened.'

All these years he'd been home. Herself gone, Bridie gone.

'Have you ever wanted to leave?'

'Why would I leave?'

'You might find a girl.'

'There's no telling,' said Eamonn, as if he'd never given it any thought to speak of.

'You must get lonely at times,' she said.

'Maybe I do.'

450

'I get lonely,' she said.

As she said these words she caught a sight of the world of home that was new, and shocking. In place of the green rain-soaked hills she saw a desert. In place of the whitewashed cottage she saw a prison. Here they had led starved and lonely lives, among ignorant and unhappy people.

'Is this the life you wanted, Eamonn?'

'You get what you get,' he said.

She remembered him as a boy, captivated by a Superman comic.

'You were going to go to America.'

'I would have liked that,' he said.

'Oh, Eamonn.'

It made her angry. This good hard-working man with his wasted life. But who could you blame for it? Not Mam, widowed by the age of thirty.

'God owes you more,' she said.

'You tell him, Mary.'

'You've done the right thing all your life. When's it your turn?'

In this new bright light she saw her family, and the people of her village, and the great crowd of pilgrims, and she understood that they had all been abandoned by God. They didn't yet know it themselves, but they feared it with a terrible fear. That was why they reached out to her. They wanted a miracle, a touch of God in their hard lives. It needn't be much. Just a little magic to promise them that they weren't lost and abandoned after all.

Make God real to us, they begged her. Don't leave us in this mess of a life without the promise of some shining glory to come. Give us a sign. And if it's to be the great wind that sweeps everything away, so much the better. The end of the world strikes for the great as well as the small. We'll all be equal in the apocalypse.

But the truth is we're all lost and abandoned. There's no glory to come. The whole giant edifice of faith is a story made up by a child.

She wanted to shout out loud, to shout at God, to shame him for having taken advantage of her.

'Fifteen years,' she said. 'That's enough, isn't it?'

She started to shake. Suddenly the emotions flooding out of her were too strong to control.

I should have had a life of my own. I should have had babies of my own. I was a child, a stupid child! Why did you have to take away my life?

They were sitting squeezed tight together on the tractor seat. She could feel her body shaking against Eamonn's big strong body, but he didn't know how to put an arm round her.

Slowly the moment passed.

'You want to go back now?' Eamonn said.

The light was fading. Mary looked down at the shore. It was low tide. The crowd in Buckle Bay would be lighting their candles, shuffling forward over the wet sand, waiting for their miracle.

If none of it's true, why not give them what they want? In the absence of eternal glory, put on a show. Then when the show's over, they'll leave at last.

'Eamonn,' she said, looking down at the white surf as it rolled in and then withdrew. 'At low tide your tractor can go out on the beach, can't it?'

'Go anywhere, this one,' said Eamonn.

'Could it go round the headland from Kilnacarry and into Buckle Bay?'

'If the tide's far enough out.'

'Could you take me into Buckle Bay, over the sea?'

'Like you're Jesus, coming over the water?'

'Just like that.'

'I can give it a go.'

He started up the engine, and turned the tractor about. They rumbled back over the coast path and into the village. Lights were glowing in the shop and in the pub. He dropped down onto the harbour road and followed the slipway where the fishermen hauled in their boats. The tractor wheels swished in the shallow water. A few men loitering on the harbour wall stared to see the red tractor drive into the sea, but Eamonn didn't go far. Hugging the coast, he followed the strip of beach round Buckle Head. He couldn't see the ground over which he was driving because it was under water. Now and again the tractor hit a big rock and gave a lurch.

'You all right there? Hold on.'

'I'm fine, Eamonn.'

The grey cloud-filled sky was fading into night. Eamonn was steering more by feel than by sight.

'Don't want to damage your tractor, Eamonn.'

'Take more'n this to hurt her', he said.

'You have headlights?' she said.

'You want 'em on?'

'Not yet.'

At their deepest point the water came halfway up the great wheels, and the bigger waves broke against the side of the tractor and splashed their legs. Then they were round the headland and making for the beach, and the water was receding once more.

'Told you she'd do it,' said Eamonn.

There ahead was Buckle Bay. Paraffin lanterns, electric torches, candles, glowed among the figures crowded onto the beach. The strains of a hymn came over the water. This was how the pilgrims passed the long hours. They said the rosary together, and they sang hymns. They had guitars and harmonicas. It was a sort of beach party in honour of the end of the world.

Mary had made no plan. It was all the impulse of the moment. The anger she had felt on Dawros Head was still with her, burning inside her like a liberation. She no longer cared what she did.

'Turn on the headlights, Eamonn.'

He clicked a switch. The tractor's lights weren't strong, but coming out of the sea like that, bouncing over the water, they created a sensation in Buckle Bay. The singing stopped. Voices cried out. All eyes were on the approaching brightness.

'Keep driving till I say stop.'

She wanted to be close enough for them all to hear her. The sky around was deep twilight, a rim of violet on the horizon. The crowd on the beach fell still, filled with amazement. The sound of the tractor's engine was lost in the deep roar of the sea.

Just where the rolling waves broke into spume Mary told Eamonn to stop, and cut the engine. Then she stood up on the tractor seat, bracing herself between her brother's strong shoulder and the upright of the high roll bar. Now her slim figure was in silhouette against the last of the daylight.

'This is Mary Brennan,' she said.

Her voice rang clear over the water. They all heard her. A sound went up from the crowd like a sigh. The messenger of the Lord had come out of the sea.

'I have a new message.'

Another gasp rose up. All across the beach the people were dropping to their knees.

'The voice of God came to me over the water,' she cried. 'The Lord said to me, "The people's faith pleases me. I will not let my people perish. There will be no great wind. Your faith has saved the world."'

Hearing this, the pilgrims began to cry and call out.

'Thank you, Lord! God be praised!'

454

'Go to your homes. Tell everyone. The world will not end. The world will live. Now make it a beautiful world.'

They were crying like babies on the beach. Cries of joy.

'God bless you, Mary Brennan! God love you! We're saved!'

To Eamonn, in a low voice, she said, 'Now drive us home.'

Eamonn started up the tractor and powered it through the shallow water and up the beach. The crowd parted to let it past. Mary remained standing, waving back at the crying faces below.

'Pray for me!' she called out. 'Pray for me! My work here is over! It's all over now!'

When they were past the crowds, and rumbling up the track to the cottage, Eamonn said to her, 'That was a fine message, Mary.'

'I said it to make them go home.'

Eamonn said nothing to that.

'I'm a wicked woman, Eamonn. I just made it up, in my wickedness.'

'So the world could still end tomorrow?'

'It could.'

'And they're thinking they're saved.'

That made him laugh. His rich deep laugh filled the night air. She hadn't heard him laugh for a long time.

55

'Who did this? On whose authority?'

Khrushchev was appalled by the news. Here, at this most delicate point of negotiation, some trigger-happy cowboy in Cuba had done the exact thing he had been so careful to avoid. He had fired the first shot.

'General Pliyev claims to know nothing about it.'

It was Sunday morning. Marshal Malinowsky was briefing Khrushchev in his Kremlin office, where he had slept that night.

'An American pilot is dead?'

'Yes.'

'The Cubans did this? With Soviet weapons?'

Khrushchev continued turning over the pages of the report that had been prepared for him overnight.

'What's this? What is Castro saying?'

'He's convinced the Americans are about to invade.'

'What does he mean, I must not let the United States strike the first nuclear blow? Does he want me to start a nuclear war?'

'He appears to be very agitated.'

'He's lost his reason. What's happening, Rodion Yakovlevich? Has the whole world gone mad?'

By now Khrushchev was badly frightened. He summoned a meeting of the Presidium at his private residence at Novo-Ogaryovo on the Moscow river. As he prepared for the meeting he received a further report, of a letter from Kennedy containing an offer of a deal. It appeared to be in answer to Khrushchev's first long letter. Kennedy proposed to trade a promise not to invade Cuba for the removal of the missiles.

'What about my second letter? What about the missiles in Turkey?'

'He says nothing about that,' said Troyanovsky.

'Why not? I don't understand.'

'I think this is what we call the Kuragin ploy,' said Troyanovsky. 'He pretends to have received from you the offer he wants.'

Khrushchev stared at him.

'You'll remember, Chairman, in *War and Peace*, how the father of the lovely Hélène Kuragin becomes frustrated by Pierre's slowness in making a marriage proposal. In the end the father bursts into the room and congratulates the young couple, just as if the proposal has taken place. Pierre is too embarrassed to object.'

'Yes, of course.'

Khrushchev had not read *War and Peace*. He knew only that Hélène Kuragin's most famous attribute had been her magnificent bosom.

'Nobody dazzles me with tits,' he said. 'This is all a catastrophe. We can't have a war over Cuba. It's out of the question. You know why?'

'Cuba is not our homeland, Chairman.'

'Because we'd lose.'

They drove together to Novo-Ogaryovo. As the big Zil limousine pulled up before the pillared porch of the house, Khrushchev said to Troyanovsky, 'I need more Lenin. Tell me when Lenin retreated.'

457

'Brest-Litovsk, March 1918. Lenin surrendered territory to the Germans to win a breathing space during the Civil War.'

'Yes, of course. I remember.'

The members of the Presidium were seated on either side of the long polished oak table. Gromyko was there too, and Malinowsky, and Ilyichev. Khrushchev wanted to be sure that every one of the top leadership was implicated in what might be construed as a climb-down.

'Comrades,' he told them. 'I believe we are face to face with nuclear war. I do not believe any of us wants to destroy the human race. At Brest-Litovsk in 1918 Lenin ordered a tactical retreat, to save the Soviet Union. Today we must order a tactical retreat, to save the world.'

He laid before his colleagues the hard facts of the crisis. An American pilot had been killed by a Soviet ground-to-air missile. There was mounting evidence that the Americans were preparing an invasion of Cuba within hours. Fidel Castro was behaving increasingly erratically.

'The time has come to do a deal,' said Khrushchev. 'I propose that we respond positively to Kennedy's latest offer. We agree to dismantle the missile sites, in exchange for a guarantee from the Americans that they will not invade Cuba.'

'We trade weapons for words?' said Mikoyan.

Only the great survivor could have dared speak aloud what they were all thinking. Khrushchev, who had feared just this reproach, responded with anger.

'What are you saying? That I should go to war for the sake of Cuba? No, Anastas Ivanovich, much as I love Cuba, I love my country more. I have given my life for this great experiment, this dream of Marx, made real by Lenin. You keep Cuba if you wish. I choose to save the world!'

Mikoyan shrugged and said no more.

'Moreover,' said Khrushchev heatedly, 'correctly understood, this is a real victory. Who would have predicted, nine months ago, that we could force the imperialists into a pledge never to attack Cuba? It was unthinkable! Why should they give such a promise? But because we have been bold, and resolute, we now stand on the brink of achieving that very pledge!'

At this point Troyanovsky entered, looking flushed.

'Comrade Chairman,' he said. 'A cable has just come in from Ambassador Dobrynin. He has had a meeting with the brother of the president.'

Troyanovsky read out the cable. Dobrynin reported that Robert Kennedy had come to him in a state of great agitation. The president was facing unbearable pressure from his chiefs of staff to order an invasion of Cuba. He needed a response from Khrushchev without delay. He repeated his pledge not to attack Cuba if the Soviet missiles were removed. He added that the Jupiters would be taken out of Turkey in exchange, but not at once. This would take place within four months, but most importantly, this was to be a private part of the deal. The president could not be seen in public to be sacrificing NATO allies to American strategic needs.

The Presidium members asked Troyanovsky to read the cable out again in its entirety.

'Why must the Jupiters remain secret?' said Malinowsky. 'That would be a trade the whole world would understand.'

At this point the Secretary of the Defence Council was handed a phone message. It was another intelligence report. President Kennedy was due to make a televised address to the American people in four hours' time.

Every man in the room believed this to be the declaration of war.

'Enough!' cried Khrushchev, banging the table. 'Bring in a stenographer! I will reply to the president.'

Before the entire leadership, Khrushchev poured out a third

459

letter to Kennedy. He spoke of their joint responsibility to the world, of the honourable intentions with which the Soviet Union had set out to defend Cuba, of the hostility the United States had shown to that brave island, of the provocations the United States gave to world peace with its intrusive flights over neutral territories and its piratical actions on the high seas. And so at last he came to the point.

'The Soviet government, wanting nothing but peace, has issued a new order to dismantle the weapons which are described as offensive, and to crate and return them to the Soviet Union.'

Gromyko then cabled Dobrynin in Washington to alert the Kennedys. A favourable response to their message would be read out over Moscow Radio shortly.

Two copies of the chairman's letter then left Novo-Ogaryovo. One, carried by Mikhail Smirnovsky, head of the Foreign Office's American desk, sped off to the American embassy. On arrival, Smirnovsky found his limousine blocked by demonstrators placed there by his own orders, shouting 'Hands off Cuba!'

The other copy of the letter was carried by Leonid Ilyichev, Secretary in Charge of Ideology, to Moscow Radio. Ilyichev's black Chaika made record time into the city, but once inside the building, his elevator got stuck between floors. Unable to get out, he passed the letter page by page through the bars of the cage's grille.

At 5 p.m. Moscow time the letter was read out live, without rehearsal, by Moscow Radio's best-known *diktor*, Yuri Levitan. His was the voice that had announced to the Soviet people the start of the war against Nazi Germany in 1941, and its victorious end in 1945; the death of Stalin in 1953; and the triumphant space flight of Yuri Gagarin in 1961.

'This is Moscow speaking,' he began. 'I am now going to

read to you a letter written by Nikita Sergeyevich Khrushchev, First Secretary of the Presidium of the Communist Party and Chairman of the Council of Ministers, to John Fitzgerald Kennedy, president of the United States.'

56

In London, three hours behind Moscow, Pamela was sleeping late that Sunday morning. When at last she came down for breakfast it was well after eleven o'clock, and she found only Emily in the kitchen. Emily and Harriet had returned from Dorset the previous evening.

'Do you know when Mary's coming back?' said Emily.

'No,' said Pamela. 'I've got no idea.'

'She said she'd be gone a few days. It's already eight days. That's not a few.'

Pamela made herself a cup of Nescafé. Emily wandered off. As she drank her coffee and smoked her first cigarette of the day, Pamela found herself thinking about Susie and Logan and his proposal. The champagne, the ring. 'How about it, old girl?' Then she thought about André, and how he had wanted his party to be 'joyful'. Then she thought about Bobby, who said, 'It's fun or it's nothing.'

What was wrong with men? What was wrong with the world?

She had forgotten that there was going to be a nuclear war. Instead she was wondering whether or not to call Stephen, who had invited her to lunch at Cliveden. She didn't much want to go to Cliveden, but nor did she want to stay here, now that Harriet was back.

Then Harriet herself appeared.

'Oh, Pamela, you're up. I wonder whether you could come into Hugo's study. We'd like a word.'

No one ever went into Hugo's study, least of all Hugo. Pamela did as she was asked.

Hugo was in there, standing by the mantelpiece, an abstracted look on his face. Outside the tall window there was sunshine on the railings, and on the grass between the trees. Hugo glanced at her as she entered, and gave her a slight shrug.

Harriet closed the door behind them, and went over to stand by Hugo's side. She had a strange bright smile on her face. She took hold of Hugo's hand.

'Hugo and I are very lucky,' she said. 'It's not just that we have a strong, committed marriage. We're also each other's best friend. I think that's rare, don't you? I can always tell what Hugo's thinking. And you see, because I know him and love him, I trust him.'

She nodded her small elegant head as if to say that all this was as it should be. Then she turned to Hugo with the look of a fond teacher addressing a naughty but favoured child.

'Of course, he's not perfect. He's as human as the rest of us. But then, neither am I perfect. I can't begin to imagine how tedious it must be to have to put up with all my little troubles. But dear Hugo forgives me, as I forgive him.'

She turned back to Pamela.

'You're still so young, Pamela. I hope that one day you'll have a marriage of your own that's as close and forgiving as ours. Then you'll understand that nothing can break it.'

'I'm sorry,' said Pamela. 'I don't know what you're talking about.'

'Oh, I think you do,' said Harriet. 'I know it's just a game to you. You have no idea what damage you could do with your light-hearted games. But fortunately Hugo and I have no secrets from each other.'

463

'What am I supposed to have done?'

'Let's just say that you are a very pretty girl, and Hugo's a normal red-blooded man, and he's very sorry if he forgot himself for a moment or two. Men have their games, too. You'll understand better when you're older.'

She smiled up at Hugo. Hugo stared down at the fender. Pamela found herself drawn helplessly into Harriet's world, where they were the combatants, and Hugo the neutral ground.

'Why doesn't he speak for himself?'

'Well, I think he's just a tiny bit ashamed, don't you?'

'But he's done nothing to be ashamed of.'

Harriet wrinkled her brow.

'I think I'm being rather unusually understanding here, Pamela. I've talked it over with Hugo, and I'm willing to forget all about it. As far as you're concerned, I should have thought some sort of apology was in order.'

'Then you'd better tell me what Hugo says I've done.'

'Hugo has said nothing. A gentleman never lays the blame on a lady. But of course, I knew at once.'

Hugo cleared his throat and spoke at last. He spoke without lifting his gaze from the fender.

'She smelled you on the sheets.'

'Smelled me!'

Pamela broke into a short laugh.

'I have a very sensitive sense of smell,' said Harriet. 'I'm glad it amuses you.'

'But nothing happened,' said Pamela. 'Didn't he tell you that?'

'You may call it nothing if you wish,' said Harriet.

'I was frightened, because of the missiles in Cuba. You do know what's happening? There's probably going to be a nuclear war. You do know that?'

Suddenly it seemed to Pamela that the coming war was more

important than anything. That in its light Harriet's accusations were rendered petty and ridiculous.

'I do follow the news.'

'We could all be dead tomorrow.'

'Well, that's as may be,' said Harriet.

'Don't you believe me? It's true. Tell her, Hugo.'

'The international situation is very serious,' said Hugo, still not looking up.

'Oh, Hugo, don't be so silly,' said Harriet. And to Pamela, 'I think it might be more comfortable for all of us if you found somewhere else to stay while you're in London, don't you? I expect one of your new friends could help you out.'

Still the sweet reasonable tone. Pamela struggled with mounting anger.

'Is there anything else you want to say to me, Pamela?'

'May I use the phone?'

For a moment she caught a look of cold hatred in Harriet's pale-blue eyes. Then the smile returned.

'Yes, of course.'

Pamela went out of the study, leaving the door ajar. She picked up the phone in the hall and rang Stephen.

'It's Pamela,' she said. 'Come and get me as soon as you can. Please.'

Then she stayed in the hall, one hand on the telephone table, breathing rapidly. She could hear Harriet in the study.

'So insolent. So selfish. You saw how she looked at me? There's something wrong with that girl. Do you think it's because of her father?'

Then Hugo's voice, murmuring low.

'She's just young, that's all.'

Pamela went slowly up the stairs to her room. There she changed into smart day clothes and made up her face and brushed her hair. Then she sat and gazed into the dressing-table mirror until she no longer recognised herself.

I am nothing. I don't exist.

Nothing happened. Nobody needs to know.

In time she heard a car pull up outside. She ran down the stairs and opened the front door before the bell rang.

'Just take me away,' she said. 'Please.'

Stephen asked no questions until they were on the road west.

'Bad day?'

She nodded.

'Could be a bad day for the world,' he said.

'Good,' said Pamela.

'Like that, is it?'

'Oh, Stephen.' Her anger dissolved into self-pity. 'I'm making such a mess of everything.'

'Don't we all,' he said. 'Being human.'

'Is there a cure?'

'There's a sort of a cure. It's called not minding too much. You'd be surprised how much fun there is to be had once you stop minding about things.'

'I've tried fun. It wasn't much fun.'

'Is this André?'

'Among others.'

'Taking on André qualifies as jumping in at the deep end. Better to start out where you're still in your depth. I told you. You can have any man you want.'

'What if I want a man I can't have?'

'No such creature.'

'He might be married.'

'Darling! You think married men aren't to be had? They're the easiest of all.'

'Honestly, Stephen. Don't you have any morals at all?'

'I'm the most moral man I know. I believe in truth, and kindness and peace between nations. I abhor violence, and lies, and the hypocrisy that makes a misery of most people's lives. What exactly is the point of fidelity in marriage if there's no love? God knows, life is short enough. And, as you may or may not know, there's a strong chance it'll all be over by Wednesday.'

'By Wednesday?'

'Tomorrow the Americans invade Cuba. Tuesday the Russians invade Berlin. Wednesday the missiles fly. Goodbye and good luck.'

'Will that really be the end of the world?'

'It'll be the end of Europe and Russia and the United States. But I suppose life will go on in Africa and India and Australia.'

They turned into the drive to Cliveden, and took the right fork that led to the big house. Stephen parked the car by the water tower.

Pamela followed Stephen from the car. In the immense hallway stood two large bronze statues of goddesses, or perhaps muses. They were naked but for a wisp of covering around the loins. Their breasts were a brighter honey-gold than the rest of their bodies, as if passing guests had fondled them for generations.

The company was gathered in the long drawing room, which looked over a broad terrace and a great open view of countryside beyond. They were mostly middle-aged or older. They spoke in the assured tones of men who are accustomed to being heard.

'Harold has shown no leadership whatsoever.'

'When the balloon goes up I shall hunker down in my place in Scotland. I'm a fair shot. I'll not starve.'

'Ah, Stephen,' said Lord Astor. 'Now we can all cheer up.'

Stephen introduced Pamela. The mood perceptibly changed. The old men stood straighter, and smiled upon her with varying degrees of fatherly interest.

'Any news?' said Stephen.

'The word is the Russians are going to make some sort of a

statement at two o'clock.' This was a balding white-haired man who was something to do with the *Daily Telegraph*. 'Just the usual propaganda rant, I expect. My chaps are saying Kennedy has to go in.'

'We've got a television in the library,' said Astor. 'We can turn it on when it's time.'

A small ugly man addressed himself to Pamela.

'Do you have an estate in Scotland to run away to?' he said.

'No,' said Pamela.

'Nor do I. I take the old-fashioned view that the captain should go down with his ship.'

'Are you a captain?' Pamela said

'Of a kind. Did I see you at Jack Heinz's do the other day? I'm sure I did.'

'No,' said Pamela. 'I don't think so.'

Eugene Ivanov now appeared from the hall, just arrived, still shedding his outer coat. He was visibly agitated.

'The situation is very serious,' he said. 'Why didn't your government listen to me? Now we will all pay the price.'

'I don't see how you can blame us, Eugene,' said a tall old man. 'It's your chap who started it all.'

'My chap!'

'Khrushchev. With his missiles.'

Ivanov threw his coat angrily over a chair, from where a servant retrieved it.

'We have missiles all round us! Chairman Khrushchev had the courage to stand up to the Americans! How can you say he started it?'

'Even so, you've got to admit it was a rash move.'

'I admit nothing! Chairman Khrushchev has shown foresight and self-confidence! I applaud him!'

'Give the man a drink,' said Stephen. 'That's enough, Eugene. We all know whose side you're on.'

468

'Ah, Stephen. If only they'd listened to us.' His gaze now took in Pamela. 'If only they'd listened to your friend.'

'So what's going to happen, Ivanov?' said the *Telegraph* man. 'If Kennedy sends in the troops, what will Khrushchev do?'

'He will fight back, of course,' said Ivanov. 'We will witness the clash of the Titans.'

Over lunch in the ornate gilt-mirrored dining room, conversation ranged more widely. Stephen Ward and one of the other male guests swapped anecdotes about the Eversleigh club in Chicago in the early thirties.

'My God! That was quite a place! Solid gold spittoons!'

'And the two elderly ladies who ran it! I don't recall their names, but I remember I was told they were the daughters of a parson.'

'The costumes the girls wore! I'll never forget sitting at one of the dining tables and seeing these princesses, these goddesses, just strolling by as if they didn't have a care in the world.'

It dawned on Pamela that they were talking about a brothel.

'I like Chicago much better than New York,' Stephen said. 'It's more American.'

On Pamela's other side sat the ugly man who had said he was a kind of a captain.

'You should have been here for the Fairbanks party,' he said. 'That was the most spectacular affair. Practically the whole royal family, from the Queen down. Jock Whitney. Lee Canfield, Jack Kennedy's sister-in-law. A whole mess of Rothschilds. The Maharaja of Jaipur. Flaming torches all up the drive. Fireworks at midnight. It was Daphne Fairbanks's coming out party. They had her name in fireworks, as high as the house. I guess she was just seventeen years old then. About your own age.'

'I'm almost nineteen,' said Pamela.

'Oh, well then. Quite a woman of the world.'

He looked across at Stephen Ward.

'Friend of Ward's, are you?'

'Yes,' said Pamela.

'He's an amazing fellow. I had lumbago, crippled by it. Three goes with Ward and that was that. All gone. But I don't suppose you even know what lumbago is.'

'No,' said Pamela.

'You don't want to know, believe me. So where do you live? Are you available to be taken out to dinner? The Connaught's my watering hole. They've got a new man there who actually understands how not to overcook beef. I promise you, you won't eat better anywhere.'

'And after dinner, would we go back to your place?'

'If the mood took us that way.'

'And would we go to bed?'

'Well, I must say!' He sat back in his chair and wiped gravy from his mouth with his napkin. 'You don't beat about the bush.'

'I can't think of any other reason why you'd want to take me out to dinner.'

'The pleasure of your company, of course.'

'What's my name?'

A slow smile spread across his face.

'You really are quite something, aren't you? You're right, of course. I don't know your name.'

'I need some air.'

She got up and left the dining room. The long drawing room was empty. She went out through French windows onto the terrace. The air was crisp, the river sparkling in the autumn sunlight. She took out a cigarette and lit it, and as she smoked she felt the turmoil within her subside.

So many ugly men. Let the world end. Let them all perish.

They're much nicer to you before than after, Christine said.

They fondle your tits till they shine.

She wanted to hate them for their hungry gaze, for the cruel game they called 'fun', for their intimacy where no one knows your name. But if she wasn't desired by men, what was left of her? A semi-educated young woman with a taste for the good life and more than a touch of pride. She couldn't cook. She couldn't type, or do accounts. She had only the one talent, which was to use her good looks to her own advantage. This one talent gave her power and enslaved her at the same time. Whatever her destiny, it could only come through love. Love must be her gift, her purpose, and her means of support. She would be courted, she would fall in love, she would marry. That was as far as her dream had ever reached.

If you're lucky you get fun here and money there and love now and again.

That was Bobby, her first lover, who had made love to her without loving her, while André watched.

Nothing happened. Nobody needs to know.

She walked the long terrace of Cliveden, and smoked cigarettes, and felt the darkness closing in. We must love one another or die. But there is no love. We are already dead.

There were people in the library now. She heard voices, and the tinny boom of the television. Then she heard loud cries. The French doors flew open, and Ivanov came out, distraught.

'Impossible!' he said. 'There's been some mistake!'

Stephen followed.

'Looks like it's all over,' he said. 'Khrushchev backed down.'

'Never!' cried Ivanov. 'There will be more! You will see! This is only one move in the game!'

'He's announced he'll take the missiles out of Cuba,' said Stephen.

'So there won't be a war?' said Pamela.

'Doesn't look like it.'

The other guests were all now emerging onto the terrace.

'Harold had a Cabinet meeting called for just about now,' said the tall old man. 'They needn't have bothered.'

'Extraordinary!' said Lord Astor. 'Good for young Jack Kennedy. Held his nerve till the other fellow cracked.'

'No!' cried Ivanov. 'You wait and see! There'll be a deal. Khrushchev's a tough guy. He never cracks.'

'Poor old Ivanov,' said Astor. 'Looks like you lost this one.'

'This is not the end,' said Ivanov. 'You will see!'

The little ugly man sidled up to Pamela.

'Your name is Pamela,' he said.

'Yes,' said Pamela. 'It is.'

'I think you've cast a spell over me, Pamela. Just now, while the television news was telling us all that there would not after all be a nuclear war, my only thought was, Then I can see Pamela again.'

'And now you have.'

'Away from here. In private.'

Pamela had been avoiding meeting his gaze, but now she turned to him and looked him up and down. He was at least sixty years old, with a stooped body, shorter than herself, and an ungainly lopsided face. Why would such a man suppose she would want to pay him any attention?

'Are you very rich?' she said. 'Or very important?'

'Both,' he said.

'I'm sorry. It turns out the world isn't going to end after all.'

She began to laugh, without knowing why. She laughed uncontrollably. The ugly little man frowned, visibly offended.

'Forgive me, I misunderstood. Stephen's friends are usually easier to please.'

He dipped his head, and turned away.

Slowly Pamela's wave of nervous laughter passed. Now she wanted to cry.

She looked round the group scattered over the terrace. Lord

472

this and Lord that, all millionaires, all accustomed to having their own way. How can they be expected to love? What they want, they get. Desire puts down roots in stony soil.

She went to Stephen.

'I'd like to go, please,' she said. 'Whenever you're ready.'

In the car back to London Stephen was in philosophical mood.

'You know, for a while back there Ivanov and I, and your friend Rupert, we really thought we could make a difference. But we might as well not have bothered.'

'I don't see why anyone ever bothers about anything,' said Pamela.

'Oh, I know that feeling, all right.'

'I was quite looking forward to a nuclear war.'

He laughed at that.

'You think it's a pretty rotten old world, do you?'

'Well, don't you?'

'Sometimes, yes.'

'Everyone's just out for themselves,' she said. 'No one really cares about anyone else. People talk about love, but they don't really mean it.'

She said it so he'd tell her she was wrong, but he didn't.

'I'm afraid love isn't what it's cracked up to be,' he said. 'Expect too much and you're bound to be disappointed.'

'Is that why you've never married again?'

'I suppose so.'

'But don't you get lonely?'

'No, I wouldn't say so. I've just lowered my sights. I don't expect love anymore. But there's always good company.'

'Good company.'

It seemed to her to be a small sad substitute.

As they approached Hammersmith she said, 'I expect I won't be seeing you again.'

'Why's that?'

'I'll be leaving London.'

'I'm sorry to hear that. Where will you go?'

'Home, to start with. After that, who knows?'

She gave him a hug when he dropped her off.

'Thanks for everything, Stephen. You're one of the good ones.'

'Oh, I'm not so sure about that.'

'Yes, you are. I've never forgotten how we first met. You were in that café, where all the men were drawing the nude model. And you were just drawing her face.'

'Yes,' he said, smiling, pleased. 'I've always liked faces.'

She let herself into the house and went directly up to her room, not stopping to see who else was in. She pulled out her suitcase and began to pack her belongings. It was past four in the afternoon. The trains ran once an hour. She could ring from a phone box on Victoria station, and Larry could pick her up at Lewes. She could be home in time for supper.

She took out her black chiffon dress, and held it up to let the light fall through the fabric. She wondered if she would ever wear it again. Then she folded it carefully, and packed it. She packed her black lace underwear. She packed her Dutch cap.

What had it all been for?

Good company, Stephen said.

She sat down on the side of the bed and put her hands on her knees and held her head up high. She remained like this, motionless, for a few minutes. She was reassembling her sense of herself, like the victim of an accident feeling her body to know what if anything has been broken. Life was going to go on, it appeared.

What have I learned?

You make your own luck. And good men are hard to find.

So she made a decision. She would use the only power she had, to achieve the only goal she now wanted. She would plant her future like a bomb.

When she came down the stairs, carrying her suitcase, there was Hugo standing in the hall.

'So you're leaving,' he said.

'Yes. I should say goodbye to Harriet.'

'She's got one of her headaches. She's upstairs.'

Pamela put down the suitcase and went back upstairs. Hugo watched her go.

Harriet's bedroom was in semi-darkness, the curtains drawn, a single lamp glowing with a low-power bulb. Harriet was in bed, half sitting up, supported by a mass of pillows. She had a folded damp flannel over her eyes.

'Who is it? Is that you, Hugo?'

'No,' said Pamela. 'It's me. I've come to say goodbye.'

'Oh. Are you going?'

'And I've come to say sorry.'

'I'm sure you meant no harm,' she said.

'I didn't really mean any of it,' said Pamela. 'It was a strange sort of madness that came over me. I couldn't stop myself.'

'Well, it's all over now.'

But it wasn't over at all. It was only just beginning.

'You see,' said Pamela, speaking clearly and carefully so that Harriet would miss nothing, 'the truth is, I've fallen in love with Hugo. I know that doesn't make any of it right. But I wanted you to know. It hasn't just been a game.'

Harriet reached up one hand and slowly drew the flannel from her eyes. She looked at Pamela sharply.

'You've fallen in love with Hugo?'

'So you're quite right. It's best that I should go.'

'But this is absurd. This is what we used to call a crush. You'll have forgotten it in a week.'

'I hope so. I just wanted you to know that I was serious.'

Harriet gazed back at her, trapped by Pamela's combination of contrition and confession.

'Thank you for all you've done for me.'

Pamela left the room, walking softly. Hugo was still waiting at the foot of the stairs.

'How was that?' he said.

'Fine,' said Pamela. 'She'll tell you.'

She picked up her suitcase and made for the front door.

'Would you like me to walk you to the tube?'

'No thanks.'

She had the front door open now.

'When will I see you again?' he said.

She looked at him and she wrinkled up her nose and half-shut her eyes and gave a little lift of her shoulders.

'Why don't you give me a call?' she said.

Then she went out onto the step and closed the door behind her.

57

Mountbatten looked round the table at the faces of the members of the crisis team.

'Well, what would we have done? If the Russians hadn't pulled back, what would we have done? Do we know?'

There was no answer.

'We've got to work this one out.'

'Are we absolutely sure the danger is past?' said Shaw.

'We're sure,' said Grimsdale. 'Soviet radio's playing Beethoven's "Ode to Peace".'

There was relief, but no triumph. No one in the room felt that they had won a victory. The events taking place in the long week of crisis had been outside their control. There was no answer to Mountbatten's question, because Great Britain, one of only three nuclear powers on the planet, was effectively powerless.

'It's a miserable business,' Mountbatten said to Rupert, after the meeting had dispersed. 'Christ knows what lesson we're supposed to learn from it.'

'Maybe the horror of nuclear war is self-cancelling,' said Rupert. 'No sane world leader is going to press the button.'

'Until an insane one comes along.'

'Or a man of faith.'

'You and your religious wars,' said Mountbatten.

'Well, nuclear war is essentially suicidal. Who would accept mass suicide as a price worth paying? Only someone who believes in a better life after death. They're the ones to watch. The ones who really believe they know the mind of God.'

Back in his office, Rupert put in a call to Father Flannery in Donegal. He wanted to know when Mary was coming back.

'She left this morning,' said the priest's voice, thin and high and far away.

'How is she, Father?'

'Oh, she's grand. You should have seen how she delivered her last message from the Lord.'

Rupert could hear the priest's tinny chuckles coming down the line.

'Came into Buckle Bay on a tractor, she did! Over the sea!'

'Good heavens!'

'Told the faithful their faith had saved the world. There was to be no great wind after all.'

'When was this, Father?'

'Last night. Saturday night. That girl really does have the Almighty whispering in her ear. Today we heard it on the news. It's all over. And that makes Mary Brennan a prophet all over again. If it really is all over.'

'It's all over,' said Rupert. 'It really is.'

'Then we shall have our chapel at Buckle Bay soon. You'll see.'

'I'm sure you will. Father, do you know what time her flight gets in?'

'I don't know anything about flights. She told me she'd be safe in her lodgings by this evening.'

The great army of officials who had gathered in Whitehall to manage the crisis were now all departing for what was left of the weekend. Rupert too went home, to rest and to think.

478

Mary Brennan was coming back. He could see her this very evening. Suddenly it seemed to him that this was a critical moment. It was for this that the world had not ended.

'If there's anything you ever want,' she had said, 'you have only to ask.'

But what if I want more than she has to give? After all, she had said to the nuns that she wanted to live a life of her own. Now she was free at last. Why would she choose to tie herself to a middle-aged man with an ungainly appearance and no prospects?

Oh, but it was hard. How did other people manage these things? I need a back channel, he thought, to sound out the response before I expose myself too far. The risk is so immense.

He remembered then the talipot palm in the Botanical Gardens that didn't bloom for forty years. He was forty-four. Overdue for blooming.

Am I to say to her, 'I love you, Mary'? Is that how it is? And if she doesn't want my love, what is she to say? It would distress her very much to think she was hurting him. He would say to her, 'I don't expect you to love me out of gratitude.'

No, he'd say no such thing. He'd smile and say it was just a passing idea, and it had seemed worth trying out. Then he would say goodnight, as he'd said goodnight to Joyce all those years ago, with a peck on the cheek. He'd come back here to Tachbrook Street, and sit here, in this armchair, and . . .

After that there was a blank.

He forced himself to wait until after six. The clocks had gone back in the night, and darkness came early. He phoned Hugo's house at last. The number was engaged.

He walked down the road, round the back of Victoria station, and into Elizabeth Street. Here there was a French bistro he liked, which he knew would be open. He went in and explained, with a little embarrassment, that he might want a table for two a little later in the evening, but he might not. There was no problem. The restaurant was not busy on Sunday evenings.

Back in his lodgings, he called Hugo's number again. The line was still engaged. It must be out of order.

He was sure Mary would be back in Brook Green by now. If he left it much later, she would be sitting down to supper with Hugo and Harriet. The thought of postponing the fateful encounter for another twenty-four hours galvanised him into action. He would go round there now. He would say he couldn't get through on the phone, he wanted to celebrate her success in averting the end of the world. They could flag down a taxi on Hammersmith Road, be in the restaurant by eight.

He made the journey west by tube. As he walked up the road from the tube he asked himself for the first time what Hugo and Harriet would think of him turning up like this, unannounced. They'd guess, of course. Perhaps they'd already guessed. Then if it all came to nothing they'd pity him. Poor old Rupert, never had any luck with the girls. But it was too late to protect himself now.

The lights were on in the house. He rang the doorbell. No one answered.

He rang again. After several minutes he heard shuffling footsteps within, and the door opened. It was Hugo, looking wild-eyed.

'Oh, hello, Rupert. Come in.'

His hair was on end, as if he'd been trying to pull it out.

'Sorry,' he said. 'Bit of a crisis here.'

'I came to welcome Mary home,' said Rupert.

Emily appeared. Her face was wet with tears.

'She's up with Harriet,' said Hugo. 'Off you go, darling.'

Emily disappeared again.

'I seem to have chosen a bad moment,' said Rupert. 'Shall I make myself scarce?'

'No, no. Good to have you here. Maybe you can talk some sense into me.'

Mary appeared at the top of the stairs.

'Harriet wants to know who's come.' She saw Rupert and as always her face lit up with a smile. 'Oh, hello, Rupert.'

'Hello, Mary.'

He could barely see her in the shadowed landing, but just hearing her voice made him happy.

'Don't go,' she said. 'I'll be down soon.'

She returned to Harriet.

'Come and have a drink, old man,' said Hugo.

He stuck his head into the schoolroom.

'Get into your pyjamas, darling.'

'I haven't had any supper,' said Emily from within.

'We'll all have some supper soon. Get into your pyjamas.'

He led Rupert into the drawing-room and poured them both a brandy.

'Here. Knock this back. You'll need it.'

They drank.

'Trouble with Harriet?' said Rupert.

'You could say that,' said Hugo. 'It's all about Pamela.'

'I rather thought it might be.'

'She's gone. She left today. Harriet sent her packing. I'm afraid I made my regret a little too obvious. Now I don't know what to do. I feel as if I'm going mad.'

'Harriet taking it badly?'

'Very badly. Hysterics, really. Mary's the only one can calm her down. Thank God she came back. What am I supposed to do, Rupert? I feel as if I can hardly breathe.'

'I suppose she'll get over it in time.'

'Yes, but what do *I* do?'

'Oh, I see.'

'I realised it as soon as she left. I'm in love with her, Rupert. I'm wild about her. I don't think I can live without her. I expect that sounds like I'm off my trolley, but I mean precisely that. And what's so stupid about it all is I've no reason to suppose she'd have me even if she could.'

'Oh. Right.'

'Yes. So there you are. It's a horrible mess. And there's Emily to think of. I don't know. What do people do?'

Mary came downstairs.

'She wants to see you,' she said to Hugo.

'Right,' said Hugo.

He left them. Mary came into the drawing room. From upstairs came the muffled sound of raised voices.

'Is she in a bad way?' said Rupert.

'She's hysterical.'

'You came back from the airport and walked into this?'

'She was upstairs, screaming.'

'I tried to phone.'

'I think she's taken the phone off the hook. She doesn't want Hugo calling her.'

'Pamela?'

'Yes.'

'Hugo says he's in love with her.'

'Yes.'

Their eyes met in a moment of silence.

'Good of you to come, Rupert.'

'I was going to welcome you back. Take you out to dinner.'

'I can't go out. Not while she's like this.'

'No, of course. I do see that.'

'I thought I'd make some omelettes or something. You could stay and join us.'

'Wouldn't I be in the way?' he said.

'I think it might help. Hugo seems to be very confused.'

'All right,' he said.

'Sorry,' she said. 'Not quite what you had in mind.'

Emily came in, now in pyjamas, and took Mary's hand in hers.

'I don't like the shouting,' she said.

'Of course you don't, darling.' Mary stroked the child's head. 'But all it is is shouting. It does a body good to have a shout from time to time.'

'Mummy hates shouting. It gives her a headache.'

'How about you help me make us all some supper, Emily?' said Mary. 'I bet you're hungry.'

'I don't know,' said Emily. 'I might be.'

Mary turned to Rupert and found his eyes on her.

'And Rupert can help too.'

They moved into the kitchen. Rupert gave himself the job of laying the table. Mary and Emily started cracking the eggs for the omelettes.

'Will Harriet come down to eat?' he said.

'I don't think so,' said Mary. 'Shall we have cheese in the omelette? Emily, you can grate it.'

Rupert laid for four. He put out knives and forks, water glasses and wine glasses, salt and pepper. He even found some cloth napkins.

Then they heard the sound of a door flung open upstairs, and Harriet's voice, shrill with pain.

'Have you lost your mind? She's a child!'

Then Hugo's voice.

'So why are you making such a scene about it?'

'It's just a game to her. Just because she thinks she's in love with you!'

'What did you say?'

'She's half your age, Hugo! Have you no shame?'

'She said she was in love with me?'

'Hugo!' Harriet's voice rose as if she was calling to him across a great distance. 'Hugo! Come back!'

'She said that?'

'She's a child!'

Then the sound of footsteps coming onto the landing.

'Hugo! Come back!'

'I'm going downstairs. I want my supper.'

The slam of a bedroom door. Hugo came downstairs, into the kitchen. He looked dazed.

'I'm sorry about that.'

He took in the sight of the table, as laid by Rupert.

'Looks like a restaurant in here.'

'It's to celebrate Mary's success,' said Rupert.

'What?'

'She saved the world.'

Hugo shook his head, bewildered.

'I did no such thing,' said Mary.

'That's the word in Kilnacarry,' said Rupert.

'Oh, Kilnacarry. What do they know? More than that, Emily. We want lots and lots of gooey cheese in the middle.'

'Maybe you should go to her, Mary,' said Hugo.

'I'll go after supper,' said Mary. 'You'll be looking out a drop of wine for us, Hugo.'

'Yes, of course.'

Rupert marvelled at the way Mary managed them all. Himself too. And all the time so calm, so lovely. Even when he wasn't watching her he was intensely aware of her every movement. He could tell when she turned to look at him.

'Rupert, you have to advise Hugo. You've got a sound head on your shoulders.'

'We'll talk later,' said Hugo, glancing at Emily.

Mary made one giant omelette and cut it up to share between

them. Emily pecked at hers, but ate very little.

'Is that all you want, sweetheart?' said Mary.

Emily nodded.

'Then come along. We'll say goodnight to Mummy, and I'll tuck you up safe in bed.'

When they were gone, Hugo refilled their wine glasses. He drank his wine and said nothing. Powerful emotions were at work within him.

At last he fixed his gaze on Rupert and said, 'She's in love with me.'

'Pamela?'

'That's what she told Harriet. My God, Rupert! Isn't that something? That changes everything. She's so much younger than me. And so beautiful. I hadn't dared to hope. She loves me!'

He was transformed. The haggard look was gone.

'When Harriet said that, I felt as if a bomb had gone off inside me. Can you believe it?'

'Poor Harriet.'

'You know what? I'm tired of all that poor Harriet stuff. I've had it, Rupert. Earlier, when she was screaming at me, I realised something I've never admitted to myself before. There are times when I hate her. I actually hate her.'

Mary returned.

'I think Emily would like you to kiss her goodnight.'

'Yes, of course.'

Hugo left. Now Rupert was alone in the room with Mary.

'It seems like you're the only one who knows what to do,' he said.

'I feel so sorry for them,' said Mary. 'For all of them.'

She was smiling at him, her face tired but so beautiful. He wanted to reach out and touch her, but didn't dare.

'How have you been yourself, Rupert?'

'Well, the world didn't end.'

'There's a mercy.'

'And I'm happy you're back.'

'I couldn't have stayed there a day longer. Do you want to hear a terrible thing? I got angry with God.'

'Why were you angry?'

'Oh, I was angry with him for stealing all those years from me. I haven't had a youth, Rupert. And now it's too late.'

'It's not too late.'

'I'm twenty-nine years old! I'm not young any more. Not young enough to get drunk, and stay out late, and fool about with the boys.' She laughed and blushed as she heard herself. 'Not that I'm the sort boys fool about with.'

She was laughing, blushing.

'Why wouldn't they?'

'Oh, I'm not fishing for compliments. I know I'm no pin-up. Mam says my face shines with the light of heaven. Who'd want to fool about with that?'

She was so unafraid with him that it made him afraid. Did she see him as the older man who presented no threat, the father, the uncle?

'I wouldn't know,' he said. 'I'm not exactly love's young dream.'

As he spoke these words he had a sudden memory of sitting in the Chinese restaurant in Kandy, saying to Joyce, 'No one's going to pick me out in a beauty parade.'

Not again, he thought. Never again.

'What are you talking about?' said Mary. 'You've a fine distinguished look about you.'

'But I'm not like you, Mary. You're beautiful.'

She blushed at that, visibly pleased. Her pleasure gave him the courage he needed.

'Is it too late for me?' he said.

Mary looked down, and then up to meet his eyes. He saw it then, how her face was shining with happiness. Her lips parted, but before she could speak, Hugo rejoined them. Mary looked down again.

'What am I supposed to tell Emily?' Hugo said.

He sighed as he sat down at the table across from Rupert and took up his wine glass. Mary sat down too, by Rupert's side.

'She says to me, "Everything will be all right, won't it, Daddy?" What am I supposed to say?'

'Maybe you all need some time,' said Rupert.

They heard the pad of light steps coming down the stairs.

'Emily! Back to bed!'

But it wasn't Emily. It was Harriet.

She was fully dressed, her clothes crumpled; her face smiling, but ravaged by pain.

'Hello, Rupert. Good of you to come and see us.'

Mary jumped up.

'Shall I make you some supper? We've had an omelette.'

'No, thank you, Mary. I'm not hungry.'

She fixed her eyes on Hugo, who didn't look up.

'I expect you've heard,' she said. 'We've had a little trouble. It's all about nothing at all. Hugo's been quite unkind to me. But I know he doesn't really mean it.'

Hugo frowned, and drank his wine, and said nothing.

'We love each other,' said Harriet. 'In the end, that's all that matters.'

'How can you say that?' said Hugo quietly.

'Because it's true.' She spoke in the tone of one who won't brook contradiction, but her voice was shaking. 'Please don't start again. Not in front of others.'

'They know,' said Hugo.

'Of course they don't know,' said Harriet. 'What happens in

a marriage is private.' She looked across brightly at Rupert. 'I'm sure Rupert agrees with me.'

'I've been saying to Hugo,' said Rupert, 'that maybe you both need a little time.'

Harriet seemed not to hear him. Her bright smile returned to Hugo.

'Hugo, darling,' she said. 'You've said some very unkind things to me this evening. And you've said them in a very loud voice. Emily heard. Mary heard. You did, didn't you, Mary?'

'Yes,' said Mary.

'I think,' Harriet went on, still in that high tight trembling voice, 'that you owe me an apology.'

Hugo frowned at the table.

'I'm sorry I shouted at you, Harriet.'

'Thank you. I'm going to go to bed now. I don't want to make anything of it, but I am in fact in a great deal of pain.'

She left them. Hugo put his head in his hands and groaned.

'It's unbearable,' he said.

'There's nothing to be done tonight,' Rupert said.

'I could get in the car and drive down to Sussex,' said Hugo.

'And arrive when they're all asleep?'

'I know. I know.'

'What do you think he should do, Mary?' said Rupert.

'I think he should go away,' Mary said, sitting down again. 'For several days. A week, maybe. If you're apart from someone for a while, you find out what you really feel about them.'

'I've found that too,' said Rupert. 'Someone goes away, and you realise how much you miss them.'

'I suppose I could go on a buying trip,' said Hugo, not sounding at all eager.

'Then when you come back,' said Rupert, 'it all seems much simpler. You've found out how you feel. You just have to say, "Here I am."'

Mary's hand dropped down by her side. Rupert's hand followed. Her hand found his hand and held it. That was all, but it was everything. He sat still, wanting never to move again.

'Oh, I know how I feel all right,' said Hugo. 'I just can't see any way out of this that doesn't create a godawful mess.'

He lowered his hands from his face and gazed at them ruefully.

'This must be such a bore for you.'

'You're the one having the rough time,' said Rupert.

'I suppose I am,' said Hugo. 'But at the same time, I'm walking on air. She loves me. You've no idea what that makes me feel.'

'You feel everything's come right at last,' said Rupert, holding Mary's hand in his.

'Yes.'

'You feel you can be the person you really are for the first time.'

'That's just how it is.'

'You feel your life has just begun.'

Hugo shook his head, amazed.

'You really do understand! How can I say no to a chance like this? It would be like saying no to life itself. It would be like choosing death over life. We're not made to do that. We're made to live.'

His eyes shone.

'I'm so glad you came over, Rupert.'

'Well, I really came to see Mary. To hear about her time in Ireland. But I should be going, now.'

'I'll walk a little way with you if you like,' Mary said. 'Tell you all the news.'

Rupert rose from the table. Hugo reached across and clasped his hand.

'You're a good friend,' he said.

Mary put on her coat and walked with Rupert down the

street. For a little while they walked apart and in silence, in case anyone was watching from the windows. Then Rupert took her hand in his, and they walked a little way hand in hand. In deep shadows, where a tree hid the light of the street lamp, they came to a stop and he took her in his arms and they kissed.

'My first kiss,' she said.

Then they kissed again, long and slow, in the dark beneath the tree.

58

The little red MG climbed the winding road out of the valley, up onto the high Downland. It was a windy day, the sky streaming with clouds in motion, grey against grey. Pamela said nothing as they drove. Ahead was the dark bulk of the Beachy Head Hotel.

'Do you want me to park by the hotel?' said Simon Shuttleworth.

'Yes,' said Pamela.

They got out and walked in the wind across the road, over the close-grazed grass, towards the cliff edge. There was no one else to be seen. Beyond the cliff stretched the sea, its various shades of sullen grey merging beyond the blurred horizon into the grey of the sky.

Pamela tied her flapping scarf tighter round her throat.

'Why are we here?' said Simon.

'Because,' said Pamela.

She didn't know why she'd come herself. Maybe she just needed distraction. She was waiting.

They came up to a low brick structure built near the cliff edge. Simon found a weather-stained plaque on one outer wall.

'The Dieppe Raid,' he said. 'Wasn't your father on that? Wasn't that where he won his VC?'

Pamela stood beside him and read the inscription.

> This plaque also commemorates the epic Dieppe Raid
> in 1942, which was partly controlled from the radar station
> on this headland. Beachy Head is once more in peace.
> But the devotion and patriotism of those who operated
> on this stretch of Downland will not be forgotten.

'What if we want to forget?' said Pamela.

'You wouldn't want to forget your own father,' said Simon.

'I might.'

She walked away from him, moving fast along the cliff edge. The wind was coming off the sea, but even so it was scary.

'Do be careful!' Simon called.

She didn't answer.

She was angry at herself for coming to Beachy Head. It certainly wasn't an act of filial piety. She came to a stop, close enough to the edge to see the cliff face, and the lighthouse far below, tiny as a toy. Did it take courage to keep walking?

Still the war hero. Still storming that fatal beach.

It felt to her like cowardice, not courage. It was a kind of giving up, the very worst kind. She knew then that she had come to Beachy Head because she wanted to forgive him, but she couldn't.

The unhappiness is in me. Your bequest to me, Daddy.

Then quite quickly the darkness closed in round her. Why do I fool myself? What am I waiting for? There's no hope in the world, and no joy. Alone, with ceaseless effort, we toil onwards to nothing.

'No!'

She cried out loud, striking with her arms against the darkness. Fight! she told herself. Fight! Don't let them take it from you!

But who were they, who so threatened her? And what was it that she defended so fiercely? Some stubborn core self that would not give in. This was no philosophy. This was the kick of the legs in deep water when the body refuses to drown. Instinct at its most primitive, that commands, 'Do anything, hurt anyone, abandon everyone, but live!'

And can this be done alone?

She found she was weeping. The wind on her face made the tears cold against her skin.

Simon appeared before her, looking wretched.

'What is it, Pammy? Please tell me.'

She shook her head, turned away. There was the fatal edge: so close, so easy.

He took her hand. Without meaning to, she went into his arms. He held her tight, and for a few moments she allowed herself to be grateful for his solidity, his ordinariness.

'I think we should go back,' he said.

She let him lead her back to the car, like a docile child. There was nothing more to do here. In the car, he glanced at her as he drove.

'What was all that about?'

She shook her head. She didn't want to explain.

'I've never seen you cry before,' he said.

'It was private,' she said.

'Yes. Of course. Sorry.'

The wind vibrated the hood of the car over their heads, making a steady thrumming sound.

'I've been promoted,' he said. 'From January I'll be getting over three thousand pounds a year.'

She said nothing.

'I know that's boring,' he said, 'but it means a lot to me.'

493

'It's not boring,' she said. 'Money's important.'

'Well, it is.'

They drove on, past the Golden Galleon, up the rising road into Seaford.

'I expect this is completely stupid,' he said, 'but I'm going to say it anyway. You've always been the only girl for me, Pammy. Might you ever, not now of course, sometime in the future, think of marrying me?'

'Oh, Simon.'

She was touched and saddened at the same time. He seemed so infinitely far away. But wouldn't that be the same with anyone? Today it seemed to her impossible that any two people could find happiness together. There were only arrangements. Alliances against the loneliness.

'You don't need to answer,' he said. 'I just want you to know I asked. To know I'm there for you.'

He could hardly have said anything more perfect for her current mood. And why not Simon? she thought. He was decent, he was solvent. Marry Simon and become a country solicitor's wife. Where was the shame in that?

And where the glory?

Of course she knew it was out of the question. That stubborn core self that wouldn't die was also ambitious. She was still ascending that crowded staircase, approaching the moment of her entrée, when all eyes would be on her, and there would be applause.

She was still waiting.

'I don't want to marry anyone right now,' she said. 'Ask me again in five years.'

'Can we cut the difference and say two?'

'I can't stop you asking,' she said.

They had now reached Edenfield. He drove up the side lane to River Farm.

'You know, it's a funny thing,' he said, 'but if you hadn't

494

cried up there on the cliffs, I'd never have got up the nerve to say what I said.'

'Thank you for taking me, Simon.'

She kissed his cheek.

'When can I see you again, Pammy?'

'I don't know,' she said. 'Not for a while. I'm going away.'

He looked crestfallen.

'Call me when you're back.'

Off he drove, a young middle-aged man in a red sports car with his life laid out before him. With his life already over.

Pamela went into the house.

It was not true that she was going away. She had nowhere to go. She had only this giant need to go – somewhere, anywhere. The longing for her life to begin.

Her mother called out from the study.

'Pammy, darling, Hugo phoned for you. About half an hour ago. He said he'd call back.'

Pamela closed her eyes and lowered her head. She drew a long deep breath. Eight days. She had almost given up. But now everything was going to be all right after all. The waiting had come to an end.

She sat by the phone so she could be the one to answer it when it rang. She felt calm and still and right.

When it rang she let it go for two rings, and then picked up the receiver.

'Hello?'

'Is that you, Pamela?'

'Yes. It's me.'

HISTORICAL NOTE

This is a novel, and the central characters are fictional, but the historical details are as accurate as I've been able to make them. Actions and opinions ascribed to historical characters – McGeorge Bundy, Oleg Troyanovsky, Mountbatten, Macmillan, Kennedy, Khrushchev, and others – are all sourced from contemporary accounts. Ivanov and his attempts to create a 'back channel' with the help of Stephen Ward are real, though Rupert Blundell's involvement is of course fictional. The world of Stephen Ward in the novel is based closely on what is known of the reality.

In the months following the period described in the novel, a political and social scandal overtook many of its real-life protagonists. In June 1963 the Minister of War, John Profumo, admitted that he had had a brief liaison over a year earlier with Christine Keeler, a known associate of the Russian spy, Ivanov. Profumo resigned in disgrace. The press began to carry stories of orgies rumoured to have taken place at the Astor estate of Cliveden. Senior members of the establishment were implicated. Police hunted in vain for evidence of criminal acts. Appalled and fascinated, the British public called for the guilty men to be punished. But who was to blame? The newspapers, the establishment, and the police all required a focus for their anger and revulsion. They picked Stephen Ward.

In July 1963 Stephen Ward was put on trial for living on immoral earnings. The police applied pressure on Christine Keeler, Mandy Rice-Davies, and a number of known prostitutes to testify that Ward had procured their sexual services for money. The prosecutor Mervyn Griffith-Jones, who had unsuccessfully prosecuted *Lady Chatterley's Lover* two years earlier, described Ward and his world as 'the very depths of lechery and depravity, prostitution, promiscuity and perversion.'

Ward's many friends, terrified by the bad publicity, deserted him. Faced by the mass of fabricated evidence, Stephen Ward realised the case would go against him. His career was over. On July 23, 1963, he killed himself.

In October 1963 Harold Macmillan, tarnished by the crisis, resigned as prime minister. In November 1963 John F. Kennedy was assassinated. In October 1964 Nikita Khrushchev was forced from power, in part because of the catastrophic failure of his Cuban gamble.

The secrecy surrounding the deal that defused the Cuban missile crisis created the impression that President Kennedy had won a victory by unwavering firmness. 'By keeping to ourselves the assurance on the Jupiters,' wrote McGeorge Bundy in 1988, 'we misled our colleagues, our countrymen, our successors and our allies. We allowed them to believe that nothing responsive had been offered.' This sent a message to the American people that a confrontational policy was more likely to succeed than one of diplomatic negotiation. This myth has proved enduring.

Today the nine countries known to possess nuclear weapons hold around twenty thousand warheads, with a total destructive power of over six thousand megatons, or six billion tons of TNT. For comparison, the destructive power of all the bombs dropped in World War Two is under three megatons.

All these countries – the United States, Russia, the United

Kingdom, France, China, India, Pakistan, North Korea and Israel – describe their nuclear arsenals as defensive. All say they continue to possess such devastating destructive power for the purposes of deterrence, not for actual use.

ACKNOWLEDGEMENTS

The story of Mary Brennan and her visions has its origins in the true story of Conchita Gonzalez. In 1961, at the age of twelve, Conchita and three other children saw visions of the Virgin Mary near the village of Garabandal, in northern Spain. Garabandal subsequently became, and remains, a place of pilgrimage. In my days as a documentary producer for the BBC I made a film about Conchita, who by then was living on Long Island with her husband, the owner of a pizza restaurant, and her children. I have never forgotten her honesty, her humility, and her beauty. I have no reason to suppose that, like my fictional character, she had come to doubt her visions; but she had certainly sought to escape the fame and pressures of being a visionary.

I'm indebted to my wife, the social historian Virginia Nicholson, who has been working on her own book about the experiences of women in the 1950s as I've been writing my novel. Her researches have guided and informed me in countless ways. To give one small example: the incident at Mountbatten's Irish retreat, Classiebawn, in which Mountbatten takes over Rupert Blundell's car and controls his manoeuvre, reversing out of the castle yard, is lifted from a memoir Virginia stumbled on in the course of her own researches. I love this glimpse of Mountbatten's character. Real life is always so much richer than anything I can imagine.

I'm also indebted to Janet Lovegrove for her precise memories of fashion in 1962.

Readers may like to know that some of the characters in this novel have appeared in my earlier novel, *Motherland*, set in the years 1942–1950. Pamela Avenell is born in this book, and reaches the age of seven, and sees Hugo Caulder kissing her mother. Larry and Kitty Cornford's love affair is the heart of that novel. Lord Mountbatten appears as a minor character, as do Rupert Blundell and his sister Geraldine.

Guy Caulder, who appears in my novels *The Secret Intensity of Everyday Life*, set in 2000, and *All the Hopeful Lovers*, set in 2008, is the son of Pamela Avenell and Hugo Caulder. Guy's daughter Alice Dickinson appears in three of the novels. The village of Edenfield in Sussex appears in all five novels.

As will by now be apparent, I am slowly building an ambitious sequence of interlinked novels that explore both the past and the present.

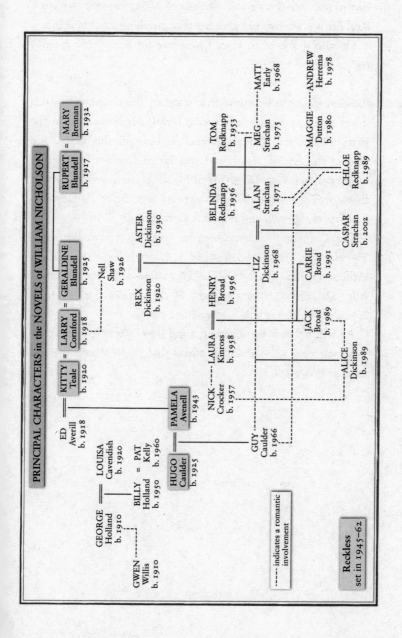

PRINCIPAL CHARACTERS in the NOVELS of WILLIAM NICHOLSON

GWEN
Willis
b. 1910

GEORGE
Holland
b. 1910

LOUISA
Cavendish
b. 1920

BILLY = PAT
Holland   Kelly
b. 1930   b. 1960

HUGO
Caulder
b. 1925

PAMELA
Avenell
b. 1943

ED
Averill
b. 1918

KITTY = LARRY = GERALDINE
Teale   Cornford   Blundell
b. 1920   b. 1918   b. 1925

Nell
Shaw
b. 1926

REX
Dickinson
b. 1920

ASTER
Dickinson
b. 1930

RUPERT = MARY
Blundell   Brennan
b. 1917   b. 1932

TOM
Redknapp
b. 1953

MATT
Early
b. 1968

MEG
Strachan
b. 1975

BELINDA
Redknapp
b. 1956

ANDREW
Herrema
b. 1978

MAGGIE
Dutton
b. 1980

NICK
Crocker
b. 1957

LAURA
Kinross
b. 1958

HENRY
Broad
b. 1956

LIZ
Dickinson
b. 1968

ALAN
Strachan
b. 1971

CHLOE
Redknapp
b. 1989

GUY
Caulder
b. 1966

JACK
Broad
b. 1989

CARRIE
Broad
b. 1991

ALICE
Dickinson
b. 1989

CASPAR
Strachan
b. 2002

----- indicates a romantic involvement

Reckless
set in 1945–62

SELECT BIBLIOGRAPHY

My researches for this novel have been extensive, but I have relied most heavily on the following books:

Bird, Kai, *The Color of Truth: McGeorge Bundy and William Bundy, Brothers in Arms*, London and new York: Touchstone Simon & Schuster 1998.

Clausewitz, Karl von, *On War*, London: Penguin 1968.

Crathorne, James, *Cliveden, the Place and the People*, London: Collins & Brown 1995.

Crawford, Marion, *The Little Princesses*, London: Cassell 1950.

Dallek, Robert, *John F Kennedy, an Unfinished Life*, London and Boston, MA: Little, Brown 2003.

Dobbs, Michael, *One Minute to Midnight*, London: Hutchinson 2008.

Frankel, Max, *High Noon in the Cold War*, Presidio Press 2004.

Fursenko, Aleksandr and Naftali, Timothy, *One Hell of a Gamble*, London and new York: Norton 1997.

Hennessy, Peter, *The Secret State*, London: Allen Lane 2002.

Ivanov, Yevgeny with Sokolov, Gennady, *The Naked Spy*, London: Blake 1992.

Kennedy, Robert F, *Thirteen Days*, London and New York: Norton 1968.

Kissinger, Henry, *Nuclear Weapons and Foreign Policy*, New York: Harper 1957.

Knightley, Simon and Kennedy, Caroline, *An Affair of State: The Profumo Case and the Framing of Stephen Ward*, London: Jonathan Cape 1987.

Schelling, Thomas G. *The Strategy of Conflict*, Oxford: Oxford University Press 1960.

Scott, L. V., *Macmillan, Kennedy and the Cuban Missile Crisis*, Oxford: Palgrave 1999.

Sykes, Christopher, *Nancy, the Life of Lady Astor*, Collins 1972.

Taubman, William, *Khrushchev, the Man and his Era*, London and New York: Simon & Schuster/Free Press 2003.

Twigge, Stephen and Scott, Len, *Planning Armageddon*, Newark, NJ: Harwood Academic 2000.

Wilson, Jim, *Launch Pad UK*, Barnsley: Pen & Sword, 2008.

Ziegler, Philip, *Mountbatten*, London: Collins 1985.

Praise for *Reckless*

'An explosively interesting novel which I found hard to put down'
Daily Mail

'Fielding a team of characters as famous as the ones who appear
in this novel is in itself pretty reckless. But William Nicholson
copes with his usual effortless brilliance'
Daily Express

'Nicholson's strength is his capacity to make you care about his characters
as they struggle towards self-knowledge, love, honesty and courage'
Spectator

'Nicholson writes with a relaxed charm, and seems to like his
characters, especially the female ones . . . a satisfying, ambiguous
and surprising conclusion'
The Times

'Gripping . . . a carefully crafted and immaculately controlled style.
This is a fast-paced, cinematic-style narrative'
Metro

'Nicholson has a talent for capturing the minutiae of life.
Reckless weaves together complex issues and manages to maintain
suspense and intrigue throughout'
New Statesman

'Thoughtful, compelling . . . a complex work that mixes high politics
with the most touching of love stories'
Good Book Guide

William Nicholson's plays include *Shadowlands* and *Life Story*, both of which won the BAFTA Best Television Drama award of their year. He co-wrote the script for the film *Gladiator*, and, more recently, he has scripted *Les Misérables* and *Mandela*. He is married to the writer Virginia Nicholson. They have three children. William Nicholson lives in East Sussex.